CEDRIC M

Love
Without
Spoiling,
Discipline
Without
Nagging

"The
Ultimate
Indian
Parenting
Book"

TODDLERS TO TEENS

wisdom
tree

ISBN 81-86685-86-3

Published by
Wisdom Tree
C-209/1, Mayapuri II,
New Delhi 110 064
Ph.: 28111720, 28114437

Printed at
Print Perfect
New Delhi 110 064

Published by *Shobit Arya* for Wisdom Tree; Edited by *Manju Gupta*; Designed by *Kamal P. Jammual*; Typeset at Icon Printographics, New Delhi-18 and printed at Print Perfect, New Delhi-64.

*I dedicate this book
to the
memory of my dear mother*

Clara Rose Kenny

Table of Contents

Section 3
RAISE HAPPY KIDS

Section 4
RAISE WISE KIDS

Part I

Part II

Section 5
TWEENS & TEENS

Part I

Part II
ACADEMIA

Appendix
2 Case studies

Acknowledgements

I am very happy to offer my profound gratitude and thanks to several people whose support, advice and encouragement has shaped this books in important ways.

At the top of my list is Shobha Arora, my associate and partner at *Tender Feet,* who has been at me for a long time to write this book. Shobha's zeal, dedication, passion and high energy levels in bringing out the best in toddlers through numerous innovative play-forms are indeed phenomenal. Her inspirational charm in touching the souls of children, and drawing parental support forms a very large portion of this book.

The most gratifying part of my work has been working with toddlers since July 1983. Many of them, now in their preteens and teens, excel in many fields, including academics. Their success rate as achievers is testimony of the early grooming and directions they received at our institution, *Tender Feet*. Today, as young adults, they have grown to be great achievers.

I have learnt a lot from discourses and writings of modern thinkers, philosophers, and management theorists. Those whom I have cited in the text have their relevant works listed in the bibliography; and there are others that I gleaned from journals, magazines and newspapers who remain anonymous. To all of them I am particularly indebted, and this is a recognition of my gratitude to them.

Ugar Sain Arora has been a great support in all our efforts at *Tender Feet*. His patience and understanding of human weaknesses and strengths have taught me lessons that reflect in the pages of this book. Ugar is my computer consultant *par excellence* who offered technical support, especially in keeping my computer going, and retrieving lost material, after the lights had gone out.

I am grateful to Jayati Rajgarhia who read the manuscript through its infancy stage till its completion and offered very valuable suggestions along the way, and I thank Shikha

Sarbadhikary for her editing assistance. I thank Manju Gupta, editor, Wisdom Tree for giving the book its final shape.

If a picture is worth a thousand words, then Charles M. Shulz's *Peanuts* comic strips are priceless for their wealth of mirth and message. I thank Anil Bhasin of *Asia Features* for granting me permission to reprint the *Peanuts* comic strips which I'm sure will bring you immense delight and 'intellectual relief'.

Lastly, how can I forget the help I received from Gopal Kochhar and his associate Rajiv Kakria. While Gopal's ready wit helped us to overcome hurdles, Rajiv's marketing inputs have helped us to launch this product. To them and to all others who were instrumental in the making of this book, I offer my heartfelt thanks.

Foreword

The year is 2025. Space, the final frontier, is heavy with traffic. Spacezones and astrolanes are buzzing with spacecrafts. Inter-planetary travel has come to stay as a reality. A delegation of Martians is visiting planet Earth on a goodwill mission. The Martians meet with our scientists who show them around. They visit many scientific and technical institutions and observe many areas of creative enterprise that our men and women in business and industry have established. They are impressed by the astonishing progress made by humans in the field of technology, medicine, science and its myriad applications.

But when the Martians are introduced to a cross-section of humans, in their home set-up, they are in for a shock. While in *Academia*, as students, the delegation had done a thorough study of humans from the earliest civilisations to the present societies, and while on this mission they were expecting to learn from the humans the *Art of Living*. Instead they were baffled. How could a civilisation of humans be endowed with such brilliant intellectual powers, and yet be so ignorant in its application to a healthy life and living, they wondered? They saw how humans brought upon themselves misery and unhappiness; they saw greed, sefishness and power rooted in the actions of humans, and the humiliation of those trampled underfoot, including their own kith and kin and others. They also saw how humans treat interpersonal relationships so casually, while madly trying to climb the high ladder of success.

Before the Martians get here (by the time your children will grow up to be parents), you have the opportunity to put your house in order. *Toddlers to Teens* will show you the way. Cedric M. Kenny has used his long years of experience in dealing with children and with their parents to write this very practical book. Survey after survey has revealed that young adults of our society, with high levels of world-class competence are victims of stress-induced ailments. So many, and among them, the very well-to-do, are suffering, though they may suffer in comfort. Kenny's book is directly addressed to this urban educated class on the upbringing of their children. He tackles the issues of confronting contradictions and bringing clarity to areas of confusion and darkness. Without being prescriptive, he uses everyday situations to bring home some basic lessons of life and wellness of living.

The topics he treats are catchy and relevant. To name a few, *Build a Loving Home, Raise Healthy Kids, Ways to Pre-empt Learning Disabilities* are some examples of contemporary interest to parents and educators. The section on Tweens and Teens should hold special interest for many parents who find themselves at their wit's end, searching for ways to deal with their teenage son or daughter. Kenny raises practical issues and suggests solutions to reduce stress, and to make children winners. He deals with eating disorders, anorexia and obesity (which are major concerns in our present society among the young). He has also an extended treatment on *Language Development, Study Skills,* and many more. Indeed, a wide-ranging menu, served as a buffet and you can pick and choose what is of interest to you.

The book is not theory but breaks theory into practice and that is the merit of the book. I feel that *Love without Spoiling, Discipline without Nagging* will be welcomed gratefully by many parents and educators who are experiencing that something is terribly going wrong with those under their care, and how to deal with issues of parenting. I congratulate Cedric M. Kenny for this timely publication, dealing with such a variety of topics eagerly sought for.

— T.V. KUNNUNKAL

T.V. Kunnunkal is former Chairman, CBSE, consultant to the Ministry of HRD, Director of National Open School, and recipient of the prestigious national award, Padma Bhushan.

Preface

Being parents is a terrific experience, but parenting could be terrifying for most parents. Raising kids is a daunting task by any standards. What works for one may not work for others because kids aren't mathematical equations where two plus two adds up to four. Worse still, when they are born they don't come with a *User Manual* to guide you on parenting: on how to operate a kid's upbringing, and which buttons to press. So, you have to charter your own path, unique to each family, as you make your way through the labyrinth of choices of what is right and what is wrong.

I hope the pages of *Love without Spoiling, Discipline without Nagging* will open your mind to find all the answers you need to raising kids: healthy, happy and wise in the twenty-first century, and to some of life's puzzling questions. When we enjoy so much convenience and comfort, and have access to so much information and knowledge, then why are we so ignorant on ways and means to overcome selfishness, meanness, hatred and anger? Why are we victims of guilt, depression, stress, anxiety and a host of psychosomatic ailments when there is so much advancement in comfort levels, psychology, psychiatry and medicine? In the words of Francis Collins, director of the Human Genome Project, "We have now got to the point in human history where, for the first time, we are going to hold in our hands the set of instructions to make a human being... previously known only to God." Imagine, we have reached the point where we can touch the face of God with our *thinking brain,* and yet we struggle to cope with many emotional issues, including our ignorance and confusion at something as basic as raising kids. On the one hand we are very clear on our career goals, and on the other, we are very confused about commitment, loyalty and dedication, whether at our job or at home. Do we know where exactly our path leads us to, or are we stuck at the crossroads of life? Before we clone the perfect human being, we will have to perfect ourselves in order to strike the perfect balance between head and heart.

Love without Spoiling, Discipline without Nagging is divided into five sections. The first section emphasizes the importance of a loving home which nurtures empowerment. Many parents rush into parenting duties without first setting their homes in order. This section invites you to reflect on family values, marriage commitment, careers and relationships with parents and in-laws. These core factors impact individual parenting styles.

The second section is about raising healthy kids. You may have read in magazines and tabloids about depression, stress and hypertension as heart-related ailments. Yet, none have linked sleep disorders as the root cause leading to those ailments. Mostly out of ignorance, parents *nurture* a 'weak sleep drive' in their children who then grow up as potential candidates for heart-related ailments. After I have shown you how to administer the daily dose of sleep as a refreshing health tonic, I have laid bare the area of disciplining children. If you have been looking for ways to handle your children's tantrums, stubbornness and negative behaviour, the chapters in this section will enable you to understand the techniques of implementing behaviour modification skills. Since 'correction' in never administered in a vacuum, you must offer children positive alternatives—something constructive to do. The third section will show you ways of raising happy kids.

When kids perform little acts of antics or service, you applaud in order to encourage them to repeat those actions. In doing so, you automatically teach them to be 'givers'. Psychologists are of the opinion that it is healthy to involve toddlers in little household chores—not as disciplinarians but as fun-loving enthusiasts. Language development is important at this stage. Using short expressions, spoken clearly, with correct grammar, pronunciation and diction helps the child to 'imbibe' and mimic proper sentence structures from infancy onwards. I have come across many children diagnosed 'slow learners' in schools, or who developed language problems (inability to read or write fluently) because grownups indulged in garbled baby-talk, or generally spoke badly or incorrectly.

The fourth section has two parts. In the first part, as your toddler gets ready to enter nursery school, you are made aware of some of the core concepts that form the nursery school culture, and what to expect from nursery schools. The chapters will guide you on how to prepare toddlers *before* they enter nursery school, as well as how to allow them space to explore a new world of school expereinces—with an emphasis on parents bonding with the schools in trust and support.

The second part is related to learning disabilities. In my attempt to enlighten you on this problem, I have only touched the tip of the iceberg which should suffice to send a cold chill down the spines of parents and educators to take cognizance of this growing ailment among our students. While the West woke up to handle this malaise long ago, many in India are still not aware that such a malaise exists. The number of students who fare badly in schools is astronomically high. In rural and backward areas the reason is malnutrition. But in towns and cities the reason is more mind-related than starvation. If today's urban children are hyperactive, it is because of the urbanites stressful lifestyles that cause it. The tension triggers a deadly cocktail of stress chemicals like cortisol and dopamine into the bloodstream which children inherit from their parents. Now, you know the reason why doctors say that blood pressure levels are much higher in today's children than ever before. But you need not despair. This section offers many guidelines to *pre-empt* hyperactivity and other learning disabilities in children.

The fifth section is dedicated to raising tweens and teens. The chapters in the first part relate to problems adolescents grapple with: parental authority and carving their own unique identities. When correcting adolescents, haven't parents at some point wished if they could get inside their children's heads to see why they behaved the way they did? Their wish has come true. In this section, you will read about the new breakthrough in brain research. The findings of this research will compel parents, educators and social scientists to be more tolerant and understanding of tweens and teens as they struggle to reach maturity.

Part two of section five will show you some tried and tested methods to teach adolescents to *bond* with the schools. The bonds will strengthen between home and school as your tweens and teens master study skills and do well without getting stressed out at tests and examinations.

Lastly, the *Appendix* will give you hope in knowing that the adolescent years, though tough on parents—also tough on adolescents—need not be the years of alienation between parents and kids. With large dollops of love and patience, and lots of application of the ideas from the pages of this book will bond you with your children and the family.

How should one approach reading this book, you may ask? If you attempt to read this book in one setting, you may miss out on some finer points. I suggest that you read, perhaps a section, chapter and ponder over it. In doing so, you will gain a lot of insight in its application to your present situation. Some portions of the book may slow you down and lead you to a spiritual journey as you begin to look for answers in your inner self. And in the process, if you find answers to some of life's vexing problems, then there is no better reward than the satisfaction of knowing that some of these pages have lightened your burden. It is commonly said, 'like father like son' and, 'like mother like daughter.' In other words, you are expected to raise your kids the way you are. But, you may want to give your children something *more* in life; something more than what you received so that they can reach for the stars.

As we grow older, we fondly remember songs which we recall as our favourite collection from our childhood days. We cherish those songs because they touched our feelings and moods when we were teens. Through those songs, we carved ourselves a philosophy that gave us an identity. All parents dream dreams and I would like you stay with your dreams—however impossible—as I share with you a song, *The Impossible Dream,* from the film, *The Man from La Manche* adapted from the original Spanish classic, *Don Quixote* by Cervantes.

The Impossible Dream
(THE QUEST)

To dream the impossible dream,
to fight the unbeatable foe,
to bear with unbearable sorrow
to run where the brave dare not go;
to right the unrightable wrong.

To love, pure and chaste, from afar,
to try, when your arms are too weary,
to reach the unreachable star!

This is my Quest to follow that star,
no matter how hopeless, no matter how far,
to fight for the right
without question or pause,
to be willing to march into hell
for a heavenly cause!

And I know, if I'll only be true
to this glorious Quest,
that my heart will lie peaceful and calm
when I'm laid to my rest.

And the world will be better for this,
that one man, scorned and covered with scars,
still strove, with his last ounce of courage,
to reach the unreachable stars!

Author's Note

There are numerous stories in this book about people I have encountered during my years of practising as a teacher, administrator, corporate trainer, counsellor and consultant. Many stories in this book come from discussions I have had with numerous experts in diverse fields of study and research, be it educators, psychotherapists, doctors, career professionals, entrepreneurs, students, and common people burdened with problems. The fact as I relate them here are accurate, but some of the details have been changed and the names of individuals, too, in an effort to keep the identities of all concerned private and confidential.

Testimonial

A.P.J. Abdul Kalam
President of India
Rashtrapati Bhavan
New Delhi

Thank you for your letter inviting me to participate in the launching function of your book *Love without Spoiling, Discipline without Nagging*. I have gone through the manuscript of the book and liked particularly the thoughts on "the intelligent brain and the emotional brain must be trained to work in cohesion".
My greetings and best wishes to you,

Yours sincerely
Sd.
A.P.J. Abdul Kalam
President of India

Dr Rajeev Sharma
Chairman
Ravi J. Mathai Centre for Educational Innovation
Indian Institute of Management
Ahmedabad

Love without Spoiling, Discipline without Nagging is a unique book which combines traditional wisdom, modern scientific knowledge with the experience of an insightful educator. Mr Cedric M. Kenny, an educator and counsellor for more than two decades, has put together his experiences and learning in a very lucid yet authentic form. The book will be useful for parents, teachers and all those who have concern for children in the rapidly changing society.

Sr. Taurina Vaz
Principal
Mater Dei School
New Delhi

Raising kids is undoubtedly a daunting task and there couldn't be a better handy manual for ready reference than Cedric M. Kenny's *Love without Spoiling, Discipline without Nagging*.

- definitely are investment towards values, beliefs, ethics and spirituality.
- calls for greater and stronger family bonding which is indeed the need of the hour, in today's fast paced IT world.

Dr Gul Jagtiani, MD
Paediatrics
New Delhi

Love without Spoiling, Discipline without Nagging is a handy book for parents and educators. It deals in a concise and comprehensive manner the problems affecting modern-day parents. Cedric Kenny's hands-on approach as educator, family counsellor and management consultant will help parents find answers to many problems they face in rearing toddlers to teens.

A lot has been written on child rearing, but unfortunately children who face problems coping with studies are written off as retarded. The chapters on *Learning Disabilities*, *Underachievers*, etc. should go a long way in helping teachers and parents to assist children with special needs.

Indeed, a *must read* for all those concerned in the care of children and youth.

Charlie Dias S.J.

Principal (Primary Section)
St. Xavier's High School
Ahmedabad

I sincerely feel that *Love without Spoiling, Discipline without Nagging* will go a long way in catering to the needs, requirements and expectatons of parents who are eagerly looking to provide the best possible environment for their children.

'Build a Loving Home' mentioned in the first chapter of the book, puts family life in the right perspective, with an emphasis on love. I am confident that parents will find the book a handy guide in directing their children to face the challenges of this century.

Congratulations to the author on this wonderful attempt.

Dr Kokila Mathur

Reader, Delhi University

Love without Spoiling, Discipline without Nagging, is an eminently readable book. The crisp idiom invites us to turn the pages excitedly to gain invaluable insights into the awesome task of parenting. Kenny helps parents create a nurturing family environment wherein he emphasizes the emotional welfare of children as the cornerstone of their educational and future development. In great detail, he discusses positive parenting with its stress on values of truth, integrity, dedication and commitment as perhaps the ultimate levers. The author's keen and sincere desire to help parents is evident in the *Academia Section* which deals systematically with preteens and teens acquiring study skills. His is a voice that is so masterful and reassuring for parents as it is culled from his vast experience as a value educator.

S E C T I O N ①

BUILD A LOVING HOME

My son, when you were just a child,

you asked me, "What is Heaven?"
I answered, "Our blessed home,
where love and understanding roam,
and peace makes our roof a dome,
of these things, God makes Heaven."

My son, when you were just a boy,
you asked me, "Where is God?"
I told you, "Mother's selfless ways
that guided you through childhood days,
her sacred love, her words of praise,
these are akin to God."

And now that you are a man, my son,
you make my life—a Heaven.
The love I give, which you return
through righteousness, you chose to learn,
the 'good name' which you strive to earn,
bringing me a glimpse of Heaven.

Each day, as you mature, my son,
you bring me close to God.
The humble things you do and say,
the 'unseen' voice that you obey,
the 'love thy neighbour' you display,
through these, my soul sees God.

— Lud Isaac

Family Empowerment
RAISING CHAMPIONS

I have always believed that how people feel about themselves inside is the real key to using their talent and releasing their potential. And how they feel about themselves is largely a function of how they are seen and treated by others, particularly their parents.

—STEPHEN R. COVEY *(Principle-centred Leadership)*

The day you became parents, God planted a seed in your hearts. When you held the little infant, whose body was knit inside yours, in your arms you felt God-like; you had worked with God, as partners, to procreate another human being, with a mind and soul, whose destiny you will to some extent shape. And yet, at that moment, you felt so humble when the awesome responsibility of raising a child dawned on you. This child would grow from an infant to a toddler, to an adolescent, to an adult and whose life would impact many other lives depending on the vision you had envisioned for this child. That seed, which God planted in your hearts, is called *parenting*. As you discover your new role, many thoughts come to you in a rush. Can you frame a vision which will guide you to raise a family of champions? Can you nurture the seed of responsibility, over several years, as the child grows from infancy to adulthood? Parents have those sublime thoughts, and I am sure you, too, dreamt those dreams.

I believe in people. I believe that all families want to provide their children opportunities to touch the stars. But to achieve those goals you will first need to know what you want for yourself and for your spouse, and then, with your finger on your children's pulse, know in your heart what you really want for them. It is obvious that the most important role you play in your busy life is that of a parent. A parent's role has never been as challenging as it is today. Parents are faced with innumerable problems as they keep pace with the fast-moving world of changing values and reckless demands. On your shoulders lie the awesome responsibilities of raising kids, putting them through school and college, managing home and keeping the family happy. More than ever it is in these changing times that you have to teach your children how to cope with pressures and tensions, how to make right choices, how to accept responsibilities, and how to solve problems so that they don't end up becoming problem adults.

As parents you are the primary educators of children. You will always be their source of inspiration and influence. The relationship you enjoy with your spouse, parents, in-laws, relatives and friends has a bearing on child rearing. If your relationship is

> *You are your child's role-model; and he becomes what you are, eventually.*

lukewarm, hostile or negative then you will have to change drastically; indeed, an essential investment for your children's sake. As you are their living example, they are learning through your positive behaviour to value themselves; to be self-reliant; to be free from stress; to forgive others; and to feel a sense of purpose in this world. You can nurture a family of champions. You have the power within you to make it happen—provided you want it to happen.

Wanting it to happen is not good enough. You will want to know *how* to make it happen. I will hand you a set of keys. But, none of the keys will fit the keyholes of your specific problems. The keys will enable you to unlock the doors of your mind where you seem to be trapped and enable you to find your own unique solutions to your specific problems. You could use these keys to empower yourself, your spouse and your children, and raise a family of champions, or simply put them away and forget about it. The choice is yours.

YOUR SET OF KEYS

Key to Success

Most families are affected by financial worries, and the man who is money-minded is affected the most. When money becomes the main focus, the role of a husband and father automatically gets reduced to a shadow-play. Since he believes that economic demands come first, he conveniently assumes that he has the family's full support in reaching his goal. While he works on amassing wealth, he expects his wife to attend to family commitments, concerns, child-upbringing, schooling, and running the house. Whenever things do not go his way at work, he belittles his wife's efforts, and yells at and punishes the children for letting him down in achieving his goals.

The impact of such paren-ting on the minds of vulnerable children is devastating. These hostile parenting images remain etched on their mind for the rest of their lives.

Children absorb quickly the negative role-models their parents project—the lies, bluffs, threats and abuses. As they grow up, they will magnify their parents' actions to suit their own convenience.

Success in a career, business or profession cannot compensate for failures in a marriage, childcare, or family relationships. Success should be all-encompassing. You are truly successful if you are an ace at your work and an ace with your family. Such a success does not happen automatically. Both spouses have to set their minds to make it happen, by creating *support systems* for one another and for their children. Such spouses develop a sixth sense of perception that sensitises them to anticipate the other's needs and fulfil them with enthusiasm. Furthermore, when parents make it a point to be available to the family whenever and wherever they are needed, the children perceive them to be dependable and trustworthy.

Key to Marriage Commitment

In the world of 'arranged' marriages, some adults embrace marriage as a long-term commitment, ready to live their vows and make the relationship work to the best of their abilities, while some adults enter into marriage simply because they see it as one of the milestones along the path of life. Due to parental or social pressures, they consent to marry. For them marriage serves as an umbrella to shield off social stigma, if any. In such a scenario, relationship with the spouse usually is of indifference, use or abuse. Precious moments of one's life are spent in trying to sort out, or get out of the tangled mess they got themselves into. One of the most wasteful and vicious cycles of life is the cycle of marital strife with frightful consequences for the children.

In most 'rocky' marriages, two-way communication is the first casualty. There is more to a marriage than sharing a bed. Meaningful communication between spouses bonds them to a meaningful commitment. Anthropologist, Desmond Morris, in *The Naked Ape,* talks of facial mimicry among married couples. If living together can alter one's facial contours to look like the spouse's over a period of time, then living together (in that same period of time) and sharing thoughts and aspirations with one's partner can also lead to a union of minds. In order to 'discover' each other, both partners have to make an effort to discuss their hopes, desires, concerns, and apprehensions about

> *Marriage commitments are reinforced when two-way communication channels remain unclogged and in working condition.*

the here and now of their lives. Over a period of time, many spouses forget the art of conversing with each other. Maybe they need to begin from scratch and chalk out their specific roles: role of the husband and father, role of the wife and mother. Thereafter, they will have to talk about raising children and agree upon their upbringing, morals and discipline. In money matters, they must talk about savings and expenditures and living within their means. They will also have to develop a mutual understanding with regard to relatives, in-laws and their social circle of friends. The 'discovery' touches the climax of compatibility when they discuss strategies on how to solve problems, cope with pressures and deal with stress and anger.

Key to Emotional Banking

I would like you to meet a working couple who has been married for five years and think the world of each other. Jacob works as a branch manager in the State Bank of India, and his wife, Anna, teaches in a high school. Jacob had developed the concept of *emotional banking*, and had introduced the concept to his wife. He said, "Relationships are about cheques and balances—about deposits and withdrawals. In order to withdraw money from the bank, you've got to first deposit the money in it. I pamper Anna a lot before I make a small demand on her."

As soon as I saw the catch, I interrupted him, "So, you manipulate each other?"

According to Anna, each family creates its own unique *emotional bank*. Some retain large emotional deposits in the bank, while others regularly overdraw and strain the relationship. She said, "Family banks go bust and end up in discord or divorce when spouses habitually overdraw through acts of selfishness, anger, hatred, rudeness, manipulation, duplicity, hypocrisy, or physical and verbal abuse."

Jacob took over, saying, "Conversely, families that value personal integrity, honesty and sincerity automatically generate substantial emotional deposits in the family bank through acts of understanding, caring, and sharing."

The family bank had obviously helped Anna and Jacob

to focus on their marriage and their relationship. By maintaining a high bank balance, withdrawals did not rock the marriage boat. Anna added another dimension to their banking system, "Whenever I have my blues and sulk, or am impatient, or irritable, I tend to make withdrawals from our bank. Jacob reaches out to me, starts pampering me by treating me to an outing or something. With that little extra he does for me, he is putting in deposits to keep the bank from going bust." Indeed, they had developed their own unique banking system.

"Simultaneously," said Jacob, "our expressions of love and tenderness, or running errands for each other earn us rich dividends and huge emotional reserves." Jacob was a thorough banker. Through emotional banking both had learnt how to invest in trust and harmony.

Key to Self-esteem, Dignity and Pride

These are basic values we have to develop in children. When a child has high self-esteem, a good measure of dignity and positive pride, there are literally no obstacles to his total fulfilment as a human being. With self-esteem, dignity and pride flow the qualities of self-respect and confidence. When children are declared poor performers in schools, parents look for ways and means to improve their academic perfomance, but never to improve their self-esteem. It is a universally accepted fact that poor performance in children is linked to poor self-esteem. As soon as these negative factors are eliminated, you will see how children begin to perform well in studies as well as in other areas. They begin to radiate joy, enthusiasm, happiness, excitement and cheer all around.

Wherever there is pessimism, negativity, violence, abuse or indifference, children develop low self-esteen, and their overall performance levels drop.

Key to a Sense of Purpose

In raising children to become champions, an important key is to help them feel a strong sense of purpose in their lives. With a sense of purpose comes satisfaction and gratitude.

A sense of purpose flows from the soul of an individual. It comes from feeling a deep inner satisfaction and contentment. Such individuals have found the meaning of life. Without a sense of purpose, people run in the rat race, feeling lost, aimless and question why they are there at all.

Most children by nature tend to be self-centred. They take all that their tiny hands can hold and then ask for more; they revel in the company of 'I, me and myself'. To give them a strong sense of purpose, parents have to guide children to transcend their personal wants by engaging them in the service of others. Suppose, Father just comes home from a business tour. Instead of allowing the children to grab their gifts, Father should expect from them a warm reception of hugs, cuddles and kisses. After that may come a glass of water, then they could bring him his slippers, and talk about whether the trip had exhausted him, and how much he missed the family. In this manner the focus is shifted from their physical wants to what makes others happy. With this kind of training, children will gradually learn to think less about themselves and their physical wants, and instead focus on how their actions will help improve the quality of life for others. Indeed, in training them you, too, along with your children would have attained the sense of purpose to live life to the full.

> *The more they will concern themselves in pleasing others the more satisfaction they will receive from their actions.*

Key to Stress-free Upbringing

In this age of cut-throat competition our children are being raised in an atmosphere of stress that is taking its toll on their mental and physical health. Many children receive psychiatric help in some form or other. They are growing into adults with higher and higher blood pressure readings, and suffer from obesity, coronary problems, ulcers, migraine, and other mental and physical afflictions. To cope with stress and anxiety, many tweens and teens experiment with cigarettes, drugs, alcohol, antidepressants and tranquillisers.

Many stress management experts blame stress *per se*

and the present-day lifestyles for causing the problem, rather than *stressful thinking*. My approach to counselling people suffering from stress has always been to help them to identify the 'trigger' that generates stressful thoughts. Once they are able to place their fingers on the stress-trigger, they are able to take control of the stress and face life's challenges through a very simple age-old method of *positive thinking*.

Stress thoughts get drilled into the children's minds in their growing years by parents and teachers. Parents push children in the pursuit of excellence at the cost of enjoying life, as though the pursuit of excellence cannot be enjoyable. Look at corporate houses—they pay hefty fees to training consultants who adopt fun and games techniques to teach difficult and complex global market theories to employees. If children could be taught through fun and games techniques, it would surely take the stress out of schooling. Many parents have complained to me that the child "is not worried at all about the coming Board exams". The parents are upset because the child is not 'worried'. In such an environment, children are groomed to worry, to have anxiety thoughts before the exams. It seems the more anxiety he feels the better prepared he is to take the exams. A breeding ground for stress and anxiety is created when parents punish children unreasonably, compare them with other children, correct them in front of other people, become angry and abusive, set unrealistic goals, emphasise the importance of material wealth, talk disparagingly of others, constantly complain, whine, gripe and grumble about living in an unfair world.

Family Empowerment

To raise a family of champions we will have to unlearn old habits and relearn new methods. To raise stress-free children, parents will have to first rid themselves of their old ways of *thinking*, and subsequently their archaic ways of raising children. We must learn to appreciate the small things in life (like the sunset, or the blush of colours on the petals of a rose) and in doing so, we will come to accept the world as God's perfect creation. We have to learn the ways of touching our souls and our minds with sublime thoughts of love, peace, harmony and togetherness. These sublime thoughts will fill us

> *Parents and teachers will have to learn to relax and de-stress themselves. Yoga and meditation will help us to see the world in a new perspective.*

with inner serenity, and help us learn new ways to deal with the challenges of life. An inner tranquillity will flow out of us to touch the souls and minds of our children and our families. And, they, too, will respond likewise. Yes, you can nurture a family of champions.

Marriage Commitment

Let me not to the marriage of true minds
admit impediments. Love is not love
which alters when it alteration finds ...

— WILLIAM SHAKESPEARE

If marriages are the bedrock of families, then why do marriages become a casuality, you may ask? More and more couples are riding their marriage caravans on dirt-roads full of potholes, and end up shaken, separated or divorced. Why were marriages, say some fifty years ago, sustainable than they are today? Was it because fifty years ago, and before that, people considered marriage as a period of life when couples performed their duties to society by raising a family? And today, have couples changed their perspective and look upon marriage simply as a means for personal pleasure and gratification? John Gray, marriage therapist and author of *Men are from Mars, Women are from Venus*, says, "Marital malcontent stems from a colossal shake-up in men's and women's roles. Women don't need men the way they once did. A woman today doesn't need a protector—she can carry her mace; she's got police forces; she's got lawyers, what does she need a guy for?" Gray, a, former celibate monk, who is now married with three children, says, "Women are having careers to support themselves and be independent. They're feeling the same responsibilities their fathers felt, but they also want to create a beautiful relationship and have children and a home. Women are carrying a weight that is heavier than any woman in history has ever carried. Naturally, they are going to be unhappy." Do husbands know what to do to keep their wives happy? Gray, who holds a doctorate and counsels families, says, "After listening to couples again and again, right before they're about to get a divorce, the message I hear from men is, 'I've given and I've given and I've given and no matter how much I give, it's not enough to make her happy.' Women, when they're ready to give up, say the same thing—'I've given and I've given and I've given, and no matter how much I give, I don't get back. I feel empty. I have nothing left to give'." To make marriage a lifetime commitment, couples may need to forge a new vision of intimate relationships in order to find lasting love.

The Essence of Effective Communication

A marriage is between two people, and when they interact with each other, they foster a relationship between them. Relationships between people get woven around interactions which are sustained through communication. So, relationship, interaction and communication are interdependent. Since time immemorial, communication between couples has sparked friction. That is because each one considers his communication skills to be perfect, while the other's to be imperfect. Due to this attitude, the essence of the message being communicated gets blurred or lost. How does one know the message one is imparting is the exact message the other is

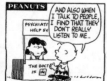 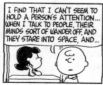 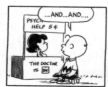 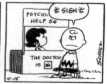

© United Feature Syndicate, Inc. 1965

receiving? You may have heard of a certain wife who told her husband, "John and Mary are married, and dressed to attend the wedding." But, the husband heard, "John and Mary are buried," and so he dressed for the funeral.

Relationships get soured when communication between husbands and wives become strained, indifferent, hostile and abusive. Relationships get bonded when interactions between partners are peppered with affection, trust, understanding, patience, tolerance and love. Family members have to forge bonds through positive interactions in order to ensure that their children grow up into wholesome individuals—happy, generous and friendly.

False Macho Pride

When relations between husbands and wives break down, when the marriage fabric begins to show wear and tear with hostility, rejection or abuse, then the children, in all likelihood, grow up to be hostile, anti-social and dissatisfied with themselves. There was an era when dowry harassment leading to deaths or wife-beatings were considered beastly. But what is shocking is that educated urbanites, who are sophisticated people, do not refrain from committing such dastardly acts. Bizarre as it may sound, a lot of affluent urbanites and socialites, with all the trappings of refinement, regularly abuse their marriage vows. Housewives, and now career women, get a raw deal from their spouses. The crux of the problem is that it is difficult for a man to accept a wife who is smarter and more efficient than he is. He has always prided himself on being in-charge, in control, and the traditional patriarchal decision-maker. When the partner sees through his pompous mediocrity and refuses to bow to his level of mediocrity, then conflict and friction abound. Snide comments and sarcasm are commonly used as forms of humiliation— "You're an MBA? How come they didn't teach

> Men who have been used to lording it over women are becoming more and more uncomfortable when women show that they have a mind of their own. Career women are seen as a threat since they bring in the moollah—in some cases much more than the hubby—which humbles his macho pride.

you at B-school to fill a simple form?" Conflict and friction ultimately lead to physical violence with him attempting to destroy her self-esteem and confidence.

Marriage of Convenience or Commitment?

There are marriages of convenience and marriages of commitment. The marriage-formula doled out by Mumbai's tinsel town, Bollywood, where pretty girls and macho guys chase each other romantically, then bash up villains along the way and finally end up tying the knot, sounds as silly as this old ditty:

Many marriages break up
when the husbands wake up
to find their wives without makeup.

What makes one couple vibe, and another take a jibe? How is it that a few seem to have found the road map to a successful marriage, while others are groping in search of the road map to a successful marriage? Marriages work out very well when both partners share a common goal, either of convenience or of commitment. When two people marry for convenience, in all probability that marriage may succeed because both partners share a common focus: they are *committed to convenience*. Similarly, when both partners marry for commitment, the marriage will work because they both share a common focus: a commitment to share their lives with each other and reach self-actualisation through their marriage vows. In both cases there is mental compatibility between the spouses. In the first instance, both partners are fully focused on their personal careers and find complete satisfaction and fulfilment in pursuing their careers even if self-actualisation through interpersonal relationships is missing. Since interactions with each other are rarely intimate, there is no room for conflict or discord. Their expectations of each other are to the minimum. In the second instance, both partners, through their ups and downs, for better and for worse, in sickness and in health, will find fulfilment in their 'togetherness'.

Marriages tend to break up quickly when one partner marries for convenience and the other marries for commitment; when two partners share separate visions, then conflict is bound to arise in the relationship. These conflicts can get very ugly and at times violently brutal, too, if left to fester like wounds. Both partners may need to be counselled under the guidance of an experienced marriage counsellor. Through therapy, each partner will come to touch the other's soul where emotions of hurt and pain have accumulated since childhood, and now threaten not only their marriage but other relationships as well. Psychologists point out that when couples bare their hearts and souls to each other, they learn how to deal with their partner's psychological wounds and in the process build a successful relationship. But when a partner is obstinate and refuses to get psychological help, and continues to torment and brutalise the other, then it is better to quietly dissolve the marriage on grounds of 'incompatibility' rather than on grounds of brutality. We are only humans, not gods, so we're bound to commit mistakes; but let us never bind ourselves to our mistakes and make our lives a living hell.

Take a look at family and social commitment from *The Monkey's Viewpoint*, and as you enjoy the jest of it, ponder over the facts contained in it.

Three monkeys sat on a coconut tree
discussing things as they're said to be.
Said one to the others, "Now listen, you two,
there's a certain rumour that can't be true,
that man descends from our noble race—
The very idea is a disgrace.
No monkey ever deserted his wife,
starved her babies and ruined her life;
and you've never known a mother monk
to leave her babies with others to bunk,
or to pass them on from one to another
'till they scarcely know who is their mother.
And another thing you'll never see—
A monk build a fence round a coconut tree
and let the coconuts go to waste,
forbidding all other monks to taste.
Why, if I put a fence around this tree,
starvation would force you to steal from me.
Here's another thing a monk won't do—

Go out at night and get on a stew,
or use a gun, or club or knife
to take some other monkey's life.
Yes, man descended — the ornery cuss—
but, brother, he didn't descend from us!"

— ANON

Upbringing Impacts Marriage

At the time when two people join themselves in the bond of matrimony, they promise to love and care for each other forever. Keeping the commitment alive depends on the way each of them was brought up as a kid. People mostly live their marriage commitment like the way their parents did; for example, how they treated each other as husband and wife, and how they raised their children. When children grow up having difficult relationships with their parents, then those difficult experiences will pepper their relationships in their adult life, towards their spouse and children, unless they heal themselves through counselling, meditation, or yoga. To build lasting relationships, spouses need to take a journey into their inner selves and touch their heads, hearts and souls to discover their inner strength and emotional growth. Susan Forward, a leading psychotherapist in the field of family relationships, has developed a self-help guide in her book, *Toxic Parents*. Take a moment to look into yourself and answer the following questions as honestly as you can. For the sake of simplicity, these questions refer to parents in plural, even though your answer may apply to only one parent.

When you were a Child ...

Did your parents tell you that you were bad or worthless?

Did your parents use physical pain to discipline you?

Did you have to take care of your parents because of their problems?

Were you frightened of your parents?

Were you afraid to express anger at your parents?

Did your parents do anything to you that had to be kept secret?

Now that you are an Adult...

Do your parents still treat you as if you were a child?

Do you have intense emotional or physical reactions after spending time with your parents?

Do your parents control you with threats or guilt? Do they manipulate you with money?

Do you feel that no matter what you do, it's never good enough for your parents?

Are you afraid to disagree with your parents?

Do you believe that some day, somehow, your parents are going to change for the better?

According to Susan Forward, if you have answered 'yes' to even one-third of these questions, it means that you carry scars from your childhood which will affect your behaviour and relationship with your spouse and children.

A marital relationship is about behaviour between two persons. Behaviour is expressed much more through body language (actions) which reveals what the mind is thinking and what the words are trying to conceal. Actions express attitude. Harmony is the tune shared between married couples. To touch the note of harmony in your lives, both of you as individuals will have to fine-tune your attitudes so that your actions will measure up to each other's expectations. Couples who have attained harmony in their marriages, experience security and warmth in their relationships.

Music in Your Marriage

Think about it... just like the house we live in needs regular maintenance to avoid major cracks and breakdowns, so also does every couple need to attend to 'marriage maintenance' from time to time.

Such a description of a 'marriage relationship' may sound good to the ears, but at the same time is hard to practise. I have asked many young parents, whom I had counselled, to go back in time and recollect the days of their courtship. Whether the courtship lasted for a few months or years is immaterial. I would guide them to recall and *feel* those feelings they had experienced during the courtship days for each other. As they re-lived that era of courtship and began to *feel* the 'old' desires to be in each other's company, to talk to each other, and to go out together, their faces began to glow, as they shared secret smiles remembering those old exciting memories. I then asked them if they would call those moments as a period of 'sweet music' in their relationship? Oh, they would readily agree because they had loved the music they shared which their relationship had created. My next question was, "How much of that *music* do you hear today?" Most couples (married for about three years and above) would admit that the music they had created together had warped over the years like the decades-old slate records. One husband spoke of the constant staccato rhythm of grunts and groans which had crept in the music of their relationship; another talked of the sound of bongo drums without melody. One wife confessed that the music died immediately after marriage; all she heard was heavy *rap*—static sounds of snubs and sarcasms.

The music you created together should not die out on you; it should die with you. Yes, there should be music in your relationship, but how are you going to keep it from fading off? Unfortunately, the pressures and tensions of the daily grind take away the joys of a relationship. You may like to know if you could start afresh. Yes, it is possible to put music in your marriage.

In spite of the present-day work pressures, couples must set aside at least one entire evening every month exclusively for themselves. No children, no relatives and no friends; just husband and wife having fun together. Maybe a leisurely walk, or sitting face to face with each other in the park, by the lake or by the sea, or watching a sunset together, or may be an overnight holiday; in fact, couples should stretch their imagination to find ways and means of sharing moments together away from the hustle and bustle of daily grind. The more they enjoy each other's company the richer their relationship will get. The rough edges of their personalities will automatically get smoothened and they will begin to savour each other's company like vintage wine.

FOUR LEVELS IN A MARITAL RELATIONSHIP

Spending time with each other can either be very enduring or frightening for husbands and wives. A marriage is not just an act of stripping naked before the partner; that is the easy part. The difficult part is to strip and bare one's heart and soul to each other which could be frightening since all humans have some private pain or shame to conceal. Imagine the pain and fear of persons with skin blemishes, burn scars, or other skin disfigurements who undress before their spouses for the first time. The fear of rejection makes them die a thousand deaths. Similarly, baring the heart and soul to reveal one's emotional scars and blemishes can be scary. And yet, if couples want not just to stick it out, but to make a go at strengthening the bonds of marriage as a lifetime commitment, then they will have to bare not only their bodies but also their hearts and souls to each other. The road to transparency is rough, but you could reach your destination with a road map to guide you through the four levels that constitute the anatomy of marital bliss.

First Level: Physical Attraction (Infatuation)

There is a lot more to a marriage relationship than to marriage *per se.* One has to understand the mechanics of marriage from the time the two persons first meet, get to know each

> *Infatuation is often mistaken for love. Infatuation is short-lived, a passing phase. What was attractive yesterday may not be so today or tomorrow.*

other, then get married, and thereafter try to live up to their vows till 'death do us part'. When two people first catch each other's 'eye' and find themselves drawn together, their body language immediately goes into an overdrive mode, sending multiple signals and messages back and forth. This fierce attraction is physical and carnal, and is called infatuation. In infatuation there is an intensity which could be self-destructive. Infatuation is a basic sexual attraction; it is pleasure-oriented, and rooted in the mammalian (*emotional*) brain, while love is felt in the heart. Blaise Pascal, the French philosopher, has aptly summed up the feelings of love that well up in the heart when he says, "The heart has reasons which reason knows nothing of." For infatuation to grow into love, both partners will have to care for and accept each other without allowing 'intruders' into their relationship.

Second Level: Love

At this level the spouse outgrows being 'in' love with the partner and begins to love the partner. When infatuation matures into love, physical attraction begins to mellow, and care and concern make their presence felt. That does not mean physical intimacy is lost and platonic love takes over. Instead, lovemaking becomes less frenzied and more fulfilling. But, your investment of love may be at risk since this state is not constant. At this level, spouses experience feelings of well-being and openness and the bond of commitment to each other gets reinforced. But all that depends on the level of openness they share with each other. Every time they conceal their inner feelings, or reveal their innermost thoughts to each other, they swing between feeling cold to feeling warm towards each other. Just like the heartbeat that has its highs and lows, so do partners go through the highs and lows of married life. Love, also, is said to be fickle by poets and lyricists. There are times when you worship the very ground on which he stands, and there are times when you want to give up on him and call it quits. The marriage boat rocks frequently, depending on the demands or tantrums of one or both partners. At one time, rough, stormy winds keep blowing leading to a tornado, and at other times all is peace and tranquil. Love has its own way of opening your hearts and minds to the other, and when you submit to love, you float on clouds of peace and tranquillity. This feeling envelops you only when you touch your inner self in the quiet solitude of your heart and mind. But when you get wrapped in the clutter of plots, plans and schemes, and you find no time to savour the silence inside you for fear that love will make you vulnerable, your marriage boats starts to rock. Echhart Tolle, in *The Power of NOW* asks, "What is the greatest obstacle to experiencing this reality?" Tolle answers, "Not to be able to *stop thinking* is a dreadful affliction, but we don't realise this because almost everybody is suffering from it, so it is considered normal. This incessant mental noise prevents you from finding that realm of inner stillness that is inseparable from being. It also creates a false mind-made self that casts a shadow of fear and suffering." For a marriage relationship to anchor itself on the sea of trust, love has to mature into friendship.

Third Level: Friendship

When the boat of marriage is anchored on the sea of friendship, then there is constancy in that relationship because friendship is rooted in the intellect. The intellect is not emotional, i.e. the blow hot and blow cold type. The faculty of the intellect is constant, never wavering. Whenever disagreements, arguments, and fights crop up (as they're bound to be) between two vibrant people whose lives are intertwined intricately and intimately with each other, there will be no rage felt, and neither will they threaten nor feel threatened by each other. At this level, spouses go beyond the false facades that one puts up from time to time (in the first and second levels), and both partners connect at a deeper level. Their openness leads them to the path of intimacy as they surrender their hearts to each other. You've heard people say, "I'm completely at ease in her company," — meaning that she has accepted you for what you are and you don't have to pretend to be someone else. Conversely, when relationships stay entangled in infatuation or in the second level of love, then any small disagreements or arguments have the tendency to flare up into ugly fights, where partners trade insults, abuses (verbal and physical), and humiliations; they strip one another of their self-esteem, dignity and pride. In such situations, the one who is victimised, or the one who has already worked out alternate options, may want to opt out of that relationship. But, on the other hand, when love matures into friendship, fights never get ugly. And, partners never strip each other of their pride, dignity or self-esteem because trust has crept into the relationship. As they share trust among themselves, they sort out their differences with maturity. They maintain the code of quiet dignity as they grow to become soulmates.

Fourth Level: Soulmates

I wish to take you to a fourth level in your marriage relationship. From your level of friendship you can aspire to reach the heights of *belief* in each other. While it is tedious to climb from the level of love to the level of friendship, it is somewhat easier to scale the heights of *belief* in each other from the level of friendship. I say it is 'somewhat easier' because you have already experi-enced peace and tranquillity inside you when you 'surrendered' and bared your heart to each other in the third level. Now, you will have to bare your soul to your spouse. Of course, surrendering your soul takes a lot of courage; most of all to be transparent to each other. The very notion of baring one's soul with transparency is frightening; it's frightening because by being transparent you will reveal to the other your true identity. Your identity is an intrinsic and intimate component of who you really and truly are; it is the region where some of the most painful emotions reside—the region called, 'soul'. Robert A. Johnson, in *Owning Your own Shadow*, writes, "We are born whole, but early on our way, we begin the shadow-making process: we divide our lives. We sort out our God-given characteristics into those that are acceptable to our society and those that we have to put away." Johnson says that though we can conceal these experiences very well, they do not go away. "They only collect in the dark corners of our personality. When they have hidden long enough, they take on a life of their own," erupting from time to time, "as an overpowering rage or some indiscretion." To understand how we create the dark corners of our personality, John Welwood, in *Love and Awakening*, explains that, as children, we build a psychological shell around us to protect ourselves from feeling pain. Born open and loving, as children we are often taught that some

> When spouses open their pain to each other and touch those dark, secret inner feelings of fears and anxieties, hopes and dreams, they will experience greater self-acceptance, and enjoy the feelings of warmth and support which will draw them more intimately to each other.

> *Like a diamond, a marriage relationship also has many facets. It will be difficult to polish each facet daily. And, yet, to keep it lustrous and sparkling, you will have to take good care of it; and so it is with your marriage—you cannot take it for granted. To initiate the process of marriage maintenance, you may have to be romantically inclined towards each other.*

aspect of our self is unacceptable. Or, maybe we were taught to behave in a certain way in order to be good. This adaptation which is necessary for our survival and integration into the family, forces us to build a false personality that we struggle to maintain throughout our lives.

But as you grow from the levels of infatuation to love, and from love to friendship, and from friendship to being soulmates, you enter into a deeper level of relationship; and as you begin to connect your soul with your spouse's, you grow in belief. By believing in yourself and in your spouse, you surrender your souls to each other and connect yourselves as soulmates.

Romance: The Marriage Aphrodisiac

Aatmik and Shiren make a super couple whom I would like you to meet through their story. Aatmik and Shiren are in their early thirties and have two children. Aatmik loves life. He is the life of every party, Shiren admits. With his rich baritone voice he sings *ghazals*, reels off jokes, teases his friends (including their wives), and enjoys his scotch. In the mornings, he is punctual like the clock at his ultra-modern factory, ready to lead the hundred-and-sixty odd employees who work for him. Aatmik manufactures hi-fashion garments and exports them to some of the leading fashion houses in Europe and the USA, and he has never missed a deadline in the eight years since he built his export unit from scratch. Shiren has often heard her friends talk of how hard their husbands worked and the problems they faced. She never heard of a single problem Aatmik has had to face at the factory. He keeps it all to himself. Shiren is the opposite. She complains to him about everything that affects her—the kids, the in-laws, the servants, whatever. Every evening he is home by seven-thirty, unfazed, for his kids, his parents and his wife. When I asked him from where does he get the strength to carry everyone's burden? He said, he looks at life philosophically. "My parents are not easy people to live with, and Shiren has won them over. They dote on her. She gets impatient with the kids, and I keep telling her to soften up or else they'll turn into brats. She's a tough Mom. Oh, I've told her so many times not to call me at the office. There I'm sitting with my agents, or foreign buyers and I've to take a call and listen to Shiren and Aamer badgering each other over finishing a silly lunch. I guess what can't be cured has to be endured. Yes, the two of us go out at least three times a week because I understand how claustrophobic Shiren gets at home. I keep my philosophy simple: work hard, play hard. Life is too short to carry a grudge." Shiren said, "He gives me a lot of attention, and I love it. But, I tell him more times than he tells me, 'I love you'!"

On the surface, Aatmik and Shiren may seem like any couple to you who are still working at establishing compatibility. Sure, they have their share of fights and disagreements. They met me because they wanted to extract a lot more out of their marriage. When counselling them, I caught the dazzle in their eyes and the soft, warm tone in their voices as they talked for each other and about each other. That was ample testimony of the sublime level Aatmik and Shiren had reached in their seven years of marriage. They kept the romance going as they forged a union of hearts and minds. Their easy compatibility underlined the fact that they were soulmates.

> *Marital bliss is not a destination you arrive at. Instead, it's like driving on the hills. It's a winding road with ups and downs. And as you drive around, you soak in and savour the sights and smells that unfold before you.*

A Union of Hearts and Minds

When does one get to be a soulmate? Can one start at thirty? Forty? Or, at seventy? There is no age barrier to becoming soulmates. It has nothing to do with age; it has to do with your state of mind. You have got to keep your mind young and vibrant. You will have to 'want' to strengthen your marriage bonds and relationships. When both spouses begin to give due importance to 'marriage maintenance' then they automatically glide into the fourth sublime level of being soulmates. Marriage maintenance is about fun-loving romanticism. As you begin to enjoy each other's company and believe in each other, you experience a great measure of warmth in your relationship. You will develop infinite patience, trust, understanding and love for one another. Your thoughts are her thoughts and vice versa. You vibe so closely that at most times, words remain unspoken (at the thought level) and you know the other's mind so well. You will enjoy a union of hearts and minds. Such a 'union' is indeed a reservoir of wealth for a contended married life and for effective parenting. You will begin to 'feel' saturated by your *love* for each other, your *friendship* for each other, and your *belief* in each other. So saturated will you become, that your love, friendship and belief will naturally spill over and wash over others, especially your extended family of in-laws and parents. "You've mellowed so much," people close to you will affirm. Furthermore, it will spill and wash over the teachers who, in partnership with you, bring up your child in school. Your friendship and belief in the teachers will ignite them to reciprocate your vibes and help you bring out the best in your child. The love, friendship and belief which you offer to the school will be a spontaneous *outpouring* from the reservoir of your relationship at home.

CHAPTER 3

Relationships in Joint Families

My father wants me to be a photographer,
my mother wants me to be a saint.
My brother wants me to be a geographer,
my sister wants me to paint.
My grandfather wants me to swim like a fish,
my grandmother wants me to fly.
And one of my aunts would like me to dance
but none of them hear my cry ...
Oh leave me alone, leave me on my own
I just know what I want to be,
I want to be free to sit on a stone
and walk by the side of the sea.

— PIERS PLOWRIGHT *(The English Teaching Theatre)*

Geeta felt 'absolutely suffocated' living with her in-laws. Geeta found her in-laws to be overbearing and interfering. In her in-laws' view, Geeta couldn't do anything right. She could not feed the baby right, or bathe the baby right, or put the baby to sleep right. But according to Geeta, her in-laws had an 'attitude' towards her. She was always reminded and corrected sharply about the common sense of child-upbringing. Earlier she would swallow her anger, but now she gave it back from time to time. She was upset to see that her baby who was barely twenty-two-months old had grown more attached to *Daadi* than to Mom. Whenever Geeta corrected or scolded the child, both grandparents appeared on the scene instantly: they would chide her for being harsh and impatient with the baby, and would take the child away from her. As a result, the child became defiant and threw tantrums for which Geeta was again blamed as being the cause of that bad behaviour. Her relations with her husband become strained since he didn't want to take sides. Whenever she complained to him on his parents' attitude, he would shrug her off, saying, "Don't involve me. And stop complaining about them all the time."

And there is Karma. She openly admits to all her relatives and friends that the best package deal that came with her marriage was her in-laws, since they are in absolute sync with her. Whenever they have their regular dose of disagreements, after a while they put those differences aside, and get on with life. Karma swears by her in-laws. "As baby-sitters and caretakers, I couldn't find a better pair," she teases them. And when the kid gets out of hand and needs to be corrected, she has learnt to quickly march the kid off to her bedroom, shut the door, and administer the correction without anyone's interruption. She has learnt from past experiences that whenever she raised her voice at the kid, the grandparents would rush to the scene. It was not the correction that bothered them: it was her sharp tone of voice, she realised. Whenever she shouted at the kid, both her in-laws' hearts would go into a flutter and they would want to take over immediately. So, instead of fighting them off, and getting snubbed in return, which would benefit the child (as in Geeta's case), she decided to censure the child in private, and praise him in public. In other instances, whenever the child misbehaved in the company of the grandparents, she trained herself never to react to the misbehaviour. Oh, that was the hardest part, Karma admits. She left it to the grandparents to deal with the correction, and they dealt with it pretty well. Her teeming mind was always juggling with ideas so as to stay one step ahead of the child.

If we were to look deeper into Geeta's problem we would see that the cause of the problem was not the typical 'in-laws' tiff which seemed so obvious on the surface. The problem was the strained relationship between husband and wife. He would come home from work and would watch television with a peg or two of whisky, night after night. He would be annoyed to see Geeta get after the poor kid's life— "Do this, do that." After a while, it would be "Not this, not that." Why couldn't she give the child space, he would wonder as he watched TV and sipped his drink! Many times he would shout at her and tell her to shut up. That would bring on a fight. They would fight and argue about how the kid should be raised; she would nag him for not spending time with the kid, and how horrid his mother was. A number of times he had to slap her hard to shut her up.

Grandparents have to be won over—not by using the child or the spouse in a tug-of-war game. Grandparents have their set of flaws just like other human beings. Having aged, they have slowed down physically and mentally when compared to a parent's youthful standards. So they hold on to their old ways because the old ways hold meaning to them in the present changing times. Their old ways and habits give them a sense of security and continuity. Geeta had problems on two fronts: her in-laws and her husband. Instead of treating each problem separately, she clubbed them together as a single problem. Knowing that her husband was cold and indifferent to sharing household responsibilities, she should have worked on her in-laws and tried to charm them and win them over. Geeta, unfortunately, found them and their ways intrusive and hostile. She had succeeded in alienating herself from the others. Now she seemed absolutely fed up of life and had begun to feel sorry for herself.

Karma, on the other hand, found her in-laws to be a real asset. She learned to keep her husband in check with the help of her in-laws. Whenever she got into an argument with her husband, her in-laws would barge in and tell him to behave himself. She befriended them, charmed them with her lavish praises, humoured them, and shared responsibilities with them. Being younger and malleable, Karma learned to accept them as they were, and as a result, they got along as a team. Karma literally worked very hard, since the days of her courtship, to bring about this relationship with her in-laws. It was much easier then. She had realised that to have them eating out of her hand, she would first have to eat out of theirs. While she made those overtures, her in-laws too made adjustments, however slow, to love and accept her as wife, daughter and mother of the household. A bond of trust and friendship grew out of that give-and-take relationship which was very rewarding for the whole family.

Staying Married

Nothing comes easy in life, at least not the things we yearn for most of all. We all have dreams, and we see ourselves in our dreams as happily married. When that does not happen we feel cheated in life. When you go through this period of pain and uncertainty, the worst injustice you do to yourself is to entertain thoughts to break the relationship. You must not give up so easily; at least for your children's sake put your best foot forward to make the marriage work. You owe it to your children to work at it continuously—giving in sometimes, and making sacrifices most times. To keep the marriage commitment going, it is important for both partners to remind themselves not to be greedy about receiving marital rewards. If your spouse has done you a thoughtful act, a kind or gentle deed, then don't simply savour and hold dear the memory of that moment till the next deed comes along, but extend yourself and give back in return something of yourself. Living moment to moment, by giving and receiving, is one of the key ingredients to a contented married life.

> Marriage is a two-way contract; to stop the marriage boat from rocking, or getting submerged, it will take both partners to actively support the relationship.

Marital strife, coupled with daily bickerings and disputes, does take its toll on children's emotional and intellectual well-being. It is only when families begin to realise the full impact of the damage and hurt they bring to their children when they fight that they attempt to patch up their differences and behave as mature adults. Experts point out that the most important thing parents can do to help their kids grow up into well-adjusted individuals is to stay together. Sara McLanahan, sociology professor, whose writings are published in educational and psychological journals in the USA, says, "Children growing up with only one biological parent are twice as likely to do poorly in school or drop out of school altogether. They're less likely to get top marks, less likely to finish college and more likely to get in trouble with the law. As adults, they're also less likely to establish a stable relationship."

Coping with Stress

For the present generation, stress is a silent killer disease. Stress not only puts a strain on relationships in joint families, however close and intimate, but also destroys the individual's body and mind. Healthcare experts point out that families who live in a state of constant stress are prone to a number of ailments related to cardiovascular diseases. Whenever tension keeps gnawing at us, a wave of stress hormones are released into the bloodstream which weakens the body's immune system. The human body was created to live life to the full and not to self-destruct; but stress, like a malignant virus, eats into the immune system and systematically weakens it, which eventually leads to its destruction. Doctors are of the opinion that when you are infected by the stress virus you become more susceptible to indigestion, heart-burns, asthma, chest congestion, migraines, orthopaedic ailments and memory loss.

Time-out Technique

Just as when children manifest high stress symptoms, they are isolated and placed in time-out zones to cool off or calm down, so also should grownups isolate themselves to a solitary area where they can practise yoga and meditation in order to cool off and calm down. You can either do this on your own and find your rhythm of peace and harmony, or join a 'centre' where experts teach you how to relax. They will

> *Learn to count your blessings as you enumerate the strengths of the family members rather than dwell on their weaknesses. By doing so, you will surely find peace and harmony in your mind and body.*

explore with you a number of relaxation techniques which you will have to try out regularly until you establish your own rhythm. When you find your own rhythm, which calms your nerves, you would have succeeded in coping with stress. Maybe, for you it's not meditation, yoga, or breathing exercises, instead it could be listening to *ghazals*, classical music, or playing a musical instrument. You could also take a walk, sit under a tree, run, jog, do aerobics to find your rhythm of peace and harmony inside you. Whatever be your technique, whether it's meditation, music or the outdoors you will be focusing on being positive, and slowly but surely become a positive person. The past is over and behind you, while the future is not in your grasp. All you have is the present moment to make the best of. You can take control of the present by feeding your senses with positive vibes.

Parenting Guidelines for Grandparents

If we knew each other better,
we would praise where now we blame,
we would know each bears his burden
wears some hidden cross of shame.
We would feel the heartaches bitter
they so long alone have borne,
if we knew each other better,
we would have praise instead of scorn.

If we knew each other better,
you and I and all the rest,
seeing down beneath the surface
to the sorrows all unguessed,
we would quit our cold complaining
and a hand of trust extend;
if we knew each other better
we would count each one a friend.

We can know each other better
if we take the time to try,
little deeds of loving kindness

make a better by-and-by;
just a look of understanding
brings a touch with all mankind;
we can know each other better—
Yes, seeking, we shall find.

— ANNETTE DENSTED

The import of this topic is not to sound presumptuous and take on grandparents by framing a set of 'Guidelines on Parenting' for them. They have been around for so long as parents and they have had first-hand experiences on 'parenting'. So why tell them what they already know? Since a lot of it is common sense and a lot of it is taken for granted, I guess, that's why nobody has bothered to tell grandparents how to 'behave' with their grandchildren.

A SPECIAL RELATIONSHIP

Many parents do not realise it, but it is true that grandparents have a very special relationship with their grandchildren. It is almost like a 'friendship' between two equals. It is spontaneous and light-hearted, unlike the relationship a child has with his parents. It could be that the kids are smart enough to know that grandparents don't bother about discipline. At times, a very strong bond grows between the child and a particular grandparent, or grandparents—maybe because they share a similar outlook on life or have the same interests.

You could take this friendship further with your grand-children and be their teacher. No matter what your relationship with your son, daughter, son-in-law, or daughter-in-law is, you could extend yourself to teach values to your grandchildren. In your own lifetime, you have seen the world and you have been through ups and downs, through good times and bad times. Times change and no matter how quickly they change, certain needs never change—the need to live our lives in joy and courage; the need to get along with our fellowmen; and the need to hold on to those values which show us how to grow, to learn and to become better people. Why can't parents teach their children those age-old values? After all, your parents had taught you those values when you were a child, and you in turn, had passed those values to your children. But in your time when you were a parent, life was a little more simple and straight. Today life is very complex and complicated. Caught in the hustle and bustle of life—of making two ends meet—it would be a great loss to your grandchildren if they missed those lessons altogether. So, why take a chance and wait for the parents to pull up their socks on value education when you could, at your own pace and through your own example, softly, lovingly and gently teach your grandchildren life's essential values. Dr Wayne W. Dyer, renowned psychologist and author of *What do You Really Want for Your Children*, shows many ways to guide children to reach their goals and grow up into wholesome individuals. A lot of that advice by Dyer may sound familiar to you and easy to use because you may have used those very principles to raise your children. Now, you may have to do the same for your grandchildren because I believe grandparents make the finest teachers children could ever have.

Happiness

The first lesson to teach your grandchildren is to be happy. Though happiness may not be your life's greatest goal since you cannot be happy all the time, but you can get into the *habit* of being happy. You have seen people sail through a sea of misery by being happy, and you've also seen another set of people who, in spite of having the best things in life, are cribbers because of their inherent inability to enjoy life. What wouldn't you give to see that gleam of joy and delight in your grandchildren's eyes? You would like them to live happy lives.

> *Can children be taught a value such as 'happiness'? If anyone can, then I am sure it's the grandparents who can. All you have to do is allow children the space to make their own fun, and then teach them to hold on to it.*

In the *New Testament*, Jesus Christ told his disciples, "God loves a cheerful giver." Well, who doesn't? To create that 'cheerful giver', you will have to soak your grandchild in a tub of joy and leave him there to have fun. Happy experiences make generous and outgoing personalities. Those 'lessons' will come from your own examples as you make the best of life: enjoying yourself and enjoying your world. The joy you radiate will be infectious: your grandchildren will catch it from you.

Integrity

You can teach integrity to your grandchildren only by setting examples by the way you live. Children imitate adult behaviour very quickly, especially the grey areas. To convey 'integrity', you have to lead honest lives. It means that in the family you don't lie to each other; you are fair to all, without bias; you keep your promises, however inconvenient; you uphold family *rules*; the affection you profess is genuine and the praise you lavish is honest. On the other hand, when you relax inconvenient rules, or cover up for your grandchildren by offering alibis and lies for unfinished chores, you inadvertently teach them to be irresponsible and dishonest. When you say that a particular person has 'integrity', it means he has the quality of being able to be depended upon or trusted. Can you trust your grandchildren to speak the truth, especially when they have to own up for something naughty they did? Can you depend on your grandchildren to complete the chores on their own? If you can, then you have touched the hallowed milestone of integrity in your grandchildren's formative years. Their character reflects on your family and the values they uphold.

Courage

For your grandchildren to live with integrity, they need to learn to be courageous. They will also need the courage to sustain life's sufferings and failures without succumbing to them. Many of us try to shield little children from these by creating a pretence world saying that these things don't exist. When we do this we are not being honest. You may ask, is it too early to tell children about pain and suffering? I don't think so. Even a little child finds out that a family member dies, or a pet gets hurt. The best way to explain to little children, without complicating issues, is to speak in simple words like, "These things happen." The greatest gift you can give your grandchildren at such time is to reach out to other suffering people and help to alleviate their pain. When they grow to be adults, they will heal their pain by reaching out to people who need their help.

Spirituality

Spirituality is about meditation and prayer: to give your grandchildren a dream to hold on to, read to them every night a passage from the holy scriptures. When you sit to meditate or pray, get them to sit beside you and teach them how to pray. Touch their souls by giving them the sense of awe and reverence for things sacred. Show them how to converse respectfully with grownups. As you listen to their aspirations and hopes, guide them to cherish their dreams in simple ways. Open to them the world of books, music, art because these are the birthplaces of many a good dream.

Love

There is so much of love around and yet we can't have enough of it; that's because we get a blast of it from time to time and then nothing—it blows away, leaving us high and dry. You don't need to spend time teaching your grandchildren about love. Toddlers know what love is, that is why they keep telling you, "I love you." But a moment later, when you ask them for a hug or a kiss, they may turn their backs on you. Children have to learn not only about love, but also about becoming loving persons. Love is not a trading skill to bargain with. Teach your grandchildren how to hold on to love, how to sustain love, and to be loving persons. As a result, when they grow up to take their place in the world, they will know how to keep love alive around them.

> 'If I give you candy will you give me a hug?' doesn't make children loving persons; it will make them calculating and manipulative.

UPGRADE YOUR PARENTING SKILLS

As loving, doting grandparents, you have in you the wisdom and infinite patience for bringing up your grandchildren in the best possible way. You are now more relaxed than you were as parents a few decades ago. Whatever your feelings and thoughts are about parenting, just keep in mind that your grandchildren are so unlike their parents you raised some thirty odd years ago. Today you are dealing with super-intelligent kids who learn about the good, the bad and the ugly, and use that knowledge to their advantage (one-third being positive and two-thirds being negative). So, get savvy and modernise your ways of thinking to meet the challenges your techno-modern grandchildren throw up from time to time. You can't serve values in compartments; you cannot go gung-ho on your grandchildren and not see eye to eye with their parents. If you don't have good rapport with their parents, then the kids have already made a sucker of you and them. And if your relationship with them is more than congenial, then you've already got the grandchildren eating out of the palm of your hands. It all depends on the prevailing climate at home and your contribution to it.

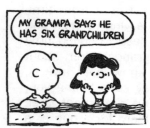
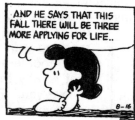
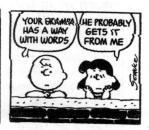

Try Not to Step on Toes

I have always looked upon grandparents as a great asset to family life. They are solid, like the Rock of Gibraltar. And I find it very heartbreaking to know, in a number of cases, that this 'great asset' has turned out to be a 'great liability' to a harmonious family life. If, through these pages you feel inspired to iron out the crinkles in your family relations, then sharing these thoughts with you would prove a worthwhile endeavour.

Whenever you see a pond or a well, you don't jump into it even though you may be an experienced swimmer. Similarly, when you see your grandchildren you need not take over the reins simply because you're an experienced parent. Lots of parents worry that grandparents spoil children. But how can anyone spoil the child with love and attention, you may ask? To win the confidence of parents, you may have to assure them that in the upbringing of your grandchild, you will maintain some basic ground rules. Some of these 'ground rules' are: You will NEVER

- *interfere when your grandchild is being corrected or disciplined*
- *contradict or overrule commands, however strict or misplaced they may be*
- *let her watch television (soap serials) with you*
- *let her stay up late at nights to play with you*
- *give her ice-cream, chocolates, custards and puddings in excess*
- *encroach upon her parents' space*

You may have heard the old saying, 'By the time the son realises that his father was right, he already has a son who thinks he is wrong.' So, don't be sore at me for telling you of the six never-dos, at least not yet. You see the children you raise (not the grandchildren) are a bundle of contradictions. When it suits them, they lean upon you for advice, and you readily give it. Then they turn around and say you're always interfering in their lives. This can be very painful to stomach. The trouble is you've seen them always running to you for advice since they were children, and now when your sixth sense warns you of the impending trouble, and you rush in with help and advice, they resent it and, you feel snubbed.

There is no need to hold a grudge against your children for their seeming intolerance. Being older and wiser, it is expected of you to avoid raising mental barriers. The mind is a very complex machine, and when it indulges in 'mind games', you may find it difficult to match your wits against their skills. If your children are seeking to establish some degree of independence from you, then allow them the space to achieve it. Your relationship with your children (who are married adults) should ideally be based on mutual respect for each other, rather than have a relationship based on control.

Perhaps, you are in a situation where your son or son-in-law works for the family business—a business you established, or lives under your roof along with the wife and kids. In such situations it would be very difficult for you to maintain a relationship of mutual respect. After all, respect flows from the ability to work and live independently. The situation may worsen if the daughter-in-law displays a mind of her own with her so-called independent thinking. You may be tempted to remind her that all her allowances come from the family coffers of which you are the CEO. Maybe, you don't say it in words, but your attitude could be saying it louder.

In your wisdom, you may have realised that there are times when your daughter, daughter-in-law, son, or son-in-law have felt your overpowering presence, that they can't do things right, and you make them feel inadequate as parents. Of course, you wouldn't do anything like that—at least not intentionally. All you wanted to do was share your years of parenting experiences with them and they can't even appreciate your concern, which causes unnecessary conflict in the family. It is so confusing, this whole issue of offering help and support—when to offer and how much to offer. Unfortunately there are no books, leaflets, or crash courses to guide you on how to turn on your tact, or your diplomacy, in an effort to stroke ruffled feathers. More than anyone else, you can be counted upon to offer mature counsel when required. Your aim when offering counsel is not to create a divide in the family but to bond the family together; so, be tactful rather than tacky, and avoid sarcasm or condescension in your choice of words or tone of voice. Your efforts will not go waste; your children will look up to you in admiration, and your grandchildren will learn to walk in your footsteps.

Working Mothers

For women who don't achieve a balance, who let their career become the number one priority to the exclusion of all other interests, the results can be disastrous.

— RONYA KOZMETSKY *(Women in Business)*

Balancing between Home and Career

Can working mothers be effective parents? Of course, comes the pat response from a chorus of working mothers. If we shift the question to make it child-oriented and ask, "Do the children of working mothers feel neglected, develop complexes, and struggle with school work?" Career Moms may become a little cautious in answering, no or yes! So why do mothers work? Some out of necessity are motivated to supplement the much-needed income. For others, the motivation could be psychological. Entering into a male-dominated arena, and exercising control over that male preserve stimulates high doses of positive self-image, personal satisfaction and social status when compared to a 'housewife' whose work revolves around the house. Another reason could be that mothers want to work in order to keep their creative juices flowing.

They are dynamic, intelligent and gifted with a natural urge to explore and exploit their skills and talents. They fear that if they take a sabbatical on their skills, their creativity will shrivel up. Unfortunately, many working mothers suffer from a guilt complex. There is always that dark lurking thought gnawing in their minds, 'I wasn't there when my baby needed me.' This guilt is much more in mothers whose motive for working is not monetary, but social status and personal satis-faction (self-actualisation). The next question is: Do housewives make better parents than working mothers? Or, are non-working mothers efficient home-makers? In either case, the answer cannot be generalised. I would like you to meet three non-working housewives—Gayatri, Sushmita and Swarna who lived three different lifestyles: one felt trapped in her marriage, the second chased after social trappings, while the third embraced marriage as a full-time commitment.

Immediately after completing her MBA, Gayatri was married into what was commonly called a conservative family. While Gayatri wanted to work, her in-laws opposed her by saying, "There is enough money in the family for everyone to live on." On occasions when she tried to draw them into a discussion on a career, they put their foot down firmly with a strong 'no,' and a rider: "You must have a baby soon." Gayatri felt like she was on a leash. The daily household chores were the only activities she was allowed to absorb herself with. As the years passed by, she had three children, but that did not lift the dark shroud of depression from her shoulders. She resigned to blaming fate for being stuck in such a sorry state. As mental lethargy had set in, she felt less challenged, empty and bored. Being dissatisfied and disgruntled, her children began to manifest her ennui. The teachers at school would complain about the children's falling grades. In no time their emotional and intellectual growth got stymied and they became underachievers.

Sushmita hated the idea of a working woman, and never wanted to take up any career. When Sushmita was twenty-one, she was married off into a wealthy family. After marriage she had no need to make the slightest adjustments since she had married into a family that was marginally wealthier than hers. The lifestyle she was used to before marriage was pretty much the same as the one after marriage. She loved shopping, eating out, partying with friends and doing her workouts at the gym. As for minding home, there were 'elders' around, plus there were ample servants to look after household chores, as well as individual needs. After a couple of years she delivered a daughter, whom she named Charu. Nothing much changed for Sushmita, except for a new maid who was hired to keep the baby company day and night. Over the years, the child grew up under the care of the maid-servant who acted as a surrogate Mom, while Sushmita kept herself busy between remodelling the interiors of her home, to shopping, entertaining her friends and being entertained. Occasionally, the newspapers would flash her pictures in what is known as the 'Page 3' socialite columns. The servants were always there to welcome Charu from school. The maid performed her duties conscientiously. She fed the child, bathed her, dressed her, watched television with her and put her to bed every night. As for studies there were other helpers available, like tutors, who were hired to teach Charu and do her homework. Since everyone's needs were taken care of in one way or the other, Sushmita was looked upon as a successful socialite.

Swarna was married for seven years and blessed with twins. Her husband had his own business. Swarna was a bundle of energy and drive. Swarna had just started practising law when she got married. After marriage, she opted to give up the law practice and chose to run the house. She would organise her time by allocating fixed slots for housework, family, childcare, and friends. Swarna was also actively involved in social work. She was secretary of an organisation that ran an institute for destitute women. She was so structured with her time that every morning she would set herself tasks on a priority basis. She would arrange her schedule by (a) clubbing together chores that she must do, (b) the chores which she must get done, and (c) the not-so-important ones which could be attended to later. Operating under this priority-based time structure on a day-to-day basis, Swarna would efficiently execute her work in a relaxed manner; she was never hassled or frustrated because she always stayed organised. She radiated the joy of being available to do chores, however big or small, to her husband, children, in-laws, parents, relatives, friends and at the charitable institute. On the one hand, the family absolutely depended on her, and on the other, she was much sought after by relatives and friends. With the support of her husband, Swarna had a very active social life, too. But, no matter how busy she was, Swarna was always home to welcome her two children from school. After lunch, she would sit to guide them in their studies but never spoon-fed them. After studies, around five or six in the evening, she sent her children for sports and hobby activities. Her home was her centre, and everything revolved within the walls of her home. Naturally, the children blossomed under such an atmosphere, and measured up to the parents' expectations as they grew up.

The Guilt Trap

Whether mothers are career-bound or house-bound is of little consequence. You can't toss a coin for an answer as to who's more effective—mothers with careers or mothers who stay at home to raise children. "Pitting stay-at-home Moms against work-outside-of-the-home mothers makes everyone a loser," says Hillary Clinton in her book, *It Takes a Village*: "There is no magic formula for raising children. You will find successes and failures among parents who do the work of staying home with their children and among those who leave home to go to work. What makes the difference is whether parents have the competence and commitment to give children what they need for healthy development ... If you want to open the floodgates of guilt and dissension anywhere ... start talking about child care. It is an issue that brings out all of our conflicted feelings about what parenthood should be and about who should care for children when parents are working or otherwise unable to." It's the quality of life you live. If you opt for a career-marriage, then make a success of it for all the right reasons. And if it is to be a housewife's role, then give it your hundred per cent. It is only when your motives get mixed up and life's vision blurs, then guilt, like a virus, eats into you. Guilt makes you feel inadequate as a parent. Your inherent inadequacies remind you that you are doing injustice to our children. You feel guilty and blame yourself for all the shortcomings your children manifest. This negative attitude rubs off on the children. Mothers who suffer from guilt pangs attempt to cover their guilt by 'giving in' to their children's demands and tantrums. Some trade guilt with gifts, outings, movies, or eating at fast-food outlets.

So, should mothers not feel guilty? Rather than nurture guilt pangs, which are reactive and non-productive, they should, instead, constantly assess their strengths and those of their children, restructure schedules, and prioritise chores to achieve optimum satisfaction on all fronts. Many working parents, who feel guilty, often express platitudes like, "I spend quality time with my children." These parents may put aside, say, one day on every weekend to be available for the child, or may take the family for a weekly outing. But what happens to the child who needs your attention or help on a day outside the weekend? Since it doesn't fit in with your weekend plan, should the child learn to wait his turn? After all, we remind ourselves that parents need *space*, too! Quality time doesn't mean the quantity of time spent with the child when it suits you, or at your convenience. He may have needed you last Wednesday, but you were not there for him because you had planned the Sunday outing for him (refer to Chapter on *Quality Time*).

> Quality time should be measured in terms of being there when the other needs you—no matter what the day or the time.

Managing Efficiently

Whether you're a business woman, a career woman or a housewife, when you set high goals for yourself, stress can seem as much a part of your life as eating or breathing, so much so, that you don't realise you are feeling it. Many workplaces prefer to remain oblivious of women playing the balancing act between office and family. And employers may not want to show any consideration, understanding or compassion about children's illnesses and doctor's appointments. Surveys conducted about the working conditions of working women show that generally women in lower-paid jobs found their workplaces less family-friendly and flexible than women in executive and management positions. As a professional working woman, you may not be able to break job commitments or appointments in order to attend to home matters. "My version of every mother's worst nightmare happened one morning when I was due in court at nine-thirty for a trial. It was already seven-thirty, and two-year-old Chelsea was running a fever and throwing up after a sleepless night for both of us. My husband was out of town. The woman who normally took care of Chelsea called in sick with the same symptoms. No relatives lived nearby. My neighbours were not at home. Frantic, I called a trusted friend, who came to my rescue. Still, I felt terrible that I had to leave my sick child at all. I called at every break and rushed home as soon as the court adjourned. When I opened the door and saw my friend reading to Chelsea, who was clearly feeling better, my head and stomach stopped aching for the first time that day." (Hillary Rodham Clinton, *It Takes a Village*).

Staying in Top Form

We live in a society that is addicted to performing at high levels of efficiency and speed. Thirty-four-year-old Priya Jain, who is a senior vice-president in a Delhi-based multinational company, recently discovered that she was a victim of stress-related ailments. Her hectic job has her breezing in and breezing out of cities, attending conferences and meeting clients across continents. Apart from constant jetlag, eating hotel meals, and regular partying, she also has to squeeze in time to attend her child's PTA, supervise his homework, and cook his gourmet breakfasts and sometimes, dinners when her husband is buried in work at the office. When the company signed her in for a mandatory executive health check-up programme, she was shocked by her state of health. The results showed she was overweight, suffered from high blood pressure and thyroid. Dr R.P. Soonawala, gynaecologist at Breach Candy Hospital, Mumbai, says, "It's not coincidental then that just so many more are coming in with complaints of irregular menstruation and unbearable pre-menstrual syndrome. Drinking, smoking and tension are impacting fertility and birthing processes." The housewife doesn't have it any easier either.

The home schedule could be equally demanding. She may start the day by ensuring that her in-laws, husband, children and servants are humoured and kept happy, which in itself is no mean task. Many housewives begin their day in the wee hours of the morning, and wind up late nights. They pack a good fourteen to sixteen hours of toil every day—from getting the children ready for school every morning and supervising their homework every afternoon, to keeping the household fed at fixed times, to entertaining friends and relatives, and, most of all, doing the delicate balancing act of keeping everyone from warring. No wonder at the end of the day it seems like they don't have time for themselves at all. To live life to the full, it is important that you stay in top form, physically and mentally. It is only when you are in top form that you can give the best of yourself to your spouse, children, career and home at trying times. To get the better of yourself you will need a little space—a mental space—for introspection and rejuvenation.

Indulge in 'Active' Relaxation

More than anyone else, you know what tension feels like as it builds up—it's that pounding headache, ailing back, or insomnia. When tension hits you, your body reacts in milliseconds. You breathe faster, and your heart rate and blood pressure rise. Your senses sharpen and your muscles tense up as you prepare yourself for action. These responses give you the energy you need to finish preparing a special dinner in record time after your husband walks in one evening with three unannounced dinner guests. That can be stressfully gruelling. If you keep pushing yourself in that energised state for too long, it will eventually take its toll on you—generally by striking that part of your body that is genetically or developmentally most vulnerable. Dr Kenneth Greenspan, Director of the Centre for Stress and Pain-related Disorders, at Columbia-Presbyterian Medical Centre in New York, says "When you're under a lot of stress, all your muscles tense. But if you have a weakness in your lower back, it's backache that you'll feel first, because that's where your 'weak link' is." Once you learn to recognise the stress 'danger signals', the only way you can rid yourself of them is through relaxation techniques. Make an all-out effort to take time out every day to do something that calms you. You may go cycling, swimming, running, rowing, anything and you will find that exercise actually changes your body physiologically to keep you feeling good and, at the same time, builds up endurance. Research shows that specific physiological changes take place in your body when you exercise vigorously that may temper the ravages of stress. Through 'active' relaxation you can make your bad days easier to get through and your good days better than ever.

When You're Stressed

When you feel threatened or anxious, your body switches to 'fight or flight' mode to gear you into action (*see* Chapter on *How the Mind Works*). For instance, here's an office situation you can identify with: Mehar Tyagi heads the marketing department of an export company. She's upset and wants to give a piece of her mind to a colleague whose casual attitude messed up a deal that was almost sewed up. Mehar is on her way to the colleague's office. As she nears the cabin, Mehar's brain senses the stress and sends a message to the hypothalamus, the main control centre in the brain, which in turn signals the pituitary gland and the adrenal medulla. According to healthcare experts, these glands simultaneously send out chemical signals and stress hormones (epinephrine [adrenaline] and norepinephrine from the adrenal medulla and cortisol from the pituitary) pour into the bloodstream. Mehar feels the heady effects of these chemicals immediately. They speed up the heart rate, increase blood pressure, dilate pupils, increase blood volume and the sodium level in the blood, and direct blood to the muscles and the liver for quick energy. In short, Mehar is fully ready to deal with the errant colleague in a stressful and threatening situation. But when she reached her colleague's cabin she finds her sobbing at her desk. Instantly, Mehar reacts differently towards her. Instinctively, she reaches out a conciliatory arm to her colleague. When Mehar left her colleague's cabin it was only after comforting her, minus the showdown. Though the stressful event has passed, but the potent chemicals it triggered are still circulating in Mehar's bloodstream.

Mehar's body is capable of controlling the alarm response and bring itself back in balance. That's because when her brain senses that blood levels of any of these stress hormones are too high, her body automatically reverses the stress reaction after the 'threat' is over, so that her blood pressure and heart rate drop and return to normal. However, if Mehar is exposed to stress repeatedly—for instance, when Mehar gets back to her office only to find that another huge order just fell through because of the delay caused in one of her production units—her body turns back on the red alert. More stress hormones are released, while her recovery mechanism is short-circuited. When she reaches home in the evening there are more complaints to attend, including a warning note from her son's class-teacher. If the stress continues without a break for long periods of time, Mehar's body can no longer recover from the alarm response and she begins to feel the pain of tension-related symptoms, like migraines or backaches. But Mehar is one smart cookie. She uses stress to beat stress through stressful exercises. Every morning she runs in the common park near the house. She runs vigorously till the blood soars in her veins and her heart pounds as she breaks into a panting sweat. This regular 'active' relaxation not only makes Mehar feel better and more relaxed in the short term, but it also helps her body respond better to stress in the long run.

Exercise: Your Stress Buster

Researchers studying stress and stress-reduction techniques are of the opinion that when you exercise and break into a sweat, your body releases beta-endorphins—a powerful morphine-like substance that has been linked to that feeling of well-being known as 'runners high'. These neurotransmitters are released at the same time as the stress hormones, but they temper their effect, to keep your body stabilised during the alarm reaction. According to Dr George P. Chrousos, senior investigator at the National Institute of Child Health and Human Development in Bethesda, USA: "Endorphins have a very agreeable side effect: they make you feel good. When you exercise regularly, you get a very nice dose of endorphins. If you don't exercise, you never get that boost. This effect can be so powerful that when well-conditioned people stop exercising, they experience withdrawal symptoms—that crabby, crazy feeling you get if you miss a workout."

Scientists are still unravelling the mysteries behind endorphins. "When you work out on a regular basis, more endorphins get into your system in a shorter amount of time and stay there longer," says Kenneth Cooper, aerobics guru and founder of the Institute for Aerobics Research in Dallas. Those of you who exercise regularly reap the benefits of a well-toned body in excellent condition. If your body is in good condition, endorphins are released at the same time that you experience stress—that's when you need them most to stabilise your body and minimise pain. But if you don't exercise regularly, your body responds by increasing endorphin levels *after* a workout. That's too late to derive maximum benefit. And of course, if you're not in the habit of exercising, you won't get the repeated positive feedback of endorphin release that you would if you did.

A NOTE OF CAUTION

Over-exercise can kill. It has been reported that professional sportsmen whose fitness and activity levels were much higher than average persons, have died of cardiac arrest while playing. Dr Naresh Trehan, Director and chief cardiac surgeon at the Escorts Heart Institute & Research Centre, New Delhi, is reported saying, "The most common cause of sudden death from cardiac causes during activity is hypertrophic cardio-myopathy where the septal or cardiac muscles are thicker than normal and which cause obstructions in heart flow. Since vigorous exercise leads to more stress on the heart, people with an undiagnosed condition may collapse during exercise." Dr K.K. Talwar, Head of the Department of Cardiology at the All India Institute of Medical Sciences, New Delhi, says, "Even teenagers, who get symptoms of dizziness, fainting spells and acute shortness of breath while running should get their hearts evaluated." Be careful not to start a programme of vigorous exercise if you are not already in good physical condition. Consult your doctor for advice and gradually build up the level of exercise.

Do You Sleep Well?

Gunjan is a thirty-seven-year-old career woman with an insomnia problem. She says, "Even with my eyes shut, I know it's the middle of the night. What woke me up? A dream? Cramps? The noise of the air-conditioner? It doesn't matter. I'm awake. Although one side of my brain yearns for sleep, the anxious side has already started stacking a multitude of should-haves and what-ifs. I think of my mother-in-law who's unwell. What if she has cancer? Could tumour be the cause of the headaches? How would I keep the job if something happened to her? Without my job could we afford the good education we give our three children? Am I neglecting the youngest? She's only in playschool ... which reminds me, it's time to get them ready for school. I look at my watch. It's only 3.35. I tell myself if I don't catch some sleep, I'll be a wreck at work the whole day." "And, what about your husband," I asked her? "He's fast asleep," she says. "Though we share many stresses, it doesn't seem to affect him. He snores into his pillow every night." It is true, lots of men have the ability to switch on and switch off their stress buttons and snore through the night.

Guard Your Sleep Zone

Your sleep zone is your bedroom—a room to make love and to sleep; and not a place to programme your TV, your worries, or your office. Gunjan not only brought her office into her bedroom but also watched TV in the bedroom and entertained friends. According to Gunjan, "The bedroom was a cosy sitting-room for close friends." There was nothing wrong with entertaining old friends in the bedroom except that they left

> To reduce stress at bedtime you should banish the TV, the cellphone the office paperwork and entertaining friends in your bedroom.

behind the stink of stale cigarette smoke, which made her turn up her nose in distaste. All these are reminders of entertainment, excitement, or tension. You must be selfish enough to guard your sleep zone. Like Gunjan, many working women bring home the workload and run a second shift at home in the bedroom, especially when they have major deadlines to meet. Establish a ritual of activities that will slow you down at bedtime, such as sipping a cup of light herbal tea, or a warm bath, or both. Research points out that a warm bath before bedtime relaxes tense muscles and leads to deep sleep.

BUILDING A DAD-FRIENDLY HOME

With both parents working in today's stress-ridden jobs, it is only natural that all their juices get sapped at the office and they both come home drained every evening, looking for relaxation, peace and quiet. But in most cases the woman ends up doing the kitchen work, as well as supervising the children's studies, while the man of the house takes a shower to wash away the day's fatigue and then sits to watch television as he patiently waits for his supper. Father dear has already proved that he is unable to cook or assist in the kitchen, and since he is short-tempered and irritable after a day's hard labour, he is unable to coach or supervise the children's studies. It is obvious that Mother dear has to be blamed for making her husband a nincompoop at home, who otherwise is a very successful career professional at the office. Since the time the baby arrives, the woman switches her role from being a wife to being a mother. She mothers the child, she mothers the pets, and she *mothers* the husband. She sees how awkwardly he holds the baby, changes the diaper and is helpless when it comes to quietening the infant. So, she quickly takes over from him because things have to be done in the right way—her way! Many fathers have confessed to me that they're unable to communicate and bond with the tiny creature, so they keep themselves 'busy' with office work, pet hobbies, reading newspapers and magazines, whatever. Some fathers are at a loss for ideas when it comes to spending time with children.

Building Family Support Systems

To succeed in one's career and goals, as well as for children to succeed in school, each one needs the support of family members. When families get wrapped around with love, friendship and belief in each other, they create 'support systems' for one another to succeed. Sacrifice, tolerance and acceptance come easy to them. They are so primed to the others' needs that they always happen to be there; they are around, helping, supporting, or doing simple chores to generally assist one another. Perhaps, you could relate to the example of Rahul, a thirteen-year-old who has to catch the school bus every morning at 7 o'clock. Be it winter, summer or the monsoon season, Rahul has never missed the school bus. For Rahul to succeed in making it to school by the school bus, his parents wake up at five-thirty every morning to create the support system. As they are up early, they wake up Rahul at six every morning. The toilet is kept free for him to use. They are around to see that he is well taken care of: has a hot breakfast, wears a fresh set of clean clothes, all the books, school diary packed in the bag, with nothing forgotten, and he is at the bus stop well in time to board the school bus. A warm send off every morning is an essential tonic for Rahul, and for every child to start the day right and bright.

What a boon it is to mothers, especially working mothers, when their husbands pitch in with both hands and feet to build a support system around the family. This can happen when both spouses keep the communication lines alive. In most marriages, communication is about assigning blame. So, get to function like a team and talk about your roles as husband and wife; and then talk about your roles as father and mother, and subsequently go ahead and play those roles. Being a good father is never easy. That's why both spouses have to be equally committed to ensuring that the children enjoy a good father-children relationship. You have a winning team at home when fathers get comfortable spending time in the kitchen, as well as supervise the children's studies, or walk to the bus stop with the child in the mornings, and from time to time do chores and share responsibilities, big and small. You can be assured that you have a healthy marriage and healthy, happy children, who in turn will play similar roles when they grow up.

Bonding with Fathers

What shall I give to one small boy?
A glamorous game, a tinselled toy,
a Barlow knife, a puzzle pack,
a train that runs on curving track?
A picture book, a real live pet...
no, there's plenty of time for such things yet.

Give him a day for his very own -
Just one small boy and his Dad alone.
A walk in the woods, a romp in the park,
a fishing trip from dawn to dark,
give the gift that only you can -
The companionship of his Old Man.
Games are outgrown, and toys decay-
but he'll never forget if you "Give him a day".

— ANON

We were passangers in transit at Delhi airport. I was surprised that he instantly recognised me even after a gap of twelve years. We latched on to each other since all the flights were cancelled due to the heavy January fog. We exchanged pleasantries, then our business cards, then some snacks, and while we snacked, S.M.Jha spoke about his family. Three hours later when the fog cleared, and before we parted company, he urged me to correspond with him with the hope of inspiring his kids to better performance.

Shauriya Mohan Jha ran a successful export business in Patna. At forty, he was a contended man, he told me he had amassed a huge fortune in a span of nine years, yet he was restless: looking for more, demanding more, expecting more. He lived in a sprawling bungalow in Pataliputra Colony, considered to be among the fashionable residential areas in Patna. His fifteen-year-old son, Vedant, studied in St. Michael's High School, and his thirteen-year-old daughter, Sehr, studied in Notre Dame Convent. Shauriya Mohan Jha gave his children the best schools the city offered. But, with disappointment showing in his voice, he said that the two kids were not 'sharp' at all. "Sehr is a waster, and Vedant a drifter. When fathers can run a complex business well, why can't mothers run a simple home?" he wondered. Obviously, he blamed his wife for the kids' failures, and the kids for failing him. He wanted to know if it was too late for his wife to learn new ways to guide and motivate the kids to be achievers and go-getters.

Father's Hand in Parenting

When it comes to parenting, fathers may put on a superior air of 'I handle only important jobs.' They want others to believe that they are on this planet to perform great things without compromising their mission on mundane chores like parenting children. Worse still, they are quick to identify problems at home and know whom to hold accountable for those problems. Mothers, who else? Like Shauriya Mohan Jha, they see the 'mess' at home and lord it over their wives to clean up the mess. After all, it's *their* job, they say. Unfortunately, they choose to take a very simplistic view of the mess without owning responsibility, or assist in finding solutions to overcome the problems. How can fathers be responsible for the mess when mothers are handling the day-to-day affairs, they ask with smug innocence? Just as they don't expect their wives to assist them in running the office, the wives shouldn't expect their husbands to come home from office and assist them in housekeeping. Without lending a hand, husbands expect their wives single-handedly to keep a clean house, keep the children disciplined without screaming, or smacking them, attend to their studies, attend PTAs, attend to their ailments, including doctors' visits, and ensure that the kids eat well, sleep well, and behave well at home and in public places. From time immemorial, fathers had chalked out for themselves the type of role they would play as parents: they will be the 'providers' and mothers the 'nurturants'.

Why the Reluctance to Play a Nurturant Role?

An Anthropological View

According to anthropologist Margaret Mead, "Fathers are a biological necessity, but a social accident." To better understand a father's role in the human family, we may gain some insights by observing the behavior of the father's role in non-human species where after procreation his function primarily is the protection of the mother and the offspring. Research carried out by Desmond Morris and other zoologists point out that except for isolated instances in the animal kingdom, as in mammalian species of the mountain gorilla, the father does not engage in the daily responsibilities of child rearing. In most non-mammalian species, the father rarely assumes any important functions related to the nurturing of the offspring. However, the wolf has been observed occasionally to baby-sit and feed the young while the mother is away from the den. One study of monkeys, father, mother and offspring, in the laboratory-setting showed how the father participated competently in the caretaking process of the young ones, so unlike of monkeys living in the wilderness. The study pointed out, the infant monkeys reared in such conditions developed extensive social patterns of behaviour.

A Historical Perspective

Strange as it may seem, maternal dominance in child-rearing is not an age-old practice. In fact, fatherhood was considered pre-eminent up until the mid-1700s when fathers worked in or near their homes (farming communities), and played an important role in child-rearing. It wasn't mothers, but fathers who were considered more competent a parent, and held responsible for how the children turned out. Books and manuals on parenting were written chiefly for fathers. The effects of paternal dominance were felt till the 1990s when courts routinely awarded fathers the custody of children in cases of divorce.

During the Industrial Revolution, more fathers began working outside their homes and were effectively removed from domestic duties. In *Fathers and Developmental Psychopathology*, Vicky Phares wrote how industrialisation brought about the "feminisation of the domestic sphere and the marginalisation of father's involvement with their children." Professor Phares further added, "By the mid-1800s, child-rearing manuals were geared towards mothers, and this trend continued for the most part until the mid-1970s."

By the turn of the twentieth century, the psychology of parenting was considered exclusively as the psychology of motherhood. Psychologists like Sigmund Freud, who believed fathers figured predominantly in children's development of conscience and sexual identity, dismissed the idea that they had any impact until well past a child's third year. Other psychologists said that a father's contribution consisted primarily of providing income, discipline, a masculine role model, and periodic outings—an exposure of the 'real world'—as experience of the world outside the home.

By the 1920s, the 'feminisation' of child-rearing began to show its cracks. Studies point out that hardly was there any hard evidence of unique maternal instincts involved in child rearing. There were none of the evasive masculine excuses that mothers are biologically better equipped than fathers to nurture children. As societies became industrialised, mothers took over the reins of parenting because fathers were not around, or unable to attend to child-rearing duties. And, instead of being content with the shift in duties, fathers began blaming mothers for all the emotional and behavioural problems of their children. By the 1940s, psychologists, and many more mothers, were asking whether fathers might share some of the responsibilities of child-upbringing.

Family sociologist, E.E. LeMasters, in his book, *Parents in Modern America*, castigated the father's role in child upbringing for the following reasons: a) A father is poorly prepared for his parental role; as a boy he was not taught the duties and responsibilities of a father outside of his economic role as provider. b) There is no biological basis for the father-child relationship, as there is for the mother-child relationship. c) The success of father's parental role depends upon his success in the pair-bond with his wife.

If we call the present the age of the 'Electronic Revolution' in order to showcase the advancement of science as a triumph of the human intellect, then according to one investigator, this triumph and advancement came at the cost of family life since many fathers today spend far less time with their children than at any other period in history—and that's not because for want of competency, but because of the stressful lifestyles they have embraced. Due to job constraints, fathers are just not physically available to connect with their children. Regrettably, these fathers have been stereotyped as uninterested in and uninvolved with young children. But, mothers need not lose heart; recent research points out, fathers are becoming interested in and involved with young children and, furthermore, they are as nurturant towards them as mothers are. Another research, refuting Frued's theory, has indicated that infants seek the proximity of their fathers rather than that of strangers and do show a pattern of attachment to the father.

Father's Influence on Children's Upbringing

The father's role in society has changed during the last twenty years, with a trend towards acceptance of a nurturant father who is more involved in childcare responsibilities. Many fathers help in feeding, bathing, changing diapers, putting the child to bed, reading stories, dressing, disciplining, playing, and calling the doctor when the child is sick. In addition, he also helps with household duties if and when the mother has to return to work outside the home.

A father's involvement in child-upbringing impacts the development of children from infancy through adulthood. When

> *Fathers who are more involved in infant caregiving, have infants with greater cognitive development at one year of agen than fathers who are less involved.*

researchers compared the development of pre-schoolers, pre-teens and teenagers, they found that when fathers were involved in care-giving and valued education, the children's verbal ability, relationships, intellectual development and school grades were better than those whose fathers did not spend time reading to them, or were not involved.

Three simple ways to be a positive father:

◆ **Be a Fun Dad:** Encourage children to potter around the house and do chores for you, and applaud their achievements, however small. The time you spend in their company should contribute to happy memories to last a lifetime. Tickle them, hug them, cuddle them, rock them on your lap, toss them in the air, or swing them around to invade their physical space and to help them overcome their physical and mental inhibitions. Encourage laughter around you.

◆ **Be a Fair Dad:** Bond with your wife so that you not only endorse the limits she sets, but also respect those limits, and she does the same for you. When setting limits, ensure that your children are given fair chances to measure to your expectations—they should never feel cornered or bullied by your method of discipline. Never be afraid to admit your mistakes to your children, and they will love you for being a 'human' Dad with 'warts and all'. When dealing with siblings, don't pacify one at the cost of the other. Project fairness so that your children perceive you to be a fair Dad.

◆ **Be an Involved Dad:** Be there to organise your children's birthdays as it is the most important day for them. Put aside your personal work to attend PTAs, and other school events, games and activities. The more time you spend in their company the more easy you will find to get under your children's skin to help them talk things over which are of interest to them, or help them with their studies, or with some problem they are facing in school, or with themselves. Change your approach as the children grow up. You cannot play those games with your teenagers which you played when they were toddlers. You will have to grow up emotionally. As an involved Dad, you are expected to be sensitive to their growing years and how they view the world.

The Father Factor

Kyle Pruett, M.D., professor of psychiatry at the Yale Child Study Centre, USA, says that mothers are inclined to relate to their infants in a more soothing, loving, and serious way, while fathers hold their children differently and engage in new and exciting games which are stimulating to the child. Researchers are studying whether these patterns are gender-related and arise from neurobiological differences in the way stimuli and pleasure are linked in the male and female brains.

Never mind the origins of gender differences, studies show that the father's jocular, playful approach has far-reaching consequences on children's development. When playing with toddlers, for instance, fathers tend to be physical, wrestling, running, jumping, playing football, and other games of physical contact. Mothers, on the other hand, engage in verbal exchanges, reading, and playing with toys. Psychologist, Michael Lamb, research director at the National Institute for Child Health and Human Development in Bethesda, Maryland, USA, says, "Fathers are more likely to get children worked up, negatively or positively, with fear as well as delight, forcing them to learn to regulate their feelings." In other words, through the father's behaviour, children learn to develop a more complex set of interactive skills. Children learn to 'read' their father's emotions by observing his facial expressions, tone of voice, and other non-verbal cues and respond accordingly. 'Is Papa in the mood to play with me, or is he tired? Is he angry at me for pulling his moustache? Is Papa going to throw me over the ceiling fan, or is he joking?'

After the children have learnt to read emotional cues, they then learn to communicate their own emotions to others. For instance, children who are bored by the same old game being played may wander off, pick a new activity, or turn their back as a sign of having lost interest. Another child may start crying to let her Papa know that the boy is playing rough or is scaring her. One investigator pointed out that children also learn how to 'listen' to their own emotional state. A common example is of a child who learns that if she gets too worked up, starts crying, or throws a tantrum, she may drive her play partner away.

Psychoanalysts point out that the consequences of such emotional mastery are far-reaching. They are of the opinion that when children successfully cope with a mix of emotions at an early age through quality father-child interactions, children develop skills and abilities to explore new activities, manage frustration, engage in problem solving, and are adventurous in their pre-teen and teen years.

Fathering Adolescents

If you ask, does a father's parenting style draw adolescents closer to him? The answer is probably no. The closeness is felt more with the mother. From infancy to adolescence, the mother's intimate, need-related approach to parenting continues to cement her bond with the children, while a father's playful and stimulating style of functioning gradually loses its appeal. By the age of ten, a child may already be angry at his father's teasing. Ross Parke, Ph. D., of the University of California/Riverside Centre for Family Studies, USA, who has been mapping the psychology of the father-child bond, says the joking, playful style that serves fathers so well during children's first years may begin to alienate teens, giving them the impression that their father doesn't take their thoughts and needs seriously. Conversely, research suggests that preteens and teens of both sexes continue to rely on their mothers for intimacy and needs, and increasingly view her as the favoured parent for topics requiring sensitivity and trust.

If fathers are inclined to relate to their children in less intimate ways, then they may naturally be less capable of building and maintaining strong parent-child bonds, you may conclude. While researchers acknowledge some degree of gender-related parenting differences, they also emphasise cultural factors. For example, parents raise their children the way they were raised because the most important models of parenting are their own parents who may have raised them along traditional lines. Without advocating or suggesting a complete shift in parental roles and duties, both parents can adopt new strategies to strength the father-child bond.

Three Tips to Pave Your Own Road

Start at the Very Beginning: Data gathered from experienced fathers tell us that fathers who take the plunge in the parenting pool from birth onwards tend to get closer to their children. Be there for your wife when she is expecting. Try and keep office work to the minimum around the time the baby is born, and take leave from work at least for a few days when mother and baby come home from the hospital in order to practice parenting skills and overcome anxieties about handling the baby. Some fathers avoid interacting with their babies for fear of hurting the baby, or being unable to calm the child when it cries. The longer the father waits to take the plunge, the longer he will take to learn and master parenting skills. A father should hold and soothe his baby at least once a day.

Cement the Bonds with Your Spouse: It is extremely essential that both partners learn to accept each other's parenting styles as distinct and different from each other. So accept your partner's style and aproach to parenting without criticising one another. Families should take advantage of the difference between men's and women's parenting approaches which benefit the children immensely. Most mothers regard the father's playful style as rough and insensitive. But if you criticise him at this point, you will succeed in not only shaking his confidence, but also shake him off his parenting duties which he would like to perform.

Create Your own Niche as a Father: If you are serious on fathering the child then you, and more so, your wife has to be sure of the exact time and duration you will spend with the infant. Make a schedule and fix the hours for each day you will spend taking care of the child, and encourage your wife to go out of the house for a breath of fresh air, or shop for groceries while you father your baby. This will give you an opportunity to fine-tune your parenting skills as you learn to tune to your baby's needs and not rely on the mother to decode and encode the baby's signals. As you gain mastery over picking up cues of your baby's needs, you will build your confidence, as well as build solid bonds with your baby.

Parenting Tweens and Teens

"You come highly recommended," was how Janet introduced herself over the telephone when she asked for an appointment. Who could resist a compliment? I couldn't. And, so we met. There was an aura about Janet—someone who has been blessed by God in a special way, someone who couldn't have asked for anything better in life. She was 'contentment' personified. I don't think she got much out of meeting me that morning, but I got a lot as she shared with me a few facets of her life. I take the liberty to share with you some of those nuggets which I am sure you will find inspirational.

Tony and Janet D'Souza lived in New Delhi with their two children. James was fourteen-years old, and studied in St. Columbas School, and Jessica, eleven, studied in Convent of Jesus and Mary. Tony owned a men's apparel retail shop in Connaught Place, and Janet had a full-time job at home. Their son, James, needed special help with his studies; after several tests at the VIMHANS hospital, he was diagnosed ADHD. He hated studies and his teachers, loved playing the fool, had a fiery temper, was destructive, at times violent, held grudges and sulked for days on end. Jassica, on the other hand, was the opposite of James. She was an A+ student, independent, hardworking and liked by all.

Janet spoke of her husband with a lot of warmth. "Tony has always been very supportive of me and the children. He is a terrific husband and father. His job is such that he is totally tied down to the shop, and can't come home early to help James with his everyday schoolwork—much as he would like to. But, he is a great motivator, and gives us lots of encouraging inputs on coping with homework, schoolwork and general behaviour. After supper, we give him daily reports of what we have accomplished during the day. This gives the children an opportunity to revise and review what they had learned in school and at home. He is a great example to them, showing how he enjoys those special learning sessions from his children. Tony has infinite patience with James. If James has made any progress at all, it's because of Tony. He has a knack of getting James to perform, and I'm still learning those skills from him.

"At times, I get so sapped; not from doing the household chores, but from helping James cope with his studies and with his world outside the home. Parenting tweens and teens can be quite an ordeal at times. When frustrations and disappointments wear me down, I look forward to the evenings for Tony to come home from work. It's magical! He hugs me, listens to me without jumping in to criticise me, or to tell me I was over-reacting. After I have finished my say, either he would have some suggestions which he would softly murmur, or he would express confidence in my ability to find a solution to my problems. And, when, after supper, he sat to review the day's work, he never admonished James for his behaviour. He made it a point to give James the father the child sought in him. Whenever James had those rebellious moods, the evenings would stretch longer as Tony would spend more time helping James finish all the schoolwork, encouraging, guiding and applauding his efforts, and I shared that time with Jessica, who is a 'no fuss' child.

"On Sundays, after Church, Tony spends the day with the kids. When he's in the mood, he goes into the kitchen to prepare lunch for us. On holidays, when the weather is pleasant, we gather a few friends and go out to Lodhi Gardens and share pot-luck. On certain evenings, Tony picks up meals and brings them home, though not every night, but often enough. The children enjoy the variety, and it lessens my work in the kitchen. And, there are those evenings when the two of us go out to visit friends. Unlike some of my friends who do everything single-handedly without their husbands support, I don't feel tied down as a housewife at all."

According to Janet, some married men were either husband material, or father material. And, many were neither husband material nor father material. And, to have a husband and father rolled in one, was indeed, God's gift to woman. Janet was grateful to God for the gift of Tony who was a great husband and a great father, "indeed, a two-in-one combination," she laughed. No family gets all the goodies on the platter. Janet had her cup of woes in helping James master his moods. But, with Tony's support and encouragement she lived each day with the hope that tomorrow would be another day to start afresh!

Conclusion

A quip on fatherhood is, "If Adam had been a better father, things might have turned out differently for Cain and Abel." To be better fathers than Adam, fathers today, need lots of courage to make a transition from the traditional role of provider and the dispenser of discipline to being sensitively involved and nurturant. Even the most dedicated of fathers find the road to fatherhood strewn with obstacles either because of a lack of set rules and guidelines, or because of career constraints and personal lifestyles. Admitting, the road to fatherhood may be more confusing and open-ended than ever before, but for those willing to take the risk, the possibilities of connecting with your children are endless. A father's role is an important one that has a profound influence on the emotional, social, and intellectual development of the children. Mothers and fathers interact with the child in unique and different ways; neither do these roles overlap, nor are they equal or interchangeable, and each makes his or her own special contribution to child development. Caring for and being involved with the family is as important for children as it is for both mother and father.

Single Mothers
STAYING STRONG FROM WITHIN

When things go wrong as they sometimes will
when the road you're trudging seems all uphill
when the funds are low and the debts are high
and you want to smile, but you have to sigh,
when care is pressing you down a bit
rest if you must, but don't you quit.

It's hard to keep smiling when troubles are piling
their weight on your neck till it's sprained;
it's hard to keep grinning when others are winning
the prizes for which you have strained.

It's hard to be cheery on days wet and dreary,
when everything near you looks drowned;
it's hard to be sunny when all of your money
is sunk in a hole in the ground.
But how will it aid you, when woe has waylaid you
to rumble and grumble and swear?
There's nothing that's healing in kicking the ceiling,
or hitting the rungs of your chair.

It's hard to look pleasant when anguish is present,
and yet it is strictly worthwhile;
not all of your scowling and fussing and growling
can show off your grit like a smile.

— ANON

Sheila's marriage started as a fairytale love story in college and ended rudely on the rocks four years later with an infant to care and nowhere to go—but to her parents' home. Her husband wanted her and the kid out of his life so that he could marry an another woman.

Times have changed. Trends have changed, too. Quite a number of men nowadays don't seem to be good at marriage, steady relationships, commitment, fatherhood, home-minding, faithfulness, love, tenderness, sensitivity and the whole list of life-affecting activities. Their 'easy come, easy go' attitude has reduced the sanctity of the marriage vows and family commitment to a soap opera.

Many single mothers could identify with Sheila's plight in some form or the other. The nightmare, trauma, pain and humiliation seemed so unbearable at that time. Among other thoughts, the most depressing thought that haunted Sheila was, 'Will my child grow up wholesome without a father?' Walking alone into the dark hostile world, thoughts of doubts assail you. You begin to doubt your own judgements. Did you act in haste? Should you have waited a little longer? But, how much longer? These are the most painful fears single mothers live through. "Even in the best of circumstances, it is difficult for any one of us to raise children alone," says Hillary Clinton in her book, *It Takes a Village*. "And, when single parents try, they have to perform roles outside their usual repertoire, or get others to take on those roles. Even families with two parents rely on the 'village' (or community) for functions that are beyond their scope." You yearn for the support of people to help you raise your child, and you wonder where will that support come from.

Listen to Yourself

I am sure you could recall many situations where you took decisions and something inside you said, 'This doesn't feel right.'

But you were so busy and wrapped up in the daily household chores or in office work that, time and again, you ignored that inner voice. Looking back in hindsight, you've realised that you ignored that 'inner information', after knowing intuitively what to do, but didn't do it. Many times, women seek my counsel to share their concerns about their emotional health. Intuitively, they are aware that something was out of balance, or not right but are unable to validate their doubts and suspicions, and yet don't know who to talk to or what to do. In some instances after opening up to a friend, they regret having confided so much in that person, or in cases where the advice given has badly boomeranged and worsened the situation. In other cases, where there is no one to talk to, the problem gets inflated into a mountain from a molehill. The only common factor is: they looked strained, stressed and carry 'pain lines' on their faces. Look at yourself in the mirror and *listen* to your body. After listening to others talk, and after weighing the pros and cons, withdraw inwardly and listen to yourself. That's where your intuition lies. The more you listen to yourself the more you will come to rely on your intuitive instincts.

Your Path to Empowerment

- *Quickly pick up the pieces, put your life together and make plans for the future. That would be empowerment in the true sense of the word.*
- *Avoid breaking down in front of your child. It will make your child insecure and frightened.*
- *You have a lot of untapped inner strength, strength of character. Use it now; talk to yourself and remind yourself of your inner strength.*
- *Teach yourself professional skills and prepare to take up a career.*
- *To listen to your body, use techniques such as meditation, Reiki, yoga and prayer.*
- *Never feel inadequate. Just be the mother you are. You don't have to be the father for your baby. Your baby will grow up as wholesome as any other child.*
- *Cultivate a sense of humour. Your child will grow up happy and cheerful.*

- *Never feel guilty or sorry when correcting your child. You will end up feeling sorry for yourself.*
- *Count your blessings: you have so much more time, real quality time, to spend with your child on a one-to-one basis.*
- *Your personalised attention would have improved your child's manners, behaviour, and general attitude. Your child will emulate you in doing chores around the house and will grow up independent.*
- *Look at the families where parents fight with each other, the children grow up confused and devious. From that point of view, you are better off being a single parent.*
- *Offer help and do chores for your parents and relatives despite the tough schedule you live. By helping out, you will not be seen as a burden on your parents.*
- *Your parents and other relatives could pitch in from time to time to give the child the extra physical and emotional wrap-up which may be required, especially when you are at work, or at an evening school trying to secure a degree or diploma.*
- *Focus on growth in its varied forms: intellectual, economical, emotional, spiritual, social, etc.*
- *Look your best at all times. Be strict with your diet and exercise regularly.*
- *Believe in yourself so that you can believe in your dreams.*
- *It is said, 'Time is a great healer'—provided you want to be healed.*
- *'Once bitten twice shy' should never be your mission statement. All men are not brutes, so don't suppress the qualities that give you your special identity. Continue to be friendly, social and trusting, as you were earlier. Or, if you were an introvert before, teach yourself to become an extrovert. Remember, you are the role model for your child. Your child should inherit qualities of being a happy and wholesome person, who is able to accept responsibility for his/her actions.*
- *Make decisions that are positive, not anxiety-based or fear-based.*
- *Lastly, if and when you decide to marry again, it should not be as an act of sacrifice—for your child's sake. It*

should be for your own sake. You have to admit to yourself that you have healed. You come first and yours is a primary need; your child's need of a father-figure is a secondary need. You must have faith in yourself that you are a wholesome person and you want to enter a relationship with 'Mr Right', the man of your dreams and there is nothing wrong with that.

Opting for a Flexible Work Schedule

As a single mother, more than anyone else, you will want a flexible work schedule so that you can have more time to spend with your children at home. Recent survey shows that there is a new wind blowing: the current trend is changing in your favour. "Many companies today are very committed to their employees and go to great lengths in retaining the best employees with the most sought-after talent by being family-friendly in areas of flexitime, child-care resources, job sharing, sick-child care and elder-care resources," says Jill Kirschenbaum, editor-in-chief, *Working Mother,* October 2003.

Design a Vision for Yourself

To design your own vision you will have to do some brainstorming, like the marketing departments or the advertising agencies. Brainstorming is a practice of coming up with ideas or solutions to problems without ruling out any possibilities at the beginning. So, jump out of the square, or snap out of your tunnel vision and write down all the thoughts that come to your mind—from the commonplace to the bizarre. Don't sift or rearrange your ideas at this stage. If you want to carve yourself a unique vision, you will have to dream dreams. "Dream, dream, dream," says A.P.J. Abdul Kalam, President of India, in *Ignited Minds—Unleashing the Power within India.* "Dream transforms into thoughts. Thoughts result in action ... if there are no dreams, there are no revolutionary thoughts; if there are no thoughts, no actions will emanate." To be a visionary you have to dream. Maybe your dream is to work out of your home so that you can pick up your children from school at 1.30 in the afternoon and give them a hot lunch. Or may be you envision going to work for three days in a week so that on the other days you are available to take the children for tennis, swimming, horse riding, extra coaching classes, whatever.

One sultry afternoon, Yamini Goel packed a suitcase along with a few shreds of dignity, then bundled her two children into an auto-rickshaw and walked out of her marriage while her husband was at work. Since she didn't want to be a burden on her parents, she asked her brother to give her shelter. According to Yamini, the situation had worsened at home. She was brutalised by her husband, abused by her mother-in-law, and humiliated by her brother-in-law who glowered her lecherously. The three would gang-up to make her life a living hell. For six years, she covered her bruises, scars and her humilitation with a smile. The breaking point came when she was beaten and locked up in the store room on the terrace for twenty-eight hours without food, water or a toilet.

When she met me, with her confidence in tatters, she softly pleaded, "I'm a single mother, help me to put my life on track." Yamini was determined to make it good for the sake of her children. She wasn't going to waste time licking her wounds. At thirty-one, she wanted to move ahead. Endowed with creative skills, she loved reading, writing and drawing, she wondered how to put those skills to use. She was twenty-four when she earned her diploma in commercial art and got married. Now, she was going to put that diploma to use. But how? How was she going to find the time between her children's education, and doing housekeeping chores, and yet find a job that will pay her mounting bills? She wanted to pay her brother a small allowance for accommodating her; instead, I told her to offer her services to tutor his three school-going children with their studies. Thereafter, other families began to send children to her for regular tution. To celebrate her child's birthday, Yamini made some very creative invitation cards by recycling scraps of coloured paper. Parents soon approached her with orders for cards, decorations and ideas for theme parties. These small jobs were more therapeutic than the money she earned. In a span of three months she was gaining confidence.

Then, a big break came her way. One evening, her

brother asked his friend who had dropped in unannounced to join them for supper. After the introductions and pleasantries were over, the visitor shared his office problems. A product his company had launched, with a huge budget, had bombed in the market. Yamini's brother told his friend how impressed he was by the TV commercial. The next day, Yamini saw the TV commercial and wrote her critique on how the ad agency had messed with the product message. She also drew a dozen sketches on how the product should be highlighted. She put the 'concept sheets' in an envelope and gave it to her brother to pass them to his friend. Soon, the job offer came to her, but she politely declined saying that she would never be able to do full justice of raising kids and commit to a nine-to-five job. But, she offered herself as a freelancer to do all their promotional art works.

Yamini had quickly mastered the concept of 'flexitime'. She works only from home. She not only continues to give tuition to children, do birthday events and theme parties, but she also designs brochures, newsletters, desk calendars, logos, product concepts for half-a-dozen blue chip companies, and yet has time for herself and her children.

Fight Off Depression

As you battle it out to get on with your life, do not succumb to self-pity and depression; these two demons stay lurking inside your psyche, waiting for an opportunity to knock you down and destroy your self-esteem. To keep these demons under control, you will have to believe in yourself and in your abilities.

We all have our ups and downs. It may seem to us that some may have more ups than downs. If that's true, then they have learnt how to hide their 'downs' from us, or to put it positively, they've mastered the skills of holding themselves well, while they're down, from the strengths they received while they were up. Maybe, if you hold on to a rose and forget about the thorny stem, the chances are you will learn to savour the fleeting moments of joy for a much longer time, and the memory of those joyful moments will bring you solace in times of depression.

A Case to Consider

After years of being abused and beaten, Shaael Devi was finally abandoned by her husband. She returned to her mother's house with her two children, broken in mind and spirit. Her mother, who had her own income, took care of all the bills while Shaael looked for a job. Within eleven months she had worked for seven companies, from being private and personal secretary to front office receptionist. When nothing seemed to give her satisfaction, she taught English language to middle school children from home. After a while she gave that up and joined an automobile company as a 'sales executive.' Once she talked her mother into buying her a laptop so that she could work from home. Later, she sold it to pay off her creditors. When Shaael came and met me, about four years ago, she wanted to end her life. She said she hated going home because her mother humiliated her and her children drove her crazy with their stupid fights and demands. She was up to her neck in debt, had pawned her jewellery and was considering possibilities of secretly mortgaging her mother's house to clear the huge debts that had accumulated.

Something in Shaael had snapped. That was quite obvious. She had to gain her dignity, pride and self-esteem back. She also had to accept responsibility for her actions. Furthermore, she had to drastically reduce her expenses. Shaael's childhood friends had rich backgrounds and married into rich families. She still entertained them and tried to imitate their lifestyle and standards. Her mother paid the two children's school fees which were a princely sum since they studied in Delhi's popular private schools. Shaael never let the children feel any want. Their birthdays were celebrated with pomp, on the same lines as her friend's children. As her mother's servant was too strict, according to Shaael, she had to hire one maid to mind the kids and another to do the cooking and the cleaning. The children made demands for special food, so three separate menus had to be prepared. The food cooked for lunch couldn't be served for supper as it had turned 'stale'. Fresh food for three separate taste buds had to be cooked twice a day. Movies and outings on every weekend sent her mother's car bills spiralling.

Through tears and desperation, with six sessions spread over fours months, Shaael painfully came to terms with herself. She had to accept responsibility so that her children could grow up to be responsible. Also, she had to learn about discernment—the art of making right choices. So far, she had made some damaging wrong choices. And, as she learnt the dignity of labour, she had to realise that to live poor was not a slur on one's self-pride; living in debt was. At the beginning she hated my guts for driving those nails into her head. But in a few months I knew she was on the road to recovery. First, she sacked the two maids, then she dumped some of her childhood friends, and began to talk of her mother with warmth.

RAISING CHILDREN TO BE RESPONSIBLE

Single mothers, more than any parent, want their children to be self-reliant, competent and responsible. Being the only parent and with a job or a career to mind, it is impossible to be at their children's sides throughout the day. It is not enough for single mothers to know that their child is responsible enough to make her bed or set the table without supervision; they want their child to be truly responsible, to have competence in handling situations when things go wrong.

As a single parent, Rupali Bindra wanted to know: "When problems arise, how do I train my child to search for options so that she makes right choices?"

On her day off, Rupali took her twelve-year-old daughter Simmi to shop for clothes. Simmi accompanied her mother without complaining through several shops, as she waded through crowded sale counters, trying out sweaters and jackets. Rupali finally liked a burgundy-coloured sweater which looked smart on Simmi. She had the sweater packed and they were on their way home.

A week later:

Rupali: It's going to be chilly today. Wear that new sweater you got.

Simmi: But I want to wear the black one.

Rupali: That black sweater is too thin for this weather.

	You've got to wear a thick one. And, what's wrong with the new sweater you've got?
Simmi:	I like the black sweater; it's my favourite one.
Rupali:	But you look so nice in the burgundy sweater we bought last week. It's the in colour, and you look so smart in it. Your friends will like you wearing it.
Simmi:	But Mom, it's too thick in the middle. It puffs up in the front and looks awful.
Rupali:	If you really want to wear the black sweater, you may. (On the surface she realised her daughter was being impossible and she had no energy to argue with her.)
Simmi	(*wearing it and standing in front of the mirror*), I look cool Mom. I look thin in this sweater.

Seeing how pleased she was, Rupali realised for the first time how self-conscious her daughter was about her weight. That was the turning point for Rupali. From then on, she decided to let Simmi have a greater 'say' in selecting her own clothes.

But it wasn't easy, at least not at that time. Thin on patience, Rupali wanted to snap at the child and say, "Then why did you let me buy it if you don't like it?" But she swallowed her anger. Her sixth sense warned her that if she insisted on getting her way, the message she would be communicating to her daughter was, 'My likes are more important than yours.' Instead, she chose to let her daughter take the decision.

In Search of Independence

Rupali went back in time to recall a number of incidents which brought on a clash of wills. She distinctly remembered the day Simmi, a twenty-two-month-old toddler issued her first loud and emphatic "No" — she unwittingly had issued her first declaration of independence. With that 'no', the parent/child relationship became a game of tug-of-war which was to continue for many, many years. Indeed, it was a conflict of wills. In addition to the conflict of wills with her kid, there was this internal conflict of the parent who, on the one hand, was already experiencing a strain in her relations with her husband, and on the other, a tussle with her in-laws, who sought every opportunity to put her down. It wasn't easy to bring up Simmi during those tumultuous years for Rupali. There were times when she wanted to hold and there were times when she wanted to let go. At other times she just wasn't sure. And, a number of times, she let go for the wrong reasons, like giving in to the child's demands in order to buy peace and quiet. After the divorce, Rupali was able to give Simmi her undivided attention, and in the process she had learnt to listen to her child and know when to let go. To make the 'let go' process gradual and less difficult, parents should offer *studied choices* in small but significant ways in the early stages. Learning to *let go* is one of the toughest challenges facing any parent but it is one of the best ways to make a child independent.

Take Pride in Your Child

Children from the age of eight and above like to make their own decisions but at the same time may ask you for your point of view on the subject. As you give your child more opportunities to become independent, you will notice that they may fall back on you for advice. Your aim should be to make them self-reliant rather than dependent on you. Many parents get irritated when the child asks for advice from the parents and then ignores it. "If he asks for my help," ask miffed parents, "then why doesn't he accept it?" Having confidence in a child's decision-making ability is difficult if parents are too busy worrying about the child's ability to commit mistakes. You can minimise that problem by letting your child develop her skills on relatively inconsequential choices. It sometimes takes great strength not to do things for your child. You may feel a sense of loss—you may

> The best thing to do when children seek your advice and yet resist acting upon it is to let them know that you have faith in their ability to decide what is best for them. That would be your moment of reckoning as a parent.

feel less needed as you stop selecting their clothes, dictating their schedules, making decisions for them. But ultimately, it is gratifying to see children develop the inner resources to trust themselves, to be able to say in a difficult situation, "I think I can find a solution." When you do less for your child you give her a great gift. You convey the message, 'I have faith in your judgement.'

Chapter 8

Quality Time

Lots of time for lots of things;
tho' it's said that Time has wings,
there is always time to find
ways of being sweet and kind;
there is always time to share
smiles and goodness everywhere;
time to send the frowns away,
time for a gentle word to say;
time for helpfulness, and time
to assist the weak to climb;
time to give a little flower,
time for friendship any hour;
but there is no time to spare
for unkindness anywhere.

— ANON

Though the doorbell rang while she was having supper, eight-year-old Ragheshwari ran and opened the door. She knew it was her father returning after a business tour of two days. She always missed her father when he went on those long tours. Ever since she had come home from school that afternoon, she was waiting for this moment to run into his arms and show him the special remark of excellence the teacher had written in her maths copy, and all her other achievements, in the craft class and the swimming pool. In a gush of excitement, almost incoherently, she tried to tell him everything at one go. He kept punctuating her tide of words with, "Wait a moment—hold on—just a minute." While in the background her mother kept saying, "Papa is tired—let him shower and relax—you finish your supper." Gaurav shook his daughter Ragheshwari off him and went to his bedroom, while she swallowed down her supper and her enthusiasm.

Half an hour later, having refreshed himself and sitting to watch television, he asked Ragheshwari to show him the maths copy. She was not interested any more. The mother sharply told her to listen to her father and bring the maths copy. She replied indifferently, "It's in the bag." "Then, go and get it," Anjuma snapped at her daughter.

While in Mumbai his clients had hosted a party in his honour. After the usual business talk on the state of the economy, investment climate, recession and depression, they began to discuss the poor state of education and stressful family life. Gaurav shared his pet views on 'quality time' with his hosts. He told them that he reserved weekends entirely for his family. Saturday nights were outings with family and friends, and Sunday mornings were exclusively set aside for spending 'quality time' with his daughter.

Ragheshwari's Perception

Ragheshwari would have loved her Papa to cuddle and hug her and ask her to bring out the school bag. More than anything else, she would have loved it if he would go through all her books and give her a special hug for every 'merit star' and 'special remarks' she had earned in school. But for all those 'special effects,' she had to wait till Sunday morning. She had so much to show off to him but he was tired. Her mother came home from work when she was in the middle of her evening tuition, so she never got to 'chat' with her Mom. Ragheshwari was a little scared of her mother because she would lose her temper with the house servants. What about the time she spent with her father on Sunday mornings?

Sundays were okay; she would show him all her workbooks and Papa would be so proud of her. Thereafter, when she wanted to do anything on her own, Papa would insist that she sat near him while he read his magazines.

Anjuma's Perception

Ever since she took up the part-time job a year ago, which was at stone's throw distance from her house, Anjuma felt she could 'breathe' again. She had natural organisational abilities and working made a lot of sense because why should anyone waste one's talents? Gaurav is a good father—sensitive and caring. He works very hard, especially when he has to travel so much so often. Those nights, when he was out of town, the child would miss him very much. One has to make some sacrifice for all the comforts he affords the family, was Anjuma's reasoning. She knew of his temper and how he would get irritable when he was tired—after all, holding a sensitive job and staying at the top would wear anyone down. When he would come home tired and Ragheshwari wanted his attention, she had to 'intervene' lest he'd snap at the child. Yes, he was very particular about spending 'quality time' with Ragheshwari. He never missed a single Sunday when he was in town to be with his daughter for two hours. Those two hours were special for him. He did not want to be disturbed at all, so he never answered the phone. While he spent that time with Ragheshwari, Anjuma would be free to attend to the household chores—cleaning and cooking. Gaurav knew that she found it a little too much to mind the child, the house and the job at the same time. He did his best to relax her by taking them out on Saturday nights.

Gaurav's Perception

A man has to slog like a dog, and Gaurav loved his job and worked very hard at it. By the evenings, when he got home, he would be so fagged out that he just wanted time to be by himself to chill out. Most of his friends were hooked on to the Net; he preferred to watch a few light shows on television and then crawl into bed. "Ragheshwari is a growing child," he would remind everyone, "and she needs a father's special attention." So he would make a conscious effort to spend 'quality time' with her on Sundays for two hours. During those two hours of uninterrupted time he spent with his daughter, he would go through her workbooks and she would chat about school and her friends. Gaurav also found Sunday mornings quiet and relaxing; it felt good to laze around in the house, without answering phone calls, and catching up with the magazines that would pile up unread during the week. Anjuma was a terrific wife; she allowed him plenty of space to orbit in; she was doing a good job with the kid (the kid was doing very well at school and was well behaved); she kept a good house, and enjoyed the part-time job in the neighbourhood. With his wife's support he was able to concentrate on his career.

Parents' Illusion

You will notice that whenever time spent on children is in short supply, or is rationed out, calling it 'quality time' makes parents feel better. The term 'quality time' was first conceived in early 1970s, when working parents carried with them guilt pangs of child-neglect as they rode the career elevators. A wave of research scholars who studied the situation came up with a solution by breaking up time into two parts—quality time and quantity time. Applying business management techniques to home management, they argued about the advantages of spending short bursts of time (quality time) as against spending long hours of time (quantity time) with children.

The architects of 'quality time' had concluded that a child only needed an hour or so of a mother's close, loving attention each day. Guilt pangs quickly vaporised as non-issues as soon as couples found quality time an immense help in juggling two careers and a snotty nose. But not everyone agreed with this theory. "Children need vast amounts of time and attention," says Ronald Levant, author and psychologist. "It's an illusion to think they're going to be on your time-table and that you can say 'okay, we've got an half hour, let's get on with it.' Some educators and psychologists are more blunt about it, "There's no such thing as quality time; it's just a myth to help working parents feel less guilty."

'If I had more time, I'd have more fun,' we like to tell ourselves, but this is seldom the truth. To test the validity of this assertion, ask yourself how much time you allot each week to fun: pure, unadulterated, nonproductive fun? For most, fun is something they avoid almost as assiduously as their creativity. Why? Fun leads to creativity. It leads to rebellion. It leads to feeling our own power, and that is scary. 'I may have a small problem with overwork,' we like to tell ourselves, 'but I am not really a workaholic,' says Julia Cameron in the *Artist's Way*.

Children cannot be raised on short (scheduled) bursts of attention and love. No matter how much you may wish to schedule quality time into your day, when it comes to it, other practicalities often interfere. Your child may be too tired, or simply uninterested. You may have planned some activities to enjoy together, but your child has other ideas or simply wants to play on her own. Since two plus two never adds up to four in the human equation, dishing out parental time in measured medicinal doses at fixed times was never a practical solution to bridge career and child-rearing. Children are not office gadgets that can be turned on and turned off; they demand time and attention at random and sometimes they want more and more of it.

It is obvious that most of the important elements of parenting get dumped when quality time substitutes for quantity time. By subscribing to quantity time, it is not true that parents who have nothing else to do spend endless hours in the company of the child attending to each and every moment of her growing years. For a moment, forget about the controversial notions of quantity time and quality time—just enjoy spending 'time' with your child. Once you get into the spirit of spending time with a child, you will notice that on any given day you can give your child just that much of close attention, and nothing more. On the child's part, she does not need you hovering over her *all* the time, and if you persist in doing so, she will turn her face away from you and focus her attention on some other object. Try and tempt yourself to maintain a diary for a day to see how much time you give the child. Barring feed-time, bath-time, and bedtime, the rest of the time would be very fragmented—

two minutes here or three minutes there, when you share those special moments of love through hugs, kisses and cuddles.

You May Count That Day, by George Eliot, shows how to make each day worth your while.

> *If you sit down at set of sun*
> *and count the acts that you have done*
> > *and counting, find*
> *one self-denying deed, one word*
> *that eased the heart of him who heard—*
> > *One glance most kind,*
> *that fell like sunshine where it went*
> *then you may count that day well spent.*
> *But if, through all the livelong day*
> *you've cheered no heart, by yea or nay—*
> > *if, through it all,*
> *you've nothing done that you can trace*
> *that brought the sunshine to one face—*
> > *No act most small*
> *that helped some soul and nothing cost—*
> *Then count that day as worse than lost.*

The Guilt Trip

One of the reasons why children get emotionally disturbed is not because their parents are working, but because the parents feel guilty about working. So when the father returns from his business trips, he brings home toys and chocolates for the child. The overt message is: 'I was thinking of you while I was away.' The covert message is: 'I feel bad abandoning you. I hope these gifts will compensate for my absence.' After a while both parties play the 'compensation game' to perfection; the child prefers his father to be out working so that when he returns home, he brings in the booty. If at all he 'forgets' to bring home the goodies, the child throws tantrums to remind him of the 'guilt pact' they had worked out as a mind game. Similarly, when the mother comes home from work, she smothers him with hugs and kisses and brings home little love tokens in spite of knowing that he was at his worst behaviour throughout the day. The smart kid has both his parents neatly wrapped round his little finger. On returning from work, none of the parents want to take on a defiant kid, so they put up with a lot of his nonsense. In normal circumstances, had she not been on a guilt trip, she would have firmly and consistently dealt with his tantrums. When parents are on guilt trips, children quickly learn how to control working parents.

Dr Benjamin Spock says, "Some parents think that the more elaborate, the more expensive the plaything, the more fascinating it will be to children. That is simply not true. What children love most of all, and what will keep them busy longest is an opportunity to be creative, and this why a box of crayons, a wad of paper, and a box of good blocks will keep children imagining and building week after week, month after month."

An important element of parenting is to have a consistency pattern in your programme. Once you have studied your child's highs and lows, then fix a routine of domestic rituals centred round the child's needs. From the child's point of view, your day is structured around her needs—your availability provides a safe, secure and dependable haven, called home. Steffen Kraehmer, author of *Quantity Time: Moving Beyond the Quality Time Myth*, recommends that parents concentrate on routines and rituals. According to the author, families should make every effort to eat together at least once a day, with the TV off. Rituals, which could include everything from holiday celebrations to making Sundays a regular pizza afternoon, will give the kids the structure they need.

When you come across teenagers who experiment with alcohol, drugs, smoking, sex, or have had a brush with the law, do not be quick to judge them; just stop and look to see if their parents are around. In practically every case of juvenile delinquency, you will find that the parents had long ago opted out of their parenting responsibilities. Just because your kids have grown up

Parents who rush home from work, and head straight to the computer or the television set, are making it perfectly clear where their priorities lie, and the kids carry the scars.

to be teenagers does not mean that they can do without parenting.

Parenting may not be the same as when they were toddlers; at this stage, monitoring is very critical to their emotional stability. You will need to monitor their schoolwork, home chores, the friends they hang out with, and what they do in their spare time (*see* Chapter, *Teenagers: Face of the Future*).

All those who believe in quality time must realise that its very essence is to be available when someone needs you, no matter how inconvenient it is to you. You have to be available to others when you are needed. In many households, children are put to sleep for a couple of hours every afternoon to keep them awake at nights. The reason being that since the father reaches home only after 9 o'clock, he gets to spend 'quality time' with the child at that time. On the other hand, if the child was kept awake in the afternoons and if he slept at a normal hour after supper (say, 8 o'clock), then the father would be denied his hour of fun and games with his child. After all, this is the only hour when father and child can spend time together every day. This is stretching the concept of 'quality time' to a ridiculous point, where the child is made to adjust his normal schedule to meet the parent's needs. Imagine the strain on a school-going child who sleeps late and has to wake up early for school (in some cases the father is fast asleep at that time); it will be very difficult for him to concentrate on classwork. In such a situation, where parents are unable to reach home in time to 'play' with their children in the evenings, instead of upsetting the child's schedule, parents should wake up early enough in the mornings to romp and play with them. Such a morning routine would be excellent wake-up tonic for the entire household.

Time goes, you say?
Ah no!
Alas, Time stays; we go.

— HENRY AUSTIN DOBSON (*The Paradox of Time*)

SECTION ②

RAISE HEALTHY KIDS

Sleep: Your Health Tonic

Only about 20 per cent of people living in industrialised countries have no sleep disturbances at all. About 25 to 35 per cent suffer from severe sleep-related problems that require medical attention. The rest of us have minor, often recurrent sleep disturbances, for an average of at least five nights per month.

— PROF. EDZARD ERNST *(Sleep, Help Yourself to Health)*

The question many ask is how much sleep does one need to stay healthy? This is the core question which needs to be addressed. It zeroes in on the core area that the child's sleep pattern needs attention. Children, between eighteen months to twenty-four-months of age, who do not get ten to twelve hours of 'uninterrupted' sleep every night, would naturally wake up in the mornings less cheery, more cranky, irritable, having low appetite, somewhat passive, and easily susceptible to common ailments than those who sleep fitfully. To stay healthy, it is not the quantity of sleep you measure; instead it is the quality of sleep that is important. What four hours of uninterrupted sleep can do to invigorate the body is something to marvel at, that not even ten hours of restless sleeping can do. So, let's take a look at two peoples' sleeping habits to understand the importance of the quality of sleep to stay healthy.

Hari the Snoozer

Hari, a fourteen-year-old lad, is a bundle of energy. He plays football with his friends every evening. He dreams of being the world's greatest soccer player. Hari goes to bed at 10 o'clock every night, and wakes up at 6 o'clock every morning so that he doesn't miss the school bus. He sleeps for eight hours in twenty-four hours. At the turn of the first hour, Hari has dozed off and is entering the REM (rapid eye movement) mode, or the dream stage. The REM sleep mode is stimulated by a region in the brainstem called the pons, and the midbrain area. Imagine a vast multitude of workers, called *neurons,* waking up inside Hari's brain and reporting for duty as soon as Hari falls asleep. Some neurons in the pons and the midbrain are activated and immediately control muscle tone and other aspects of REM sleep. The neurons render Hari immovable by de-activating his large muscles: arms, legs, neck and the back. Otherwise, Hari would physically act out his dreams and hurt himself in the dark. If, by chance, he wakes up at this point, he would vividly remember his dreams. Hari would alternate between REM sleep and N-REM (non-rapid eye movement) sleep. The N-REM sleep is regulated by the forebrain.

As Hari progressively slips into N-REM sleep, he will cycle back into the REM sleep after every ninety minutes. The N-REM sleep mode goes through a succession of four stages. The depth of sleep increases from stage one to stage four.

As Hari slips into a *deep, deep chasm of sleep*, he literally is 'dead' to the world. If a burglar were to break into his bedroom and steal his TV and stereo system, he wouldn't stir. The total N-REM stage lasts for about four to five hours. In this mode, his breathing and heart rate slows down, his body temperature and blood pressure decreases. The 'workers' begin their repair and maintenance work while Hari is in this deep sleep mode called the N-REM mode. These 'workers' work non-stop for ninety minutes and then take a break. At break time, Hari enters the dream stage.

At the start of the repair work, some of the 'workers' in the forebrain punch buttons to activate the pituitary gland to release a secretion from the *growth hormones,* enabling the worn out cells in the blood to get replaced and replenished with millions of new cells. The new cells bring in a surge of fresh oxygen into the blood. They rejuvenate the cells in the tired muscle tissue and invigorate the body. After having slept for eight hours, Hari wakes up refreshed and renewed. Sleep was therapeutic. With a spring in his stride he's looking forward to the inter-school soccer league match which he has to play this evening.

Sanjay the Insomniac

Sanjay, a forty-five-year-old shopkeeper is overweight, but not obese. He is a typical worry-bug with high blood pressure. Sanjay's pet comments on life are: "The weather is awful. The money market is tight, and the country has gone to the dogs." He enjoys a bottle of beer every evening after work, then he has a glass of water with his supper, watches TV and goes to bed by 11 o'clock. Sanjay's constant whine and worry is that he doesn't sleep well at nights. He craves for sleep as he closes his eyes, wondering whether the markets will open up and business will get better! The two children are doing badly in school, expenses are mounting and the future seems bleak. As he dozes off, it is past midnight. Sanjay had just begun to cycle between REM to N-REM mode when his tight bladder hits the 'alert button' which triggers an emergency signal to the brain—'Wake up! It's pee time.' The neurons (the little workers) who were about to start the rejuvenation and repair work in the body had to quickly abandon duty and run for cover due to the red alert signals. But Sanjay fights off the red alert message as he tosses and turns in bed. But he soon begins to feel restless and uneasy. Reluctantly, Sanjay gets up and goes to the bathroom to relieve himself. Returning to bed, he reaches out for the jug of water near his bedside table, pours himself a glass, drinks it and lies down. Two hours later, the pattern repeats itself. Just as he was entering the N-REM stage, for the second time, the tight bladder sends red alert signals to the brain to wake up. Due to his water drinking habit, Sanjay never enters the deep, deep chasm of sleep as Hari does. He has conditioned himself to drink water every two or three hours, as he believes that water flushes his system and thus keeps visiting the bathroom.

> It is only in the deep N-REM sleep that the neurons activate the growth hormones for the repair of worn out tissue and cells.

It's only natural that every morning Sanjay wakes up tired, stressed and without zest. He has made himself a 'surface sleeper', so he never gets into the deep chasm of N-REM sleep. Sanjay's blood cells and muscle tissue have not undergone any rejuvenation or replenishment, so he wakes up feeling haggard, rather than refreshed. Sanjay is irritable with his wife, over-anxious about the children's future, has difficulty in concentration, and keeps brooding absent-mindedly. For him, sleep is a luxury he eagerly craves for. He could perhaps help himself to a good night's sleep if only he could limit his water intake.

When a person cannot sleep fitfully, physicians prescribe painkillers and sedatives so that the body and mind can repair themselves in the nocturnal hours. To enjoy that four-to-five-hour chasm of uninterrupted sleep, it is very important for Sanjay to employ sleep inducement techniques to lull himself into sleep. Some lull themselves into sleep through reading, some count sheep, some with a dose of sex, and some through meditation techniques where they have learnt to keep their minds blank. Avoid worrying. Most perfectionists play out entire scenes of their day's actions, or of the actions they will enact the next day, the moment they get into bed. They keep arranging and re-arranging the scenes to the minutest details, keeping their brains hyperactive through the night. Some drink and eat (night partying) to the extent that they become uncomfortable. In such circumstances, no amount of lulling or loving will help.

Hazards of Sleeplessness

Research shows that people who are unable to sleep well

have decreased levels of leptin—a hormone that tells the brain to switch off appetite, and we stop eating. Due to leptin deficiency, people end up eating more than their body needs; they crave for sweets, starchy and salty food, and run the risk of being overweight (*see* Chapter on *Obesity in Children*). Michael Sateia, a psychiatrist who studies sleep disorders, says, "Virtually everyone has at least a transient period of insomnia that lasts a night or a few nights. Some snap out of it after a while and begin to sleep normally. And, some never do." The one agonising thought at bedtime that plagues those who have difficulty in sleeping is the fear of not falling asleep. Rachel Manber, a Stanford University psychologist, says, "The worst enemy for a person who isn't sleeping well is trying harder to sleep." It is a proven fact that obesity, cardiovascular diseases and diabetes have their roots in sleep disorders.

Early Sleep Patterns

Like any behavioural pattern, sleep also has patterns—very definite and determined. And, like any behavioural pattern, the sleep pattern, whether restful-sleep or restless-sleep, gets ingrained in the body's system. Unfortunately, many people don't consider sleep as a behaviour pattern. Instead, they treat sleep as a 'tuner switch' to be tuned on the moment they get into bed. Without realising it, people relate to sleep in the same way as they relate to eating. Many people eat not because they have hunger pangs, but because they feel an urge or an impulse to eat. Similarly, they expect to sleep at will, too—from the moment they shut their eyes. Instead, they end up staying awake in bed for hours on end.

Probable Causes of Bed-wetting

The causes for bed-wetting could be psychological, as well as physical. Anxiety could be one of the psychological reasons of bed-wetting. When both parents are career-occupied, children may feel insecure, neglected and clamour for parental attention. Of the many ingenious ways to get attention, bed-wetting could be one of them. Another reason could be nervous tension. In cases of parental friction, hostility, violence, or abuse, children develop nervous traits, and bed-wetting could be one of the relief outlets for children. Another common reason for children to bed-wet is when either one or both parents lead stressful lives, or are perfectionists. They communicate tension around by picking on one another's faults and blowing them out of proportion. While children learn to 'control' themselves during their waking hours, they bed-wet since they are unable to control themselves while asleep.

'Tight bladder' could be one of the important physical causes for bed-wetting. Some children are habitually given milk, juice or water at bed time. All this liquid eventually ends up in the urinary bladder making it 'tight' and uncomfortable to sleep peacefully. Since sleep patterns get ingrained from infancy, it is not difficult to understand why Sanjay, at forty-five, suffers from a weak sleep drive.

In all probability, when Sanjay was a toddler his mother put him to bed with a bottle of feed. After a couple of hours, with his bladder full, he would wet the diaper. On feeling uncomfortable, he would whimper, toss and turn, or cry in his cot. His mother would wake up, change his diaper, fill the bottle with milk, thrust it into his open mouth, and go back to bed. As soon as the child became comfortable and sucked on the nipple he would fall asleep. Soon, the same waking-up cycle would repeat itself as his bladder would get tight. The tight bladder triggers the brain to wake the body to relieve itself of the discomfort, while hunger pangs don't trigger the brain to wake the sleeping body. As a child, was he really hungry for feeds at night? In all probability the answer would be a 'no'. Over a period of time, this habit gets ingrained in Sanjay, and the nocturnal drinking and peeing habit will stay with him.

Structure Proper Sleep Patterns

A newborn baby sleeps for about eighteen to twenty hours in a day. Children who are between two years to three years of age sleep daily for about ten to twelve hours. And as they grow older they settle down to about eight hours of sleep. When you look at fourteen-year-old Hari sleeping, you want your

> What our grannies said was true: "The baby grows most when she sleeps best."

children to sleep like that. You can make it possible if you begin to 'structure' your child's sleep habits as early as possible.

Asha is a thirty- baby. She is fed supper at 7 o'clock and put to bed at 8 o'clock. By 8.30 p.m. she has dozed off to sleep. By 9 o'clock she gets into the REM stage and begins to dream. You may see her smile, gurgle or grimace in her sleep. At times she may shake her limbs vigorously, or stretch herself rigidly, or simply wake up frightened on having had a nightmare. By 9.30 p.m., Asha is fast asleep. She now enters into the deep chasm of sleep which will ideally last for about seven to eight hours. She will cycle back and forth between the REM sleep mode and the N-REM sleep mode in those eight hours. The N-REM sleep mode lasts for a much longer period in little children than in adults, because at thirty months, Asha is growing at a very rapid rate, in fact, at a furious rate when compared to an adult. The bone and muscle tissue, blood cells and bone marrow cells have to multiply at an extremely rapid rate— into several billion cells—to keep pace with the rapid growth rate of the child. The brain centre sends messages through its neuron network to activate the pituitary glands to stimulate the release of growth hormones to repair and replenish tissues and cells, and the growth hormones get activated only when a child is in deep slumber. By 5 a.m., Asha 'surfaces' from the deep chasm of sleep. Though her eyes are closed, you will see her smile, grimace, clutch her fingers into a ball, or keep changing her posture, depending on the nature of her dreams she is wrapped in. By now her bladder would be tight from the liquids she ingested at suppertime. She may or may not wet the bed. Girls have better bladder control than boys. At 6.30 in the morning, Asha wakes up. Her face is lit up with a radiant smile. Since she slept well the whole night, she will be full of bounce and energy throughout the day. If she continues with her regular sleep pattern, she will be an active child who will quickly burn her calories and develop a good appetite for food. This, in turn, will give her a good constitution, building a reserve of antibodies to fight off common ailments like, colds, fever, chest and nasal congestion.

Those of you who wish to change the child's sleep pattern from, say late nights, and bring it up to 8 o'clock every night, will need to first effect a change in your own lifestyles. Let's say the toddler is two-years old and sleeps after 11.00 p.m. But, you would like him to sleep at 8 o'clock. To bring about the change, you may have to stop the short naps, or the long siesta he has got used to because he already has a *weak sleep drive*, which means he has irregular sleep hours, is restless in bed, or wakes up at nights. Put a stop to his napping habit; keep your child happy and active, especially during those hours when he is used to taking a nap in the daytime. In the evenings, take him out to the gardens and parks and tire him out by playing games where he has to run around. By doing this, you are literally 'regulating' his *biological clock*. And that's only forty per cent of the effort. The sixty per cent effort comes into effect when you attempt to regulate his *activity clock*.

Though your toddler can't tell time, he sure knows when it's time to sleep. That's because his brain registers the evening routine by closely absorbing the activities of the household. In this case, around eleven every night, all activities at home lead to bedtime, so he gets 'conditioned' to get into the sleep mode at elevenish every night. To change his sleep hour to eight every night, you will have to make a detailed note of all the activities that take place every evening between 9 o'clock and 11 o'clock, and then enact the nine-to-eleven activities two hours ahead to trigger his 'sleep switch'. After having had a full day of outings, you will surely succeed in putting him to sleep at 8 o'clock every night.

For how long will this exercise go on, you may ask? Let's say, for the duration of about ten per cent of your toddler's existence on this planet. So, if your child is two-years old, this exercise must be carried out consistently for two continuous months, without a break.

Sleeplessness—The Mother of Ailments

Some may still recollect the good old days of the 'family physician' who believed that the root cause of most ailments lay in the digestive system. Their norm was 'heal the stomach in order to heal the body'. They probed the patient's stomach region with their fingers and prescribed medication and a diet to heal the stomach. Having counselled numerous parents over several years, I firmly believe that the root cause of most common ailments, affecting people from infancy to old age, is lack of proper sleep habits which eventually lead to insomnia, obesity and other ailments connected to cardiovascular diseases. After seeking my advice, many parents who had succeeded in regulating and modifying the sleep habits of their infants, later reported to me that they had noticed an immediate change in their children's behaviour and health patterns. The children woke up happy, ate well, played well, and slept well.

A Parent's Nightmare

* *Child sleeps around midnight.*
* *Wets the bed or diaper.*
* *Wakes up hungry in the middle of the night.*
* *A light sleeper; gets disturbed easily.*

Some Causes of Disturbed Sleep

The brain never sleeps even though the body is asleep. Instead, the brain acts as a sentinel and 'watches' over the defenceless sleeping body. The brain, while listening to sounds, noises or smells, runs security checks through its senses in order to categorise them as familiar, or unfamiliar, friendly or hostile, and takes decisions whether to wake up the sleeping body or to allow it to sleep. Often we have woken up with a start from deep sleep. The brain was able to sense danger and wake us up. While the body was being woken up, the brain had simultaneously activated the body's defence mechanisms to neutralise the danger posed possibly by a fire, a burglar, or any other impending disaster.

Many children hardly sleep well at night. In many families infants and toddlers share the same bed with their parents. A parent's tossing and turning in bed will obviously disturb the sleeping child, as much as the child's turning or whimpering will wake up the parents. Many children share the same bedroom with their parents, although they sleep in their own little cots. Watching night TV, or movies in the same room, or in the adjoining room can be disturbing for a child who has fallen asleep at 8 o'clock. At times, parents who return home from a late night party will put on their bedroom lights, however dim, to get ready for bed while the child is asleep in the same room, or worse still, on the same bed. Lights, shadows, footsteps, murmuring, hushed noises are bound to disturb a sleeping child in the room.

There are situations where a parent regularly works late at office and reaches home after 10 o'clock. In many families, it's a normal scene to have the child awake to welcome the father. As soon as he reaches home, the father and child are wrapped up in fun and games. From the parent's point of view, this is the only moment when the father gets to spend 'quality time' with his child. Indeed, it's a delightful sight to watch father and child wrapped up in excitement, laughter and merriment. After that magic moment is over, the father hands over the child to the mother or to the maid, to be put to bed. Now, with so much adrenaline pumped into the child, who is high on excitement, it's going to take quite a while before the child settles down to sleep.

Certain foods that excite and stimulate the brain, like chocolates, ice cream, and sweets with artificial colourings and preservatives must be avoided at nights. Furthermore, children who are in the habit of drinking milk at night, may not just get their bladders tight, as pointed out earlier. Milk residue, as research points out, clings to the gums and teeth causing chemical reactions, which hasten tooth decay. Instead of the bottle, give your baby a hot bath just before sleeping. With a hot bath, as the body temperature rises, the veins, arteries, capillaries and blood vessels expand, the muscles begin to relax and the flow of blood normalises. Gradually, as the body temperature lowers, it brings about a therapeutic effect in relaxing the body at bedtime.

Preparing for Sleep

In an ideal situation the toddler is fed supper at 7 o'clock, taken to the bathroom at 8 o'clock, and thereafter put to bed by reading a story (without dramatisation). But many mothers strongly believe that the child needs those intermittent catnaps during the day, or the post-lunch siesta. The need for sleep can be measured by the fact that if the short naps or the siesta *eat* into the nightly 8 o'clock sleep hour, then those day-naps are superfluous. But, after all the dozing, and the cat napping, and the siestas, your child still sleeps at 8 o'clock every night, then it's obvious that your baby requires that much of sleep. If your two-year-old sleeps for *more* than twelve hours daily, then you have reason to worry.

Like all behavioural patterns, the sleep pattern is also habit-forming. Hence, parents have to caution themselves regarding their personal convenience and their child's need for excessive sleep. Many parents put their children to sleep in the afternoons so that they could catch a short nap themselves, or get some home chores done while the baby is asleep. The old saying is, 'If you snooze, you lose'. Parents must activate themselves as entertainers to keep their child engrossed in fun-filled work in the course of the day. Or else, they would have to nurture a sleepy, listless adolescent.

Coping with Home Parties

Many a sleep-programme gets jettisoned when there's a party at home and friends drop in late in the evenings. Look at it from your toddler's point: he's had his usual 'active' day at the playschool, then after lunch he played with his toys, did colouring, watched television, then went out and romped in the playground with other children. By seven, he's tired and is fed supper. But the poor mother has a hard time putting him to sleep because his sixth sense keeps him awake, though he is very drowsy. He is in a state where his body is tired and a part of his brain wants him to sleep, while another part of his brain picks up uncoordinated signals which he can't figure out. But he has gathered enough data to warn his cautious brain that it's not a regular, normal evening. Then, people start dropping in. There are so many guests around him who are giving him all the attention. And also, there is so much of food and drink, fun and laughter around him. He is free to do what he likes. As the party goes on in full swing, Puploo is in a very excitable mood with all the attention he's getting. But at the same time, sleep is overcoming him; he feels cheated of the fun he's having. As he keeps fighting off the demon of sleep; he gets cranky and demanding. Mother picks him up and takes him away from the crowd. She makes a heroic effort to lull him to sleep. Will she really succeed?

There are two ways to handle such a situation:

Plan 1:   Put him to bed in the afternoon, so that he wakes up fresh, and enjoys the adult party which will wind up late in the night.

Plan 2:   Get smart: Puploo shouldn't pick up any 'party signals'; then make sure your child is put to bed at the regular time before the guests arrive. His bedroom should be away from noise and disturbances so that he gets his uninterrupted sleep for the next ten to twelve hours.

Count Your Blessings

It is very important for parents to regard sleep as the single most important healer of the entire body system, whether they are infants, children, adolescents or adults. You must nurture in your children proper sleeping habits from infancy so that they will grow up healthy and stay in control of their lives. Apart from reaping health benefits, your children will enjoy high energy levels. The results of the sleep tonic are that they will:

* be better focused and attentive in class;
* untiringly complete their homework on coming home from school;
* find time for hobby classes;
* enjoy outdoor games; and
* rarely get 'under the weather' or sick since their body's immune system will grow stronger to ward off ailments.

Indeed, your children will be better off than the present generation of adults. Today, people at the age of thirty sleep less and take more pills as they toss and turn in bed, praying for a good night's sleep. Their symptoms are: stress, tension, low concentration, anger, impatience and rage, simply because their mothers didn't inculcate in them proper sleeping habits when they were young.

C H A P T E R ②

Dreams & Nightmares

Tell me your dreams and I will tell you what you are.

— SOCRATES

There is a lot of mystery attached to the world of dreams. We often wonder what could cause dreams, and what is the significance of dreams? Some people admit that they dream a lot in their sleep, and they can vividly recall their dreams and describe them in detail. Others admit that they don't dream at all, or can never recall their dreams. And, there are the miniscule few who, gifted with extra-sensory perception (E.S.P.), can recall a dream of an impending doom with chilling detail. It is uncanny how they are able to *foresee* in exact detail, while asleep—an accident, an incident or a disaster that will happen (usually to someone they know, or at a place they had visited).

A CHILD'S DREAM WORLD

REM, or dream sleep, occurs in infants, toddlers, children, as well as adults. Ultrasound scans have shown that the foetus begins to have REM sleep as early as the twenty-third week of pregnancy—about seventeen weeks before coming into the world, an unborn baby dreams in the womb itself.

In the infant's first year, total sleep time drops from about sixteen hours to about thirteen hours in a day cycle, and half of that time is spent in REM sleep. Since the N-REM (non-REM) sleep remains the same at about eight hours, this means that REM sleep, or dream sleep, gets reduced by about three hours between birth and the first year. As the child grows up, the dream sleep continues to decrease until he reaches adulthood, when approximately a quarter of the total sleep in made up of REM sleep.

Nightmares

Four-year-old Aishwarya's parents were a worried couple. They were worried and anxious because their li'l darling would wake up screaming, choking and terrified almost three to four nights every month. They tried ways and means to rid the child of her nightmares. Aishwarya would wake up screaming and choking, and sit up in bed with her eyes wide open, convinced that she could see something frightening in the room. The parents seemed as frightened of the nightmares affecting the child as much as the child was. While counselling them, it became apparent that the father had an easy-going nature while the Mom was a bundle of nerves. Outwardly she was cool and calm. She was also very competitive about her child. Aishwarya had to be better than the best, after all Mom was 'sacrificing' her best years in devotion to the child's upbringing. Good wasn't good enough. She was paranoid about any breakdowns in the child's routine and would split hairs analysing pros and cons.

As a matter of fact, Mom should know that it takes a good twenty minutes before the child 'wakes up' to the realisation that the nightmare is over. In such a situation, take the child out of the bedroom for a little while, may be to the bathroom to freshen up, or to the kitchen for a sip of water. Assure the child that all is well, and no more bad dreams will haunt her. Hug, cuddle and caress her as you put her to bed, and lie down with her till she falls asleep.

The following day, you may discuss the previous night's events with your child, and ask her if there is something that is troubling her. Don't be surprised to find out that she fails to remember anything about the nightmare—that's because she had slept soundly thereafter.

Research points out that nightmares occur frequently in children between the ages of four and six. And children between the ages of six and twelve may continue to have bad dreams. It is quite common for children to have an occasional disturbed night. If your child wakes up distressed in the middle of the night, comfort her with a cuddle. Take her gently in your arms and softly reassure her that it's only a dream, that whatever it was that frightened her, was not real. Lie down on the bed with her and explain to her that the bad dream is over, and she will soon fall asleep. Stay with her till she falls asleep and then tiptoe out of the room.

If your child has repeated nightmares, then it is obvious that something is wrong, either at home or at school. On the home scene, if you and your spouse are not getting on well, or if you live with your in-laws and there is tension between you and them, then your child may have disturbed nights. But, if all is well on the home front, then check out the school scene. Ask your child if she is worried about anything. Maybe she is not getting on well with friends, or has broken up with her best friend. Maybe she is losing confidence since she is not good at certain games as some of her friends are, or has skipped homework. Maybe the teacher ticked her off and it has upset her no end.

> When parents are overly strict, or regularly fuss over small details, then the child may have uneasy nights.

Night Terrors

Anita told me about her three-year-old grandson who would often spend his weekends with her. "It was about 2 o'clock one night when Ayushman woke up screaming. I ran to his room and switched on the lights. I was out of my wits as I watched Ayushman sit up in bed, eyes wide open and shrieking. I held him close to comfort him but he got more agitated. My heart was thumping as I broke into a sweat, wondering if my baby was having a seizure. I ran to get a glass of water, to splash it on him or to make him drink, God knows what. But just as suddenly as the shrieking had started, it ended in the same manner. Ayushman stopped screaming, lay himself down and closed his eyes. When I came to him and caressed his forehead, he was sleeping peacefully. The next morning he remembered nothing." Anita wondered if Ayushman could be cured of those 'traumatic' dreams.

Night terrors can be awfully traumatic to witness. Both, nightmares and night terrors can shock the daylights out of parents and grandparents. Knowing how to cope with them will help you and your child sleep easier. Night terrors belong to a class of sleep disorders called *parasomnias*, which occur when a child is partially aroused from deep slumber. Even though their eyes may be wide open, they are not awake. Dr Jodi Mindell, associate professor of psychology at St. Joseph's University, Philadelphia, and author of *Sleeping Through the Night*, says "A night terror isn't a dream. It happens during deep sleep, when a child is not dreaming, and he doesn't come fully awake." Symptoms of night terror include screaming, and signs of fearfulness and withdrawal when touched. And, though a child who's having a nightmare can be easily comforted by being awakened and held, a toddler having night terror is almost impossible to rouse. Doctors suggest it is better not to touch the child; instead, just stand by and wait till the terror passes, and keep him from falling off the bed if he starts to walk around. Sleep walking is related to parasomnia. Try and secure the bed by adding a railing around it, or lay pillows or a thick rug on the floor to buffer his fall. If his bedroom is on the top floor, then put a gate across the stair landing. By the time the child is eight to nine-years old, night terrors taper off into oblivion.

Obstructive Sleep Apnoea

What triggers this odd phenomenon of being caught between slumber and wakefulness is yet not clear. Some doctors are of the view that it is related to a medical condition called 'obstructive sleep apnoea'. This is a disorder in which blocked or narrowed breathing passages cause people to snore or stop breathing while asleep. Some children have apnoea simply because their tonsils or adenoids are enlarged. Untreated, the condition can lead to developmental and behavioural problems, including an increase in night terrors in a child who is already predisposed to them. Removal of adenoids and tonsils can be very effective.

A quick check of the points below would enable you to see if your child who suffers from night terrors has obstructive sleep apnoea. The symptoms are:

* Snoring—it's the most common sign.
* Pauses in breathing during sleep.
* Breathing through the mouth, both while asleep and awake.
* Contorted sleep positions, as your child unconsciously manoeuvres himself to try to breathe more easily.
* Noisy breathing, coughing and choking while asleep.
* Short-term wakefulness in sleep due to interrupted breathing.
* Unusual grumpiness in the morning.
* Persistent bed-wetting in a child who snores loudly and frequently while asleep.

If any of these symptoms are visible, then consult an ENT specialist for appropriate treatment.

SWEET DREAMS ARE MADE OF THESE

Keep your child happy. A child's mind should not be cluttered with thoughts of conflict, fear or anxiety. Children fall asleep easily when they feel loved and secure. Kisses and cuddles before bedtime are very therapeutic in helping a child to relax. Reading a short story with a happy ending will also have a settling effect on the child's mind. At times, the onset of a cold or flu could bring on disturbed nights, so try and be very patient.

Children should be comfortable. Make sure that the bedroom is not too hot or too cold. The ideal room temperature should be twenty-one degrees Celsius. At suppertime the child should not be overstuffed with food and drink, nor should she go to bed hungry or thirsty. Avoid late night snacks of cheese, chocolate or drinks containing colourings or additives (preservatives). Some children are prone to nightmares after consuming these foods or drinks at bedtime.

Ensure that your child spends a fun-filled active day. Cut out the afternoon naps for toddlers and older children so that they naturally fall asleep at night. If they feel drowsy in the afternoons, then try and occupy them with exciting activities which will keep them engrossed in some creative work. A romp in the garden or park every evening will accelerate a healthy fatigue. Children should be tired enough by the evenings and wanting to sleep every night.

The time after supper should not be noisy or excitable for the child. Bedtime is the time for peace and quiet. Children should not be disturbed with television noises, people chatting, traffic sounds, dogs barking or the neighbours yelling. Shut the windows and doors to eliminate the sounds, draw the curtains so that headlights from vehicles do not cast strange shadows in the room. Assure your child that these sounds and lights won't harm her or him in any way.

Children sleep well when they follow the same routine before bedtime every evening. The fixed routine will send 'sleep messages' to the billions of impulse centres in the brain and the central nervous system, enabling the child to fall asleep quickly. So, set a fixed time for a hot bath after supper, then put on the night-suit. Between the bath and dressing up for bed, talk about the day's events to see that nothing is worrying the child—no fights with friends nor home quarrels. Thereafter, tuck the child in bed for a bedtime story followed by a goodnight kiss, and then put out the reading lamp.

The room where the child sleeps should have a soft night lamp. If there is no provision for a night lamp in the room, then the light in the passage, near the bedroom door, may be left on so that its soft light (not the glare) enters the child's bedroom. Children don't like to sleep in dark rooms. A dark

> *Set a bedtime routine and follow it religiously: it is the key to good sleeping habits.*

room gives an eerie feeling and often has an unsettling effect on children. Children do get scared of the dark. With the night light on, they feel reassured by the familiarity of the bedroom and its dimensions.

Disciplining the Child

Anyone can become angry—that is easy. But to be angry with the right person, to the right degree, at the right time, for the right purpose, and in the right way—this is not easy.

— ARISTOTLE *(Ethics)*

Two-year-old Mandira kept tugging at her mother's leg in a shop, whining for a cola drink while the mother was keen to purchase something more nutritious. The whining escalated to whimpering, then crying and finally erupted into a wide-mouthed from-the-bottom-of-the-guts S-C-R-E-A-M, and then for effect she rolled on the floor. Here was the quintessential test of parenting on the shop floor. Mandira's mother, anxious to cut short the tantrum quickly, surrendered. "It's so damn exasperating," she explained. "Either you give her the cola, or you have a big scene. So what do you do? You buy the thing." For the mother it was just a matter of giving in to a cheap treat to keep the child quiet and happy, but a lesson learnt in expedient parenting points out that such decisions are signals to bigger problems in the future.

Your toddler whom other mortals call, 'a sweet bundle of adoration', has grown into a headstrong and utterly shameless brat. She is stubborn to the core. She screams. She whines. She hits. She throws tantrums. She hates to say *please*, and loves to say *no* with a capital N. Your actions and reactions to her antics have got you wondering whether you're helping to create a confident and a caring child, or a brat? You're in a dilemma.

A Parent's Dilemma

* *She is stubborn and defiant*
* *He is hyperactive and destructive*
* *Daily demands new toys, adornments, clothes*
* *He is hot-headed, violent and vicious*
* *She is an ace manipulator*

The 'dilemma list' can be further expanded with more tidbits of the negative behaviour without an answer in sight. Parents are absolutely confused when it comes to using, what psychologists call, 'behaviour modification' techniques. Is spanking the right way to discipline a child? Or is it better to reason out with him? How do you ignore a tantrum? What about giving the brat a 'time-out' in the bathroom? While confusion reigns on *how* to discipline and *when* to discipline, you know your child is getting more and more naughty because your blood pressure is rising and your patience is declining. In the last couple of decades, lines have been drawn between discipline and punishment which were not drawn earlier. People are less certain and more confused about disciplining the child today than ever before. While in search of a better way, parents continue to discipline children with their own unique mix of threats, bribes, shouts, love and humour.

Discipline and Punishment

Often when parents seek advice from childcare and healthcare specialists on 'reforming' their child, they are often advised to give the child some more time, so that the problem will sort out by itself. This kind of 'advice' puts the parents in a dilemma. It's like being caught in a circus cage, with you as an inexperienced trainer, training a tiger cub a few 'civilised' acts, which will win the cub social acceptance, approval and applause. You, the cub trainer, ask for 'tips' on training skills from the experts, and you are told to give the cub 'some more time'. In turn, the trainer is painfully aware that the cub's aggressiveness will become ingrained as a behaviour pattern with the passage of time. Eventually the trainer realises that he's losing control over the cub, and being at a loss on how to gain control over the cub, the trainer in desperation begins to *flick* the whip. The cub snarls and snaps back. The trainer and the cub are now at loggerheads.

Shouting, ranting, slapping, cuffing, or locking up the child is plain punishment and has nothing to do with discipline. Actually, the spirit of discipline is opposed to corporal punishment. In order to discipline one has to be self-disciplined: to stay in control of one's emotions and one's faculties. There is a difference between discipline and punishment. Child psychiatrist, J. Gary May says that the distinction is basically simple. "Since punishment is used to cause pain, the child will always look for ways to 'pay back' the individual who inflicts the pain, and may do it in a way that is just as cruel, harsh, and uncaring."

> Discipline promotes a sense of self-esteem; punishment destroys it.

It's usually a weak parent or teacher who administers corporal punishment, because that person wants to exercise control over the child by inflicting pain. Parents and educators must be willing to learn new techniques to channelise a child's energies, and not to curb or control them. To channelise is to give wings to their growth. To control them is to clip their feathers of expression and stymie growth.

Discerning Right from Wrong

It is every parent's wish that their children grow up knowing the difference between right and wrong. Generally speaking, parents are well aware what morals their children should imbibe, namely, they should be honest, never lie, cheat or steal; they should be obedient and considerate to others. Unfortunately, the two-year-old who is throwing his fourth tantrum in two hours is so selfish and demanding that parents pause to wonder if he'll ever learn to be obedient or considerate of others!

We seem to miss out on one very basic fact. Children learn about right and wrong at a very early age, from infancy onward, and that the learning process spans the whole of childhood. Today's children are not just intelligent, they are super intelligent beings. If we were to compare our levels of awareness and vocabulary when we were, say three-years old, vis-à-vis, today's three-year-old, we could be rated as duffers. The evolution of being is an ongoing process. Never before in its history has the human race been swept along in the strong eddy of technological inventions, as it is now. Every day we hear of some startling new breakthrough in science and technology. Today, we've mastered the secrets that constitute 'genome mapping' and the DNA, as well as the secrets of the *entire* universe. All this knowledge definitely has its impact on the zygote and in the formation of the embryonic brain. Today's three-year-old is a highly evolved individual who is aware of his environment and is articulate about his needs. He knows how to play his cards with nimble fingers and an astute mind.

Two pickpockets met on a subway train,
each picking the other's pocket.
The woman crook got his pocket book,
the man got her diamond locket.
Admiring each other, they fell in love,
they married, but that was worse.
They wished for a child who could snatch a bag
or pilfer a Scotsman's purse.

Their wish came true, and a boy was born,
a slick-looking, sly-faced mite.

But, alas, alack, with a crippled hand—
the fingers were closed uptight.
The heartbroken parents hurried the child
to a famous specialist;
and offered him watches and precious gems
if he could unclench the fist.
First thing he did was to tie a string
to a wristwatch with jewelled band,
and wave it steadily, back and forth,
just over the crippled hand.
As the fingers opened, the Mother and Dad
began to dance and sing.
For there in the palm of the baby's hand,
was the midwife's diamond ring!

— ANON

TEACHING GOOD BEHAVIOUR

From Admiration to Imitation

Children identify strongly with their parents whom they admire and love, and they imitate them so that they can become like them. Later, they will identify themselves with people they admire outside the home, like teachers, film stars sports persons and television characters. Parents are tickled when their little girl steps into her mother's high heels or plays with her nail-polish or lipstick, or when a little boy wants to dab an after-shave cologne on his cheeks or wear trousers like his father does. The admiration and imitation to become like their parents also spreads to other types of behaviour, for instance, when the child uses swear words, argues or loses temper just like the parents. When children want to be like us, then we have to set an example with our behaviour.

> We must make sure that we do not tell lies over the telephone or in person, or get angry when the child is around.

A child is confused when he sees that adults get away with unacceptable behaviour while he gets punished for imitating that same behaviour. If we want to encourage honesty, kindness and consideration in our children then we must set that same pattern of behaviour in ourselves. And we should make it a point to defer handing out physical punishment because it only encourages more aggression in the child.

> *You say that Father writes a lot of books, but what he writes I don't understand.*
> *He was reading to you all the evening, but could you really make out what he meant?*
> *What nice stories, Mother, you can tell us! Why can't Father write like that, I wonder?*
> *Did he never hear from his own mother stories of giants and fairies and princesses?*
> *Has he forgotten them all?*
> *Often when he gets late for his bath, you have to go and call him a hundred times.*
> *You wait and keep his dishes warm for him, but he goes on writing and forgets.*
> *Father always plays at making books.*
> *If ever I go to play in Father's room, you come and call me, 'What a naughty child!'*
> *If I make the slightest noise you say, 'Don't you see that Father's at his work?'*
> *What's the fun of always writing and writing?*

> *When I take up Father's pen or pencil and write upon his book*
> *Just as he does—a, b, c, d, e, f, g, h, i—why do you get so cross with me then, Mother?*
> *You never say a word when Father writes.*
> *When my Father wastes such heaps of paper, Mother, you don't seem to mind at all.*
> *But if I take only one sheet to make a boat with it, you say, 'Child, how troublesome you are!'*
> *What do you think of Father's spoiling sheets and sheets of paper with black marks all over on both sides?*

— RABINDRANATH TAGORE *(An Anthology)*

Model Your Lives Accordingly

The easiest way for parents to get their children to behave is by modelling their lives according to the behaviour they want. In other words, if you don't want your child to hit out at his sibling then you shouldn't hit or spank him—ever. If you want him to say, 'please', 'thank you' and 'excuse me', then you should often use such words yourself in conversation. Right actions will generate right reactions, and vice-versa. Parents should look upon discipline as a teaching opportunity and not as a power struggle which breeds conflict and hostility in children.

Establish Clear Rules

Rules that seem crystal clear to an adult may seem pretty complicated to a child. For example, a mother tells her eight-year-old son, "Go to your room and finish your studies." The child spends an hour in his room and later joins the family to watch television. After supper when the mother frees herself from watching her favourite TV serials, she calls for his school-bag to check his work. When she sees he has done practically nothing, she lashes out in anger, "How many times must I tell you...?" The child is ashamed and confused. He tries his best to 'finish his studies'—up to a point. On the one hand he couldn't understand some of the things he read, and on the other, everyone was having a great time watching TV—so he put aside his books and discreetly joined them. In the first place, the mother should have sat with him to get him started on his studies, then praised his efforts as he picked up momentum, and later checked back from time to time on his progress, with more showers of praises for his achievements. So, instead of ordering him to finish his studies, the appropriate thing to do would be to sit with the child and guide him on how to follow instructions:

    (i) complete the homework, and

    (ii) revise what was taught in class.

    Only after the child has comprehended clearly the order, "go to your room and finish your studies" that the child should be left to handle the responsibility by himself.

Rewards as Reinforcement

Consider the following conversation between two cousins, seven-year-old Selma and six-year-old Omar:

    Selma: Where did you get that chocolate bar?

    Omar: Mama gave it to me.

Selma:	Why?
Omar:	Because I wanted it.
Selma:	So ... she gave it?
Omar:	Oh, I started screaming.
Selma:	(*confused*) You mean because you screamed, your Mama gave you a chocolate bar?
Omar:	(*smiling*) I guess that's the way it works.

Will Omar scream again? Of course, he will; in fact, louder than before. Wesley C. Becker, in his book *Parents are Teachers*, says "The basic point of reinforcement is that any behaviour followed by a reward will automatically be repeated." So, how should Omar's mother have reacted to his screaming to decrease the chances of getting his way in similar situations? According to Becker, she should have ignored the screaming (acted indifferent), or sent him to his room, or cut off his TV watching for some period of time (acted negatively). Studies point out that by acting neutrally or negatively to a person's behaviour often reduces the likelihood of the person acting the same way again in subsequent encounters. A set of reinforcement principles referred to as *Grandma's Rules* by Becker were developed by psychologist David Premack: "A less-preferred activity that is performed before a more-preferred activity is reinforced positively by it." Examples of *Grandma's Rules* are: "If you do your homework now, I'll give you a chocolate bar later," and "After you take a bath, I'll take you out shopping." On the other hand, "Eat your chocolate bar now and do your homework later," may not get the homework started at all. If eating the chocolate bar, a more-preferred activity is permitted before doing homework, which is a less-preferred activity, then it won't have a positive reinforcing effect, according to Premack.

Be Consistent

If children are going to learn that some behaviour is right and some behaviour is wrong, then it is important that you are consistent in applying an identical response every time something *right* is done, and an identical response every time something *wrong* is done. When a mother changes her approach or the degree of response in dealing with a problem

> *When the father or grandparents belittle the mother's efforts, the whole exercise of teaching a child right from wrong gets further complicated.*

say, of disobedience, her inconsistency will hardly reinforce right from wrong. You can't censure a child for doing something one day, and allow her to do it the next day. Reinforcement must come from the other family members, too. Everyone at home should be in agreement of what is acceptable behaviour and what is not. Usually in families where both parents are involved, supportive, satisfied with their roles, and who teach children appropriate behaviour by drawing examples from their behaviour, in those homes discipline is most likely to flourish.

Positive Parenting

Raghav and Sukriti, with two sons, aged seven and four, were going round the bend and feeling the strain of it all. Just when Sukriti got the elder boy to behave and do her biding, the younger one would throw up a fuss. After she had met the younger one's demands, the elder child would accuse her of loving the sibling more. She blamed her husband, Raghav for not pitching in enough. According to Raghav, the mother was doing enough damage without his help. She severely punishes them: she shouts, slaps, locks up the kids to teach them a lesson. Raghav said he neither contradicts nor intervenes when Sukriti corrects the children. If he stepped into the kitchen to cook a couple of his favourite dishes, she'd shoo him out, he said. He loved cooking, he admitted shyly. If he humoured the kids and played with them, she'd accuse him of going soft on them, instead of disciplining them. I asked them if they spent time exclusively with each other as a couple? Sukriti said, after minding the kids the whole day, where was the time? Raghav said, that a few times he had wanted to surprise her, had even bought cinema tickets for a night show. She refused to go out saying the kids needed her. Once, when he took her to Bangalore for three days, she cribbed and cribbed about being away from home. Sukriti admitted that the elder kid had stopped eating and the younger one had developed high fever in her absence for which she will never forgive herself. Raghav said that she called home at least five or six times every day to find out the mischief they were upto. Then she would scold the children over the telephone and end the call by saying how much she missed them and loved them. Sukriti said she didn't want the kids to trouble their grandparents in her absence. According to Sukriti, her in-laws who lived with them, were non-interfering, complying and doted on the kids. Of course, they took good care of the kids but they also spoilt them, she said.

Instead of the children, it was Sukriti who needed help. She had to change herself: soften up and mellow down. She had managed to put her husband and the in-laws in their places. Unfortunately for her, the kids were playing mind games with her and refused to buckle down under her wrath. Sukriti needed to be a positive person in order to be an effective parent. That negative force in her was like toxic energy which had to be dealt with first. She saw everyone around her as 'problem' people whom she had to set right. To begin with, the first tough lesson was she had to 'let go' of controlling their lives. Indeed, it was going to be a hard toil for her to make that roundabout turn: to trust her husband and in-laws and accept them for what they are. Without intending to, she had destroyed the husband's culinary skills, and criticised his positive parenting ways, while she reduced her in-laws to puppets who danced to her tune. Sukriti came for advice on how to better her kids; instead, she was advised on how to better herself by becoming a positive person. I don't think she was ready for that sort of advice. Would she have the humility to see herself in another light? Humility comes at such a high price. Through meditation, introspection and yoga she would learn to touch her inner self and discover the music within her, and blend it in harmony with the music of her loved ones. I assured her that her children's behaviour would change automatically after she had learnt the power of praise.

Parents have to realise that disciplining children is not to simply get them to conform to rules. Rearing a flock of obedient sheep is not what positive parenting is all about. We want our children to be dynamic as opposed to being submissive.

And the truth is, children are greatly inspired by the behaviour and attitudes of their parents. Debashis Chatterjee, in his book *Light the Fire in Your Heart*, says, "When the molecules of carbon are rearranged, we get diamond. In physical form, carbon and diamond look very different, yet they are merely different expressions of the same potential. This is the story of people who may appear to be very different from what they can be. With a little internal reorganisation in their values, beliefs and attitudes, people can be truly transformed." Like most parents, Sukriti has a lot at stake and a lot to lose if she doesn't change herself. Children have the potential to be transformed into diamonds and the potential to remain carbon.

How and When to Correct

> You can't solve a problem on the same level on which
> it was created. You have to rise above it to the next
> level.
>
> — ALBERT EINSTEIN

Parents and teachers ask, "Isn't correction, disciplining?" They usually link correction to a negative activity where children have to be scolded, smacked, locked in bathrooms, thrown out of class, punished or detained in order to be taught lessons in good behaviour. As management trainer and consultant, I am hired by corporate houses to identify attitudinal and behavioural problems, offer solutions, and rectify negative behaviour. You may ask, "Do the participants sit with their heads bowed in shame while I harangue them on behaviour and attitudes?" In fact, the reaction is opposite; the participants in my workshops laugh at the modules on mind games and, at the same time, know they are laughing at themselves, while rejuvenating their resolve and determination to function better. In this chapter, I will share with you the techniques used by trainers in corporate houses to bring about behavioural and attitudinal changes. Once you comprehend its principles, it will not be difficult to apply those techniques at home.

DYNAMICS OF CORRECTION

The Concept of Coach and Referee

The precondition for any correction is to first project to the other your sincere feelings, "I care about you. I value you. You are important to me." If this precondition is not met, then the very meaning of correction is lost, and the exercise tapers into a 'ticking off' session, which could result in exchange of hostilities. Offering corrections is one of the most important ingredients to improve human nature. Ask the world's major corporations, and they'll tell you of the millions they spend annually on hiring lead consultants to improve human resources. When the child perceives the projection of your love and care for him, he will also perceive you upholding his self-esteem, his dignity and his pride. Behaviour is strongly rooted in emotions. To effect any change in behaviour at the emotional level, children want to tangibly feel that grownups believe in them. Parents and teachers must understand that whenever they execute a correction they have dual roles to play:

1. referee
2. coach

As in any game, when a player commits a fault, the referee blows the whistle; similarly, when you play the referee's role, you 'blow the whistle' for one brief moment when your child commits a fault. As a referee, you must learn the skills to reprimand. Kenneth Blanchard and Spencer Johnson, in *The One-Minute Manager,* lucidly illustrate techniques to correct aberrant behaviour in people. The same principles will work if applied to home situations. The authors split correction (reprimand) into two halves. The first half of the reprimand relates to the referee's role and the second half relates to the role of the coach. According to Blanchard and Johnson, "The one-minute reprimand works well when you:

Tell people *beforehand* that you are going to let them know how they are doing and in no uncertain terms.

The first half of the reprimand:
- Reprimand people immediately.
- Tell people what they did wrong—be specific.
- Tell people how you feel about what they did wrong— and in no uncertain terms.
- Stop for a few seconds of uncomfortable silence to let them *feel* how you feel.

The second half of the reprimand:
- Shake hands, or touch them in a way that lets them know you are honestly on their side.
- Remind them how much you value them.
- Reaffirm that you think well of them but not of their performance in this situation.
- Realise that when the reprimand is over, it's over."

Given a span of one minute, you have ten seconds to execute 'the first half of the reprimand', and fifty seconds to execute 'the second half of the reprimand'. You have to understand, as a coach, that reprimanding does not mean persecuting, instead, every effort is made to make the individual realise that a particular bad behaviour has to be eliminated and not the person's self-worth. The 'player' is made to realise that he is a very valuable player in the team and his contribution is vital to team effort. This becomes possible when the coach in you communicates special warmth which the player *feels* in a tangible way. With patience and affection, the coach teaches the 'player' the method of playing the game correctly. This implies that the coach:
- upholds the self-esteem and dignity of the players
- has infinite patience as a trainer
- has the ability to inspire the team
- knows the rules of the game

These qualities can be summed up in one sentence: *He loves to coach, and he loves those he coaches.*

Many parents are at a loss to know how to get their child to obey them.

Radha, an architect, who works from home, was talking to her client over a cup of coffee in her hall. Her two-year-old

Sarah kept playing with a fairly large ball in the hall. Radha kept reminding the child not to play in the hall. But the child continued playing without heeding her command. After a while, the ball fell over a flower vase and brought it down. Radha jumped up, her patience having run out, excused herself, scolded Sarah as she picked her up physically, then smacked her across the bottom, and locked her in the bathroom. With some variations this could be a familiar scene to many parents. The ideal situation would be such that the mother, before she sat down to entertain her client over a cup of coffee, should have informed the child of the meeting and organised her time. The child would then stay busy in her room playing with her LEGO set—happily constructing a spaceship while the mother conducted business with her client. Both situations are possible.

Coaching is Positive

In the first situation, Sarah displayed stubborn traits because her mother lacked structure, functioned on the level of convenience, and failed to project consistency. When Radha had no guests or clients, she did not mind where the child bounced the ball—be it the kitchen, bathroom, bedroom or on the outdoor lawns. So, what's right today may become a wrong tomorrow. If she wants Sarah to respond to her commands, she must first be definite and clear in her own mind. Playing the role of a patient coach, Radha must consistently and persistently demarcate the play zones. Outdoor games, which involve big, outdoor equipment, must be played outdoors. Blocks, mazes, puzzles, dolls, kitchen sets, dinky cars, crayons, etc. must be played within a specified territory in a specific room. Not any room. Radha may spread a bright coloured vinyl mat or rug in the child's bedroom for the child to sit and play, to demarcate the 'activity area' in the room. To reinforce this 'area', Radha must constantly guide Sarah on which toys must be played outdoors and which toys on the vinyl mat in her bedroom. If these simple and direct commands can be carried out with consistency for about two months (that's about ten per cent of a two-year-old child's existence on this planet), the 'pattern' of accepting directions will be firmly imprinted in the child's brain cells by then. And, the child will rely of these positive 'imprints' when called upon to respond to future commands.

Refereeing is Negative

You will soon notice that shouting, ranting, or smacking the kid won't get you positive results, because every time you keep blowing the whistle like a strict referee, the child antagonises you further with his negative behaviour. The end result of hostile correction is that the child ends up crying or sulking without completing the activity. In his own scheming little way, he knows he's won and the parent has lost. The mother stimulating the child, and the child responding to the mother's stimuli gets imprinted in the child's brain cells as a complete behaviour module or 'script'. This 'script' immediately enters into his synapses, the brain cells, for recording and cataloguing, which the child will effectively apply to get his way in other areas when negating commands. In fact, *shouting is verbal abuse.* Parents shout at children to get simple chores done, like "have your bath", or "eat your food." Delay tactics, in the child's response to the command, obstruct the parent's schedule who has so much more to do (than to administer a bath, or feed the child), and there's so little time to attend to many other chores piling up. Cleverly, he pretends not to hear anything and continues playing his own game. Our super intelligent child is quickly mastering the technique of power games. He is learning the art of holding his ground, while his synapses are busy filing and cataloguing the tug-of-war going on.

> *Shouting commands doesn't accelerate any positive action from the child.*

Let's take a closer look at the situation.

Raja is three-years old. He is excitedly playing with his toys when his Mom for the *nth* number of times has told him, "Come, have your bath." Finally she shouts at him and drags him to the bathroom with toys clutched in his hands, crying and howling, for his bath. According to his Mom, this is a regular scene. At first she cajoles him, then coaxes him, but since he stays adamant, indifferent, uncooperative—that's the final straw that breaks the camel's back—she screams at him, and then physically picks him up. "He's just plain stubborn," she says in a tired voice.

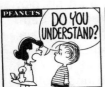 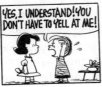 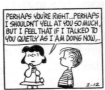 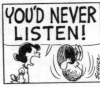

Stay Consistent, or Else

Let's reconstruct the scene. It's 6 p.m., it's Raja's bath time and he's playing with his toys. As his Mom gets the water ready for the bath, she tells Raja, that in five minutes he has to get to the bathroom. Raja can't tell time; but his Mom wants to instil in him the sense of time. As she gets his bath ready, water to the right temperature, soap, towel, talc, she then organises the clothes he will wear after the bath. Once she knows she has set the bath ready, she says in a bright, musical voice with excitement and warmth, "Let's put all the toys away in the box; then put the box under the bed, and let's run to the bathroom." She now playfully sits with the baby to execute what she said, picks up toys and starts dropping them in the toy box. Deftly, she guides the child's hand which is holding a toy, and with a sing-song tone, shakes the little hand over the box to drop the toy therein. Once the toys are in the box, she makes rumbling noises as she helps the child push the box under the bed. Thereafter, with a dazzling smile, coupled with lots of laughter she firmly holds her child's hand, and making loud pitter-patter footfalls, she races him to the bathroom. In a jiffy she takes off his clothes and begins to splash water over him. Keeping up her tempo of the nonsensical jabbering, she lathers him, and then washes off the soap. She dries him up with the towel, powders him, and dresses him up in the clothes she had earlier laid out on the bed. Clean and groomed, Raja is ready for his next activity, which his Mom has programmed for him.

Be an Accomplished Coach and Referee

Let's analyse the situation: Right from the beginning Mom stayed focused. She wanted the bath scene to be a matter of fact, a functional exercise, and not a play situation. The child was already playing. To drag a child away from his play and take him for a bath would build resistance to the bath. So, she sent out an early warning message, "Darling Raja, bath in five minutes," and simultaneously she went to prepare the bath: water with the right temperature and the right quantity; soap and towel handy, powder, comb and clothes ready and laid out. Since she was 'focused', she had a ready check-list running in her mind, and a consistent methodology of approach. Heading the list, is the first rule: "Get several *yes responses* at the very start." With joyful exuberance, she will offer an array of distractions in quick succession. She will firmly lead the child to a particular activity without giving the child choices, and at the same time, she will project to the child, with easy banter, that she is introducing a new activity. Just as it is important for the 'distraction technique' to be delightful, speed is of importance, too. With lots of excitement in her voice, and laughter ringing in her words, she tells Raja, "Darling, your five minutes are up!" (Though she could have spent anything from five to twenty-five minutes preparing the bath; it doesn't matter). "Let's put the toys in the box, and push the box under the bed." Before Raja could react to that command, with enthusiasm and spontaneity in her actions, she quickly picks up Raja's toys and puts them in the box. She gets him to 'help' her when she shakes his hand holding a toy, over the box, and lets the toy fall into the box. Once the box is pushed under the bed, she grips Raja's arm firmly, and runs him to the bathroom. Raja feels the pressure on his arm; he looks at his Mom's face, and her eyes. She isn't angry. She is laughing happily; she's having fun. Indeed, two contradictory messages, firmness and fun, are sent to Raja's thalamus glands. Simultaneously, numerous similar messages, of firmness and fun, are rushed to the cerebral cortex within that span of two to five minutes. Before Raja can make up his mind to resist the change in the activity, he is already in the middle of his bath. Overlapping in quick succession,

Raja's circuitry registers happy, joyous and exciting happenings. The pituitary gland secretes a little adrenaline into Raja's blood which make his eyes bright with excitement, and the whole body is indulging in fun— a reflection of Raja's overall muscular responses; the mammalian brain is at the centre of this enjoyable activity. It sends positive messages to all the nerve centres in the body, which respond with positive feelings to the activity. The baby's having lots of fun with Mom, the entertainer, in the lead.

But, had his Mom goofed off or had Raja 'ignored' Mom's commands, and had Mom made the attempt to steer Raja to the bathroom forcefully, and, in turn, had Raja shaken off her hold, then it was obvious that his muscular system had already negated her command. The reptilian brain by then had taken total control of all the responses, and no amount of 'reasoning' would have helped because the reptilian brain would jam or 'doctor' all the messages to the cerebral cortex (*thinking brain*). At lightning speed, the emotional brain would join the reptilian brain in warding off a second attack. When Raja's Mom would make a second attempt to physically pick Raja and carry him to the bathroom, Raja would scream his lungs out and flay his arms and legs in obstinate protest.

Block Negative Responses

His Mom knew that if she got the 'no response' to the bath, then immediately Raja's muscular system would respond to that negative verbal message and that would be displayed through physical resistance. The cerebral cortex would track the 'resistant messages' and imprint it as a 'pattern' for future reference. At the same time, the mammalian brain would instantly pick up the signals from the verbal negation and the resistance put up by the muscular system, and lend its emotional flavours through howls and sobs. The reptilian brain would instinctively take over with lightning speed, shutting off any inputs from the cerebral cortex. Instantly, the pituitary glands send messages of red alert to all the systems. The adrenaline gets the blood rushing to the whole body—the face is flushed, the muscles get tense (to levels of catatonic rigidity, if need be). The whole body is set to fight the commands tooth and nail. All this activity takes place in a matter of milliseconds. Indeed, we have here a brilliant child who uses his keen intelligence to beat his parents at their game of one-upmanship. In due course of time, the imprints or patterns of these power games, emanating from hostile parenting, become firmly rooted in the cerebral cortex, and like a computer virus, it will quickly chew up and destroy all the discs of positive data. Alas, a lot of valuable inputs, over several months, come to naught as the toddler becomes impulsively rebellious.

Entertain as You Teach

Parents and teachers will have to be 'entertainers' in their approach to disciplining children. They will have to apply the skills of a creative entertainer consistently. By being 'creative' I mean that you can't repeat the same script of words and actions for bath, bed, toilet, meals, games, etc. again and again. Let's say the 'bath activity' has a *specific script.* This script, with its actions, you will use for bath alone and you will not use it for another activity, say, bed or toilet. Your creativity will urge you to compose a ditty or a jingle to captivate your child's imagination for the next activity. As an 'entertainer', you will never display impatience, irritability or anger. Your goal as an entertainer is to touch their pleasure zones to bring forth positive responses from your children, not their stubbornness. So, you cannot afford to touch their negative zones. Lastly, it is equally important for you to remain consistent in your personal behaviour, so that your children are consistent in theirs.

Law of Consistency

I had mentioned earlier the need for consistency in adult behaviour and expression in order to channelise the behaviour of children. Perhaps we could understand the concept of 'consistency' better from a feathered friend, the parrot. From the dawn of creation to the present times the crows, sparrows, parrots, etc. have made their nests exactly the way their 'ancestors' made them millions of years ago. Their nesting habits like all other habits have consistency.

One bright sunny morning, Vidur's parents brought home a parrot in a cage. Eight-year-old Vidur adopted him as a pet and taught him to whistle and mimic a few words which drew laughter from everyone. A year later, Vidur developed a skin allergy. The doctors advised them to get rid of the pet. Unable to keep the pet any more, with a heavy heart, Vidur opened the cage to let the parrot fly away. But the parrot was in no mood to fly away. When Vidur pushed him out of the cage, he began to flap his wings with much difficulty. Poor parrot, he couldn't join the company of other parrots since he had 'forgotten' the parrot language (he had learnt instead, 'Pretty Polly—how do you do!' and to whistle), and he couldn't fend for himself. As for making his nest, that was just impossible. Being denied access to his natural habitat for so long, this little bird was in a 'confused' state. All that once came natural to his instinct as a parrot was now inconsistent with his nature. The poor parrot had developed irreversible aberrant behaviour patterns. His behaviour had been modified to suit the human habitat. In his natural habitat he was a total misfit. Outside the cage, he would live his life in isolation and die in loneliness.

The law of consistency is 'imprinted' in the brain cells of birds, animals and humans. Our eating, drinking, mating, sleeping and community habits are consistent like those found among the birds and animals. Upbringing is about training, and in order to train, one has to understand the law of consistency imprinted in our brain cells. When we contradict the law of consistency, like Vidur's parrot, our child lands in a confused state, but with a difference. The child is not bird-brained like the parrot. He has evolved into a superintelligent being, and he will use his intelligence to improvise on the existing 'contradictory' data and use it to suit his convenience—to control and manipulate others in order to have his way.

SOME CAUSES OF AGGRESSIVE BEHAVIOUR

Toys, TV Characters and Family Squables

Volumes have been researched and written about the importance of play in early childhood development. Precious little has been written about the influence of toys and games on children's behavioural patterns. While girls are given dolls and kitchen sets, boys are given macho toys to play with. Toys of violence like guns, swords, knives, etc. or toys of combat, like soldiers, tanks, warplanes and helicopters expose the child to war games where killing and hurting is just a game. Boys grow up playing the bang-bang or *dishum-dishum* games. Movies like the *khoon-pee-jaounga* types, reinforce violent behaviour in children. Cartoons, such as, *Popeye* and the *Tom and Jerry* kind (even adults love them), are loaded with bashing and with themes of one-upmanship. Parents watch soap serials which depict family intrigues and hostilities. Furthermore, they argue and fight with each other when the children are around. At times, they insult, abuse or hit one another in front of children. If children play combat games with toys of violence, or watch TV shows that project hostility, or get entrenched in family squabbles where parents fight, for such children interaction with others would naturally be an expression of hostility and aggression. In such circumstances, children usually grow up to be hostile and destructive.

Cable TV

When parents are hooked to soap serials, very soon their children get glued to TV sets. This gives rise to TV wars at home. While parents want their children to watch Cartoon Network, National Geographic and the Discovery Channel, the children know what they want and take to watching, among other channels, M-TV, WWF, Baywatch, Fashion TV and movies with adult themes. Till date, there is an ongoing debate between parents, educators and psychologists on the decadent influence of cable TV on the minds of growing children.

Violence: Cable or Familial?

Sometime in the mid-1990s, leading Delhi newspapers carried a news item about a student who got into a fight with another child on the school playground. He beat the child mercilessly with a stone. The rage was cold-blooded and the stone large enough for the child to be declared dead upon arrival at the hospital. In another incident, a few years later, the same papers reported a student who pulled out a gun from his pocket and pulled the trigger just before the morning assembly on the school grounds. The bullet lodged itself in the back of a student's head (quite some distance away), killing him instantly. Both these incidents took place in schools that were known to be conservative. For weeks, the newspapers and magazines aired views of the city's leading psychiatrists, psychologists, educators and parents. They were quick to conclude that cable TV must be blamed for the violence and rage the children experience and express at home and in school.

There could be another point of view. Why blame cable TV alone? It could be too pat an answer as a cover-up for a society's malaise where perversity and rage have risen to alarming levels. Of course, it is true that TV watching does influence behaviour, and so does the lack of family values and ethics. To take an impartial view, let's say that a million or more children watch the so-called 'decadent' television channels. If this is true, then on an average, we should have some tens of thousands of children, who are influenced by these serials, beating the brains out of other children. Fortunately it is not so. How is it that only a minuscule number of individuals develop such aberrant behavioural patterns? Why blame TV alone for all that is aberrant in us and in our society? Maybe, because it is clinically less messy to blame television than to blame ourselves and our upbringing. By making television the monster, we simultaneously give ourselves a 'clean chit' for good behaviour. By giving ourselves a good chit we don't need to change the way we live. We can continue to be selfish, violent, and immoral and still keep a clear conscience because we can always blame the environment for our aberrations. For our children's sake, we need to have courage to look inward and investigate the reasons that make us brutes, and we need the courage to take firm, concrete measures to rectify the errors in our lifestyles.

Family Brawls

Children are deeply influenced by the way their parents behave. Parental flare-ups and fights can be very unnerving to the child. Many children tremble in fear and wet themselves or develop nervous tics, or stutter when they see their parents shout, fight, abuse, and hit each other. Ideally, children should never be exposed to such ugly scenes. If and when parents fight, especially when children are in the room, they should make up immediately by hugging, cuddling and kissing each other in front of the children. If I were to see it from the children's point of view and pass judgement, I would say that if you have the *indecency* to fight in front of children, then have the *decency* to make up in front of them. In such a scenario (where you patch up your differences before your children), you will be slow to lose your cool the next time, and you will grow a little more tolerant of your spouse. This togetherness and bonding will reassure children that it is normal to disagree or to get angry provided one makes up immediately. The lessons children learn are never to sulk or hold grudges. Saying 'sorry' comes easier to children who see their parents make up with each other after an argument or a fight.

A few parents at my seminars have told me that some of the healthcare specialists had advised them against hugging, kissing or cuddling in front of the children since it was a 'Western' concept. I beg to differ, because being courteous, affectionate, loving and caring has neither boundaries nor geographical zones. But, spouses making love while the child is asleep on the same bed, or with the child on the cot in the same room is to be discouraged. We are talking about tokens and manifestations of affection and caring which we want our child to imbibe as a normal human being. If we want our children to be well-mannered, affectionate and caring, then parents, who are the child's primary teachers, will have to coach their children to show them ways on how to control anger and rudeness and take charge of their emotions.

Electronic Gizmos

Once upon a time we grew up in a family unit called the joint family. Interaction with grandparents, parents, uncles, aunts and cousins was the primary force that shaped our social skills. The secondary forces were built around our interactions with the outside world, like the school and the community. Now we have the tertiary force of influence: the electronic medium of television shows and computer games. While some experts who study child behaviour may haw and hem at the electronic medium's negative influence on children, most parents have discovered that television is a convenient babysitter. Putting the television on and allowing the child to watch his 'favourite show' is a sure way to keep him quiet and inactive. Some parents heap high praises attributing super intelligence to a child's skills at working the remote control switch, or the cellular phone, little realising that these electronic gadgets soon become tools of control. With a remote control in hand and knowing which buttons to press, children dictate to the grownups what programmes should be watched on the tube.

Much of the advertising on television aimed at children is designed to make them effective naggers. Children are unable to exercise a critical mind when watching television. They are very gullible; they are unable to differentiate between entertainment and a product sale. Today, more and more advertisements are either directed at children or have children shouting out the messages with half-truths. Since a child has no sales resistance, he nags his parents until he breaks down their resistance to buy items ranging from water purifiers and refrigerators to toiletries to toys, chocolates, junk food, and what not (*see* Chapter on *Eating Disorders: Obesity in Children*).

When children can be so strongly influenced by what they see on TV, imagine the influence of violence, sexual innuendoes and family feuds on the minds of these same kids. You can recall instances when the child behaves like the 'man of the house'. Many psychologists are of the opinion that a child who sees an example of violence is not only likely to copy that example immediately but is likely to refer to that example for future behaviour. Research points out that children who watch a lot of television are more likely to be aggressive than children who do not, and children who are aggressive are likely to watch a lot of violence on television. They do poorly in school and have short attention span. Studies also indicate that frequent exposure to plotting, manipulating, hoodwinking and manhandling depicted on the small screen erodes the sense of trust a child learns from loving parents.

Computer games and television serials cause more harm than good because they deny children the time to play outdoors. Being glued to the screen, ruins their posture, gait and eyesight. Since they don't interact with family and friends, they are less creative, less verbal, less social and less independent. We cannot turn our back on the electronic medium, whether it is television or computers, but there is more to life than these electronic tools. Since television and the internet hold a strong attraction for children, parents should exercise close supervision over what their children watch and for how long. Berry T. Brazelton of *Harvard Medical School* has observed: "Children under five are likely to show signs of exhaustion if exposed to more than one hour of television a day."

The law of moderation should be exercised in using the electronic medium. Allow the children to watch 'educational' programmes, say once a week, alongside with the parents who will explain the story-line to them, and answer their questions; then television could become a useful educational tool, and so will the use of computers.

The Way the Mind Works

*The mind is its own place, and in itself
can make a heav'n of hell, a hell of heav'n.*
—JOHN MILTON *(Paradise Lost)*

The mind is usually taken for granted. Attention is mostly drawn to the mind's functioning when parents come face to face with their children's behaviour problems. That there could be parallel thinking—not having it exactly one's own way—is hard to accept by many parents.

As parents, we want to invest in the very best for our children. We want to give our children the best prenatal and postnatal care, the best upbringing, and the best education so that they grow up to be winners. In spite of the best intentions most of our 'parenting' experiences come with bitter-sweet flavours, like a box of chocolates. Perhaps we need to know more about why children act and respond the way they do. To get to the root of the matter we will need to know more about how the mind works. Armed with this knowledge, we will be better equipped to guide and channelise our own energies and those of our families.

Your Baby's Brain Size

Anthropology is the study about the origin of being. The study of anthropology will lead you to measure head sizes. Don the cap of an amateur anthropologist and run a measuring tape around the head of say, a twenty-four month-old child. His head size would measure between fifteen to seventeen inches. Now run the same tape around your head. It would measure between twenty-one and twenty-three inches. You will find that the toddler's head size has already developed to about seventy per cent when compared to an adult's head size. At the time of birth, the brain weighs about twenty-five per cent of its adult weight. By age two, a child's brain is about seventy-five per cent of the adult brain weight, while the two-year old's total body weight is only about twenty per cent of adult weight. By age five, the brain is about ninety per cent of its adult weight, while the body weight is about one-third the adult weight.

Our Prehistoric Origin

In these pages, I have attempted to share with you the functioning of the brain as a layman. Most of us know of the brain as one composite organ, just like the liver or kidney. Actually, the brain is made up of three separate brains, each part having developed and evolved over several millions of years. The most primitive human brain is located at the base of the spinal cord, called the stem brain. It resembles the brain of reptiles, and it is also called the *reptilian* brain, and is about three-billion-years old. The *reptilian* brain's central function is the survival of the species through the fight-or-flight responses. It regulates heartbeat, breathing, blood pressure and muscle tone. Fear drives the blood into the large muscles making it easier to run. Fear immobilises us from writing an exam, or keeps us tongue-tied when we are about to deliver a formal speech in public.

The second segment of the brain is called the 'limbic' brain, or the *emotional* brain. It is also called the mammalian brain. Curled cashew-like around the stem brain, the emotional brain weeps and panics, longs and laughs. It controls all feelings, emotions, and sexual drives. It is about one-hundred-and-fifty-million-years old. The third segment that grew out of the limbic brain, a great mass of tissues that make the top layers of the human brain, is called the neo-cortex brain, or the cerebral cortex. Between three and five million years ago the neo-cortex brain developed. The neo-cortex brain is the seat of intelligence—the IQ zone where science and number configuration take place. It is also called the *thinking* brain. It sets humans apart from its nearest relatives—the apes. It enables humans to plan, learn and remember. Lust and sexual drive stem from the *emotional* brain; logic, love and relationships from the *thinking* brain. The pillars of Western learning were firmly laid on the teachings of the Greek philosophers like Socrates, Plato and Aristotle where the skills and powers of the *thinking* brain was emphasised. The study of the *emotional* brain has remained mostly ignored.

Your Brain: The Fastest Computer

The brain is capable of processing up to thirty billion bits of information per second. The human nervous system contains about 28 billion neurons, or nerve cells designed to conduct impulses. Neurons enable the nervous system to interpret the information it receives from the five senses and conveys it to the brain. In turn, the brain then transmits action messages to the nervous system, while at the same time it methodically files and catalogues its findings for future reference and use.

> The brain sifts, analyses and comprehends all that the five senses perceive, and it acts and reacts with lightning speed.

The three segments of the brain developed from bottom up. They are connected and interconnected by a network that roughly runs into nine thousand five hundred kilometres of circuitry or *neural pathways*, which carry messages and signals at a mind-boggling speed to the different brain 'centres'. It takes the brain about twenty milliseconds to receive, interpret and react to a message (that's about ten times less than it takes an eye to blink). The development of neural pathways depend on the stimulation, or nourishment it receives from the time of birth onwards (*see* Chapter on *Learning Disabilities*).

Division of Labour

The cerebral cortex has a right lobe and a left lobe with each lobe executing definite functions. The right lobe controls: recognition of faces, creativity, rhythm, visual images—their depth, parallel processing, and synthesis. The left lobe controls: language, speech, reading, writing, logic, reason, analysis and serial crossing.

You have heard the expression, 'Her heart is bigger than her head', or, 'he is all head and no heart'. Ideally, a balanced person is one whose three brain segments—the *reptilian* brain, the *emotional* brain and the *thinking* brain—process the information cohesively so that actions, responses and judgements are appropriate.

Why We get Emotional?

The fact that the thinking brain emerged from the emotional brain, reveals a lot about the relationship between feeling and thought. You've heard of people having *sharp instincts*. The *emotional* brain has developed for itself a very refined and sophisticated sub-station which disseminates information and gets the body systems to act upon it, without referring those messages to the *thinking* brain. The *emotional* brain, being instinctual in response, *hijacks* signals and messages sent by the senses by giving it an emotional flavour. When messages and signals become emotionally tainted, the rational brain stops functioning. The *emotional* brain has its own little memory bank from where it executes its *emotional blackmail* techniques. A classic example is of a child who wants a certain object. The parents say, "No." In a flash of lightning, the emotional brain takes over. The child whimpers, cries, screams, or flays arms and legs, and continues to do so until the parents relent. When the child gets his way, he has won. This technique now gets *scripted* by the *emotional* brain and remains catalogued and stored in its library of solutions for future use, with or without modification, depending on the situation.

Understanding Your Child's Brain Cells

Why do children act the way they do? Sometimes they are

praised and at other times they are scolded and corrected. One moment they are so angelic and the next, they are full of devilry. To understand how behaviour gets stored in the brain cells we may have to recall what we learnt in elementary school. We learnt that the brain is made up of millions and millions of cells, and each cell functions as an independent storeroom. Your child's behaviour patterns, whether positive or negative, gets stored, like data files, in the brain cells. You could compare your child's brain cells to the 'empty rooms' of a brand new apartment, which you have newly purchased. But you cannot move overnight into the apartment because it needs to be furnished. Fortunately, the apartment has only a few rooms to furnish. Depending on how much money you are left with after buying the apartment, you can either furnish the new home with old, rickety furniture (if you're short on funds), or furnish it with interiors of great value (if you're still left with some money). Just as the 'empty rooms' need to be furnished, similarly the baby's brain, which has millions and millions of cells, or 'empty rooms' need to be filled up.

If the parents are in conflict or confused, or fight and contradict each other, they naturally fill the baby's brain cells with junk data. On the other hand, when both parents are absolutely compatible and in full agreement on the ways and means of bringing up the child and other issues, they naturally fill the child's brain cells with data of lasting value. Unlike the rickety furnishings in the new apartment, which at some stage could be junked and thrown away, the data which the brain cells receive and store stays there permanently. When the child reaches the age of reason (adolescence), he will rely upon the data lodged in his brain cells since the time he was an infant. If his actions, as an adolescent, are considered inappropriate in certain situations, and he is scolded, beaten and punished for those actions, it is obvious that he's working with confused data. Indeed, it is a severe functional handicap for a teenager. On the other hand, a teenager whose actions win the approval of the people around him, or, let us say, he goes a step further by anticipating their needs and performs deeds for which he receives praise and recognition, it is obvious he is working with values-based data lodged in his brain cells. His actions measure up to the expectations of the people around him (*see* Section on *Pre-teens & Teens*). From the time the child is born, it is very important for all family members to have a common agreement on corrections, in order to ensure that the infant's brain cells receive and store data of lasting value.

Historical Perspective

Before the late nineteenth and twentieth centuries, philosophers and social historians contributed the most influential ideas about development since there was little, if any, empirical science of development as we know it today. Plato constructed arguments to prove that knowledge is innate. In *The Republic*, Plato says, "But then, if I am right, certain professors of education must be wrong when they say that they can put knowledge into the soul which was not then there before, like sight into blind eyes...Whereas our argument shows that the power and capacity of learning exists in the soul already," (*Book VII*).

In the eighteenth century, French philosopher Jean Rousseau, speaking mainly of the child's moral knowledge, the child's sense of right and wrong, claimed that a newborn is a 'noble savage', who instinctively and innately comprehends socially acceptable forms of behaviour without specific training. In his view, the child is born with both knowledge and the propensity to learn; hence, the child is perfectly capable of getting along in life without adult guidance. By contrast, according to British philosopher, John Locke, in the seventeenth century, at birth the child's mind is as a blank slate, *tabula rasa.* The child knows nothing at birth. All that a person knows results from learned experiences. According to Locke, all knowledge is learned, and the principal means of learning is through the association of ideas.

The writings of these philosophers reflect their concerns about the moral goodness of the child and the need for moral training. In today's language, this is translated into a concern for the child's social awareness and the need to teach the child acceptable social skills. The Dutch philosopher,

Kierkegaard, defined a 'being' as a *thinking thing*. Parents and teachers fill the blank slates of children with the indelible medium of the good, the bad and the ugly; but being *thinking things*, children put two and two together and come up with five, a baffling equation for parents to accept. Unfortunately, while one-third is the positive content, two-thirds account for the negative contents that get inscribed on the *tabula*, slate.

Outdated Parenting Methods

Parents often bring up their children the way they were brought up, relying on pleasant or unpleasant memories of their own upbringing when they were little children. Aadhiraaj's parents are in their mid-twenties, and want to bring up Aadhiraaj the way they were brought up. In fact, we now come face to face with Aadhiraaj's grandparents who brought up the kid's parents. That's going a full generation backwards. Aadhiraaj's grandparents, who reared his parents, would have relied on antiquated techniques and methods that go back another thirty years. It makes no sense in bringing up a child by using generation-old methods, when you know that the child you are grooming has to be fully equipped to function in tomorrow's world. Grandparents proudly reminisce their old days when a "no was a 'NO' in my time". Today's child interjects with a "why?" to every "no". This unnerves parents, who quickly lose patience, or feel that their authority is being challenged or undermined. The human species is the only living species on this planet where its young ones are nurtured over several years. And, parenting is about nurturing. Hence, it's very important to put our act of parenting right, so that the end result would showcase a well-balanced individual some twenty years down the lane. What could have gone wrong when the end result shows a confused individual, you may ask? The factors are many, but the core could be related to either inconsistent (permissive) parenting style, or hostile (punitive) parenting style.

Ramesh and Geeta were a made-for-each-other couple as all their friends said. They were such fine parents, too, so they were told. But, their kid was a wild one. He was destructive, disobedient and defiant. Had Geeta and Ramesh bungled up? Where? Let us admit they were both very likeable people.

While they made a very good team as spouses and parents, they had bungled up in the area called, *parenting*. They confessed they were at loggerheads when it came to child upbringing. When one said "no", the other differed in opinion. "No colas," said Mom. "It's okay in moderation," said Dad. Both parents had forgotten the one and only golden rule when it came to laying down the rules: BE CONSISTENT in the rules you lay down. When rules are laid down firmly and carried out consistently, children are not confused and they know what their parents want them to do. Every child respects the 'Law of Consistency'. Ramesh and Geeta should learn to back each other up in the presence of the child when laying down rules and policies. When Mom said, "No colas", and Dad felt that Mom was too strict or harsh with the child, he should have remained quiet, or withdrawn from the scene, and not voiced his contradiction. Arguments, squabbles, fights, disagreements between parents make for distorted data, which the child's emotional brain absorbs readily. After all, they are children of convenience; they take on their parents' worst habits and seldom their best habits, because the best habits are habits of discipline.

Many parents and grandparents have asked me, "When the child is being scolded or punished for no fault of his, then shouldn't the parent be stopped?"

Why only parents, teachers, too, are often at fault in punishing children for no fault of theirs. But, that is not the time to tell them to stop reprimanding; if you do that, children learn to rebuff authority, and will stop responding to correction. So, in trying to set one right you may spark another wrong. It is advisable that family members, who see injustice being committed, should stay out of it. At that moment, respect for authority (even flawed authority) takes precedence over concern for injustice. The family, as a unit, has to *project* consistency for the child to *perceive* its importance. Hours later, when they are in bed and fast asleep, or when they are out playing in the field, you may discuss

It is only when the whole family projects consistency that the child will perceive how important it is to respect authority.

with each other, and come to an agreement on the parenting style to be adopted in the future. Likewise, take an appointment with the concerned teacher to discuss ways to inspire the best efforts in your children.

The nurturing grounds for emotional hijackings are when family members squabble or disagree with each other over methods of upbringing in front of children. The emotional brain picks up signals and messages relating to pleasure or displeasure. It automatically chooses pleasure-related messages which are convenient and suitable to its senses, and flavours them with emotional attachments. The body instantly manifests these messages. Pleasure-related messages are projected through eyes shining with delight, beaming smiles, gurgling sounds, laughter, or contentment. Conversely, the emotional brain picks up denial signals, and manifests it through tears, sobs, cries and tantrums.

Contradictory Signals

Mothers have often complained to me that on a one-to-one basis, children behave very well; but the moment the father comes home from work, or if the grandparents are around, children begin to misbehave. They become defiant, stubborn or throw tantrums. In a situation like this, a child knows that when he is with his Mom on a one-to-one basis, she has a one-track mind with a fixed focus and she will never deviate from that focus. His mental 'library' accumulates data in areas where family members do not share his Mom's views; instances when family members have put her down, saying, either she is too harsh, too disciplined, too firm or brittle in her ways. His brain has catalogued those 'imprints' of their contradictions. At times, they have even 'rescued' him from her. With such support, it suits the child to 'cock a snook' at his Mom in their presence. Indeed, lowering another's esteem before others in the family is a very shallow display of love or righteousness. In the child's eyes, whenever his Mom is being contradicted, her authority is challenged. So, he too, challenges her authority. The contradictions he sees around him, suit his convenience. If he does not obey his Mom, especially when she orders him to do what he doesn't like doing, he knows he can get away with it because others will come to his rescue. To overcome this dichotomy in behaviour, the entire family should put their act together. To channelise the child, every member must bond together as one family, having one voice and one direction. When correcting children, the family should support each other in totality, even when they disapprove of the other's methods.

Controlling Tantrums

Tantrums, too, can be brought under control when the family members rally around each other and learn to 'ignore' the child's howling or sobbing, let's say, for something as silly as a strip of gum. To ignore a child who cries and rants is the most difficult exercise for parents or grandparents. But *giving in* to a child's demands is to encourage a tantrum, which in turn pushes negative buttons in the child's brain cells. Any child who throws tantrums has mastered the fine art of getting what he wants. He knows that if he hollers loud enough and long enough, he will eventually wear down his tormentors, and get what he has set his mind to.

Correct Children with Feelings, not Reason

Parents and teachers often forget that their own actions speak louder than their words. Whenever you discipline or correct a child, it is important to first know the dynamics contained in a 'correction' format. For effective results, parents and teachers have to touch the emotional chords in the child's emotional brain rather than the logical side of the brain. Less of reason and more of feelings should be the norm. When correcting children, most adults function from levels of convenience. It is very convenient for adults to reason with the child. It is very taxing to the adult to distract the child through child-like antics. The child is high on instinct and low on reason. Since the faculty of reason is like a sapling which will grow and function with age, parents and teachers have to reach out to children at their instinctual levels, rather than at the levels of reason. To win children over, parents will have to adopt methods to distract them with a bagful of monkey tricks.

Three-year-old Ronnie saw his mother's cellular phone on the chair and made a run for it. But Mother got there in quick strides, picked up the instrument and put it in her handbag. When Ronnie saw he was 'cheated' of his prize, he began to scream. To keep him quiet, Mother decided to teach him a lesson once and for all why he should never touch her phone. "It's not a toy," she said in a stern voice. "You cannot play with my phone. I need it to make calls and receive calls. Now, be a good boy and go play with your toys." Ronnie then howled more loudly, making strange choking sounds.

Here's another scenario, when Ronnie made a dash for the cellular phone, his mother couldn't find any toy or object nearby to distract his attention instantly. So, she burst out laughing as she threw herself on the floor and grabbed Ronnie and began to tickle him while she smothered him with kisses. She then helped him to climb on her back—while she became a 'horse'—ready to treat him for a horse ride as she took him to the other room. Ronnie, taken by surprise, began to enjoy the new game his mother played and completely forgot about the cellular phone.

When making a correction, we usually correct the child head on. We've often heard it said that while condemning the sin, we should not condemn the sinner. When children commit errors, we rush to condemn them—not condone them. From rude commands, "Stop it. Shut up. Are you an idiot? Don't be stupid"—to expletives, to slapping and smacking, and the list goes on. With such an approach the child digs in his heels and holds his ground (like a wild boar) all the more firmly. Adele Faber and Elaine Mazlish in *Liberated Parents Liberated Children* talk about the approach of Dr Haim Ginott, a child psychologist and author of *Between Parent and Child*.

> *Don't condemn the child, but focus on the action before you, and mobilise his support.*

According to Ginott, adults should avoid expressions which judge a child's character or ability, and never use words like 'stupid, clumsy, bad'. When a child spills, let's say, water colours, while engrossed in a colouring activity, parents usually snap at the kid, "You stupid nitwit. Why are you so clumsy?"

Instead, Ginott advises, "We can be sure that the child's total energy would be mobilised for defence instead of solution." The spilt water colour on the floor has to be cleaned up, so you need to act upon the solution. "Oh dear, that needs cleaning up. Let's get the sponge and mop the floor." By mobilising him in the cleaning-up action you have taught him a very important lesson—not to defend his folly but correct the wrong committed. Look at it from another angle. You take someone to a restaurant for a meal. While in the middle of your lunch, your guest reaches out for a dish and spills his drink on the table. What do you do? Chide him for being clumsy? Or do you quickly reach out for a napkin to mop up the drink so that it doesn't spill over his or your clothes? As you mop up the spilt drink, you may ask the waiter to replace the drink. And, if it happens the second time, would you lose your cool? No, you wouldn't. You may, on the contrary, cover up for his embarrassment by telling him episodes of similar accidents. Look at ourselves: We are understanding and courteous to people outside the sphere of our intimate relations, while we rush to condemn our children for the accidents they commit.

Be gentle on the child when you attempt to correct him. And, stay in control, because when you are in control of your temper you are able to choose your words and be consistent in your line of action. When you lose control, you scream, shout and display your frustration, admitting the child is beyond your control. Many parents, with the best of intentions, start the correction exercises only to give it up after a couple of hours or days, readily accepting defeat. This will further reinforce in the child new strains of obstinacy. It's like a patient who starts on an antibiotic treatment for a viral fever only to give it up after a couple of days because the fever does not climb down. Unfortunately, the virus will now develop new strains wherein this same antibiotic treatment will become redundant.

Children Imitate Adult Behaviour

When parents catch children telling lies, using bad language, being disobedient, they react immediately by shouting or cuffing the child. Parents seldom realise that it was a ploy to get attention, or a copycat manifestation of an adult's behaviour. At the breakfast table, Ram told Geetanjali, his wife, that if Mr Sharma called, she should tell Sharma that he was not at home. While in the middle of the breakfast, the phone rang. Geetanjali picked the phone. It was Sharma on the line asking for Ram. Geetanjali readily covered up for her husband saying, "No, no, no. He has already left for the office. Yes, try the office number." Incidentally, Ram had made other plans with his wife. Being a Saturday, they had planned to spend a day out shopping, with a movie and a lunch thrown in. The four-year-old had soaked in the entire script. A week later, Geetanjali caught the child brushing off granules of sugar stuck to his fingers. The sugar bowl was open, close to where he was standing. "You're eating sugar again," she cornered him. "No, no, no," he whined fearfully. Geetanjali got very angry since she could not tolerate her child telling lies. She decided she was going to straighten him out once and for all, so that he would never tell lies ever again.

We live double standards. We want our children to do what we say, not what we do. If parents live by these standards, there will be no change either in the parent's behaviour or in the child's. From one situation to another, the child will hone the parent's skills of deceit, even though the parents may rave, rant and punish the child. Many parents publicly display despair over the child's negative behaviour, and correct them in public places. When parents publicly criticise and correct children, they do not realise that they inadvertently reveal to outsiders their own private behaviour. Have you secretly watched a child enact a role-play? He will assume the parent's role, while his toys are the errant or disobedient children. He sets to correct and discipline them. His gestures, actions, and words are replayed ditto to those of the parents, or in some cases, the teacher's behaviour.

Pygmalion Effect

Pygmalion was a sculptor in Greek mythology who carved a statue of a beautiful woman that subsequently was brought to life. George Bernard Shaw's play, *Pygmalion* (the basis for the musical hit, *My Fair Lady*), has a somewhat similar theme. The essence is that one person, by his effort and will, can transform another person. Parents play the Pygmalion-like role in developing able children and in stimulating their performance. What is the secret of their success? How are they different from parents who fail to develop similar responses in their children?

In George Bernard Shaw's *Pygmalion*, Eliza Doolittle explains:

> *You see, really and truly, apart from the things anyone can pick up (the dressing and the proper way of speaking, and so on), the difference between a lady and a flower girl is not how she behaves, but how she is treated. I shall always be a flower girl to Professor Higgins, because he always treats me as a flower girl, and always will; but I know I can be a lady to you, because you always treat me as a lady, and always will.*

Some parents treat their children in ways that bring out the best in them. While others, like Professor Higgins, unintentionally treat children in a way that stunts their development and performance. Eliza Doolittle says that the "difference between a lady and a flower girl is not how she behaves, but how she is treated." When parents and teachers complain about children's behaviour, they are saying, *"Look, we're doing our best. We're okay; the kid has a problem. The kid needs to learn how to behave."* But when parents see how they *treat* their children, then the onus is upon them to stimulate children to a higher level of performance. It is unfortunate that few parents think like Eliza Doolittle when raising kids. You will admit that it is easy to teach someone to read and write, to add and subtract— *"the dressing and the proper way of speaking, and so on"*— but how do you teach someone how to *create* a poem, or how to make a wise decision? The only way to master these skills is for parents to first learn parenting techniques, which usually are not found in self-help books. These parenting techniques are: interpersonal skills, discernment, judgement, creativity, and sensitivity which develop the intuitive side of parents. These skills, when implemented, will touch the dignity and esteem of children.

Servant's Influence on Child's Behaviour

We lived under the rule of the servants. To save themselves trouble, they virtually suppressed our right of free movement. This was hard to bear—but the neglect was also a kind of independence. It left our minds free, unpampered and unburdened by all the usual bother over food and dress.

— RABINDRANATH TAGORE *(My Reminiscences)*

Most servants who work in our homes are God's own people. They are there to do the oddest of jobs, however distasteful, at the oddest of hours, and to do it without a whimper, gripe or a grumble. We hire them to help around in the house and then gradually push the full load of the household chores on to them. In some households they are blessed and appreciated, and in some they are cursed and abused. In such homes, they are treated as low status people, bereft of feelings or dignity. Most servants have rural backgrounds and live in hutments. They migrate to cities in search of employment, and to covet a job they commit themselves to do all the chores the employer dictates. They sweep and mop houses, dust furniture, wash cars, look after children, bathe and feed children, run errands, buy groceries, wash linen, iron clothes, and many more chores which keep cropping up in the household from time to time. When they are given more than they can handle, and they are unable to handle competently the responsibilities thrust upon them, then they are at the receiving end of their employer's wrath. Indeed, it is a thankless job for most servants working in our homes.

Due to personal convenience, or other constraints, many parents leave the child to the care of maids and other house servants. When the child is literally brought up by house servants, it is natural for the child to learn rural mannerisms. As a toddler his *rural bent* would not be so noticeable, or objectionable, but when he is an adolescent, his mannerisms and behaviour would stand out like a sore thumb, and he would be regularly checked to mend his ways. While in the care of servants, some of the glaring areas which need to be watched are:

Speech: The choice of words, the diction and pronunciation get affected. The child's speech would carry overtones of a 'regional' accent. The accent comes from the region the maid or servants hail. Slang words or abusive words add colour to his vocabulary. But it would cause a grave set-back to the child's language development skills if he has to unlearn and relearn language skills as an adolescent (*see* Chapter on *Language Development*).

Eating Habits: He eats his meals sloppily. While eating he squelches, spits and belches. In the rural countryside if something is unpleasant and distasteful to the palate, or if it is some hot stuff, it is spat out. In urban areas, etiquette demands that the food is swallowed down with a drink of water. It is also common practice in the villages to belch as a sign of contentment after a meal, while belching is considered gross in urban areas.

Personal Hygiene: Brushing teeth or keeping the mouth clean is never given top priority in villages, as it is in towns and cities. If parents don't handle this area with care and caution, then they could end up paying through their noses for dental care at a later stage. Bathing is another ritual that is perfunctorily performed. The hair smells rancid, and may carry lice. Undergarments may not be fresh. The ears and nostrils remain neglected, as do nails on fingers and toes. Spitting and urinating by the roadside is also common among children brought up by servants.

Dress Sense: Under the servant's influence, the child may grow up having no dress sense. Some parents are very particular to dress their children in combination sets or in matching clothes having the same colour blends. For the servants 'clothes are clothes', no matter what the colour is; whatever clothes catch their eye they will get the child to wear it. When parents are not particular about dress sense, the child is at a disadvantage because as an adult he is likely to make the wrong choice of clothes.

Class Distinction: By observing the adult's attitude towards the servants, the child knows that servants are low status people. They can be pushed around; they can be manipulated and punished. Children learn to order the servants around, bully them, treat them without respect, even kick them or spit upon them.

Total Dependence: Like parents, like children. Just as the parents become totally dependent on the maids to look after children, so do children become totally dependent on the maids for everything. For every activity the child has to have the maid to help him perform it. As he has grown dependent on the maid, he is unable to interact with children of his age. Without the maid he is unable to adjust in school, or play games in the park, or attend birthday parties in the company of other children.

Servants are very important to us. But their functions should be restricted to assisting in housekeeping, while the parents retain the child-upbringing portfolio to themselves.

Otherwise, this is what child-neglect will amount to: overdependence on servants, and aping of rustic behaviour and mannerisms. Unfortunately, many parents turn a blind eye to one or more of these shortcomings when the child is a toddler. But by the time he is seven to ten-years old, his shortcomings will be his undoing. Indeed, irreparable damage is caused to the child's development when parents abdicate their parenting duties.

A Step in the Right Direction

There are many parenting skills parents should be familiar with in order to guide their service staff correctly. In most cases, parents blindly let servants bring up the children, and react only after negative traits become ingrained in the child's behaviour. If you have no choice but leave the child's upbringing to the servants, then pay added attention to the chapter on *Cultivating Good Habits,* It will help you to guide your servants to be aware of proper habits which you want to inculcate in your children.

SECTION ③

RAISE HAPPY KIDS

'Working' Towards Happiness

One can live magnificently in this world if one knows how to work and how to love. To work for the person one loves, and to love one's work.

— LEO TOLSTOY

Fruits of Labour

I had known Francis and Annette D'Costa for many years. They had two sons, Robert and George. They belonged to the lower middle-income class, where the luxury of house servants was an alien notion. Francis and Annette were working parents with regular jobs. The two boys, when they were children, had to assist their parents in doing household chores. Both the boys were allotted specific responsibilities by the parents, and they were expected to arrange their time-tables accordingly. They had to sweep and mop the floors, wash and iron clothes, buy groceries, run errands, clean the dishes, as well as make time to attend to their studies. It may seem that the poor kids thrived on a raw deal and a rich diet of work; that all work and no play would make them dull kids. But the opposite was true. When Robert and George reached adulthood, they were better off than their childhood friends in the neighbourhood, who had been less industrious. Both brothers were well employed in blue chip companies, earned more money and had more job satisfaction than their friends, whose parents had pampered them when they were children.

Across continents, in the USA, Dr George Vaillant, a psychiatrist at Harvard Medical School, had initiated a study in 1940 to understand juvenile delinquency. The study followed the lives of four hundred and fifty-six teenage boys from a Boston suburb where they were contacted and later, interviewed again at the ages of twenty-five, thirty-one and forty-seven. When they were compared at middle-age, one fact stood out: Regardless of intelligence, family income, ethnic background or amount of education, those who had worked as boys, even at simple household chores, such as weeding the garden, keeping the house clean, carrying out the garbage, they enjoyed more productive lives than those who had not. They were happier and had better marriages and closer relationships with their children. "It's not difficult to explain," said Vaillant. "Boys who worked in the home or community gained competence and came to feel they were worthwhile members of society. And because they felt good about themselves, others felt good about them."

Those teenagers were about fifty-years old when the researchers began to tabulate the findings. For those middle-aged men the significance of what they had done as boys to how they had turned out as adults was startlingly sharp. Those who had scored the highest on the boyhood activity scale were twice as likely to have warm relations with a wide variety of people, five times as likely to be well paid, and sixteen times less likely to have been significantly unemployed. On the other hand, those parents who considered their children too small to do any chores and had no work responsibilities were far more likely to have a spat with the law, and ten times more likely to have suffered mental and physical illnesses. The researchers also found that IQ, amount of education, family, and social and economic class made no real difference in how the boys turned out.

Can the lives of boys who were born during the American depression really tell us anything about bringing up happy children in this present technology-driven age? Says Vaillant, "I believe the same principles apply today." Another psychologist, Stephen Glenn, supports Vaillant saying, "Parents who do everything for their children may actually perform a disservice to them."

Making Work A Child's Play

Some parents believe that preschool children are too young to help around the house and that they should be playing, not 'working'. But for little children, cleaning a chair with a duster can be as much fun as building a tower with building blocks, or brushing a doll's hair. Instead of rushing through the household chores so that you can make time to 'play' with your child, encourage your child to offer help and turn your work into his playtime. You will feel happier doing the housework if your child is not nagging you for attention, and he will enjoy trying out a new activity.

Set Small Targets

The household chores may be a boring routine for parents who have to perform them day after day, but for a child they are like a game—fun and fulfilling. The purpose of delegating chores isn't to get tedious tasks pushed on to the kids, or to teach them 'how to work'. A tidy bedroom, a manicured lawn, or sparkling cutlery are less important than developing responsibility, independence, self-esteem, confidence and competence. These value-added skills set the foundations of emotional well-being. Helping around in the house also helps children to understand that people must cooperate and work towards common goals. Those adults who know how to do this are happy and content with themselves and with others.

Handling Responsibility

Teaching kids how to contribute to family life is part of good parenting. Children need to be given responsibilities in the house.

Even two-year olds can learn to put away their pyjamas. And by the time the child is fourteen, he should be able to complete many chores on his own, take care of his personal belongings, dust the house, and budget his pocket money. Unfortunately, parents often make children dependent through over-indulgence and doing too much for them. Parents should organise and plan chores for children so that they become happy, productive and responsible adults.

Avoid 'Cluster Commands'

Many parents give 'cluster commands' to their kids which are incomprehensible because those commands are abstract or imprecise. When Anisha, a ten-year-old, heard her mother say, "Clean your room and keep it tidy," she had just a vague idea of what that meant. She pushed the clutter (shoes, slippers and toys) against the walls, and that was it. Half an hour later when the mother went to inspect the room, she was ballistic. She expected Anisha to have made the bed, arranged her shoes and sandals in a line by the bedside, and put the toys away. Conversely, Anisha pictured a 'clean room' with a clear path to the bed so that her mother wouldn't trip, and so she 'cleaned' the room accordingly.

Teaching the Steps

If you want to teach your child to be a happy worker, then you must break down each new task into small parts and demonstrate it one at a time. If your child is to clean her room, first show her how to do it by putting yourself in her place. If three items need to be done—first, to make the bed, then to properly arrange shoes and sandals, and last of all to keep the toys in order—then break the task into three segments and specify each segment. In doing so, you will make the job specific and manageable, and your child will have the joy and satisfaction of being able to finish it.

Praise Abundantly

You must constantly praise and reward your child's success. Praises can be lauded verbally and rewards can be lavished through hugs, cuddles and kisses. Give rewards but not bribes. Rewarding a child with money to perform household chores is a bribe. When will that child learn to share home responsibilities? Probably he never will. However, telling others how proud you are, within your child's earshot is another form of compensation. On the other hand, if you take their accomplishments for granted, or if you give your children the impression that they can never do anything right, they will lose their sense of self-worth and they will grow up feeling inadequate and incapable. After all, learning is the process of trying and failing, and trying and succeeding. If you teach your children not to fear mistakes, they will learn faster and feel free to accept challenges.

The Joy of Working and Learning

The secret of successful job sharing is to plan ahead. Think of everything you do in an ordinary day, and work out ways in which your child could be involved. Do not underestimate your child's ability; she can probably do more than you give her credit for. The urge to 'help Mummy' comes almost as soon as the child can walk. It is a good idea to break the larger tasks into smaller child-sized jobs that are easily managed by small hands and can be completed before the child gets bored. A child of three can fetch and carry, or even sort laundry, which also teaches about colours, shapes and sizes. The child of four and five can understand simple instructions, run small errands, and be expected to put away toys, pick up clothes, or remove his own dinner dishes. The seven-year-old can take on family responsibilities. For a seven-year-old child, a good first assignment is to lay the dinner table. To ensure that the child does not get frustrated laying the dinner table, to begin with, you may have to give instructions at each stage, from taking the cutlery out of the drawer, working out which utensils are needed for the meal and laying them in the right order, remembering where everyone sits and checking there are enough chairs. And then there are table mats to find and put on the table, and

> *Accomplishment makes a child confident and happy, and instils in him the quality of helpfulness.*

water tumblers, too. Children should not be rushed into jobs beyond their skills. A new task should offer a challenge, but it must also afford the child a feeling of accomplishment. Accomplishment enhances self worth and self-esteem. But if children become discouraged, they may be unwilling to try again.

Teach Children to be Task Specific

Shivangi, a four-year-old child was a fast worker. She would always show off her work ahead of the class. The nursery teacher pointed out to her mother that Shivangi would finish her colouring so fast that she would leave some portions uncoloured. When she was told to complete the page of colouring, she had already lost interest in that activity and would ask for a new activity. If she did not get her way, she would pout and get moody. When the mother related this incident to me, she also added that at home too, she would get bored with one activity and switch to the next, leaving the first one incomplete. Shivangi needed help to enhance her concentration span, to develop a 'commitment to complete' the task at hand, as well as be happy and cheerful. I suggested to the mother to get her started on baking a cake at home since it would be a new game and at the same time the entire task of baking a cake would take an hour or more to complete. I also guided the mother to first 'organise' the ingredients and all that goes with baking a cake so that the task does not turn out to be messy or frustrating. A couple of months later the change in Shivangi was noticed by all, at home as well as in class; she was less distracted and took pride in completing her tasks, and was happy as a lark. A very satisfied mother told me that every weekend they regularly baked either a cake or cookies, and each time Shivangi learnt to remember more and more about the ingredients to be used and their exact quantity. She was practically doing the mixing all by herself. It was only for safety reasons that she was not allowed to operate the oven. Shivangi looked forward to the weekend baking time since all her cousins and relatives spoke highly of the new 'family chef'.

Choosing Appropriate Tasks

Some tasks simply are not suitable for children, and there are times when the moment is not appropriate, or you are just not in the mood. These are the jobs you are better off doing when the child is asleep or happily occupied doing something else. But there are lots of things that a child can do. It is a question of choosing the right job at the right time.

The right job is one that is safe for your child to do. Some tasks are simply too dangerous, such as cutting vegetables, opening a can, sewing a button, or ironing clothes. You know what your child can safely accomplish and whether it is within his capabilities. If he is unable to complete the task, he will just get angry or frustrated. The job should also be interesting enough to hold the child's attention. It is not fair to occupy the child with some meaningless chore in one room while you get busy in another room. It is best that he occupies himself in the same room that you are, so find something suitable which he could accomplish successfully but which you will not mind if it is not done expertly. It is obvious that adults can do most jobs better than a child can. Resist the temptation to either do it by yourself or do it all over again. This will destroy your child's feelings of competence and self-worth. At the same time, children have to be taught the importance of completing a task to the best of their ability, and being sloppy will receive no praise or encouragement. Set a reasonable deadline, but don't nag them. For example, if the dinner table is not set by meal time, point out that others are waiting to eat at the table, which is not fair at all. The best way to teach kids how to do a job is by simple repetition. First explain what the job is all about, and show them how to do it; then do it with them; and after that let them do it alone with least supervision. Be around to offer advise, but don't be quick to step in. And don't interfere if they want to do it their own way.

Being Moody

There will be times when your child may simply refuse to help out when you ask him to. When this happens, the right time for your child to help is when he asks, or you feel he will accept your suggestion and enjoy it. There are plenty of opportunities for him to help around the home, so don't force him until he is ready and willing. It is much better to wait until he is in the mood, and you both have enough time. The worst time is when you are in a hurry or you are tired.

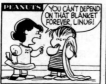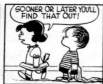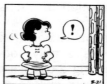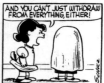

© United Feature Syndicate, Inc. 1956

INJECTING ENTHUSIASM FOR WORK

- It is important that you keep your little 'co-worker' happy and enthusiastic when he is job sharing with you. However tedious the job may be to you, make it seem like great fun to him. Even cleaning the dining table can be a sought after job if you sound excited about it. Whatever the job, give him clear instructions and explain or show him what and how he has to do. Take special care in explaining the details of the task, and stay closeby if he is doing something for the first time or is likely to make a mess, or may need your help to begin with. It is important that your child learns to do things by himself, even if it is not the way you usually do it, so that he feels a sense of pride and achievement at having successfully completed a task.
- Children can be encouraged to help around the house by making them responsible over their own things. To begin with, they can be taught to keep their school bags, school uniform, shoes and socks in their proper place when they come home from school. They could be made responsible to keep their study desk clean and tidy, as well as the toys in the room. This will teach them to care for and value their own things and increase their sense of independence.

- To make home chores exciting, keep them short and offer breaks in between. "After you've watered the plants, we'll stop for a drink, then we'll wipe the floor clean." Talk as you work together. Discuss if the plants need fertilisers or a spray of pesticide, how he is getting along with friends, or is he happy in school. Talk about yourself, what you have done and what you will do. This will make your child feel involved in the short jobs as he bonds with you, and it will increase his language skills.

- It is important to accept your child's limitations and not to rush him or expect too much from him. He needs plenty of practice to master the skills. So give plenty of praise and encouragement, however small the accomplishment. This will give him the incentive and the encouragement to finish the job.

Nature—The Eternal Teacher

Parents hold varied opinions on whether a growing child must be brought up with a sense of order in a neatly structured environment or not. Some believe it is very important for character formation; others believe that if the structure is rigid, it may backfire later on—like the child may rebel to order and neatness as an adolescent. And yet, some mothers are of the opinion that tidy habits and order are important but not for infants. I will urge you to look at Nature so that we can learn from it. There is order in Nature: day follows night, the seasons, etc. Naturally, the environment becomes the child's first teacher, especially between the ages of six months to twenty-four-months when the child learns at a very rapid rate.

> Order, not neatness, is essential to the child's overall development.

Introduce Structure and Routine

Order in a home does not mean that everything must be neat and clean. Rather, it means that belongings are kept in a manageable fashion and that the lives of the people who live there proceed in a logical progression. Young children in particular are sensitive to the regular scheduling of events—

mealtimes, bedtimes, playtimes, nap-times, story-times, and the like. Early on, they began to learn by taking in everything they saw and heard, and sorting it all out. According to Dr Theodore D. Wachs, professor of psychological sciences, Purdue University, *"In an orderly home they quickly learn to differentiate between objects, discover how to group them, and come to realise that day-to-day living is composed of a predictable series of balanced steps and procedures."* If the environment in which the child begins this learning is cluttered with haphazard commands and chores, such learning will only serve to confuse the child about order and routine. She will not be able to feel the rhythm of the day and will not learn that there are predictable places and times for certain activities. It is important to have variety in a little child's world, to stimulate her mind and her muscles with new toys, new sounds, new faces, new substances and new activities. But unless this variety occurs within ordered boundaries, the child may be overwhelmed and become inhibited and passive rather than active in her explorations of the world.

In Wachs' own words, *"In a number of tests designed specifically to assess the development levels—both motivational and intellectual—of infants, experts have measured just how much of a determining factor the early environment can be. Time and again, children coming from homes considered more orderly scored higher than those from disorderly homes. And even by the time they reach school age and have learned to control and manipulate their surroundings more and more, environment continues to play a major role. In pre-school settings, children who work and play in more ordered environments exhibit more focused social behaviour and more active involvement in tasks, which may result in more logical thinking patterns. Then, their ability to do schoolwork well and to solve problems may be enhanced. But if you still think that it cannot make any difference to an infant how clutter is piled up in her room, I can only urge you to think again. The people and things in a little person's world are the only tools she has for learning, and every one of them has an impact."*

Love's Labour Gains

The patience and love you will invest in getting children to help you to keep the house clean will bear a rich variety of fruits when they happily help around, doing house chores. While working with you they will be acquiring new skills, building confidence, learning to share and cooperate, as well as being made to feel a useful and valued part of the household. They will also relish the sense of achievement of seeing a job well done, and grasp the importance of keeping their room tidy. By giving your children the chance to help you, they will at a very young age become more skilled and task oriented. They will put these same skills to use when applying themselves to their school tasks in the years to come. Indeed, a worthwhile investment for the future—for you and for the children.

Cultivating Good Habits

I watched them tearing a building down,
    a gang of men in a busy town.
With a ho-heave-ho and a lusty yell
    they swung a beam and the sidewall fell.
I asked the foreman, "Are those men skilled,
    and the men you'd hire if you had to build?"
He gave a laugh, said, "No, indeed;
    just common labour is all I need.
I can easily wreck in a day or two
    what builders have taken a year to do."

I thought to myself as I went my way,
    'Which of these roles have I tried to play?
Am I a builder who works with care,
    measuring life by the rule and square?
Am I shaping my deeds to a well-made plan,
    patiently doing the best I can?
Or am I a wrecker, who walks the town
    content with the labour of tearing down?'

— ANON

POWER ETIQUETTE

Business schools in India, and all over the world, offer workshops to their graduating students on good habits, table-manners, grooming, dress sense, general etiquette, behaviour at parties, telephone manners, how to conduct national and international business through sophisticated social graces. Business houses, too, spend a fortune every year 'grooming' the creamy layers of management to hone good social habits through business etiquette seminars. The demand for social grooming is so great that every year a few hundred new image consultancy firms sprout up to grab a piece of the etiquette pie. *Dress for Success, Passport to Power, You are What You Wear*, are holy books used by the 'image gurus' who rake in millions teaching executives to *fake-it-till-you-make-it*.

In the whole scheme and plan of parenting, parents had somehow overlooked to incorporate in the parenting curriculum good habits, manners, etiquette, and proper grooming. So, when these kids grew up and reached the top of the office rung in their late twenties and thirties, their 'slips' were showing. The business schools they had studied in had taught them well and so they learned to *run* the business well; unfortunately, their parents had not taught them how to conduct themselves well (good habits and manners), so they were unable to *conduct* business with sophistication and suavity.

When good habits are inculcated in childhood, their expressions become an outpouring of a person's natural behaviour throughout life; there is nothing 'fake' about children using "please", "thank you", or "excuse me" in their daily expressions. Everyone likes a child who is polite, considerate and courteous. We can't help but notice the impeccable manners when our child's friends visit us for tea, and we wonder whether our child is as polite and well mannered when she's at a friend's birthday party. There is no doubt that children often behave differently when they are with other adults than they do at home, and no child can be expected to maintain good manners all day. But if we can help our child to be polite at home, not only will we feel proud of her, but we can be more confident that she will behave well with friends or at school.

From infancy onwards, children learn good habits from observing how other people behave, particularly their parents and grandparents. The way you become angry, irritated, snap and shout, the way you walk and dress, your appearance, your courtesy and tact, your personal habits of cleanliness and oral hygiene are open books for your children to read, digest and enact. Later, as they grow up, they also ape the habits of their teachers, peer groups, best friends, sports icons, movie stars and television characters. If a child's exposure at home has been of the rude, crude and sloppy type, then these habits get further reinforced. Conversely, when a child grows up in a climate of good manners, courtesy and kindness, his circle of friends, who share similar habits, further reinforce habits which are considered cultured and refined.

Good habits are formed when parents routinely talk, practise and repeat the same actions day after day until the child becomes accustomed to perform such activities on his own. Let's look at a few habits which we take for granted.

Cleanliness

In winters, some parents don't bathe their children because it's too cold for a bath. Families who can afford heat convectors to keep the rooms warm and hot-water geysers in the bathrooms for hot baths have no reason to skip a bath. Even if your child has to skip the morning bath, at least a hot bath before bed every night will have a therapeutic effect. It will help him to sleep well, as well as keep him clean. If he doesn't get into the habit of a daily bath as a child, then as he grows up to be a teenager, resign yourself to nag him to take his bath.

To help children take to cleanliness, check the following list:
- daily morning bath
- brushing teeth every night
- cleansing mouth every morning
- clean and trimmed finger-nails and toe-nails
- daily change of clothes and underwear
- regular haircuts or trims

Hair Care

Whatever be the season, cold winters or sweaty summers, your child's hair should never smell rancid or unwashed. Like his body, the hair too should have a fresh air about it. Try and avoid putting oil on the child's head *after* a bath. The oil attracts dust and dirt and gives him an 'oily' look. His hair strands should have a natural smooth look. It is a good habit to give the child an oil massage (head and body) *before* a bath. After a bath your child's hair should be brushed or combed so that he looks well-groomed, never dishevelled or messy.

Body Odours

Unpleasant body odours are very offensive to others. The reason why some emit unpleasant body odours could be due to irregular bathing habits, or due to not wearing fresh undergarments or clean clothes. After a bath, if a child has to wear the same old smelly clothes, inside or outside, the rancid stench of stale sweat from the unwashed clothes enters the skin pores and remains there. Later on, as a young adult he may bathe regularly but he will not be able to shake off the unpleasant body odour for years to come. It is the same with smelly feet. When summers get hot and sweaty, parents quickly get their children to wear sandals and slippers. It may not be such a good idea. Let me tell you why. When the weather is hot and humid, we feel clammy and wash our hands and face quite often. We wash our hands more often than we wash our face, and we wash our face more often than we wash our feet. So when a child walks and plays barefeet, his sweaty, clammy feet attract dust and grime. But if he were to wear some light footwear along with *cotton* socks, not only is the sweat absorbed by the cotton socks, but the cotton socks act as a cooling agent, a filter, allowing the air to pass through, cooling the feet and keeping them fresh. Haven't you heard people say, "My feet are killing me?" They literally suffer from 'tired' feet. Nylon synthetic socks must be worn in winters only, since they function as thermal wears. If nylon synthetic socks are worn in summers, the child is sure to suffer from smelly feet since the synthetic fibre won't allow the sweat pores to breathe, and he may also suffer from athletes' feet disease, not to mention tired feet.

Clothing

When dressing up your child the aim is not only to clothe him but also to inculcate in him proper 'dress sense'. Children should not be gaudily dressed. Care should be taken to see that the colours they wear match with one another; children carry pastel shades very well. Similarly, their clothes should fit them well. They shouldn't be tight or oversized. Some parents buy oversized clothes intentionally since "the kids grow very fast". So, a child wears a new set of clothes which are a size too big for him, and by the time they begin to fit him right, they have already become worn out with use. Unfortunately, he will never learn to look his best even in his best clothes. It is a good habit to have separate sets of clothes for separate activities. After school, the child should change the school uniform into home clothes, and to sleep he can change into his pyjamas. When he has to go out for parties, he can wear a special set of clothes kept for such occasions.

Posture and Carriage

Make a conscious effort to correct your own posture when walking, standing and sitting and you will find it easy to help your children develop a good posture and carriage. According to Nora King of the National Back Pain Association (UK), "We should be encouraging children to think about their backs—not by nagging, but by making them aware. And we should try to set them a good example." Back trouble is on the increase, and one theory is that's because of the way we live these days. Children walk less and sit a lot more these days. They use the car or bus to school. They carry heavy school bags with a single strap, instead of the two shoulder straps which are much better for posture. They should be encouraged to take up some sport or hobby, like swimming, tennis, football, ballet, *kathak* dance—something they'll enjoy, without doing it to excess.

Opening and Closing Doors

When you have to open doors and especially close them, do it noiselessly. If a door is closed when you enter a room, close it behind you; do not leave it ajar or open for someone else to close it. Always keep the door closed when you use the bathroom. If your child has a nursery room of his own, don't barge in without knocking first. You show him that you respect his privacy. He will also learn to knock on doors before entering a room, even when the doors are open. And you can train him to wait until he hears the instructions given by the person in the room. Sometimes he will be told to enter and sometimes he will be asked to wait out for a moment.

Art of Conversation

One of the main characteristics of a good conversationalist is to be a good listener rather than a good speaker. A good listener is a person who can keep the conversation going by drawing people to share and discuss their points of view with an open mind. Children have to be guided how *not to interrupt* when others are speaking and to wait their turn, and not to poke fun at others, or laugh and talk in a shrill pitch, or use slang, vulgar, abusive words. As you guide and encourage your children to speak freely and teach them the do's and don'ts of verbal and non-verbal communication they will learn from you some very basic skills of conversation.

Telephone Etiquette

The telephone rings and the children run to answer it. That's it. Whoever heard of an 'etiquette code' for home-phone users? Whether it's the home phone or the office phone, the 'rules' of telephone conversation are somewhat similar. You may teach your child a few ground rules on handling the phone so that the caller is charmed and impressed on hearing a cultivated voice having excellent telephone etiquette, and a reliable messenger. When the phone rings, and if the TV or the music system is on, first lower the volume or put it off and then answer the phone. Speak in the phone instrument with a 'smile' in your voice just like when you greet someone you know, at your front door. Never shout, or whisper, while talking. If there is a message, write it down immediately on the message-pad which should be permanently kept by the telephone. Lastly, before keeping the receiver gently in the cradle, thank the caller, or say 'bye' to indicate that the conversation is over.

Table Manners

Though we sit at the dining table to eat food, it is not considered proper to give the impression that food is the uppermost thought on our minds. It is also considered impolite to draw attention to the food other than to compliment its taste and flavour in modest terms. I have met numerous young people with excellent table-manners who've said that they were able to polish their conversation skills and social graces at the family dining-table. You, too, should introduce the family dining-table habit at home so that the family sits together at least at meal times, to enjoy a meal together rather than eat at separate hours in front of the television. The other reason is that children today have quite a busy social life of their own. They're invited by their own set of friends for lunches, high teas, birthday parties, and you would feel proud, when the hostess calls up to say, your child has excellent table-manners.

When at the Dining Table

Some of the basic rules are: don't ever keep your elbows on the table; you can rest your forearms on the edge of the table, though it's ideal to have only the wrists rest on the table's edge. Never get the food on the edge of your plate so it doesn't spill over the tablecloth. Use the napkin to wipe your lips and fingertips; never to blow your nose or wipe your face. Use the corner of the napkin to dab your lips before speaking and never speak with food in your mouth. Chew your food with lips closed to avoid making squelching noises. When you want a dish which is not near you, don't point at it but ask the person sitting near you to pass it to you. Don't try and choose the best and the biggest piece. Do not heap food on your plate; you could have a second helping later. You shouldn't waste food on your plate, at the same time never polish your plate, cutlery or fingers by licking them clean. If the food in your mouth is pungent or hot, don't spit it on your plate; swallow it down with some water. Inedible articles like bones, fruit seeds, or any other thing which cannot be swallowed, may be removed from the mouth either with your fingertips, keeping the mouth closed as much as possible. You may also slip them from the mouth onto the spoon or fork and put them on the edge of your plate. Never drop them directly from your mouth to the plate, or feed pets while eating. Oh, yes, there is a lot more on table-manners, but this should suffice to start your child on enjoying a social event like eating at the dining table in the company of family members.

Parents as Role Models

> Parents must conduct themselves with dignity and care, so that children learn from their role models how to be polite and well-mannered.

Children learn their manners primarily from their parents. If parents are uncouth, sloppy, shabby and boorish, the children turn out to be so. As you have gathered, in order to be well mannered, one has to be a socially conscious person. An individual's actions are considered acceptable when the actions gain social acceptance. On the flip side, an individual is labelled ill-mannered when his actions are frowned upon by others and considered inappropriate. People who belch loudly, break wind in public, gobble their food down voraciously, drink themselves drunk, dress shabbily, bathe irregularly, speak ill of others and commit acts which generally offend others display a lack of sensitivity to the feelings and sentiments of others. The sooner the parents realise their own role as socially conscious persons and learn the skills on how to be socially groomed, the children learn automatically to be well-mannered.

Siblings

Let me be a little kinder,
let me be a little blinder,
to the faults of those about me,
let me praise a little more;
let me be when I am weary
just a little bit more cheery—
Let me serve a little better
those that I am striving for.

Let me be a little braver
when temptation bids me waver,
let me strive a little harder
to be all that I should be;
let me be a little meeker
with the brother who is weaker.
Let me think more of my neighbour
and a little less of me.

— ANON

Next to parents, brothers and sisters are the most important persons in a child's life. And loving one another and getting along with each other are vital aspects of growing up. Oh, and how they fight, you'll say! Siblings have been fighting with each other since time immemorial. So, it is almost natural for siblings to fight. Before I discuss some of the trigger points that could turn on sibling rivalry, I would like to share an aspect of solidarity that siblings share with each other. This aspect mostly goes unnoticed by researchers since they usually study the negative aspects. Older siblings are natural teachers, showing their younger brothers and sisters new physical skills, how to use toys and play games, and the meanings of words and numbers. And, the little ones naturally look up to the older ones, accepting direction one time and refuting it the next. The mimicking is so good that you will see the little ones manifesting close to two hundred per cent the older sibling's negative behaviour. But, as they grow up, the under-current of love and affection grows, and the bonds of solidarity develop even as their behaviour goes through ups and downs. They are friendly one moment, and squabbling the next; they could be playing doctor-and-patient and manifest concern and caring, and the next moment they are teasing, fighting and tearing each other's clothes. As you are often called to sort out their squabbles, be fair to point out right from wrong without getting involved in their arguments. Your role as the trouble-shooter is to help children find *positive* ways of getting attention they need. Let us look at some of the trigger points that cause rivalry in siblings, and your role in it.

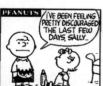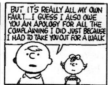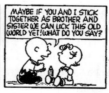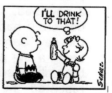

UNDERSTANDING YOUR OLDER SIBLING

There could be many reasons why the birth of the newcomer is not a happy event for the older child. Changes and changes, with so many changes; suddenly he is buffeted by a flood of changes and he is expected to keep a calm composure, and go through the motions as though everything around him is normal. There are times parents and grandparents get so preoccupied with what is happening that they take the children in the house for granted and expect the impossible from them.

Prenatal

At times, parents go into the overdrive mode when preparing the older sibling on the arrival of the newcomer. This 'preparation' may damage the cosy relationship which existed between the child and the parents. Listed below are some acts of omission and commission which may bring forth an adverse reaction in the older sibling.

Three-year-old Monica watched the parents bring out a very tiny cot and place it in their bedroom. They told her that she had slept in the little cot once upon a time when she was a teeny-weeny baby. That same little cot would now be given to the new baby. Monica, who hadn't the faintest idea that the cot was hers, claimed that she would keep the cot to herself and her dolls would sleep in that cot, but she wouldn't share it with anyone else. If the parents had brought out the cot in a matter of fact manner without assigning its ownership there would have been no problem at all.

In another instance, Shreya who was four-years old, always slept in her parents' bed. The parents began to prepare Shreya by saying, "You're a big girl. We'll get you a new bed." Shreya linked the other threatening messages her brain had been recording about 'sharing' her world with the new baby. The child knew that the issue was not about being a big girl who needed a new bed; the harsh truth was that she had to *abdicate* the bed for the newcomer. She resented the idea of giving up her territory of love and comfort; she hated moving to the new bed.

> *It is not such a good idea to have a child share the parents' bed.*

I would like to point out that the parents made a mistake with Shreya when they made her sleep on their bed, and they were now getting ready to repeat their mistake with the new baby. In this kind of an arrangement, your intimacy takes a back seat; and every time you toss and turn in bed, the child stirs up, and thereafter you wake up. In an ideal situation, the child should have her own cot, or a mattress on the floor, maybe in the same room if you are short on space.

In preparing for the advent of the newborn, parents start shopping for linen, clothes, toys, etc. They bring home the goodies, and tell the older sibling that they are for the new baby. To prepare him, they tell him that from now on he will have to share his cupboard space with the new brother or sister to come. They put the new linen and clothes in the cupboard. His anxiety and misery grows. Once upon a time he was the centre of everyone's adulation. There is so much of talk about the newcomer that it seems as though he is no longer important. The strong message he deciphers is, 'Move aside. There's someone coming to take your place.' Parents should realise that far from preparing the child to receive the newborn they are threatening the life of the existing one. Cots and cupboards can be used in a matter-of-fact manner, without highlighting, underlining or making issues about what belongs to whom.

If a mother is recommended bed-rest by her gynaecologist, then she would be unable to run around, play, or carry the child as he was used to earlier. The loss of this physical love-bond causes deep anxieties in the child. These physical changes may cause emotional scars, and the child may retaliate irrationally. And, in the case where bed-rest is not recommended, even the most robust of mothers get tired, feel faint and have mood swings. And as she nears the delivery time, she may just not be able to get 'physical' with the child. On being reminded that Mom will bring home a new baby may just cause negative reactions in the older sibling. On the contrary, the father and other members of the family must supplement lots of physical games for the child to feel that he is the centre of everyone's attention.

Finally, the time comes when the mother has to be admitted to a hospital. The child may get into a panic state. His state of hysteria could be on account of a couple of reasons. Maybe, he was never left home without the mother for a long duration, and he cries his heart out. It also could be that he was sometime admitted into a hospital. Ever since, he has been overwhelmed by the fear of sickness, pain and separation. In all probability, the anxiety levels can be brought under control by arranging for the child to be brought to the hospital to visit his mother from time to time. This will reassure him that neither has his mother disappeared, nor is she sick and ailing. Before getting admitted to the hospital, you will first make sure that the hospital rules do not forbid children the visitation rights.

Postnatal

After the mother and baby come home, things may not get better for the older sibling. It is natural that everyone is exhausted. With the new baby in the house, there is so much *more* to do. The older children are expected to cooperate. While they are told not to make any noise, or to help out, and not to seek attention, from time to time, they are scolded for being noisy while the baby is asleep. There are times when they want to kiss and cuddle the baby, they are checked not to squeeze too tight or not to suffocate the child. There are times also when instead of a kiss, the baby gets a bite; so grownups have to be very careful with little children in the house. Infants getting their eyes poked, or faces scratched and pinched are common complaints of sibling hostility. Many children ask their parents, "When will the baby go back to the hospital?" or, "Let's throw the baby out." These are warning signals for which parents are not to scold the children, but to correct themselves. They need to check their attitude towards the sibling and not so much the sibling's attitude towards the newcomer, as is usually done. Parents may encourage and teach the child how to caress and care for the newborn with the help of a rubber doll. A twelve-inch rubber doll, whose clothes could be taken off and put on, works as an ideal prop. Tenderness, affection and gentleness can be taught to the children as you guide them to bathe, dress, hug, cuddle, caress, comb, powder, kiss and put the doll to sleep. From the doll, the children will automatically learn to transfer the tender, loving care to the newborn.

Guests who drop in to visit the family give the older

child the royal bypass. All the attention is lauded on the newcomer as the baby is picked up and admired, while no attention is paid to the older sibling. The gifts they bring are also for the little baby. In such situations, parents should keep small presents handy in the house to be given to the older child when the guests come, so that he doesn't feel jealous about the attention given to the new baby.

Many mothers breast-feed the baby in front of the older sibling. In a flash he recalls that his mother never carried him in that intimate manner, neither has she played with him nor spent time with him. It is common to hear little children ask their mothers to pick them up and breast-feed them also. Since, breast-feeding the infant is not a permanent practice but a temporary one, it is best to distract the older sibling with some activity in another room while the mother nurses the baby.

When proper attention is denied to the older sibling's need of *recognition*, he is unable to cope with so many threatening factors that suddenly overwhelm him. He finds solace in reverting to baby like behaviour. Dr Eric Berne in *Games People Play*, said that a child needs to be *stroked* in order to live healthy. If a child is unable to receive positive strokes, then he will seek negative strokes through misbehaviour. It is better to be spanked or scolded than to shrivel and die, according to Berve. So the sibling will whine, crawl, talk baby talk and wet the bed to get negative strokes. Sigmund Freud called it 'regression'. Some psychoanalysts believe that children who use regression to cope with stress are neither abnormal nor unhealthy, as long as they are able to return to age-appropriate behaviour when they become accustomed to the stress.

Your Check-list

✦ A few months prior to your delivery, let him spend more time at your relative's or friend's house so that he feels familiar and comfortable in their company—even make him spend nights at their place. Then, about a month before your due date, explain to your youngster where he will go and who will take care of him while you're in labour.

- Your older child may like to help out in doing small chores with you for the newcomer, or he may not. If he is happy and eager to help out, then let him, but if he is reluctant then don't push him. Instead, you should read him books and show him pictures of children playing together and helping each other.
- Even though the two of them seem to be getting along fine, do not leave the baby alone with an older sibling or any other young child.
- Whenever appropriate, casually discuss the advantages of having a younger sibling: "Won't it be great fun when Tina is old enough to play hide-and-seek with you?"
- Feel free to commiserate with your oldest child about the baby in a light-hearted, blameless way, "When babies are tired, they sure do cry a lot, don't they?"
- Be patient and understanding with the older child for bouts of regressive behaviour; toilet accidents, more whining, thumb sucking, or reverting to the pacifier is only natural.
- As long as you remain sensitive to his needs, you will be able to prevent your older child from feeling like a second fiddle.

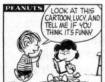 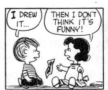 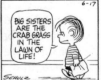

© United Feature Syndicate, Inc. 1961

MINIMISING SIBLING RIVALRY

Do not resort to corporal punishment. If you hit the child, the child will hit the sibling too.

The prenatal and postnatal actions, as pointed above, will obviously lead to sibling rivalry. As long as the stimulants continue to be pro-newborn, the sibling's behaviour will remain regressive. As soon as there is a change in the stimuli, the older child's responses will change.

Sibling rivalry can be tough to put down. It's like a parasitical plant which receives nourishment from jealousy and envy caused by the parent's indifference, neglect or ignorance. Most parents, who are unable to identify the cause for this rivalry, get so strained mentally and physically that they use force and punishment to correct the child's behaviour. Such harsh methods may further trigger a series of defence mechanisms in the child. He may learn to give as good as he gets.

You may have to give each child at least some opportunity to feel like an only child. Set aside special time each day for individual attention, say about fifteen to twenty minutes when you feel the child needs it most. Use the time to play, put the room in order, read, colour, chat, or you may want go out on an errand—any activity is fine as long as it is carried out together.

As early as you can, you should clearly lay down the house rules and consistently enforce them. If there is to be no hitting, screaming, or throwing things—then say so firmly, not once, but keep repeating any number of times. And be ready to use punishment when the rules are broken. All the rules must first be followed by grownups as reinforcement.

Treat children fairly, not necessarily equally. An older child, by virtue of age, deserves privileges equal to his responsibilities. As the younger child matures, increase her responsibilities and be sure to praise the way she carries them out.

Parent's Transparency

At the office tea-party, when Shabana was offered the chocolate doughnut, she put it aside in her bag and brought it home for her two children. "You could share a doughnut," she told them. Nargis ran to the kitchen and brought the knife to cut the doughnut. Three-year-old Aamer said that he would cut the doughnut. Nargis argued that she was bigger, so she had the right to cut it. "No," said Aamer. "Yes," said Nargis. And they fought over who would cut the doughnut. Finally Shabana intervened saying, "Nargis is right. She is older, so she will cut the doughnut. But, Aamer will have the first choice to pick up whichever piece he likes." So, Nargis got her way, while Aamer got the first choice to pick his piece of the doughnut. Of course, Nargis took her time to cut two exact halves while Aamer drooled. It was a win-win situation for everyone. Both children were able to 'see' and 'feel' their mother's fair decision. Parents must not just make right judgements. Their judgements must be *perceived* to be fair and just by all. Under this climate, children grow to trust and believe in their parents.

Unfair Parents

One weekend, Satinder brought home two gift-wrapped toys. He gave one to his five-year-old Tara and the other to his two-and-a-half-year-old Natasha. Both the children opened their packets with a lot of excitement, and as soon as Natasha saw Tara's doll, she wanted it. The parents told her that she had her own doll to play with while Tara had hers. The child was adamant. She would not see reason; she cried and cried until the parents approached Tara and pleaded with her to give her doll to the little sister. Tara, too, became upset and said she would not give her doll. They told her that since she was a 'big girl', she should be more understanding. Tara reasoned with them that her sister already had a doll to play with. The parents cajoled her and promised to give her a bigger present the next day if she gave her doll to her little sister. With a heavy heart, she flung the doll angrily at Natasha and ran to her room.

With such an exposure of the win-lose type, both sisters will grow up never trusting each other. They will never trust their parents either. In later years, Tara and Natasha will doubt their parents motives since the parents have projected themselves to be unfair and partial in their judgements. To put an end to sibling rivalry, there has to be a win-win situation for everyone. Satinder and his wife will have to restructure the scene from scratch.

Inculcate the Concept of 'Ours'

The problem was not in toy-grabbing or in toy-sharing as it may obviously seem. The cause of the problem lay in a faulty first premise: the mine and thine premise. It seemed natural to Satinder to bring home two toys for his two children so that they would not fight over a toy. And, yet they repeatedly fought over toys. When the this-is-yours and that-is-hers concept did not work, Satinder should have worked on the concept of 'ours'. Here, everything belonged to everybody, including toys. Along with the concept of 'ours' they would also need to introduce the concept of 'elders first'. Satinder will have to get the family together (it is a great game to play with grandparents around). He then brings out the wrapped packet and hands it to the grandparents. They admire the wrapping paper, spend time over identifying the objects, and gingerly pry the cellotape, in an attempt to save the beautiful wrapping paper. With a lot of care and caution, they pick up the doll from the box, and with lots of *oohs* and *aahs* of appreciation they 'play' with the doll, creating dialogue and action. They pass the doll back and forth and after having satisfied themselves, they then pass it on to the parents to play with the doll. The parents pick up the action and the dialogue where the grandparents had left off, and after lots of hugging, cuddling and sharing the doll with each other, they pass it on to the children to play. The children who had seen a live demonstration on caring, sharing and playing together, now begin to respond to play in like manner—maybe not at the start, but after a couple of months of consistent family play the children will definitely follow the family lead. Family members have to be consistent in demonstrating the 'ours' concept. Mother would be inconsistent if she would say, "Today I've made Tara's favourite custard." Tara would naturally want to take 'charge' of the custard because it was *her* favourite custard that mother had made, while the little sister would insist that it was her favourite custard, too, or, if a grandparent says, "Natasha loves burgers, let's go out and have burgers." And you will have another sibling fight to contend with.

Sibling rivalry brings out the worst qualities in children. They quarrel over an object, territory and privileges; they become competitive with each other, and vie for parental love, attention and preferences. Parents, poor things, go into a tailspin trying to keep everyone happy. When parents demonstrate more and more the concept of 'ours' through actions rather than through words, siblings will seldom fight over the nitty gritty that makes mine or thine. They will share their things with each other and learn to wait for their turn to come. Learning to wait for one's turn is one of the greatest assets one can possess if only parents could coach their children to develop.

Language Development

"Then you should say what you mean," the March Hare
went on.

"I do," Alice hastily replied; *"at least—at least I mean
what I say —that's the same thing, you know."*

"Not the same thing a bit!" said the Hatter. *"Why, you
might as well say that 'I see what I eat' is the same as
'I eat what I see'!"*
— LEWIS CARROLL *(Alice in Wonderland)*

Cradle Talk

Baby talk is not about the way a baby talks, but it is a
particular way adults talk to a baby. Adults speaking baby
talk avoid expressing the difficult consonants like 'r' and 'k',
or the double consonants like 'sp' for spoon, etc. Baby talk
is the first language the infant speaks. By the time the infant
is ten-months old, adults who indulge in baby talk should
switch from baby talk to normal speech for language structure
to take effect.

When grownups continue to talk to toddlers in 'baby
talk' they stymie the language structure development, which
may later pose as one of the problems leading to being a

'slow learner' in primary school. The language cells in the left hemisphere of the baby's cerebral brain are open to language inputs that the brain soaks in through the mimicry of sounds and facial expressions of the communicators. Parents are the child's primary language teachers, and they should realise when to switch from (a) cooing, to (b) babble, to (c) baby talk, to (d) structural form. Language structure gets reinforced when parents use simple sentences in proper pronunciation, diction, enunciation, and intonation. Inability to make these switches, or the inability to correct one's speech blemishes or facial expressions such as frowns, twitches, lisps, slurs, stammering, mispronunciation, or fractured syntax, then all of it becomes part of the language package the child imbibes, copies and expresses (*see* Chapter on *Underachievers*).

How It all Begins

Language ability in infants develops from language function to language structure. The term *language function* relates to the emotional aspect of language where infants communicate their needs through cries, gestures, and facial expressions. Adults respond through cooing and babble sounds. When infants are about two-months old they begin to mimic the adult's cooing sounds they hear. When they are six-months old they begin to babble. Continuous repetition of the same sound, "ba-ba-ba" is called babbling. This helps the infants utter their first words, which usually are made up of the sounds they babble the most. By the time they are eight-months old, infants become more attentive to what people say. Finally, at about one-year-old, the average baby speaks one or two words. By the age of two, most children put words into clusters to form simple sentences. *Language structure* is about word clusters that form sentences; it is about the rules of grammar and syntax. It is also about not mixing languages, say Hindi with English, or with a third language.

No one yet knows why some babies talk at twelve months while others have to wait till they are two-years old. Some treat it as a handicap and delay the child's entry into nursery school. Many parents link language ability to IQ. This is incorrect. Early language ability is about language function, not language structure; it is about communication, not vocabulary.

Once these parameters are understood, then parents who are concerned about their fourteen-month-old son who doesn't speak, should look at his ability and willingness to make his needs known, and to understand what others say. Those skills must be normal. From ten months onward, if the child hears enough simple language addressed to him everyday through someone reading to him, and talking to him about the pictures in the books, singing to him, talking about the food he is eating, etc. then by the time he is two-and-a-half-years old, the words will come to him in a rush and he will probably speak in sentences.

Staccato Style

To develop the conversational ability in toddlers, adults should demonstrate patience and excitement when they 'discuss' topics and issues with children. Unfortunately adults who are impatient with children use 'staccato language' (i.e. language related to specific functions) when communicating with children. Some samples of staccato language used: *Don't argue. Wish, Auntie. Say* namaste. *Don't slouch. Don't suck your thumb. No, don't you dare. Don't touch that. Stand straight. Chew your food. Stop crying. Why don't you listen? Stop it. Shut up. I'll slap you. Do this. Don't do that. Go to your room. Get out. Finish your studies. Complete your homework. I said, come here. Don't put it in your mouth. You're a bad boy. You're a naughty girl. You devil. Don't fuss. Finish your food. Clean your mess. Don't play with your food. Don't be stupid. No TV for you.* Children who are spoken to in this manner day after day, will not only turn a deaf ear to parental authority but will automatically lack conversational skills. Using staccato commands constantly is one of the major causes for language deficiency in later years.

Avoid Public Censure

Also, parents invariably end up correcting the child in public places or before relatives and friends for incorrect syntax or mispronunciation. When children are checked in front of others they feel humiliated. Some literally crawl into their shells, and grow wary of people-interaction; they become introverts.

Whether they are labelled as inhibited, shy or withdrawn, one thing is clear: they become doubtful of their own actions and words and they are apprehensive of being publicly checked and told how to speak correctly.

To give your child a lead start in speaking, both partners must converse with one another comfortably. When you read your daily newspaper or magazines, cultivate the habit of discussing some topics together. Through these relaxed discussions, you will teach yourself the art of listening. When parents have cultivated the patience to *listen* to children and when children feel relaxed to talk to their parents (without the fear of being corrected or ticked off), you can be sure that you are on the right track of developing language skills in your child.

Make Your Child a Natural Linguist

India is a melting pot of languages. Most families in urban areas speak at least two or three languages fluently. In a typical Delhi middle-class family, many parents are fluent in English, Punjabi and Hindi. The grandparents may be fluent in Punjabi and Hindi, and may speak or understand English. The servants in the house usually speak Hindi. In such multi-lingual families, parents must encourage the flow of more than one language at home so that the child could develop into a natural linguist. To develop linguistic skills in children, the precondition is that each language should be spoken in its chaste form and the pronunciation, diction and syntax should be proper.

Shiv Naraynan hailed from Kerala and had settled in New Delhi with his family. His wife Aparna was a Punjabi. Shiv was a top-notch corporate lawyer and Aparna was a highly accomplished criminal lawyer. Shiv and Aparna spoke fluent English, Malyalam, Punjabi and Hindi. Antara, their two-year-old daughter, spoke gibberish and they were very worried about her language skills. I advised them to *exploit* the languages they knew by drawing definite language codes at home. I asked both parents to speak to each other only in chaste English, while they would speak to Shiv's parents in Malyalam (being natives of Kerala) and to Aparna's parents in Punjabi. With the servants they would speak in Hindi.

And so, they would be communicating in four languages without much effort. Since the child's left cerebral lobe which controls language development is open to absorption of speech sounds, words and syntax, and it soaks in all that is spoken, the child would be absorbing four languages simultaneously. I also cautioned them that between the ages of three and five, Antara would mix Hindi, English, Punjabi and Malyalam in a single sentence, but they shouldn't get perturbed, or stop to correct the child on proper usage. At this stage it was important not to interrupt Antara's language flow because the child would literally be dipping into her language bank and pulling out little words (like nuggets); subsequently she would be clustering them to fit them into a sentence. If anyone would rubbish her attempts through corrections, the chances are she would withdraw 'expressing' herself. Instead, I had recommended that all the grownups in the family had to reinforce their own speech mannerisms by keeping their language codes chaste, while at the same time ensuring that the child's spontaneity and enthusiasm at self-expression was not curbed. If and when the child borrowed words from two or more languages to make a sentence, such as, *"Gim'me ek glass pani."* No one should directly tell her to speak correctly, because if she is corrected at that moment, the risk of putting brakes on her language development are high. See it from the child's point of view: she asks for water and instead she gets a dose of correction. Indeed, a sure way to kill spontaneity. So, shouldn't she know the correct form of each language? Of course, she should know how each language is spoken correctly so that she can differentiate between the two languages.

Teaching Technique

I would like to show you a unique way to teach your little darlings how to develop linguistic skills. To teach children to master language skills you must adopt subtle skills when making corrections, so that children are made aware of the errors and yet don't feel that they are being corrected. Instead of hitting the hammer on the head, skirt the issue. To emphasise the right form of expression from the wrong form, talk to a family member within the child's hearing,

"Papa, when you are thirsty what do you say?" And Papa replies distinctly in chaste English, "Please give me a glass of water." He also repeats the same sentence in chaste Hindi. Mother then takes the conversation further by saying, "Our darling Antara speaks so well; she too says, 'Please give me a glass of water'." And you give her a glass of water, without asking her to repeat the correct form. By affirming what you *want* her to say, and by giving her credit for what you *expect* her to say, even though she did not say it in those exact words, you not only give her encouragement but also show her how to choose her words and grammar correctly. Your positive reinforcement gives her the confidence to express herself without hesitation. Come to think of it, you regularly do something similar to this effect in your offices to your employees in whom you see potential. There is a lot of potential in your children for you to tap and exploit. So, go ahead and give them a long rope and they'll learn to handle more than one language with ease.

By the time the child is six-years old, patterns of each *language structure* automatically get ingrained in the child's language cells of the brain. Aparna and Shiv were absolutely delighted to have a natural linguist in the family. They were surprised when they went for a short holiday to Goa, Antara returned home not only with a suntan and sea-shells, but also a smattering of *Konkani*— the language spoken in Goa. Further more, since the parents regularly conversed with each other, discussed current topics at the dining table, as well as enjoyed talking, discussing and reading books to the child, the six-year old's reservoir of vocabulary had swelled to everyone's amazement. Antara, at sixteen, speaks seven (Indian and European) languages fluently. Her younger brother, Rahul, at thirteen, also is multilingual.

A Love for Reading

To help children develop their language skills, it is not enough to be talking to them. You need to read to them, also. Many parents read to their children only at bedtime when they put them to sleep. As the child grows older, parents wonder why the child gets drowsy whenever he reads a book. Poor kid, the moment he begins reading his brain is conditioned to automatically press the *sleep mode* button. To help children develop a love for reading, they have to be read to at other times, too, including bedtime, with a variety of books to hold their interest.

- *Variety*: You wouldn't give your children the same food at each meal every day. Why would you read out to them the same book repeatedly?
- *Interests*: Just as you wouldn't read a book that doesn't hold your interest, neither will your children. The most important consideration in choosing a book for your children is that you have to match their interest, reading level and attention span.

How do you make these choices? Here are nine categories of different children's books:

- *Picture books:* The first books for young children, which emphasise the alphabet, nursery rhymes and picture stories.
- *Poetry and verse books:* Rhymes and poems presented in various forms.
- *Fantasy books:* Stories about imaginary worlds and people.
- *Folklore or traditional literature:* Includes fairy-tales, mythology, legends and religious stories.
- *Science fiction books:* Stories about scientific happenings.
- *Realistic fiction books:* Stories about people or events that could have occurred in real life situations.
- *Historical fiction books:* Stories about past, but fictionalised events.
- *Biographies and autobiographies:* Stories about real people's lives.
- *Non-fiction books:* Books written to provide information.

Selecting the right books for your children is essential because they are so distracted by everything that is happening all around them that many never think of reading as a leisure activity—especially because they read so much in school on a daily basis. One cannot adequately emphasise how critical books are to your children's total development. While television allows them to be passive (they don't necessarily have to think), reading books ignites their imagination. Says Jim Trelease, author of *The New Read-Aloud Handbook*, "The ultimate objective, of course, is to create *life*time readers, not just *school*time readers—readers who are still reading and educating themselves twenty-five years after graduation."

Through a dear friend at the Indian Institute of Management (IIM) in Ahmedabad, I was introduced to Atula Ahuja, an amazing young woman. She loves books and she loves children. Fired with enthusiasm to inspire children to read and enjoy books, she started in a small way from her residence on the IIM campus, and now she has moved to a larger place. Atula recognises the importance of developing in children an early interest in reading, and she offers a well-structured reading programme that first enhances listening skills, and then develops reading and comprehension skills. Through a wide variety of books, phonics, reading games, illustrations, drama and poetry, Atula teaches children to discover the magical power of words. Children are learning to read, and reading to learn at the same time by practising and applying reading strategy lessons (students learn to comprehend, recall and analyse information), as well as by deepening their knowledge of letter and sound relationships, word families and spelling patterns. The result of her unique effort is overwhelming. Children who once disliked books, or had difficulty in reading and speaking in complete sentences, or were unable to comprehend what they read, have begun writing creative poetry and prose with enhanced vocabulary.

How to Read to Children

Nearly all parents assume that a parent sits with a child and reads aloud while the youngster listens. That is one of the ways to begin reading to children. But you can add more variety in your reading and make it exciting for your child:

- On the second or third reading of the same book, teach the child one of the *key* words and agree that every time you come to that word, you'll both read it *aloud*.
- You and your child role-play and dramatise the major events in the story.

- Ask your child to create a different ending to a familiar story or stop reading before the ending, and ask him to tell you what will happen next.
- Before actually reading the story relate it to the child's previous experiences.
- Get the child to describe the illustrations (pictures) and relate it to the story.
- Be creative. Make puppets of different characters in books and act out the stories through puppet play.
- Make colourful cut-outs of the main story characters (you need not be an artist to do this) and ask your child to arrange them in sequence to the story.
- Play soft instrumental background music, to match the mood of the text, while you read.

A Love for Knowledge

Unlike yesteryears, today there are many formats available to parents to encourage children to read books and enhance their language skills. Many bookshops in urban areas encourage browsing or reading over a cup of hot chocolate, tea or coffee. Then there are book fairs which children love to visit. Parents, who are members of local libraries in small towns, may *not* find storybooks pertaining to their child's level. Never mind. The very idea of visiting the library with your child to return and pick up books is an invaluable lesson to children on reading and caring for books as common property. Then there are illustrated story-books for children with accompanying audio tapes. The child can follow along in the books independently while listening to the audio tapes. You may consider playing tapes of children's stories during the daily travel time in the car. Parents invest money in buying CD-ROMs of children's stories, and then after a while they are junked. That's because like movies, children will view CD-ROMs only a few times and then get tired of them. For your child's sake you'll have to be techno-savvy. Chat-rooms for children to discuss storybooks electronically are available on the World Wide Web. In addition, your child can read other children's book reviews on WWW and write his own review, too.

The Power of Books

When children are eight years to twelve-years old, parents introduce their daughters to Nancy Drew and Enid Blyton books, and their sons to the Hardy Boys series believing that that's all the 'good' reading the kids require because that's what they read when they were kids. If kids today have taken to reading, we can thank Harry Potter's magical spell. Let's hope their interest in books lasts. To sustain children's interest in books, parents need to expand their own reading interests in order to stimulate their children to read worthwhile books. Reading a good book stimulates not only the imagination, but also feelings, emotions and thinking. Parents may introduce books on how other societies and races live; on racial diversity and social segregation; on how societies treat their women and children; people's contribution to their communities; hunger and poverty in the world; lives of heroes; the importance of being moral and other global issues. With such an exposure, children's horizons are no longer limited to the family, the neighbourhood, the city or even the country, because they know they live in a global society and have to play a role in that society.

S E C T I O N ④

RAISE WISE KIDS

Part 1

Children Learn What They Live

If children live with criticism, they learn to condemn.
If children live with hostility, they learn to fight.
If children live with fear, they learn to be apprehensive.
If children live with pity, they learn to feel sorry for
     themselves.
If children live with ridicule, they learn to be shy.
If children live with jealousy, they learn what envy is.
If children live with shame, they learn to feel guilty.
If children live with tolerance, they learn to be patient.
If children live with encouragement, they learn to be
     confident.
If children live with praise, they learn to appreciate.
If children live with approval, they learn to like themselves.
If children live with acceptance, they learn to find love in
     the world.
If children live with recognition, they learn to have a goal.
If children live with sharing, they learn to be generous.
If children live with honesty and fairness, they learn what
     truth and justice are.
If children live with security, they learn to have faith in
     themselves and those around them.
If children live with friendliness, they learn that the world
     is a nice place in which to live.
If children live with serenity, they learn to have peace of
     mind.

— DOROTHY LAW NOLTE

C H A P T E R (1)

Choosing a Nursery School

"An important aspect of self-esteem is self-confidence. Children who lack self-confidence spend so much of their energy fighting anxieties within that they have none left over for the business of learning. For such an unhappy child, a new experience is not exciting but threatening. Thinking that he will fail whatever he attempts, a child without self-confidence gives up on himself."

— JEAN MARZOLLO & JANICE LLOYD
(Learning Through Play)

In this chapter, I have tried to keep my personal bias on a leash and attempted to give you some objective views on how to choose a nursery school. This chapter has three sections. In the first section we will look at the nature of toddlers and their temperament. In the second section we will look at the nature of nursery school education, and how to sift the chaff from the grain. In the third section we will look at the nature of learning and development at the toddler-age for your child's optimum enhancement of social and cognitive skills.

NATURE OF TODDLERS AND THEIR TEMPERAMENT

About the Apple of Your Eye

When a child is two to five-years old, this period is usually referred to as the preschool period, or as early childhood. This period is also called the 'play years' to underline the importance of play. This doesn't mean that after the age of six, children stop playing. Play occurs at every age. But the years of early childhood are the most playful of all since children spend nearly all their waking hours playing. Through play they acquire skills, ideas and values that are crucial for growing up. They chase each other and dare themselves to attempt new tasks as they develop their bodies. They play with words and ideas as they develop their minds. They play games and dramatise fantasies as they learn social skills and moral rules.

Their playfulness can cause them to be delightful or exasperating. To them growing up is a game and their enthusiasm for it seems unlimited. One moment they are quietly tracking the path of a beetle in the grass and the next moment they are riotously tearing down the play area. You may have seen in the Shimla hills and other hill stations baby monkeys chasing, wrestling and pummelling each other; their friendly jostle may quickly turn into a brawl. Young children play the same way. Their minds too, seem playful. The immaturity of their thinking enables them to explain that, 'it rains because children need to play in the water.'

Many parents are unable to enjoy their children's antics; they expect them to sit quietly, think logically and act realistically. Don't be a fuddy-duddy, dim-witted parent to your children. If you learn to enjoy their playfulness, you may enjoy listening to them. And more than that, you may visit the library to start reading books or magazines on children between the age of two and five.

> You may have to wake up the child in you in order to reach out to your children.

Making the Right Choice

Before you get ready to look at preschools to see what to expect from them, it wouldn't be a bad idea to first understand your children's needs and know for yourself how best children should be taught at this early age. (Now you know why I want you to make that trip to the library and pick up a book about early childhood development.)

Twenty-four-year-old Balwinder Kaur was born and brought up in the USA. After her marriage, she settled in India and has two children. She couldn't get over the fact that four of her friends in her neighbourhood chose a particular nursery school, 'simply because it was near the house.' On weekends, they would compare Balwinder's child's development to their children and 'gripe about the low level of activities in the neighbourhood nursery school.' In spite of being in the family way, Balwinder spent close to five months visiting and surveying all the nursery schools in the city before she took a decision, "because that's what my parents did in the US when I was a kid." She admitted her children in a nursery school that was about ten kilometres away from her house. She and her husband were very satisfied with her choice of school.

"There are a few things that a preschool can't and shouldn't be expected to deliver," says Barbara Brenner, author of *The Preschool Handbook*. "Some mothers and fathers see preschool mainly as a place for a youngster to get a jumpstart up the competitive ladder. They choose a preschool for its promise to teach computer skills or for getting into the most prestigious private schools. These are *not* good reasons, and indeed they may have serious negative consequences for everyone in the family." Ideally though, preschools *can* be a rich experience in three areas: social, physical and intellectual development. Once parents are realistic about preschool priorities, they can begin to seek out the best possible environment for their child—and the family as a whole.

NATURE OF NURSERY SCHOOLS

About Nursery Schools

Until the late 1970s, children went to the nursery schools in metros and towns not because they were in the race to get ahead in the 10+2 schools, or for a holistic development programme. Life wasn't so complicated and competitive as it is today. In those days, children attended nursery schools because parents wanted a little time off from their children. And while the child attended the nursery school, he was expected to pick up three basic skills: learn to 'sit' in the company of other children, learn to 'speak' English by reciting a few rhymes, and get 'potty-trained'. And, many parents didn't believe in the concept of nursery schools; they considered them unessential and a waste of money.

Since then, nursery schools have come a long way. Today, nursery schools, play schools, activity centres or preschools, as they are called, are the 'in' thing. No more are they considered as a frill for some; instead, they are a staple for toddlers in cities and towns. This awareness among parents has created a dire need for quality nursery schools. Since nursery schools do not come under the purview of government regulations, people with varied backgrounds, other than education, have jumped onto the nursery school bandwagon making nursery school education a commercial venture.

The area of early childcare has grown extremely competitive with numerous new players joining in and making tall claims. In the midst of this loud babble, parents are very confused about which nursery school to choose for their children. With the nursery pond teeming with choices, pinpointing the best one among them is neither easy nor obvious. Rather than to simply enrol children in one of the neighbourhood nursery schools for the sake of convenience, parents have to realise that all pre-schools are *not* created equal. They have to go through the process of selecting a preschool for their toddlers by evaluating its strengths and qualities vis a vis their personal beliefs.

We live in the IT age where knowledge comes with a power-tag. So, you will have to become preschool-savvy and children-savvy. Numerous studies have been conducted around the globe on early childhood development and the role of preschools. Get to know what experts think about what children need to learn in a preschool to enable you to make better choices. After you have read their findings and questioned their premises, then test them with your own convictions. The more knowledgeable you will be the better choices you will make (see Chapter on *Hyperactive Children*).

NATURE OF LEARNING AND DEVELOPMENT

It is a fact that toddlers have the ability to learn all the time. A toddler's capacity to learn and grasp new skills and explore new horizons is considered to be immensely vast. Every experience they have, both in and out of school, is a source of new information used to enlarge and refine their understanding of how the world works. But that doesn't mean they can also quickly learn to adapt to adult methods of learning. Research points out that toddlers learn differently from the way older children and adults learn. David Elkind, in his book, *The Miseducation of Children*, says "Pre-schoolers learn most effectively not through the kinds of instructions many people associate with schooling. A good preschool programme does not include formal lessons during which children sit and listen to a teacher impart information ... Children this age must not be formally taught to read or write or calculate, the kind of concentrated attention such learning demands is unnatural for young kids."

Why Child-centred Nursery Schools?

Nursery schools being very small in structure and size, when compared to the high schools automatically focus on personalised attention and care and their programmes are therefore child-centred. It is impossible to receive child-centred education in high schools since many schools accommodate between two thousand to five thousand students on the campus, while a nursery school may only house a few hundred children. To successfully swim in that sea of learning called a high school, children should receive a strong foundation in a number of skills at the preschool level. As I'd mentioned earlier, nursery schools are generally not alike because they are inherently child-centred. A child-centred programme incorporates flexibility in its content and character. Some nursery schools focus on enhancing the social development of the children, while others seek to accelerate cognitive growth. Some emphasise daily, structured activities, while others let the child do whatever he wants to do, at his own pace. Some nursery schools stress group activities, while others stress individual activities. Some confine the nursery activities to classrooms, others want children learn on the open lawns, close to Nature. The list of such basic differences is almost endless. Parents expect the end-result of a preschool programme to register long-term effects of cognitive growth on children. On the contrary, research points out that by the time children enter elementary school the cognitive gains that resulted from preschool education fade off. Psychologists who have studied the impact of preschool learning on children are of the opinion that preschools that emphasise academic skills are most likely to produce temporary gains, whereas programmes that emphasise *curiosity and self-motivation* show the greatest long-term gains (*see* Chapter on *Learning Disabilities*).

Child-centred Concept: Its Theories and Practices

The concept of creating nursery schools as child-centred environments for toddlers arose from a humanistic approach to early childhood development. Humanism is a cluster of attitudes about how to view children and their growth. Maslow's (1970) theory of self-actualisation, Carl Rogers' (1951) client-centred therapy, and Gordon's (1975) transactional-analysis perspective are all examples of humanistic theories of development.

The two basic concepts of humanists according to B.R. McCandless and E.D. Evans, *Children and Youth: Psychosocial Development*, is summarised as follows:

(a) In theory, focus should be upon the *uniqueness* of child—how each is different from all others. Understanding this is more important than knowing about the general processes and factors that are common to all children and treat them alike. In practice, focus should be on warmth and sensitivity in adults. Do the teachers welcome each child at the school gate? Do teachers lower themselves to child height to talk to children? Do they listen to the toddler's imperfect words and try their best to understand? Do they *anticipate* when a fight is about to begin and find ways to avoid it? Do they initiate and monitor play activities? Are they comforting, encouraging, and guiding—all at the appropriate moment?

(b) In theory, focus should be upon the child's capacity for constructive growth and *creative potential* at the highest levels of functioning. This attitude is in contrast to a concern for understanding how the child simply reacts to the environment, behaves in predictable ways, and accumulates information already available to others. In practice, focus should be on providing opportunities for children to explore. Is the space ample and safe? Are interesting toys, puzzles, blocks, coloured beads, and books used as teaching aids? Are there activities such as nature walk, dancing to music, yoga, aerobics, sports, games, dramatics, role play, drawing, painting, cutting and pasting for which adults have to make extra effort? Is there structure or routine? Are planning, programming and assessments carried out on a daily, weekly or monthly basis? Watching television, even educational television or computers, is a poor substitute for toddlers.

These humanistic theoretical perspectives complement rather than contradict each other, because they emphasise different aspects of development. Preschool educators have to be 'eclectic', meaning that rather than adopt any one of these theories exclusively, one should make use of parts of all of them. Whatever the similarities, at the heart of each theory is a different view of the nature of the child. A child is a collection of hidden impulses that need to be expressed, understood and controlled.

The Montessori Programme

Maria Montessori was an Italian physician-turned-educator who developed a revolutionary approach to teaching young children at the beginning of the twentieth century. She began her work with a group of retarded children in Rome. She was highly successful in teaching them to read, write and pass exams meant for normal children. Some time later, she turned her attention to poor children in the slums of Rome and had similar success in teaching them. Her approach has since been adopted extensively in private nursery schools, making its greatest impact on preschool children.

Montessori's approach is simultaneously a philosophy of education, a psychology of the child, and practical educational exercises that can be used to teach children even if one does not adhere strictly to the *Montessori method*. She identifies four different sensitive periods, each containing a different facet of development: "the development of sensory and perceptual abilities, the development of awareness of order, the development of sensitivity to language, and the development of sensitivity toward movement." According to Maria Montessori, "the teacher serves as a facilitator rather than as the controller of learning, pointing out interesting ways to explore the various curriculum materials and offering help to any child who asks." (Montessori, *Discovery of the Child*, M.J. Costelloe, SJ., Trans.).

Give Your Child a Headstart

Burton L. White and Jean Carew Watts conducted a study in 1973, called the Harvard Preschool Project where they visited numerous nursery schools. Looking at toddlers they found that some children were already superior in social and cognitive skills at three years, while other toddlers were lagging behind. As you go through the characteristics of competent children, you may be inspired to channelise your own toddler as you prepare him to join a nursery school of your choice.

Characteristics of Competent Children

Social Skills

◆ Getting and maintaining adult attention in socially accepted ways.
◆ Using adults as helpful resources.
◆ Expressing hostility and affection to adults.
◆ Leading and following peers.
◆ Expressing hostility and affection to peers.
◆ Competing with peers.
◆ Praising oneself and showing pride in one's accomplishments.
◆ Involving oneself in adult role playing, or showing a desire to grow up.

Cognitive Skills

◆ Linguistic competence—ability to understand and communicate.
◆ Intellectual competence, including ability to deal with numbers, rules, and understand other points of views.
◆ Executive abilities, such as planning complex activities.
◆ Attentional ability, specifically the ability to work on one's own project while being aware of other people.

Focus on Long-term Development Gains

Parents mustn't lose the focus why they want to admit their child to a nursery school in the first place. Primarily, the investment is to secure the child's future. At the end of the two-year preschool programme, children should be equipped with skills to be able to cope with the stress and pressures of formal schools, which are usually engaged in transmitting basic academics through a rigid syllabus. Coping alone is not enough. Children have to enjoy learning in the midst of teeming classmates, and complete their tasks and tests within designated time-frames. How do the nursery schools measure up in preparing children for the future? Will they be trained

> Through all the 'chaff' of child-centred learning that preschools claim to offer, parents have to look for the 'grain' of truth.

to become little robots who will parrot answers to a set of predetermined questions? And, while they are teaching children basic skills, will they also teach them how to get along with other people—their peers and those older to them, and acquire an appreciation of aesthetics and human values? If the children are being exposed to activities that will be a source of pleasure in later life, do they simultaneously learn creative ways to sustain their interest in completing those activities, as well as the ones that bring no pleasure? With your involvement and support, the preschool years can become very rewarding for your children.

Make Nursery School Enjoyable

*"I tried to teach my child with books
He gave me only puzzled looks.
I tried to teach my child with words.
They passed him by often unheard.
Despairingly, I turned aside
"How shall I teach this child?" I cried.
Into my hand he put the key.
"Come," he said, "play with me."*

—ANON

Generating Positive Energy

Ashish Trivedi entered play school when he was thirty-months old. On the first day after school got over, the mother picked up Ashish and met the class-teacher with a battery of questions. "What did he learn today? Has he made any friends? Did he play with some children? Was he crying a lot? Did he eat anything? Was he thirsty?" Indeed, this worried mother was letting out a steam of anxiety. And, it was too much for the poor teacher to handle, especially after she had gone through three full hours of trying to settle down and entertain fifteen new children who had entered school for the first time in their lives. And now this over-anxious, paranoid mother! While other mothers were offering their appreciation, the thought crossed the teacher's mind, "Good heavens, today's only the first day. What does she expect? Will I have to give her moment-to-moment reports every day?" Many teachers, when they are badgered by parents feel that it's much easier to deal with maladjusted children than with over-anxious parents.

"You must not show so much anxiety," parents are advised. Is it possible to do so? Can one control one's feelings? Yes, you can, if you apply your mind to it. If you want your child to be independent, then fill your head with positive thoughts and your heart with positive feelings. Start by imagining your toddler taking to school happily and confidently, and begin to *feel* his joy. Your positive thoughts and feelings will fill you with positive energy which will lead you to believe in yourself and in your child. When you are filled with belief in yourself and in your child, you will pass this energy to the teachers in school. This positive energy, coupled with belief in yourself, will help you perform positive acts. First, you learn to believe in yourself, then in your child, and later in the teachers. In short, you are gradually infecting others with your positive energy.

Building Trust and Friendship

It is normal for children to feel anxious on the first day, or the first few weeks of school. While some kids walk in with a smile, others may dread to walk in at all. Crying, whining and clinging are common anxieties displayed by pre-schoolers. Some may complain of stomach aches or may puke, and those who cannot puke on cue manage to cough hard enough to bring up the puke. And, so the game is played, to-school-or-not-to-school, to test the family's resilience and resolve. If you learn to keep your cool, accept changes, and not to display your anxieties like Ashish Trivedi's mother did, entering preschool need not be such a harrowing, heart-wrenching experience. With some preparation, a little bit of luck and lots of prayers your baby could strut into class and enjoy it. The preparation bit is laid out in these pages.

As for the luck, we all need it; children are so unpredictable that at times even the best of preparations come to naught. About the prayers, it is not for your baby, but for you. May you be blessed with fortitude and courage to carry out your mission in spite of your child sensing your doubts and anxieties.

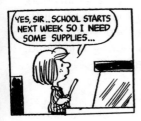
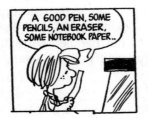
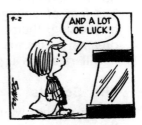

Resistance to Change

Volumes of tomes have been written on change, on transition, and on restructuring in business books and magazines. Corporate houses spend huge amounts of money to alter the mindset of their employees through corporate seminars and workshops, so that they adjust and adapt to contemporary market demands. Change and transition is about stepping from the familiar into the unfamiliar, and this unsettles many adults. When faced with change and restructuring, they gripe, sulk and whine, and also exhibit psychosomatic problems that may include acidity, hypertension, or stiff muscles and joints. In short, a lot of time, money and effort is spent by business houses to bring about corporate change—which goes to prove that change, transition, and restructuring has never been taken to kindly or willingly by humans, big and small.

Home-School Transition

Leaving the familiar confines of home to enter preschool is what psychologists call 'the home-school transition' which most toddlers resent. To prepare him to accept this transition does not call for an investment of money, but you need to invest huge amounts of time in restructuring your baby's habits to adapt and adjust to changes that the new environment will demand. The 'familiar confines of home' have other ramifications than mere walls and surroundings. It is also about the people in the house whom the child is familiar with. When he is unable to spot his own people in the new surroundings of the preschool he becomes insecure and distressed, which psychologists call, 'separation anxiety'. Some children are traumatised by the anxiety of separation. The fear of change is manifested through loss of appetite, bedwetting, thumb sucking, tantrums, disturbed sleep, terror dreams. If this fear is not handled correctly during childhood, it will raise its ugly head in later years also.

Life Scripts

Which mother would not like to see her baby take to school the very first day like a duckling takes to water? Any mother would love to hear the teacher say, "Your little ducky waddled into school so happily. In class he is so friendly and polite. He is toilet-trained..." and the list goes on. Comments like these by the teacher are music to any parent's ears. To make this happen, you would need to spend time in preparing your child for school. William Shakespeare, in *As You like It*, said, "All the world's a stage, and all the men and women are merely players." To help children perform with confidence on the stage, that you may call a 'pre-school', you would need to be familiar with the 'script' so that you can prepare the child by rehearsing the *script* in advance. The shortest and sweetest way to teach children new scripts is for parents to create an atmosphere which will be conducive to enacting the script. For example, a child should have had at least nine to ten hours of sleep at night so that he could wake up fresh and energetic for school the next day. But if he is taken to a night party and then bundled off to school the next morning, he is going to be very irritable, distracted and cranky. Similarly, if toddlers are expected to adjust and adapt to new surroundings, then they will require such exposures as will enable them to take to the new surroundings easily. Some mothers tire the children during

> If we want children to accept change, then parents will have to change themselves to the routine they want their children to change to.

the day and keep them busy in the afternoons by taking them to the shopping malls, or dropping in at a friend's house for a chat, or for a run in the parks. These outings offer him great opportunities to explore the unlimiting spatial dimensions of new areas. You will find that he takes to the home-school 'transition' in happy stride. In fact, he is thrilled to walk into school and explore the place on his own.

Overcoming Separation Anxiety

Healthcare experts are of the opinion that although 'separation anxieties' are normal among infants and toddlers, they are not appropriate for older children and adolescents and may represent symptoms of 'Separation Anxiety Disorder' (SAD). Studies show that children with separation anxiety will cling to their parents and have difficulty falling asleep at night, and also experience nightmares or fears at bedtime. When separated, they may fear that their parent, in some way, will be 'lost' to them forever, or may be involved in an accident

> When children are exposed to the world of strangers, they learn that there are a lot more people who make this world and not just the handful of familiar people at home.

or taken ill (hospitalised). The need to stay close to their parents or home may make it difficult for them to attend school, stay at relatives or friends houses, or be in a room by themselves. Why wait till they're five-years old to find out if they're infected with the SAD bug or not? You can implement a programme to expand your children's *social* horizons from infancy itself. To expand your children's *physical* horizons, you will have to take them out regularly where they freely explore open areas. Through these outdoor exposures, children learn to be comfortable in new areas which extend beyond the dimensions of the walls of their homes. If you would like them to be on their own, or play with other children with a minimum of fuss, then allow them to interact with other children as early as possible, say at ten to twelve months of age. If interactive play with other children is delayed till the time they are two-years old or more, their memories would have already *scripted the scene* made up of familiar persons within the narrow walls of their homes. This script gets imprinted in the brain, and they function from the empirical data gathered from infancy onward. Introducing them suddenly to new people at the preschool will make them afraid and insecure in the new world.

Many parents believe that when they send their children to the parks and birthday parties, the exposure is adequate to prepare them to enjoy preschool. In fact, some parents fault the school for their children's anxiety because their kids are 'quite free' at home, at birthday parties and in the parks. There is a flaw in the comparison. At school, toddlers are left to the care of the teachers (unfamiliar persons in unfamiliar surroundings), while at birthday parties or in public parks, either mothers, family members, or maid-servants accompany children. The sense of security which children associate from having familiar persons accompanying them compensates for the fear of being in a new place. Obviously, children grow dependent on the familiar persons being around them all the time in unfamiliar places. In school, when they cannot see any familiar people on whom they are dependent, they feel a deep sense of abandonment; their insecurities bring on howls, screams and cries. Since separation from a dependent (familiar) person brings on anxiety, can 'separation anxiety' be reduced or eliminated altogether? Yes, if you have the will then you'll find ways and means to either reduce or eliminate it altogether.

Vision Statement

To begin with, you will first formulate a *vision* for your child. The vision statement identifies what you want from your child. Supposedly your *Vision Statement* says, "I want my daughter to be a happy, friendly child," or another may say, "I want my child to be a tennis player." Once the vision statement is identified, then develop the *action plan* on how you will achieve your objective. Chalk out a few practical ideas which you will enjoy and can become part of your routine. You could ask two or three friends who have children, more or less, your toddler's age to come over to your place, or for a picnic lunch. Organise some eats and drinks, and with the minimum of supervision from grownups let them be on their own. It is not going to be hunky dory the first time you initiate this playgroup, and there could be screams and howls, pushing and jostling. But as they meet regularly and are left to themselves more and more, they will come to accept the routine—from being in the company of other children to enjoying the company of friends, and from grabbing toys to sharing toys and playing together. You, too, will enjoy these breaks and it will help to relax you in the company of other mothers, whose cup of parenting joys and tribulations spills over like yours. Happy interactions will result in happy memories. Your baby will not only love to play with other children, but he will enjoy exploring new places. And, school will be another such fun place to explore and enjoy.

Give Children Space to Grow

When the weather is bad, or for some other reasons you are unable to take him out and he is at home by himself, engrossed in some play or activity then let him be by himself. Just make sure the place is safe and he cannot come to any harm or hurt by being on his own. Many grownups keep 'interfering' in the child's activities by correcting, directing and helping him to do things the right way. Others appoint a housemaid to keep the child company. This interference from adults destroys his creativity and increases his dependence on others.

> *Allow the child space and to your delight he will play on his own, using blocks, crayons or imaginative role-plays.*

Children learn fastest through imitation. They take to mimicking and imitating adult behaviour patterns and habits very quickly. We have heard it said that actions speak louder than words, and yet we use harsh words to shout down the child's behaviour without realising that his actions are a reflection of our own—often magnified. Hence, if we get in the habit of putting our best foot forward, then his mimicry and imitation of our actions would benefit him immensely. Your *Vision Statement* 'script' of preparing a happy child to enter preschool will incorporate the nitty-gritty of mundane details which require your constant and consistent attention.

You will have to chalk out a *routine* much in advance and stick to it.

Daily Routine

Punctuality is a value one could befriend as a lifetime companion. To be punctual every morning, one doesn't have to go into a tailspin. With some measure of time management mixed with a dose of foresight, the whole range of activities could be joyfully covered on a daily basis. If a two-year-old child has to get about ten hours of sleep every night, then he has to be fed supper by 7 o'clock so that he gets into bed, say, by 8 o'clock. He could be woken up by 6 o'clock in the morning. Parents will have to get used to waking up a wee bit *before* the child every morning to put on some music. Potty chores, brushing, bathing, dressing and having breakfast could become enjoyable 'quality time' interactions for the whole family. Quality time is another word for time management. If you organise your time you will never suffer the 'morning rush hour'—be it at home or on the roads. With such a regular routine, you will automatically drop your child in school, much before the punctuality deadline. Your child would have done potty, had a bath, a full breakfast, and would strut into school looking well-groomed and tidy, happy and cheerful, to enjoy another day of fun and games with his friends.

Interactive Playgroups

After you have set the daily routine, you will have to look around the neighbourhood and make friends with those families that have children about your child's age so that you can form a playgroup for your child. At the playschool your child will have an emotional headstart if he can socialise with other children without any parents around. Many children break down, crying or sobbing their hearts out the moment the parents or the housemaid is out of sight. Which parent wouldn't like their child to walk into class happy and cheerful? To make that possible, for many months, prior to the date the child enters school, you must expose the child to the company of other children *sans* family members or home-servants accompanying the child. Parents have to make the effort to identify playgroups in the neighbourhood for their children to interact with. Since it is your need, you will have to take the initiative. Playing with other children will enable your child to become independent. Simultaneously, at home, you will encourage your child to play on his own, using blocks, crayons or imagination.

Transition from Play School to Formal School

Year after year, families residing in metros and towns pay a heavy price to secure admission for their children in well-known schools. The price they pay is heavy: financially, emotionally and mentally. Toddlers, on completing three years (either March-end, or September-end, depending in which state they reside), are eligible for admission interviews and tests. Educators and psychologists sit on interview panels to judge which toddlers to fail and which toddlers to pass. Parents are of the opinion that the interviews eliminate rather than select children. Since local governments have turned a blind eye to monitoring these interview-exams, the syllabus, markings/ratings, selection methodologies vary from school to school, which is an added nightmare for parents. In such a scenario, parents are under severe pressure to prepare children for interviews and tests. The admission pressure breaks many families. In desperation, parents enrol toddlers to attend tutorial classes after nursery school gives over. These tutorials have a fixed focus: they drill the child into becoming 'answering machines'. Nursery schools also change their *modus operandi,* from regular play-way methods to mock-interview classes for parents, and special drills for children to meet the demands of tense parents. The strain and pressure on the children is mostly passed on by the parents who themselves go through a harrowing time, trying to get their children admitted to reputed schools. The dearth in quality neighbourhood schools has tipped the scales in supply and demand. For approximately two hundred seats, there are about two thousand applicants. Faced with such a ratio, parents who hit the panic button, pass the panic to the children. In some cases where parents carry themselves with poise and confidence, regularly spend time with their children, and are able to handle strains and pressures maturely between themselves (without passing stress vibes to their children), those toddlers fair well in the interviews. Instead of dreading the interviews, these children look forward with excitement to show off at the interviews. Handling emotions appropriately is what effective parenting is all about.

Disarm School Stress

"A child should not be readied for school through drills, rote exercises, or memorisation. Rather, she needs to be raised in a stimulating environment, given age-appropriate toys to play with, and the freedom to experiment. With the help of her parents, such a child will internalise many—if not most of the skills that serve as a foundation for academics."

—*(Parents' Guide to Raising Kids who Love to Learn)*

Morning Blues

Many parents, when they are dissatisfied for whatever reason, instantly gripe and make their displeasure known. Take the example of six-year-old Sandeep, who after studying *several terms* in the same school, suddenly took a dislike for school.

Getting ready for school every morning was an ordeal for the family. Sandeep would throw tantrums, saying he did not want to go to school. Sandeep's mother suspected the class-teacher to be the culprit, and over the phone talked to the headmistress, telling her that the child was scared of the teacher who was harsh and cruel. The headmistress was taken aback by the accusation and asked both parents to meet her the next day. The headmistress met the parents and discussed Sandeep's tantrums. She asked the parents if any changes had taken place at home in the last fortnight? They said, 'no' to questions asked. Was anyone hospitalised? Was the maid (caretaker) sacked? House guests? Yes, they had house guests. Their relatives from Jaipur were visiting them. Yes, they had a two-year-old child. The headmistress pointed out that Sandeep may have become attached to the little cousin and wanted to play with him at home, instead of attending school. The parents, now disarmed by the headmistress, agreed with her and said the child wanted to bring his cousin to school to meet his friends. She told the parents to bring the cousin to school in the afternoons, at the time when they came to collect Sandeep, so that he could get his friends to meet his little cousin.

You may not find other headmistresses so perceptive, and that is no reason to jump the gun. When parents jump to conclusions that either the teacher punished the kid, or some child hit the kid, then such accusations may not go well with the school faculty who are doing their utmost to settle an emotionally disturbed child. Maybe, you could change your tact or approach. If your approach is soft and gentle you may find a positive response from the faculty; after all, you want your child to settle down quickly, and so would they. Look at the situation from the school's point of view: the disturbed child not only upsets the entire class of children, but brings the class activities to a grinding halt. The reasons for these tantrums could be many. First fix the origin of the problem: is it home, or is it school? Never assume the fault always lies with the school.

Toys are a Child's Precious Jewels

Out of the blue one morning, Yusuf said he was not going to school. He wanted to stay home. He hated school, he said. His friends hit him and the teachers scolded him. The grandparents got perturbed, but the parents weren't. In viral fever and in cough and cold, Yusuf would go to school. Since they closely monitored Yusuf, they refused to accept that friends and teachers were the problem. They knew the teachers were very fond of him and he had a good set of friends. So, they bundled Yusuf off to school. The next day, and the days after that, the tantrums became a regular ritual every morning. None could identify the cause of the problem. At home, too, the parents noticed that Yusuf had become sulky and selfish. He would hide his toys from his cousins, or snatch it away from their hands. It so happened that Yusuf suddenly had to cope with a new set of relatives. An uncle and aunt brought along their two brats, one who was older than Yusuf and the other was about his own age. The older one was a wild ruffian. The cousins laughed, ridiculed and broke some of his toys while playing with them. When Yusuf would take away his toys from them, his parents would correct him, scold him, and tell him to share his toys with his cousins. The cousins were sharp—good manipulators. Unfortunately, the grownups never saw them bullying Yusuf. He began to hide his toys. But they were clever cousins. They knew all his hiding places. So how could he leave his toys behind and go to school? What would happen to his toys? He had to be at home to protect his toys. They were his prized possessions, his precious jewels. There was nothing more precious to Yusuf than the toys he had treasured for so long. So, every morning when they got him ready for school, he would howl and wail, wanting to stay home and hide his toys. It was only after the cousins left that Yusuf began to enjoy going to school again.

If your child comes out of class, when school gets over, unhappy, upset or crying, it is obvious that there is a problem in the school. Maybe there was a fight in the class, or maybe the teacher ticked him off, or the child did not stand first in the class competition, maybe it is a nagging ear ache or constipation. Or, having completed the *term*, maybe the child has to enter the new class and the child prefers the former class where she is fond of the old teacher. Or, maybe the teacher had resigned midterm, or gone on leave and the child feels lost.

There are many instances where children come to school in the mornings, crying from home, and leave school in the afternoons, happy and content. In such a situation, the problem is the home environment. Maybe the elder brother or sister is at home, either sick or has a holiday and the younger child has to go to school. Or, maybe you have house guests who have children and while they are going to be home, having fun with his toys, the little one is sent off to school. It could be that the father or mother has gone on an overnight business tour, or the maid whom the child is fond of has gone on leave, or been sacked. Or, there is a sibling child whom the mother is nursing at home, or a family member is admitted to the hospital. It could be that both parents have been fighting. At times, parents 'prepare' the child to enter formal school and they tell him, "Now you're a big boy and you have to go to a big school soon." For the child, going to the 'big school' (another environment) means going there right away. There could be so many reasons why the child gets upset or feels insecure. You must put faith in the school for your child's sake. Once the origin of stress is identified, whether it's the home environment or the school environment, you must be open and frank to enlist the support of the school personnel to help your child come out of it. It is advisable to nip the problem in the bud. When you work as a team, your child will settle down faster.

Fears and Phobias

For some reason, Anita was afraid of the teacher. To complicate matters, it seemed that Anita also loved the class-teacher. This love-fear relationship baffled the parents. They had observed that Anita had an excellent equation with the teacher. She enjoyed the classes. When school would give over, and the moment the class-teacher called her out to hand her over to the mother, Anita would sob and cry. Furthermore, a few times, when Anita saw the teacher at a grocery store or in a restaurant, she got petrified and cried her heart out. Was Anita a problem child? Or was the teacher the problem? Much later, it dawned upon the mother that she had caused the problem. At the time of collecting Anita from school, the mother would daily ask the class-teacher, "How was she in school today?" When the teacher would praise the child, the mother would slip in a complaint. Shaking

Anita's arm, she would say, "Shall I tell your teacher that Anita troubles Mummy in the mornings, and she doesn't drink her milk quickly?" One day it was the milk, another day it was about a tantrum, then about a sulk, and it would go on. At home, when Anita was scolded, she was told that if she didn't listen, "Mummy will tell your teacher, you're a naughty girl." Poor Anita was in constant fear that whenever her mother and the teacher met, they would be exchanging a complaint list of her misdeeds. Anita loved her teacher. She deeply valued the relationship with her teacher who would daily praise her in class and give her 'merit stars' and 'smileys' for her work. And, she loved her mother very much, but she felt an undercurrent of threat to the twin loves she had. She didn't know how to handle her feelings, so crying came natural to her every time she saw her Mom and the teacher talking together. She did not dread the teacher, nor did she dread her mother; instead she was afraid of losing something precious whenever her mother *talked* to her teacher. Another barrage of questions followed from the mother to the teacher: "Why is she scared of you? Why does she cry every morning? She refuses to get ready. She wasn't like that before? Has someone hit her? Was she scolded?" The kind teacher got her to meet the principal who explained to the mother ways to relax her 'grip' over her daughter.

Dealing with Embarrassing Situations

The first time the child pukes in school or does potty in the pants it may be accidental or intentional. Whether intentional or accidental, the teachers must ensure that the child's self-esteem, dignity and pride does not get flushed down the drain. The teacher's attitude towards puke and potty must not show disgust or disdain. To soothe the child, their words, gestures and facial expression will offer assurance that all is well, after all. Before you rush him to the doctor, find out if the problem needs medical attention or just restructuring

> *Children should be toilet-trained so that their self-esteem, dignity and pride remain intact in school and in other public places.*

of schedules and attitudes at home. If the child forces himself to puke or to mess his pants with potty, he is intentionally using this as an escape route to go back home. (This usually happens in the first month of settling down in pre-primary schools.) If the child vomits in school, parents may ensure that the child is given a very light breakfast at least about an-hour-and-a-half before leaving home so that the light breakfast goes down and doesn't stay stuck on the chest. If it is not digested, then at the first sign of stress or strain the breakfast will spill out and that will compound the stress. If the child soils his clothes in school, then parents must personally supervise that the child has done potty every morning before leaving for school. Morning potty is an excellent lifetime habit to be inculcated at a very early age. As a precaution, children who are not toilet-trained must wear a diaper during the first fortnight of school, or till such time they are toilet-trained.

C H A P T E R (4)

Home-School Bonding

Upon entering school, the child is exposed to new patterns, styles and attitudes. When the child discovers occasional discrepancies between what the school proposes as values and those experienced at home, there can be a certain amount of conflict. However, when the curriculum and school practices and discussions incorporate the knowledge of the family and the richness of the home culture, this conflict is more easily managed and the student's self-image is enhanced.

— ALMA FLOR ADA & PAM SCHILLER
(The School-Home Connection)

Aaryan was a Class VII student. One afternoon, when he did not reach home on the school bus, his mother became very worried. When she telephoned one of his friends, she was told that the teacher had detained him in class as he had forgotten to bring his homework copy to school. Since he missed the school bus, Aaryan reached home three hours later, sullen and upset. His mother scolded him for being so forgetful. The next day, Aaryan handed his homework copy to the teacher. And, three weeks later, the teacher returned the homework copies to the students; they were uncorrected and unsigned by the class-teacher. Aaryan's mother was very upset with the teacher for returning her son's uncorrected homework copy.

Eleven-year-old Sohail was an average child. He did not have many friends and his interest in studies had dwindled. According to his parents, "He has fallen into bad company because he's in the worst section of his class. He is doing badly in maths because the maths teacher is strict." The maths teacher was willing to tutor Sohail privately, but he refused to be drawn into a discussion with his parents on the subject of extra tuition.

Thirteen-year-old Nikita was a conscientious and a bright child. Of all her subjects, she loved geography the most. It was her best subject for a number of years. Whenever she would go out on school camps or on holidays, she would enthusiastically read about the details of the place and talk about it with a dazzle in her eyes. But this year she lost interest in geography and was doing poorly in it. Nikita's explanation was: "Geography's a dumb subject. It's just doing workbook exercises and colouring maps."

All the three situations given here spelt problem. Should you talk to the child's teacher? Should you talk to the principal? Should you ask for your child to be transferred to another section? Or, should you ignore it, hoping that things will work out eventually, as a mother, who once told me, "If we constantly breathe down the teacher's back, how is the child going to learn to respect his teachers?"

Usually parents do not ask for appointments to compliment teachers. I wish they would do that. A troubled parent who is seeking an appointment to meet the teacher is definitely thinking in terms of confrontation. And, the teacher also prepares for the confrontation by digging into her memory bank, looking for the child's problem areas, which she had laid to rest. She may also gather negative data from her colleagues. So, you have two uneasy people who are very apprehensive of each other's integrity, sitting together to thrash the problem. The outcome of such parent-teacher encounters could be disastrous, if not alarming for the child's development.

Somehow parents and teachers seem to forget the common goal. The common goal of education is the development of the child. Instead of joining forces to become partners in the mission of child development, parents and teachers tend to build separate camps and spend their time finding faults and trading charges against each camp. Unfortunately, in this cold and hostile environment, the one and only casualty is the child. It defeats the very goal for which the school was instituted in the first place.

Building a Bridge between Home and School

Teachers are a breed of people who are overworked and underpaid in most countries. Many noble-minded individuals joined the teaching profession not for profit, but because they believed in education as a vocational calling. I am sure many teachers cherish memories of those students who had some serious problems, and if not for their dedication, those students would never have become achievers in life. As teachers, you know the ways and you know the ropes of how to get the best out of your students. We all like to feel important, so one of the better ways to get a child to respond in class is to make him feel happy. When he is happy, his self-esteem soars and he likes his teacher. She becomes his role model to copy, and he would willingly run an extra mile to please his teacher.

Parents have to realise that the best way to get the teacher involved in their child's development is to demonstrate their own involvement and appreciation of the teacher's efforts. In fact, it takes very little effort to strike a rapport with your child's teachers. It may not be easy making a phone call to thank the teacher, how about sending small notes of appreciation, from time to time, praising the teacher's genuine efforts in working with your child? You will see the difference it will make in your child's attitude to the teacher. The teacher will begin to give more attention to the child, and the child will begin to respond better. Who doesn't love appreciation or encouragement?

> A phone call to thank the teacher for an act of kindness, however small, will have a tremendous impact.

So give it your best shot. As much as you need it, so do your children, and their teachers, too! In an atmosphere of mutual give and take, you build bridges between home and school. The bonds of appreciation bind these bridges of partnership which will benefit your children immensely.

Mind Your Manners

When parents 'bump' into a teacher, say at a party, grocery store, cinema hall, doctor's clinic, street corner, or wherever, the questions parents frequently throw at the teacher is, "So, how is Sanjay doing in class now?" Or worse still, "Vikram is so good in English. Why wasn't he selected for the inter-school debate competition?" Any beginner's manual on the *Art of Conversation* will tell you to never interrogate. When you mix interrogation with conversation, others not only feel uncomfortable, they feel 'guarded' and it leaves a bad impression. Interrogators usually leave a rude and arrogant impression. So, instead of saying, "Why is my son not on the team?", you could say, "How is the selection for the inter-house team going? What can I do to help you?" If you have to discuss your child's behaviour or performance, then don't do it so casually in a public place or at a social gathering. In order to get something you may have to give something first. Try being pleasant and charming, or better still, offer your services, it will do wonders to your *art of conversation* skills. After you have exchanged pleasantries, as well as praise and appreciation of her work, you may say something to this effect, "If you could spare me some time, I would like to come over to school and discuss Sanjay (or Vikram). Tell me which is the best time and day so that I could ask for an appointment at the reception counter."

Team-work Works Wonders

Many teachers give up on students who avoid work or misbehave. This is what a teacher, who taught history to Class V students, once told me, "A mother took an appointment to talk to me about her son who sat sullenly through my history class, looking as though he hated me and everything I said. As the mother talked I began to get a picture of his nature and demeanour. I had mistaken his shyness for hostility. He was terrified of participating in class because the other students, especially the girls, seemed to know much more about history than he did. He was scared of being laughed at and ridiculed. The mother and I agreed to team up. While she, from home, would push him to talk in class, in school, I would involve him more and more in discussions and praise his responses. In no time his sullen looks disappeared and he made tremendous improvement in other subjects too." The moral of the story is when a student sees that his parents and teachers join forces and team up for his benefit, he can perform miracles.

When parents don't team up with the teachers, then children usually have a field day. Today's child is smarter than his parents and teachers put together. So when the child is punished for misbehaviour, he comes home and relates his version of the story on what the teacher did. Usually his is a 'doctored' version. The incenced parents rush to school the next day to protest the punishment the child is given. If the parents had kept an open mind, they would have realised that everything the child related was not completely accurate. Instead of declaring war on the school, they could seek an appointment with the teacher to get her version of the story also. To put himself in the best possible light, the child would obviously omit certain details, elaborate on a lie, or forget to relate corroborating factors. Perhaps the most helpful step in establishing a positive parent-teacher relationship is to start early, before the problems arise. In a climate of friendship there will be no question of settling scores with one another. To everyone's satisfaction, there will be a bond of trust in the parent-teacher relationship.

Bonding: A Long-term Commitment

When the child is in a nursery school, lots of parents involve themselves with school activities. They volunteer to help at major functions, as well as involve themselves in special classroom activities. Many parents interact with the teachers regularly since they visit the school twice daily to drop and pick up the child. They make friends with other mothers at the school gate and form playgroups for their children. And there are other parents who even at that early stage of

> *Parents don't realise that high-school kids need just as much attention as younger ones, if not more.*

their child's education never get involved with the school under some pretext or the other. They stay busy with their work and their lives, and they leave it to the school and the toddler to work out their equations.

As the child grows up, parental involvement with the school begins to taper off. By the time he is nine-years old there is a growing indifference amongst parents. Maybe, one of the reasons being that the child has grown independent and he can fend for himself in school. It gets worse as the child enters senior classes. Since the kids come home smiling, parents assume that everything is fine. Parents, who don't spend time with their children, often end up looking for quick solutions to infuse the kids with knowledge when their grades are low. Money can buy tutors, so the children are given extra tuition. If their grades are okay, then they are given extra allowance for entertainment. All this is to compensate for the years of parenting neglect. Many such parents do little reading and spend hours vegetating in front of the television, while the upwardly mobile parents spend their time shopping, entertainment and partying.

Tips on How to Bond

There are parents who would like to bond with the teachers but are at a loss how to go about it. Some of them are unable to get past, "How was Gurpreet in school today?" This is a hackneyed conversation-stopper—so just junk it. Bonding is about relationships. Bonding involves positive interactions. To interact positively you will first have to ignite your mind to think positive. Once you turn on the positive juices in your mind, you begin to feel relaxed and friendly towards the individual. As you warm up to the person, your approach becomes friendly and pleasant—you feel disarmed and you are able to disarm others with your charm. In this relaxed climate there are many things you can talk to the teacher about your child, such as, what your child is good at. Is this an only child who is used to exclusive attention? Are you planning a new baby? These decisions are going to affect your child's behaviour, so the teacher should be told about it. Has your child some personal characteristics which the teacher should know? Is he shy? Would he need the teacher's prodding? Is he left-handed? Your child is a meticulous worker, that is why he completes his tasks slowly— the teacher should be told about it so that she can work with your child and not write him off as a 'slow worker'. If the child has special talents, the teacher should be informed about it. "Gurpreet sings very well, or he plays the drums beautifully, or he is good at tennis." Your child writes good essays, or writes poetry. The teacher would be happy to know that your child has natural talents which she could encourage. When parents discuss their child's talents with the teachers, they pave the way to enable the child to contribute to his growth.

Volunteer Your Services

You may have developed so many personal interests, hobbies and talents while you were in school, college, before and after marriage which you could put to use at your child's school. Choose your own pace and time, which is comfortable to you to volunteer your services in, say, a read-aloud programme, tutoring slow learners, preparing theme-posters, charts and flashcards, teaching Reiki, yoga or meditation to emotionally disturbed children. If you are a professional, you could offer to give demonstrations or talks on science, math, medicine, whatever. Your involvement in the school will surely endear you to others, most of all to your child who will feel very proud of you. As a co-faculty member, you will be able to exchange views with teachers on inspiring your child to better performance.

Develop Your Children's Talents

Many children are talented in so many fields and the teachers are kept in the dark simply because parents consider those 'talents' unproductive as career goals. The child gradually loses interest in those fields and his talents get buried along with his self-worth. In many cases, children are flogged for not bringing in good marks in academics, while marks earned in non-academic subjects are written off as wasteful 'play'.

Our concentration on academics *per se* is so dominant that any interest displayed by students outside the field of academics is frowned upon and discouraged. To make children high performers, parents and teachers have to realise that by igniting the child's artistic brain, they inevitably stimulate the academic brain to perform better. Until this realisation takes root in the minds of parents and teachers, schooling will continue to be a tedious exercise for all those who find academics boring.

Some 'Never-do' Tips

A relationship gets strengthened when there is transparency. If you want the teacher to be honest and transparent with you, then the teacher would like to see the same measure of honesty and transparency in you. Lies and alibis never support a relationship. Some of the things parents should avoid indulging in:

- *Never provide cover for your kids with a 'sick' note when he has neglected to complete his homework or wants to avoid a test.*
- *Never go on a holiday or an outing on school days just because it suits your convenience, or office schedule, and then expect the teacher to help him catch up on all that he has missed.*
- *Never undermine the role assigned to him in a class function, or demand a more meaty role.*
- *Never run down the teacher in front of the child. Taking pot shots at the teacher's methods will encourage resentment of the teacher. You need not endorse everything the teacher does, neither should you voice your criticism publicly; it will affect your child's proficiency in studies.*
- *Never jump to conclusions by hearing your child's side of the story, especially those that have got him into trouble. Always cross-check to get the full picture.*
- *Never voice your ire or disappointment over the telephone. Call up to take an appointment to discuss: "Jagdish creates a fuss coming to school in the mornings. I wonder if you can help us find out what the trouble is."*
- *Don't find solutions over the telephone. And, when your best efforts are, time and again, continuously stonewalled*

by the teacher, and your child is still petrified of the teacher, it is wise to put it in writing so that the authorities can place it on record against the teacher. When letters like these sent by parents get accumulated on the teacher's record, some action will definitely be taken at some point in time.

Reach Your Goal

Teachers come in varied hues. Some hues are jarring and some are pleasing. The pleasing hues are a joy forever. But it is jarring when your child is stuck with an incompetent or an unfair teacher. It is equally jarring when the teacher is vindictive—who insults, humiliates and punishes children under some excuse. To teach a child to grin and bear it, you will have to learn to grin and bear it yourself, believing that something good will come out of this experience also. Something good can come out of it provided you make it happen. With your positive attitude you will toughen your child to accept this hardship. You can help him to become resilient by making him understand why some people are mean, prejudiced and short-tempered. Shift his focus from the teacher to the subjects. Children often lose interest in the subjects because of bad or incompetent teachers. At the time when the going is tough, it is important for you never to lose sight of your main goal: your child's holistic development. When you know your child is going through a difficult period, offer your support to enrich his learning experiences outside school. If the maths teacher is lousy, introduce your child to mathematical games and puzzles. If language, history or geography is taught badly, take him to a play, or the National Museum of Natural History, or the library where the two of you could explore and make those subjects come alive. Your support and encouragement will motivate him to draw more strength in those subjects, and learning of subjects will become more exciting than thinking morosely about one miserable teacher. One or two outstanding teachers, in his school, who combine intelligence, sensibility and compassion will be enough to infuse in him a lifelong joy in learning.

Part 2

As I Grow

Please ...

Understand that I am growing up and changing very fast. It must be difficult to keep pace with me, but please try.

Listen to me and give me brief, clear answers to my question. Then I will keep sharing my thoughts and feelings.

Reward me for telling the truth. Then I am not frightened into lying.

Tell me when you make mistakes and what you learned from them. Then I can accept that I am okay, even when I blunder.

Pay attention to me, and spend time with me. Then I can belive that I am important and worthwhile.

Do the things you want me to do. Then I have a good, positive model.

Trust and respect me. Even though I am smaller than you, I have feelings and needs just like you.

Compliment and appreciate me. Then I'll feel good, and I'll want to continue to please you.

Help me explore my unique interest, talents and potential. In order for me to be happy, I need to be me, and not you or someone you want me to be.

Be an individual and create your own happiness. Then you can teach me the same, and I can live a happy, successful and fulfilling life.

Thank you for hearing me, I love you!

—HELENE ROTHSCHILD,
(Free to Fly, Dare to be a Success)

Learning Disabilities (LD)

Be the change you wish to see in the world.
— MAHATMA GANDHI

Albert Einstein, Nelson Rockefeller, Agatha Christie, Hans Christian Anderson, Woodrow Wilson, Thomas Edison, Hellen Keller, Eleanor Roosevelt, —what did all these people have in common, other than the fact that they were famous? Well, all of them would have been placed in classes for *exceptional children* when they were growing up, if these had been available. The first four were all dyslexic. Edison was unable to master mathematics, Hellen Keller was both blind and deaf, and Eleanor Roosevelt was extremely shy and withdrawn as a child and would have been placed in a behaviourial-disorders class, had there been one at that time. Hollywood stars, Cher has *dysgraphia* (writing disorder), while Tom Cruise has *dyslexia* (reading disorder).

WHAT IS A LEARNING DISABILITY?

It is quite normal for children to be *more* active, *more* exuberant, *more* impulsive and *less* attentive than other children. If your child's behaviour problems seem a little excessive, even for a child his age, it is probably the case that he is simply a little immature and will in due time probably outgrow these problems. On the other hand, these children could be exhibiting symptoms of Conduct Disorder (CD), or Oppositional Defiant Disorder (ODD), or Attention Deficit Disorder (ADD), or worse still, Attention Deficit Hyperactivity Disorder (ADHD) at school, at home, or in relationships. These children often can be helped if parents learn how to manage their behaviour at a *very early age.*

Learning disabilities (LD) affect one in five children, making it one of the most common neuropsychiatric disorders of childhood. Experts in the field of ADHD, ADD and ODD say that, when someone is unable to process information properly, that is, when they're unable to interpret what they see and hear, or unable to relate, coordinate or link present information with information which is already stored or recorded in other parts of the brain, is said to have a learning disability. It becomes apparent when the person manifests difficulties in proper speech habits, writing and reading, or muscular coordination, or is impulsive, lacks, restraint and self-control, or is restless and inattentive. This affects their ability to learn to read, write and do math.

The Causes

What causes learning disabilities? Research suggests a number of possibilities. Some experts point to a *minimal brain dysfunction* (subtle disturbances in the brain structures and functions), that could cause learning disability, or a *miswiring* of the brain in which sections of the brain can't communicate with each other efficiently. Some experts attribute LD to heredity, where connections between the left and the right brains, or the sensory areas having to do with vision and hearing, remain impaired. Others point out to the possibility of the mother having taken a particular medication, drug or alcohol during pregnancy, or a disease contracted by the child during infancy. Whatever the causes, help is possible when parents and teachers identify the problem as early as possible, and

> Research points out that people with learning disabilities are not brain damaged. Brain scans show their cerebrums are perfectly normal.

accept responsibility by creating an environment that nurtures creativity through unconventional methods. Only then will these children adjust and respond to normal schooling. Dwelling on the *causes* of LD will be non-productive as researchers are nowhere to the truth of knowing what causes learning disabilities. But, from the child's point of view, it is important to find exciting ways and means to get the right kind of help to snap your child out of the LD prognosis through a creatively structured programme.

Identifying LD

Problems manifested in core areas like language processing, muscle coordination, attention and visual perception affect a variety of skills, such as (a) academic skills: reading, writing, spelling and arithmetic, (b) language and speech skills: listening, talking and understanding, (c) motor-sensory integration skills: muscular coordination, balance, drawing, colouring and writing. When children manifest problems in more than one of these areas, the problem spreads to other areas of learning. Academic learning disabilities are diagnosed when there is a severe discrepancy between achievement and intellectual ability in one or more of the following areas:

- Oral expression (speech and talking)
- Listening comprehension
- Written expression
- Basic reading skills
- Reading comprehension
- Mathematics calculations
- Mathematics reasoning

Christine Gorman, author of *The New Science of Dyslexia*, published in *Time*, 8 September, 2003, says "You can spot the symptoms of this learning disability even before your child starts to read, if you know what to look for."

Ages 3 to 5

Does your preschooler...

1. Seem uninterested in playing games with language sounds such as repetition and rhyming?
2. Have trouble learning rhymes such as 'Humpty Dumpty' or 'Jack and Jill'?

3. Frequently mispronounces words and persists in using baby talk?
4. Fail to recognise the letters in his or her name?
5. Have difficulty remembering the names of letters in his or her name?

Ages 5 to 6

Does your kindergartner ...

1. Fail to recognise and write letters or write his or her name, or use invented spelling for words?
2. Have trouble breaking spoken words into syllables such as cowboy into *cow* and *boy*?
3. Still have trouble recognising words that rhyme such as *cat* and *bat*?
4. Fail to connect letters and sounds (ask your child: What does the letter *B* sound like?)
5. Fail to recognise phonemes (ask your child: What starts with the same sound as *cat, dog, man*, or *car*?)

Ages 6 to 7

Does your first-grader ...

1. Still have difficulty recognising and manipulating phonemes?
2. Fail to read common one-syllable words such as *mat* or *top*?
3. Make reading errors that suggest a failure to connect sounds and letters such as *big* for *goat*?
4. Fail to recognise common, irregularly spelled words such as *said, where* and *two*.
5. Complain about how hard reading is and refuse to do it?

Age 7 and older

Does your child ...

1. Mispronounce long or complicated words saying 'amulium' instead of 'aluminium'?

2. Confuse words that sound alike such as *tornado* for *volcano* or *lotion* for *ocean*?
3. Speak haltingly and overuse vague words such as *stuff* or *things*?
4. Have trouble memorising dates, names or telephone numbers?
5. Have trouble reading small, function words such as *that*, *an* and *in*?
6. Guess wildly when reading multi-syllabic words instead of sound them out?
7. Skip parts of words reading 'conible' instead of *convertible*, for example?
8. When reading aloud often substitute easy words for hard ones such as *car* for *automobile*?
9. Spell terribly and have messy handwriting?
10. Have trouble completing homework or finishing tests on time?
11. Have a deep fear of reading aloud?

To determine that a child has a learning disability, it is necessary to administer at least two basic tests: the IQ test and the achievement test which is an academic test: reading, writing and/or arithmetic. Usually additional tests are required by a physician or neuro-psychologist to determine which specific areas are causing problems so that home and school could closely work in mainstreaming the child.

Don't Panic

There is hope. Your child will cope. So don't give up in despair. Many children manifest specific learning disabilities.

> Many of us suffer from partial dysfunction of some kind. But we learn to cope. Some of us who can't remember roads while driving, learn to memorise landmarks along the way.

Dyslexia is a term used for a child having severe reading problems. *Dysgraphia* is used for those with writing problems (children writing the letters of the alphabet in reverse form). *Dyscalcula* denotes those with math problems. Look at us. Don't most of us show some traces of 'dysfunction' at some point? Of course, we do.

Many adults who find it hard to remember the names of vegetables, spices, pulses, farm products, etc. at the grocery store carry a 'shopping list'. Those who find math difficult may simply conclude that the 'economical pack' is a money saver without actually calculating the difference in price. Those who are slow readers will look for symbols or pictures on the labels. We, as grownups have learnt to 'get along'. We have mastered ways to compensate for our specific disabilities. So, our children will also in due time, provided parents and teachers *patiently* respond by inspiring hope and trust in the child at an early age. Unfortunately, neglect, indifference or plain ignorance, on the part of the parents (competing in the rat race) and educators (burdened with large numbers of students) have magnified the problem. There is hope! Early educational intervention through a tightly structured activity-related preschool programme can benefit children even with *severe* learning disabilities to enjoy academic and social success in schools and colleges as they grow up.

WAYS TO PRE-EMPT LD

Emotional Brain versus Intelligent Brain

When Rakesh Suri, a thirteen-year-old, and his mother, Ritu attended the school PTA meeting, they met several subject teachers who were teaching Rakesh. The language teacher told Ritu that Rakesh was hyperactive. "He never sits in one place, plays the fool all the time, disturbs the class with his pranks. He is naughty and fights with the children. He gets very poor marks." The science and math teachers had identical complaints, and suggested home tuition to cope with the class-work. The games teacher told Ritu that he was a talented lad who needed to be coached and guided in swimming and basketball. The music teacher told her that Rakesh should be regular for concert practice as "he sings and acts very well". On the way home, and for the rest of that week, Rakesh was scolded day after day for not studying. All his extra-curricular activities were stopped: swimming, basketball, singing, dramatics and watching television. Two tutors were hired to coach Rakesh with his weak subjects.

Actually, Ritu and the teachers needed to know a little more about the functioning of Rakesh's brain before they concluded their judgements. By laying emphasis on the functioning of the cerebral brain, without taking into consideration the dominant role played by the emotional brain, was being a little short-sighted. Feelings play a very important part in our decision making. Feelings override the intellect almost every time. The intellect comes to naught when emotions hold sway. By cutting off the extra-curricular activities in which Rakesh excelled was an inappropriate act since the *emotional brain* found pleasure in those activities, and stimulated a flow of juices which ignited the *thinking brain* to participate in those very activities. By shutting off the juices, the flow of stimulation also was shut off. Rakesh, in due time, to keep the juices flowing, would adopt skills to sneak out, outwit and cheat on his teachers and parents so that he continued doing those acts that brought him pleasure.

Functions of the Right and Left Brain

Research conducted by neuro-psychologists indicate that the brain is divided into two hemispheres, the right side and the left side. The right hemisphere controls the movements of the body's left side, and the left hemisphere controls movements on the right. Research further indicates that each hemisphere specialises in different functions, processes different kinds of information, and deals with different kinds of problems. It has been pointed out that in the left hemisphere the logical thinking processes are found. The mode of operation of the left hemisphere is linear; that means it processes information sequentially, one bit after another, in an ordered way. Perhaps the most obvious linear faculty is language. In short, the left side controls reading, writing, logic and reason. In sharp contrast, the right hemisphere is specialised for simultaneous processing; that is, it operates in a more holistic, relational way. And, its most obvious faculty is comprehension of visual images. The right side controls the recognition of faces, creativity and rhythm. (The right hemisphere of the brain instantly recognises a face but the left hemisphere is slow in coming up with the name to that face.) The left deals with parts and specifics, the right

UNSTIMULATED BRAIN		STIMULATED BRAIN	
	Fewer neural pathways to develop thought		A rich network of neural pathways to permit complex thinking

deals with wholes and relationships among the parts. The left deals with analysis, which means to break apart logically; the right with synthesis, which means to put together. The left is time-bound, which means it has a sense of time. The right is time-free, meaning it might lose the sense of time altogether.

Unfortunately for Rakesh, neither his teachers who had computed his overall performance, nor his parents had the faintest idea that the boy's right hemisphere was more adept and alert than the left. For some reason the circuitry or neural pathways connecting the right side with the left side were not fully ignited. In this case, the brain's right hemisphere on being stimulated by positive messages, responded to swimming, basketball, music and drama, which made Rakesh an accomplished performer. As for the brain's left hemisphere, without positive stimulation, it *slept* through the language, math, and science classes.

Igniting the Brain

Parents and teachers could use the emotional brain to kick-start the cerebral brain into action. Through the use of innovative teaching methods, the right side of the brain could stimulate its circuitry to get the left side of the brain to respond, and vice versa. To achieve this, the emotional brain's involvement is essential. The student will first have to (emotionally) *like* doing something before (cerebrally) *wanting* to do it. If only classroom subjects, like language, maths, science, etc., could be made exciting for the emotional brain to *like* it, then the cerebral brain will be stimulated to *want* to do it.

Isn't it a fact that some people's right hand and leg is stronger than the left hand and leg? And, some people's left limbs are stronger than the right limbs; and the right eye vision is sharper than the left eye, and vice versa. Very rarely do people have both, right and left, limbs function with equal strength or dexterity. So also, an individual's right lobe of the brain is more alert than the left lobe. Sportspersons, who are highly motivated, commit themselves to rigorous practice sessions, using novel techniques and methods, over several months and years, to achieve dexterity over both limbs, right and left. Through strenuous practice some sportspersons literally shift the strength from the left limbs on to the right limbs, and vice versa. So, with constant and persistent application, over several months and years, we can gain mastery over our organs, and get them to function with equal dexterity. The magic words are 'motivation' and 'novel techniques'. Parents and teachers at preschool and primary school must constantly challenge themselves to be innovative, creative, flexible and spontaneous so that whatever they teach comes alive for the children. How children love to relate to what excites them! If teaching becomes a cluster of exciting games, children will definitely respond to what is taught. Our children need not grow up to be *half brained* where one half of their brain is developed and the other half remains underdeveloped.

> *Indeed, it is possible to enhance the functions of the right hemisphere and the left hemisphere to somewhat equal dexterity.*

Good with Numbers but Poor at Maths

You may recall a familiar case of a child who vividly remembered cricket scores and batting averages of his favourite batsman, in the exact years and the stadiums played in. And, that same child had trouble memorising, say seven times table. The child could compute and recall cricket scores with quick accuracy, but was unable to compute a simple math tables. Whenever an activity stimulates pleasure signals, the emotional brain sends out positive messages that are received by both hemispheres of the brain, and they rev up with excitement. But if that same activity were to stimulate stress or strain signals, the brain would sleep through those messages. So, when the cricket match is on, the left side of the brain which controls language, logic, numbers and math, gets saturated with the positive juices sent from the emotional brain, and sits up alert. And when it comes to memorising a tedious poem, or a maths table, the same left side falls asleep.

Stimulate the 'Sleeping' Brain

Let us look at the functioning of the brain's right side and left side from the parenting point of view. The child likes to watch television. The emotional brain creates a craving to watch the TV show. The right side of the brain is alerted and reminds the child to switch on the television to watch the cricket match. Then his favourite batsman comes to the crease to bat. The emotional brain switches to overdrive mode. With lightning speed, messages are relayed to billions of centres in the brain and the central nervous system, and juices are secreted which excite and stimulate the whole body. A tiny drop of adrenaline, for example, in the bloodstream makes the heart beat faster, as the breathing gets shallow, while the eyes get dilated, and large muscles get toned and firm. Oh, there is so much excitement in the entire body system; it is party time! Simultaneously, these positive messages of excitement are carried back and forth by the circuitry (neural pathways) to the right and left lobes of the brain.

If the left lobe is sleepy or lethargic, the excitement causes it to sit up alert, and join the party. After all that excitement, if the left lobe still doesn't join the party, then the right lobe takes over the functions of the left lobe. It begins to register numbers and comprehend configurations and passes on the tabulations to the recesses of the memory zone. Hence the child, at will, can recall from his memory bank, not only the favourite batsman's varied scores, but also, he is able to recall scores of previous years, as well as places where the games were played. Indeed, the emotional brain activates the two lobes of the neo-cortex brain to either collaborate together, or to function single-handedly; and in doing so, it triggers an amazing feat of tabulating numerical configurations for the child.

To compute the cricket scores, both sides of the brain, the left lobe and the right lobe may have to work in sync with each other. The emotional brain, through its excitement, stimulates such juices, which bring about a *flow* of affinity in the entire body system, including in the 'sleepy' left side of the brain. The same applies to music, dance, drama, art, craft, clay modelling, pottery, drawing, and painting where the positive messages cause a *sublime flow* in the neural pathways which stimulate the sleepy left lobe of the brain and activate it to assimilate and disseminate new data. I'm convinced that *children with learning disabilities can overcome their handicaps through intense stimulation of the emotional brain*. Once the child likes and enjoys doing those actions, he will desire and want to repeat the actions because they give him pleasure. His left cerebral lobe, which controls logic, maths, language, analysis, will automatically respond to the pleasure stimuli, and like any normal student, he will begin to respond to class-work.

Therapy for Brain Stimulation

We know that the most motivated sportspersons train tirelessly, over several months and years, to develop stamina, strength, dexterity and mastery of their skills. So should all the children be exposed, from infancy itself, to music, song, games, art, painting, role-play, etc., over several months and years, so that the right brain will function in consonance with the left brain. Such a curriculum of fun-filled activities will pre-empt learning disabilities. Restless and distracted children, labelled as *hyperactive*, will settle down to perform classroom duties as other normal children do. Children, who read, speak, write and memorise tables with tedious difficulty, labelled as *slow learners*, will gradually respond as normal children.

Remember, someone being teased 'muscle brained'? Take the cue and exercise the brain like a muscle. Muscles need constant exercises to stay well toned. Since so little is known about the brain, there is so little awareness about its maintenance. If muscles are not regularly exercised, they become slack. To keep the brain in excellent shape and to keep the neural pathways (wiring) which keep the brain centres connected at peak performance levels, maintenance is a must. The right kind of mental exercises and the right kind of foods are essential. Keeping the dreaded Alzheimer's disease at bay is motivation enough to pay attention to brain maintenance. Memory drills, brain-teasers, scrabble, chess, jigsaw puzzles, and learning to play the violin, or some other musical instrument will help. Foods rich in antioxidants, omega-3 fatty acids (cod liver oil, walnut), and low fat foods will assist in keeping the brain young and sharp for years to come.

Enhance Your Brain Power

In a recent study conducted by Dr Arne May and colleagues at the University of Regensburg in Germany, people who spent three months learning to juggle showed enlargement of certain areas in the cerebral cortex (the thin sheet of nerve cells on the brain's surface where most higher thought processes take place). They were then asked to quit juggling completely, and three months later the enlarged areas of the cortex had started to shrink.

A similar study conducted in London in the year 2000, corroborates this research. Every Sunday morning, for two years, apprentice cabbies would ride their bicycles, balancing the London roadmap on their handlebars, to familiarise themselves of London's bylanes and winding streets. The study found a change in the shape of the cabbies hippocampus, the brain module where new memories of places are stored. The MRI scans of jugglers and cabbies showed an enlargement of the grey matter (the brain areas rich in neurons), as opposed to the white matter (the circuitry that connects neurons). There is hope for students who give up easily. With consistent effort at studies, over a period of time, they can enhance their intelligence quotient.

Nurturing Intelligence

Studies conducted by a team of Norwegian and American scientists and published in the *Acta Paediatrica* (March 2002), point out that babies, particularly those weighing less than six pounds (13 kg), can grow into smart, intelligent kids if breastfed exclusively for six months. Researchers point out that infants who received only breastmilk for the first six months of life, scored an average of eleven points higher on IQ tests at age five than infants who received formula and solid food in addition to breastmilk. The findings also refute the notion that small babies will grow faster if they receive some formula and solid food from early on.

Music Intelligence

Experts who study cognitive development believe that music literally leaves its mark on the brain at all ages. Listening to music can affect a child's reasoning and thinking skills. It has been demonstrated in several studies that while listening to many forms of music is beneficial, *classical music in particular* has an even greater effect because the complex structures of certain pieces of music stimulate the complex structure of the brain, encouraging both hemispheres to work in consonance. Scientists who found that music affects spatial reasoning—the ability to see relationships among objects, believe that music ignites and strengthens many neural pathways in the neo-cortex (the higher brain centres where spatial reasoning takes place), thereby enhancing intelligence. The more classical music children are exposed to in their early years the greater the integrated balance they will experience throughout their lives. It can affect test scores, raise energy levels, improve reading and writing skills, aid in learning and retaining new material, promote coordinated body movement, and take creativity to a higher level.

The Mozart Effect

As reported by T.V. Sairam in *Alive,* March 2004, Alfred Tomatis, a French physician, who spent almost five decades studying the healing and creative effects of music, conducted clinical studies on over 100,000 patients, particularly with listening inability, vocal and auditory handicaps, as well as, learning deficiencies. He confirmed what is called the *Mozart Effect.* Wolfgang Amadeus Mozart's sonatas and concertos were found to have a healing effect in innumerable experiments conducted by his team around the globe. Tomatis found that

> *Listening to complex, non-repetitive music like that of Mozart, stimulates neural pathways, which are essential for the process of thinking, says FRANCES RAUSCHER.*

regardless of one's taste or previous exposure to Mozart, his music calmed the listeners, improved spatial perception and enabled them to express themselves lucidly. Spatial intelligence, which is crucial in higher brain functions like chess, mathematics and music, is the ability to see the visual world accurately, to form mental images of the physical objects and to recognise variations in objects. Clinical study points out that listening to *Mozart* increases spatial scores of high school and college-level students on IQ tests. In another study conducted by Frances Rauscher, it was also found that the spatial reasoning performance of nineteen kindergarten children—who received eight months of music lessons—far exceeded that of fifteen others, who were never given any music lessons.

Music has been put to therapeutic use from the dawn of civilisation. Ancient civilisations make mention of musicians playing instruments and singing ballads to soothe the nerves of agitated kings and nobles. In India, from time immemorial, different *raags* were used to bring relief to mind-related problems. Some of the *raags* used are: *Raag Durbari Kannad* to cure headaches, while *Raag Khamaj* and *Raag Kafi* to correct sleep disorders, and *Raag Bhim Palasi* is recommended to those suffering from anxiety and hypertension. A bus station in one of the cities in the USA was identified as a crime-prone area. The local authorities introduced soft music through a PA system at the bus station and the crime rate dropped. If music be the food for intelligence and therapy, and has the power to tame anger, rage and hatred then parents and teachers should introduce piped-in classical music (of joyful cadences) in homes, in vehicles, and also in recreational areas, and in hobby classes at school.

St. Ignatius of Loyola, founder of the Jesuit Order, had once advised his community of Jesuits, "To win over someone to your point of view, you will first enter through *his* door and then come out through *your* door." To win over children,

> *Before the child is taught anything, the first lesson we grownups have to learn is to make the child to like us and trust us.*

parents and teachers will first have to knock on the children's doors that open to their personal feelings. It is essential to stimulate positive messages in the child's mind through affection and encouragement. So, touch the child's emotions by introducing activities that appeal to his feelings and to his right cerebral lobe—activities that the child responds to naturally. Activities like music, rhymes, song, dance, drawing, painting, clay modelling, role-play, dramatics, concerts, catch-ball, simple yoga, aerobics, hopping, skipping, jogging and numerous other fun-filled activities your teeming mind can think of. Through these activities the left cerebral lobe will get ignited and begin to relay signals and messages in consonance with all the brain 'centres' for positive responses.

Nursery and pre-primary schools in particular can play a very vital role in stemming the growth of LD in children. They could offer guidance and counselling to parents to enhance their realisation on three aspects of parenting: (1) *early childhood development;* (2) *positive parenting;* and (3) *family bonding.* Simultaneously, they should evolve a very vibrant curriculum to stimulate all the eight intelligences in children (*see* Chapter on *Underachievers* for details on 'Eight Intelligences').

At Our Play-School, we have received excellent reports from the parents of children who had passed out, over the years, as well as from teachers in primary, elementary and high schools on the impact our curriculum has had on children. Through our experience, spanning over twenty years, our students who are now young adults, have emerged emotionally balanced with good interpersonal skills, and leadership talents in many areas. They thoroughly enjoyed academics, did homework without fuss, excelled in aesthetics, participated successfully in competitive sports and games, are well mannered and nurture a deep concern for the environment and ecology. They love celebrating all the festivals and are very family-oriented.

LD can be pre-empted if dealt with at an early age; not

through panic or medication but through a programme of structured fun and games. The programme should start at home, from the time when children are infants. It should then extend over to the preschool, and from there carried to the pre-primary school. With about six years of exposure to such an action-packed, structured activity-based programme, the children would develop wholesome personalities. Parents and teachers must call for a wider awareness of LD, and treat this virus seriously. Children with physical or organic causes may require more than this development programme. They may require medical help alongside this programme to cope with the pressures of mainstream schooling.

Underachievers

The fault, dear Brutus, is not in our stars,
but in ourselves that we are underlings.

— WILLIAM SHAKESPEARE *(Julius Caesar)*

Viren Kathuria showed his mother his arithmetic test paper. Seeing his marks, she was upset.

Mother:	What, you've scored only fifty-eight per cent.
Viren:	But, Mom, I scored the highest in class.
Mother:	What do you mean 'highest'?
Viren:	That's what the teacher said.
Mother:	I don't believe you.
Viren:	Read her remark. She's written, 'Well done!'
Mother:	Are you sure, you got the highest (with pride in her voice) ?
Viren:	You could ask her.

Setting Achievement Standards

The *standards for success* against which a child judges his performance become important benchmarks of achievement behaviour. Some children have very low standards of success, and others have very high. A family I know has two children. Both children would react differently to their grades. The elder son, Neil would fret and mope with depression on getting an overall aggregate of about ninety-one per cent, blaming himself for committing careless errors as the reason for not doing well in *all* his test papers. The younger daughter, Rieta would score an aggregate of fifty per cent and congratulate herself for having done extremely well. Their reactions were so different because their standards of excellence were different. Neil was known for being a studious student, while Rieta, a live-wire, was known to be a family entertainer.

The social interactions of children with their parents, teachers, peers and siblings often determine the standards against which children judge themselves. According to Bandura and Kupers who have said in *Journal of Abnormal and Social Psychology*, "Children exposed to models who adopt lenient standards for their performance (e.g. models who reward themselves even for mediocre work) also tend to adopt lenient standards against which they judge their own behaviour. Children exposed to models who adopt stringent standards (e.g. models who reward themselves only for superlative work) also tend to adopt strict standards." In the case of Neil, his parents and grandparents talked of competitive application to attain high laurels and a huge success in life through studious academics. But in the case of their daughter, Rieta, since the time she was a toddler, the parents would glamorise and credit her for her qualities in socialising, housekeeping and being feminine. The family had struck an excellent balance on all fronts: they were highly qualified in specialised fields with successful careers, maintained a beautiful house, and were invited to all the elitist parties in town. Their lifestyle was talked about and aped by many in their social circle. To conclude, we can say that it is only natural for children to respond to whatever standards parents set and expect of them.

> *When parents set reasonably high standards for children's academic performance, the children will strive to attain those standards. If they set low academic standards, children will be satisfied with a mediocre performance.*

Underachieving Children

Underachievers are those children who do not work to their full potential set by the school. They simply fail to work as capably as they can. I once asked a psychologist who works in one of the city's popular schools, about underachievers, she said, "They don't seem to be making enough effort to master the concepts taught in class, or do their homework right, or on time; and their grades are always poor." But I've seen some of these children score pretty high in other tests of intelligence and ability, e.g. a child may have an in-depth knowledge of the mechanics of locomotives, or is an ace cricketer. (The world's *numero uno*, master-blaster, Sachin Tendulkar, is said, never to have scored as high in classroom tests as he scores in international cricket test matches.) The obvious discrepancy between ability (aptitude) tests and actual performance in school is the main criterion for categorising children as *underachievers*. When class-teachers along with the subject teachers identify a pattern of underachievement over several terms, such children are then referred to special classes, or given some type of remedial help. In some severe cases, a child is failed and made to repeat the entire year.

Naveen was eleven-years old and had to repeat his class. His parents brought him to meet me to be counselled. Instead, I settled him in another room and discussed his situation with his parents alone. While the mother seemed tired of the kid, the father blamed the mother for negative upbringing. I asked them to start at the very beginning of the 'break down'. As far as they could remember, for the past three years, the headmistress and the subject teachers would call them in and pull them up. Finally, a year ago, they accepted the class teacher's recommendation to have Naveen undergo an intelligence test by a psychologist, who was attached to the school. After spending Rs 12000.00/- for four sessions which included two psychological tests: the IQ test and the aptitude test, the child was certified a 'slow learner.' The parents gave a copy of the certificate and the test papers to the headmistress. The certificate vindicated the school's stand: that the teachers had done their best and there was little or no hope for Naveen. The parents, too, felt justified on giving up on him since he now carried the certification of a slow learner. School and home concluded that it was useless to 'push' Naveen any more, since he lacked the IQ and the academic aptitude. Ten months later, his grades were far worse than ever, and he was detained for the whole year with a warning that if he didn't improve his grades, he would be dismissed from school. And, that's when they met me.

The Causes

How did Naveen get to be a loser? How do children become underachievers? Either the home environment or the school environment, or both are to be blamed. If you look at the home environment of underachievers, you will find that many such children have poor parent-child relationship. For example, their parents may not be happy with themselves as spouses, may show high levels of anxiety when parenting, treat them inconsistently, fail to encourage them to be independent, fail to inculcate structure in their upbringing, and may themselves not be models of achievement. According to Burton L. White and Jean Carew Watts, who studied the role of mothers whose children lagged behind in schools, reported that "some of the mothers were depressed, disorganised, and listless. They seemed to have stopped trying to provide adequate stimulation for their children. Others were overprotective, constantly interfering with their children's natural curiosity and independence. Still others were more interested in housekeeping than in their children's activities, and consequently ignored their toddlers most of the time." On the school front, for example, the teachers could be harsh and rude, quick to punish but slow to praise, bad communicators, incompetent, biased, or just plain vindictive. So, the child either feels victimised or is simply bored in class. A single negative environment is bad enough, but if both environments, home and school, are negative, then what chances does the poor kid have other than being doomed to be an underachiever?

Dissecting Naveen's Upbringing

In the case of Naveen, his father, Praveen took no

responsibility to guide his son in his studies, or discipline him. That was the mother's job, he said. Pushpa, the mother would grumble about the total lack of support from her husband regarding the upbringing of the child. She was at a total loss on how to control the child. How she wished she had a daughter instead of a son! To release her tension, she would get on the phone and talk to her friends, discussing (sometimes in front of the child) how badly he did in school, how disobedient he had become, and how bad his teachers were. Whenever Pushpa put strictures on the kid, Praveen would lose his temper at her saying that either she should, "limit the strictures to the time I'm in office, or relax the rules when I come home." After a hard day's work he wanted to enjoy the company of his son—not be a 'Hitler' in the house. Naveen was his father's pet according to Pushpa. But according to Praveen, the child was scared of the mother who was constantly breathing down his back, and the poor kid only had him whom he could 'relate' to. The father denied Naveen nothing, and the eleven-year-old knew in his bones, he would never starve nor would he need to seek a job in his lifetime since his father owned three huge factories from where the money kept rolling in. Praveen proudly said that he didn't care much for degrees since he didn't have one himself, while degree-holders were in his 'pocket', slaving for him. Actually, it was a relief to both parents when the psychologist had diagnosed Naveen to be a slow learner because they didn't have to 'push or pressure' him to study any more. But they were upset and angry with the 'school people' for giving them an ultimatum to withdraw their child from school. They felt no remorse for the child, but ashamed on how to tell their friends about the impending dismissal since the school was the city's leading institution for the 'who's who' crowd.

It was obvious that the home environment was absolutely vitiated with misplaced values. Naveen had become a master manipulator, and he was using his intelligence to control his environment. I knew the child could grow up to be an achiever, provided he was cut off entirely from the home environment. I told the parents to take advantage of the 'ultimatum' and right away admit Naveen into a boarding school, far from home (away from relatives and friends)—in one of the hill stations. I explained to them that it was better for Naveen to repeat a year in a new environment than to repeat a year in his current class. After all, repeaters and failures, whose self-esteem has been shredded, rarely top the class. Once the parents accepted the idea, I then spoke to Naveen and sought his views on a one-to-one basis, giving him inputs to build his pride. Thereafter, he visited me twice again, and at the end of that session we made a pact: he would bring me his reports and work-books whenever he'd come home for holidays from the hills. Climbing uphill those five to six seasons was very tough for Naveen as he transformed from being procrastinator into an achiever. It was heartening to see the seventeen-year-old Naveen score about seventy-seven per cent in his final Board exam.

Why the Stress on Academics?

The foundations of our education system are Western. The foundations of Western learning are primarily Greek and Roman—fashioned by the teachings of the great Western philosophers and thinkers— Socrates, Plato, Aristotle and Cicero. The emphasis was on language, logic, and reason, the chief functions of the left cerebral brain. Had the foundations of learning been established on the philosophy of Buddha, Mahavir, Jesus and other Eastern philosophers and thinkers, the emphasis would have been on caring, nurturing, meditation—the function of the right cerebral brain. But, since the times of the Greek masters to the present day, education primarily focuses on linguistic intelligence and on mathematical-logical intelligence. These two levels of intelligences came to be fixed as measures of all intelligences. Schools and universities built their curriculum of academics around the development of two fixed intelligences. Through tests and examinations, a student's mastery over these subjects was deemed as possessing superior cerebral development compared to the students who either scraped through or flunked in the subjects. The famous IQ tests still measure intelligence quotients based on logic, reason and language.

But mounting evidence through clinical studies,

experiments and research on the human brain has forever shattered the myth of fixed intelligences. According to authors, Colin Rose and Gordon Dryden, in *Learning Fundamentals,* we are not born with a single fixed intelligence quotient or IQ. The human brain has the potential to develop at least eight different 'intelligences', such as:

(1) **Linguistic intelligence**
They are the ability to read, speak and write well. This ability was highly developed in people like Radhkrishnan, Nehru, Churchill, and Kennedy. In today's context you can credit linguistic intelligence to Arundhati Roy, Bill Clinton.

(2) **Mathematical-Logical intelligence**
The ability to reason, calculate and think logically. This ability is highly developed in economists, scientists, engineers, lawyers and accountants.

(3) **Visual-Spatial intelligence**
The ability to paint, draw, take imaginative photographs, create sculptures, or to visualise three-dimensional space. This ability is highly developed in navigators, architects, and also in artists such as Michelangelo, Picasso and Anjolie Ela Menon.

(4) **Musical intelligence**
The ability to compose songs, sing, play musical instruments, create poetry, use rhyme and rhythm.

(5) **Interpersonal (or 'social') intelligence**
The ability to relate to others; you will find this ability strong in salespeople, teachers, and natural leaders.

(6) **Intrapersonal (or 'reflective') intelligence**
The ability to focus on inner feelings, draw conclusions from experiences, and make plans. This ability is strong in people who meditate, and in psychotherapists.

(7) **Bodily-Physical intelligence**
The ability to use one's hands or body. You will find this ability strong in athletes, gymnasts, dancers and craftsmen.

(8) **Naturalist intelligence**
The ability to understand and be in tune with Nature. You will find this ability strong in ecologists, environmentalists and gardeners.

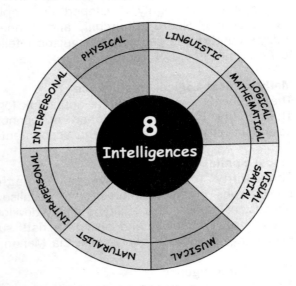

Overcoming the Problem

Till schools and colleges don't recognise the existence of eight intelligences, parents and teachers will have to help children master skills in overcoming the handicap in language, logic and reason. You will have to exercise patience to understand the root cause why underachievers are unable to cope with problems or academic material presented to them. Being restless, they divert to other activities. You've got to catch them young—when they're toddlers. If early childhood educators could identify children who either procrastinate or divert attention from one activity to another, then the problem could be nipped in the bud. Children who have difficulty in coping with classroom activities distract themselves from the task, begin to daydream, or disconnect themselves. On identifying these problems, teachers should on-the-spot creatively devise new teaching strategies to increase children's participation and initiative. The strategies could include: .

- Using creative and exciting games with small, easy tasks built into them to ensure that the children win frequently and in quick succession.
- Shower praises liberally with star ratings (star-stamps on their hands and arms) for task-related involvement and accomplishments.
- Encourage children frequently with enthusiastic confidence-building statements like, "How well you did that! I love you!"
- Through stories and game-related activities children are taught and encouraged to find solutions to problems, which will help to lay the foundations for learning in later years.

Our experience at *Our Play School* has shown that through creative activities and through personalised attention and care, even the most distracted and restless children quickly respond to performing and participating in everyday classroom activities.

Hyperactive Children (ADHD)

Human salvation lies in the hands of the creatively maladjusted.

— MARTIN LUTHER KING JR.

What is Hyperactivity?

Hyperactivity is commonly manifested in boys, and in some cases, as early as in those of two years and above. A *hyperactive* child is one who is highly excited, overly active, restless, distracted, and fidgety. More boys are prone to be hyperactive than girls. Hyperactive children are unable to sit in one spot quietly and concentrate on classwork. Restlessness, aggression, and distraction cause hyperactive children to develop a learning disability called Attention Deficit Hyperactivity Disorder (ADHD), which further compounds the problem.

Attention Deficit Hyperactivity Disorder (ADHD) and Attention Deficit Disorder (ADD) are clinical diagnosis for children whose behaviour is categorised into three segments:

hyperactive, impulsive and inattentive. A hyperactive child is always in motion and restless. The impulsive child is unable to control his immediate reactions, or think before he acts. The inattentive child has difficulty keeping his mind on a single task so he gets bored quickly.

What causes Hyperactivity?

Listed below are some factors mentioned by medical practitioners, scientists and psychologists engaged in studying ADHD.

Heredity is one of the main causes. Most hyperactive children have at least one close relative, usually the father, with a similar make-up. As a child, he was probably a late starter at school, found it hard to sit still, fidgeted a lot and was far from easy to live with. These characteristics in a parent create a difficult environment to grow up in and are often passed down to the child. The result is a complex mix of heredity and environment.

Environment could be the cause for hyperactivity. Children with no outdoor place to play may get restless. They will constantly be on the move inside the house. They play with 'movement' toys. They will imagine ordinary building blocks to be their motor cars or airplanes and invent games with them. Watching television day after day makes some children irritable and aggressive.

Temperamental differences make some children more active than others. Some children kick a lot in the uterus, run around as soon as they can walk, and want to keep active every minute of the day.

Brain injury, perhaps due to some complication during pregnancy or at the time of delivery, could be the reason why the child finds it hard to sit still or concentrate.

Brain dysfunction can make it hard for a child to relax. He may need an unusual amount of stimulation to arouse the central nervous system, so the child must keep moving in order to think clearly.

Eats and drinks also affect activity levels. Lead-based

paints, *if* used to paint toys, wall-interiors, furniture, etc. when ingested even at a minimal level, will make it impossible for a child to concentrate or think clearly. (Lead-based paints are banned in many countries). Physicians are of the opinion that artificial food colourings affect children's behaviour and school grades. According to them, colouring additives (carmoisine, ponceau 4R, tatrazine, sunset yellow), and preservative (sodium benzoate) used in children's foods and drinks make children hyperactive, restless and prone to tantrums. Vitamin deficiencies, especially the B vitamins, impair concentration. And, certain foods, such as, chocolate, sugar, and cola are known to affect restlessness in children. However, one particular research showed evidence that caffeine in coffee quietens down hyperactive children rather than exciting them.

While the exact cause of hyperactivity may not be known, a combination of some of these factors may explain why a child is hyperactive. But one thing is clear; poor parenting can cause behaviour problems; it does not cause hyperactivity, and most hyperactive children were destined to be that way from birth. However, the way you handle your child can make the problem better or worse.

Nearly all children carry mild strains of the hyperactive 'virus' in them, unless they are extremely quiet, controlled, submissive and compliant who fully concentrate on what they are doing. Listed below are some characteristics that a hyperactive child may display. Most children go through stages of difficult behaviour at some time and grow out of it. It may help parents whose children are underachievers in school to know that there is more than simple bad behaviour at the root of it. For those of you unfamiliar with ADHD, you may be guided by these typical symptoms.

Signs to Look for
Behaviour
+ Behaviour fluctuates from day to day.
+ Extremely disorganised and has difficulty in organising tasks or activities.

- Confuses left from right.
- Late in learning to tie shoe-laces, wears clothes back to front, messy eater, has difficulty in following two commands at once, or in the right order.
- Often engages in behaviour without any heed to the consequences.
- Frequent shifting from one unfinished activity to another.

Lack of Attention
- A poor listener, forgets instructions, lists or messages and is easily distracted from tasks.
- Daydreams and is inattentive.
- When reading, skips words, sentences or paragraphs.
- Makes careless mistakes in school-work, homework and other activities.
- Has difficulty in finishing chores/tasks.
- Often blurts out answers before questions are completed
- Is frequently forgetful.

Social
- Has difficulty in awaiting turn in games/group situations
- Has poor self-esteem and lacks confidence.
- Unable to make friends, butting into activities of others.
- Aggressive and picks up fights easily.
- Wants to mix as an equal but can't, and is often left out socially.
- A poor loser, speaks without thinking.
- Behaves badly to gain attention in a group.

Language Problems
- Often seems unaware of what is being said to him.
- Forgets what he is saying in the middle of the sentence.
- Interrupts others constantly.
- Talks excessively and incoherently.
- Gets confused over yesterday and tomorrow, earlier and later, and so on.

Overactive
- As infants: irritable, cry a lot, erratic sleep patterns.
- As toddlers: at school, fidgety, disruptive and distracted.
- Prefer outdoors; behaviour worsens in noisy, stressful situations, or in crowds.
- Difficulty in remaining seated.
- Often is 'on the go' or acts as if 'driven by a motor'.

Other Problems
- Clumsy and impulsive, also accident-prone.
- Specific learning problems like, reading, spelling, math.
- Finds it hard to settle at nights, and is a restless sleeper.
- Touchy, rarely satisfied, irritating yet very sensitive.
- Often losing things that are of essential use.

Coping with ADHD Children

According to Dr Russell Barkley, an internationally recognised authority on AHDH (as reported by Elaine Lerner) in *Parent Guide* magazine, June 2003; "Far too often we react to our children's behaviour, often on impulse without regard to the consequences and with no plan for what we are trying to achieve. Seeing a situation from a reactive frame of mind can somehow make things look hopeless. It is not what your child does, nor does to you that creates these problems for you, but instead it is your response. Take the initiative to change the way you react to your child and accept the responsibility to make the relationship happen in the way you want it to develop."

A lot of patience is required to work with ADHD children since they have a hard time learning from experience, whether that experience is positive or

> *When parents and teachers exercise sensitivity and understanding in working with hyperactive children to build their self-esteem, then only will they cope with their problems in a more positive way.*

negative. Being over-reactive and impulsive they are quite prone to developing a lowered self-esteem. A bruised self-esteem in turn develops traits of immaturity, interpersonal problems, conduct disorder, and poor impulse control leading to drug abuse, alcoholism, anti-social groupings and personality disorder in adulthood. Despite his tough exterior, deep down, the hyperactive child feels vulnerable and insecure. He may cover his insecurities through reckless behaviour, defiance or bullying.

One of the most important ways you can help a hyperactive child is to explain things with clarity since he has problems with concentration and listening. Before talking to him, turn off the television or radio and call out his name clearly. After you have his attention, make sure he looks you in the eye while you talk to him. Your instructions should be precise and simple; concentrate on what you are saying so that he understands your language. "Prioritise what is important and what is not important for you as well as for your child," says Barkley. "Don't get caught up in conflicts over trivial issues that cause you to win the battle and lose the war."

The hyperactive child is, by nature, very disorganised and needs a definite structure and routine. It becomes easier when parents have structure and routine in their lives and stay by it. Your child needs to know when it is time to get up, and what he will have for breakfast on the day he goes to school. If there will be multiple activities that day, he will need to know in advance, otherwise the many different activities following one upon another are likely to produce over-stimulation and thus disruption. It is important to absorb the child in household chores (as discussed at length in the Chapter on *Working Towards Happiness*). Giving him responsibilities and holding him accountable will give him a structure and a routine to make him feel useful and important. It is a sure way to enhance self-esteem.

It is very easy to lose patience with fidgety children who compulsively touch objects as they walk or run around the house, which frequently leads to a lot of breakage and mess. When they are shouted at, some get agitated and angry, while others who are sensitive may feel miserable and

> *When correcting, we must learn to keep our anger and frustration under control and deal with children in a calm manner. If we pounce at the child and shout at him, our behaviour too is hyperactive.*

victimised. In both cases the end result is shattered self-esteem. In a calm manner the child must be told firmly how unhappy you are, and at the same time to reinforce positive behaviour, you must praise him for the good acts and deeds he recently did.

It is mostly in schools that hyperactivity is identified. That is because these children find the 'school culture' restricting their movements. They have to sit in a fixed place for long periods of time. Also they have to complete assignments and pay attention to what the teachers are teaching; they find concentration most difficult to cope with. They find the school structure rigid and confining, hence they want to buck the system. Lack of concentration means that a hyperactive child has to invest twice the effort to achieve half the success of classmates. Being distracted, inattentive and disruptive, the teacher may simply write them off. Instead, the teachers should recognise the problem and address it appropriately. When parents and teachers *bond* together to exercise infinite patience and employ unconventional methods laced with love and understanding at home and at school, then in all probability, hyperactive children could settle down to the routine of doing normal class-work like normal children in due time (*see* Chapter on *Home-School Bonding*).

Cathi Cohen, a clinical social worker and group psychotherapist with extensive experience in working with ADHD children, advises parents on how to deal with ADHD children in her book, *Raise Your Child's Social IQ*. She says,

- "◆ *A multidimensional approach to your child's treatment is essential. While social skills training is a very important part of a therapy regime, it's not the only part.*
- ◆ *Medication may be necessary.*
- ◆ *It's important that you inform teachers of the skills you're working on with your child.*
- ◆ *Model the skills consistently at home.*
- ◆ *Undertake role-playing exercises regularly and provide continuous positive reinforcement and feedback.*

- *Chart progress. Give your child a reward when you see him demonstrate constructive social behaviour.*
- *Encourage your child to monitor closely his own behaviour to better understand the consequences of his behaviour.*
- *Do not have your child play sports that are too competitive for him to handle effectively.*
- *Stick to sports that are non-competitive.*
- *Encourage your child to spend time with easygoing playmates. ADHD kids tend to gravitate toward other ADHD kids, and this can mean chaos. Try to find more mellow playmates for your child.*
- *Repetition is the key. If it takes a non-ADHD child six times before he learns a new skill, it may take your ADHD child six hundred times."*

It is so obvious that raising children with ADHD puts an immense emotional strain on the family. Many parents hold back their tears of trepidation, as they painfully clutch at straws, working ways to cope with the burden of parenting an ADHD child, while many more are ignorant that the problem exists. Our country hasn't yet woken up to handle issues related to LD. In small pockets, mostly in the metros, a handful of non-government agencies (NGOs) are engaged in making parents aware of LD related problems in children and offer remedies by appointing specialised teachers to teach in schools, or through Yoga and meditation classes. Parents must search out schools, professionals, teachers and community resources to support, guide and encourage programmes designed to mainstream ADHD children.

Attention Deficit Disorder (ADD)

Every man has to seek in his own way to make his own self more noble and to realise his own true worth.

— ALBERT SCHWIETZER

Eight-year-old Uday Pathak's second trimester Report Card had comments by his subject teachers that read like this: 'Uday did not apply himself fully this term', and 'Uday has a lot of potential but he daydreams and wastes time', and again, 'He needs to focus more, and work harder in the final term'. Another comment said, 'Uday is forgetful and lazy; he distracts himself easily'. Through these comments, it is obvious that the teachers believe Uday is capable of better academic performance but is slipping due to his careless, slip-shod attitude. To the parents, such comments may seem innocuous and they may ignore them in the hope that the child will sooner or later overcome the bad phase. But comments like these should make the parents sit up.

Sometimes the missed symptoms are so severe that the child with ADD is labelled as 'forgetful and lazy' because his teachers assume he is purposely doing poor work.

What is Attention Deficit Disorder (ADD)?

ADD and ADHD are first cousins. In Attention Deficit Disorder (ADD) the child isn't hyperactive, in Attention Deficit Hyperactivity Disorder (ADHD) the child is hyperactive. Attention Deficit Disorder affects one in fifty boys and one in a hundred girls, but it can be easily missed if the child is bright enough to compensate for the disorder. The salient features of ADD are difficulty in concentrating, easily distracted from the present task, failure to pay attention, and poor functioning. In short, children lack the ability to prioritise, organise, and strategise.

Identifying ADD

You may run a random check to see if your child has ADD. Experts believe that children may have ADD if at least six of the following symptoms are manifested as shown in section A:

Section A

1. Avoids or dislikes school-work and homework that requires sustained mental effort.
2. Doesn't seem to listen when spoken to directly.
3. Fails to pay attention to details and makes careless mistakes.
4. Is easily distracted.
5. Has difficulty sustaining attention or staying focused on tasks or activities.
6. Loses materials necessary for tasks or activities (pens, pencils, cricket ball).
7. Is frequently forgetful.
8. Doesn't follow through on instructions or complete tasks or assignments.
9. Has difficulty in organising tasks and activities.

Section B
1. Did these problems start before the age of seven?
2. Have the symptoms been present for at least six months?
3. Does your child have trouble both at home and at school?
4. Was each symptom that you identified in your child present most of the time?
5. Do the symptoms cause him significant problems, like poor grades or missed assignments?

Your child may have ADD if he has manifested at least six out of the nine symptoms in Section A, and you answered yes to *all* the five questions in Section B.

IT NEED NOT BE ADD; CONSIDER OTHER ASPECTS

Daydreaming

Most children spend a lot of time daydreaming or instead of focusing on the subject being taught, they sit in class and visualise the football match they will play in the inter-school tournament after school hours. These are absolutely normal behaviours when the daydreaming is limited in amount and frequency. Only if the child is found to be constantly daydreaming or engaged in unfocused thought, ADD should be considered.

Sheer Boredom

An under-stimulating environment such as a tedious chapter explained monotonously by a dull teacher can put off even the most focused student. Under-stimulation can occur at home, as well as, at school. (When parents are at a loss as how to occupy children during the vacations, you can be certain that the children will have dull, monotonous vacations.) Many intelligent students appear to have ADD simply because they are under-stimulated in most situations. However, they would be able to concentrate well when they are intellectually challenged; the child with ADD would not.

Sleep Loss

Children who don't sleep well will naturally be sleepy at odd hours; they will have trouble concentrating and difficulty in paying attention. They may appear to be drowsy and dopey like a child with ADD. If the symptoms are due to sleep loss, the child will look tired and out of focus. Sleep loss is a major problem affecting people of all ages, rendering them unable to function at their peak potential (*see* Chapter on *Sleep, Your Health Tonic*).

Vision and Hearing Problems

All children with attention problems should be screened for vision and hearing problems because they are a common cause for 'inattention' and are often present before the age of seven. In this instance the actual cause of inattention is the failure to pick up clues from the environment, and not as a result of difficulties with concentration.

Param's parents would regularly scold her for being inattentive in class. But, unknown to them, Param was nearsighted. From her desk where she sat in class, she was unable to see what was written on the blackboard. So the notes and assignments the teachers wrote on the blackboard went unnoticed by Param. In another case, Soumiya was a partially deaf girl, who sat in the far left corner in the class. Most of what the teachers taught or explained in class went past Soumiya, since she was unable to hear well. Both, Param and Soumiya were unable to measure up to their class-work and homework. Their handicaps led to missed assignments, 'forgotten' instructions, and other symptoms mimicking ADD.

Other kinds of eye problems should also be taken into consideration if your child is a slow learner, and should be evaluated for vision-related learning *difficulties*, suggest eye specialists. To rule out LD, get an expert's opinion, if your child

- Avoids reading—gets tired, or in some cases, gets headaches or double vision. This is often caused by focus disorder, or problems with eye teaming.

- Loses place while reading or uses finger to follow. Omits, inserts, or rereads words. Poor control of eye movements brings on this result.
- Writes slowly or sloppily, or doesn't complete written assignments. This can be the result of poor eye-hand coordination.
- Confuses words, poor word recognition or spelling, reverses letters (dyslexia), poor reading comprehension. This is often the result of poor visualisation.

Tips to Overcome ADD

Since ADD is manifested in children's behaviour, parents and teachers will have to *jointly* support 'behaviour therapy' techniques to tackle the child's specific area of dysfunction. For example, if the child is doing poorly in science because she doesn't do her homework on time, *behaviour therapy* (with the teacher's support in school) would focus on techniques needed to get her to copy from the blackboard the science assignment and put the science book in the bag so that the science book gets home. During the study hour at home (with parent's support), she completes the science homework and the science book is put in the school bag so that it gets to school the next day.

Although each behaviour therapy programme will have a variety, all successful programmes will be designed to fulfil three needs: increase structure, decrease distractions and improve organisation.

Increase Structure

Children need a structure or a set routine around which the same actions are repeatedly performed in a gradual manner so that a child with ADD can automatically perform those same set of actions again and again in the same sequence. When those 'set actions' are performed repeatedly at set times, the child's response to those actions form a pattern and become automatic. Actions become 'automatic' when the child begins and completes a set of specific actions successfully, since the individual steps have not to be remembered anymore while performing those actions.

A Mother's Determination

Six-year-old Alex, before going to bed every night, goes to the bathroom, climbs on a footstool near the pot and pees in it, then flushes the pot. He then moves the footstool in front of the mirror-cabinet, opens it, reaches for the toothbrush and toothpaste and brushes his teeth. He wipes his face and hands on the towel, puts off the bathroom light, then softly shuts the bathroom door and gets into bed. The moment it's bedtime, Alex's response every night has become habitual. He follows the same actions in that set pattern automatically without having to remember the steps involved. To turn a daily routine into a 'set action pattern', Alex's mother would have practised the same routine repeatedly with him for a number of days or weeks until he could do it on his own. She had patiently and distinctly repeated, repeated, and repeated the same lessons again and again and then got Alex to repeat and repeat the same lessons again and again, verbally and physically, until they became automatic. For a couple of weeks after that she had let him do the 'bathroom' routine on his own, but closely supervised his actions. Thereafter, she gently reinforced the 'bathroom' reminders at the time she'd come to read to him in bed and kiss him goodnight, "You smell 'minty' and sweet tonight."

Decrease Distractions

A child with ADD is unable to filter out external stimuli. Alex's mother was fully aware that any extraneous sounds would distract Alex while studying, hence she would make sure that no one put on the television in the next room while he did his homework. She had stopped her elder daughter from working the popcorn machine since she loved to munch on popcorn, even though she studied in another room. The smell of popcorn would have distracted Alex, making it impossible for him to concentrate on his homework. She had appointed a quiet isolated place in the house for Alex to work, where the light was good and walls were blank, free of pictures and posters (see Chapter on *Learning to Learn—At Home*). Alex's mother had talked to the teacher in school and got her support. Whenever he was to write a test in class, he was given a special area (the back corner of the classroom) that was free of distractions from other students, and away from windows. But when lessons were taught, Alex was made to sit in the front row, close to the teacher, to decrease the number of potential distractions within his visual range.

Improve Organisation

A child with ADD is unable to perform ordinary day-to-day functions on his own, and lacks the ability to organise, prioritise and strategise. Some commonplace chores which we take for granted and consider easy-to-do could be very trying and frustrating to a child with ADD, for example, Alex's mother got him a school bag with a number of pockets and compartments to it. She stuck coloured labels on each compartment of the school bag. A blue label said, TAKE TO SCHOOL. In this compartment Alex put his books which he had to take to school after he finished his homework. The red labelled compartment said, HOMEWORK: Alex learnt to put books in which he had assignments and homework. Another label in yellow said, HOME-SCHOOL. In this compartment he placed textbooks and notebooks according to the day's timetable. The purple pocket had his tiffin-box. In the green pocket he kept his pencil-box. Inside the pencil-box there were tiny coloured stickers with markings in slots for pencils, eraser, ball pen, pencil-sharpener. Likewise, Alex's mother placed large coloured labels with coloured drawings in his room so Alex knew where to keep his toys (outdoor toys were separated from indoor toys), books, clothes, shoes, slippers, socks, as well as, soiled linen and soiled clothing. Since all the areas were labelled, Alex had no difficulty in staying organised and keeping his room tidy.

Training Alex to stay structured, focused and organised was as tough as learning to bicycle on an uphill terrain. Instead of reeling off the order in which he should do the tasks, Alex's mother would get him to describe the steps required to pack his school bag, keep his room clean, set the dinner table, or get ready for bed. Similarly, with his studies, she would encourage Alex to 'see the steps' involved with a lot of patience. Once he began to 'see' that everything has its own method to accomplish it, it became easier for him to break large complicated tasks into manageable units and organise them separately.

Children with ADD need large dollops of love and attention to master the skills that come easy to normal children. Providing Alex with extra patience, love and attention helped him to regain his self-esteem, besides adding to his sense of safety and security.

SECTION $\boxed{5}$

TWEENS AND TEENS

Part 1

Teenagers Learn What They Live

If teenagers live with pressure, they learn to be stressed.

If teenagers live with rejection, they learn to give up.

If teenagers live with too many rules, they learn to get around them.

If teenagers live with too few rules, they learn to ignore the needs of others.

If teenagers live with broken promises, they learn to be disappointed.

If teenagers live with respect, they learn to honour others.

If teenagers live with trust, they learn to tell the truth.

If teenagers live with openness, they learn to discover themselves.

If teenagers live with natural consequences, they learn to be accountable.

If teenagers live with responsibility, they learn to be self-reliant.

If teenagers live with healthy habits, they learn to be kind to their bodies.

If teenagers live with support, they learn to feel good about themselves.

If teenagers live with creativity, they learn to share who they are.

If teenagers live with caring attention, they learn how to love.

If teenagers live with positive expectations, they learn to help build a better world.

— DOROTHY LAW NOLTE and RACHEL HARRIS

Teenagers:
Face of the Future

"*How much do our school children really know about democracy, civic conduct or political responsibility? An all-India survey sponsored by the National Council of Science & Technology Communication (NCSTC) of over 50,000 high school children from 229 districts in 16 states revealed that teenagers, most of whom studied in government schools, were concerned not only about the future of the nation but also their role in shaping it... Over 90 per cent of the respondents recorded their appreciation for being given a chance to express their views on issues concerning the nation. Nearly 80 per cent of the respondents provided highly constructive suggestions for improving governance and reconstructing the nation... an overwhelming 75 per cent of the respondents preferred development of villages so that they could continue to live there rather than migrate to alien towns to work as wage labour, (and) over 90 per cent of the respondents were highly aware of the political responsibility of voting for the right candidates.*"

—ADITI KAPOOR
(Times of India)

Pay-back Time

When toddlers grow up to be adolescents, it is pay-back time for parents. They get back what they had invested in their children. In the first five years of the individual's life, the *die* that got cast and formed the mould will govern the stimuli and responses for the rest of the individual's life. All the accumulated data in the brain cells, since the time of infancy, now fructifies. In other words, behaviour and actions of teenagers are governed by the data stored in their brain cells from the time they were born. Jean Piaget is perhaps the most famous psychologist today in the field of child development. According to Piaget, between eleven and twelve years of age, children reach the most advanced level of thinking; they can think logically using abstract propositions. Teenagers use logic and reason to back their actions and behaviour. When teens use their faculty of reason, they open millions of doors in their brain cells, unlocking volumes of data stored since childhood. If the data stored is positive you have positive teenagers, and when the data stored is negative, you have problem children on your hands. When spouses put aside their personal egos and back each other (errors and all) in areas of child-upbringing, then their acts of consistency would have paid off since their teenagers live up to their expectations. "God made man in His own image and likeness," says the Bible (*Book of Genesis*). It's probably true that parents make children in their own image and likeness.

Encourage Teens to be Frank and Open

I'm a firm believer in children and in the youth. When I interact with them, I am amazed at the way they think and talk—with so much clarity and a sense of purpose. In my workshops, I have asked them time and again, about the meaning of life, the purpose in life, about fulfilling a mission in life, ethics, values and all. I've found teens to be very open; they open their books of life, ready to discuss and talk about why they do what they do, with no holds barred. The same discussion with adults brings on duplicity; they get guarded when discussing their beliefs and actions. They want others to have a good opinion of them so they lie; but not the youth. A couple once told me of the workshop they attended on 'Marital Relationships'. The instructor gave a questionnaire which had to be completed separately by the wives and husbands. It so appeared when the scores were tallied, out of the eight couples, six seemed a perfect match for each other, while two couples had problems. Three years later, the two 'problem couples' were still hanging on to their marriage vows, while the perfect ones had broken up and moved on. Adults, perhaps, lie because they are caught up with their image in society and what others think of them. The youth, on the other hand, express their beliefs and actions like the way they live it. And, I've found they talk coherently, as well as listen intently.

I recall an instance when I was invited to address high school students studying in an Embassy school in New Delhi. The school had students of many nationalities, including Indians. When I was ushered into the 'administrative lobby', I was politely asked by a senior staffer who welcomed me, what topic I had chosen to speak on. I told the kind lady the topic would emerge through the discourse with the students. She blanched, then blinked a couple of times and softly excused herself. A moment later, she returned with another lady and introduced her as the principal. The principal asked me the topic of my lecture. I repeated my earlier answer. She covered her impatience with a warning shot that two guest speakers on previous occasions were booed out by the students. With a smile, I assured her that she had nothing to fear, and with a strained smile she told me I had thirty minutes. After a while, I was escorted to a large hall where all the high school students were sitting on mats, and a microphone was placed on the stage. From the place where they sat, I asked if the last row of students could hear me comfortably without the use of the mike. They said they could, so I excused myself from going up to the stage. The teachers, along with the principal, sat on chairs which were spread over the length of the hall. My guess was they had spaced themselves in a manner that could ensure the children behaved themselves.

Every time I come face to face with children, I am

delighted by their eager faces, and bright shining eyes. I imagine the myriad thoughts running through their minds and I feel a surge of electric charge in the room. The aura is heady. As they sized me up, I asked them a question (one of the starters I use in my management workshops), and they were racing to guess the answer. There was a lot of excitement to satisfy me with the correct answer, and I was playing hard to satisfy. After analysing my question and their answers, I involved them in discussing its application and relevance to their lives. From there we discussed the concepts of responsibility, performance, authority, attitudes. And, in the midst of it, we were interrupted by the principal saying that my time was up and the students had other subjects to attend to. The students, in a chorus, asked for more time. She told them that she would have to cut down the lunch break. They agreed, and we raced on with topics that touched their value systems and personal lives. They had questions on questions; at any given time there were a dozen hands in the air waiting to ask questions. When the principal announced that it was past an hour and half, there was a shock of disbelief in the hall. I had wrecked the day's schedule. Time flew so fast that no one noticed it. While the principal spoke, there was still one hand up. She firmly told the student to put her hand down. The student pleaded, and I intervened and told the principal to allow her to have her say. She stood up and said, "I have stopped wishing my teachers because they never wish back. I have stopped doing my homework conscientiously because they never correct properly and on time. What the heck, I've just realised that I'm only lowering myself. They can go, fly a kite; from today, I'll do my best in class and wish them all. Thank you." When she sat down, there was a moment's silence followed by thunderous clapping. I hope the teachers were listening. She had summed up the essence of the hour-and-half we had spent together.

History Repeats Itself

Parenting teenagers has been a strenuous ordeal for parents all through the history of the human race. If you stepped into the past and took a peep at the *time capsule*, you will see people in the past talked just like the people today. If the present generation of parents and grandparents show despair at the behaviour of the youth, then they aren't being original. Their predecessors, too, looked down on adolescents as worthless fixtures that marred society's evolutionary process. Socrates, the Greek philosopher who lived in circa 500 B.C. complained, *"The youth today have contempt for authority, and talk nonsense when they should work. They have bad manners ... They contradict their parents and have no respect for older people."* Then you have a Greek poet called, Hestes, who lived in circa 800 B.C. He wrote, *"I see no hope for the future of our people if they are dependent upon the frivolous youth of today, for certainly all youth are reckless beyond words. When I was a boy we were taught to be discreet and respectful of elders, but the present youth are exceedingly wild and impatient of restraint."* Another great nobleman and renowned warrior, Peter Herman, who spearheaded the first Crusade, circa A.D. 1274 shared his frustration and anxiety when he said, *"The world is passing through troubled times. The young people of today think of nothing but themselves. They have no reverence for parents or old age; they talk as if they know everything and what passes for wisdom with us is foolishness for them."*

The greatest parenting blunder that gets passed from one generation of parents to the next is that parents tend to idolise their own childhood and adolescent years and consider them to be the most exemplary years worthy of emulation by their children. All through history, the contemporary crop of parents seem to suffer from chronic memory lapses of their own misbehaviour, temper tantrums, delinquency, rebellion and all the stuff that goes with the storm and stress of growing up as teenagers. Opening lines like, *"When we were kids, no one ever..."* or, advice laced with, *"When I was your age ..."* is bound to hit communication roadblocks with teenagers, because statements like these carry a stink of superiority and condescension. Now you know why your teens turn up their noses the moment you

> *Your sham only serves to confuse your children who learn to switch you off, while simultaneously learn to accept deceit as a way of life.*

> *The youth are very direct in many ways. Their honesty of expression, verbal and non-verbal, is often misconstrued as rebellion to authority.*

start to advise them. If grownups feel uncomfortable with people who put on superior airs, condescend, or patronise them, how can the youth look up to grownups, for direction and guidance, who perpetually lie in order to project themselves as paragons of virtue? If you want to reach out to your kids then knock off all the sham. To do that, you will have to get off your high moral horse and touch base with your children. Your teens know your weaknesses and your strengths and they can see through your false facades even before you complete your sentence.

Raman Jain, a Director in a postgraduate institute in Bangalore, invited me to conduct a two-day workshop for the students. When I confirmed my availability, he asked me to be his guest. Raman Jain had authored a number of books on social behaviour, and his wife, Aashna, was a psycho-therapist. Aashna had to coordinate a couple of modules into my two-day workshop. I noticed the family met at breakfast and dinner, which I thought was very commendable. Here were two masters in the field of behavioural psychology, and you would expect theirs to be an ideal family. Instead, their sixteen-year-old Rohit carried the scars of his parents' profession. He muttered when he spoke, dragged his feet, and looked dishevelled. Rohit gave the appearance of a tired young man. When they conversed with Rohit at the table, you couldn't flaw them for their words of wisdom, or the gentle, soft tones in which they spoke—but their words were loaded with authority. After Raman spoke to the son, Aashna would take over and explain Raman's point of view and the immense benefits he would reap by walking the path they paved for him. But, in the module she presented in my workshop the day previous, Aashna authoritatively spoke about the hazards of blind submission and compliance to authority; she concluded by saying that it ultimately destroys the self-esteem in the individual's psyche. There was such a gigantic gulf between her theories in class and the practice at home. Indeed, if Aashna's module was more humanistic, with a touch of realism, the students would have gained so much from it, and so would her son. If her lectures had come from the heart, she would rely less on flip charts, slides, projectors and other audio-visual peripheries. You can get away with this in the classroom or in seminars and workshops, but not at home. Oh, the youth can smell from a mile the dichotomy between theory and practice. It is only when they get slammed by parents and teachers, time and again, for questioning the dichotomy that the youth ultimately stop listening.

Parenting Styles affect Behaviour

Most of the problems teenagers face (and for which they are blamed) come from parenting styles practised from the time they were infants and toddler's. Parenting styles never change; parents who undermined their toddlers potential will continue to do so even when the child is a teenager. Conversely, parents who gave their toddlers responsibilities will do so in later years also. Steven R. Yussen and John W. Santrock in *Child Development*, elaborate on the following parenting styles:

- *Autocratic*: Teenagers are not allowed to express opinions or make decisions about any aspect of their own lives. Parents are restrictive and exhort children to follow directions, respect work, and place limits and controls on them.
- *Authoritarian*: Although teenagers can contribute opinions, parents always make the final decision according to their judgement. This style of parenting encourages children to be independent but still places limits, demands and controls over their actions. There is extensive verbal give and take, and parents demonstrate a high degree of warmth and nurturance towards the teens.
- *Permissive*: The teenagers assume more active and influential position in formulating decisions, considering, but not always abiding by, parental opinions.
- *Laissez-faire*: Teenagers can decide whether to consider or ignore parental wishes in making their own decisions.

- *Ignoring*: Parents play no role, nor show any interest, in directing the teenager's behaviour.

The 'permissive', 'laissez-faire' and 'ignoring' parenting styles place relatively very low demands, limits and controls on the teens' behaviour. They are given considerable freedom to regulate their own behaviour, with parents taking a non-punitive stance. Parents shirk from giving directions or involving themselves in their children's lives. They believe that the teens are old enough to know right from wrong, and they need to be given space to make their own decisions. When the pendulum swings from permissiveness to harsh punishment, both being extreme forms of parenting style, the children manifest behavioural problems.

In Search of Identity

Erik H. Erikson, a brilliant psychoanalyst who has shaped our thinking on social development, is an authority on identity and identity crisis faced by adolescents. He believes that the reason why teenagers are stressed and confused about themselves can be traced to the way they were treated as toddlers. According to Erikson, the ease with which the adolescent resolves his identity crises depends on how well he had fared in resolving his psycho-social crisis beginning as early as in nursery school. The first crisis is *initiative* vs *guilt*, which occurs during preschool years. Erikson believes initiative is the basis for allowing the person to become what he is capable of becoming. By developing a sense of initiative in preschool and elementary-school years, the child becomes more active, more relaxed, and makes better decisions. He frees himself from thoughts about failure rather quickly, and instead, directs his energy enthusiastically to new problems. Erikson is of the view that this sense of achievement will not be achieved if guilt feelings and a sense of self-restriction become too great.

Carving an identity can be challenging, complicated and daunting. Depending on how parents and teachers treat them, their paths are often paved with confusion and poignancy. During this period of life, teenagers are literally standing on the crossroads of two main streets: (i) they resent being treated as children, and (ii) they want to be reckoned as adults. The options they choose and the decisions they make on how to assert their identity may affect their entire lives and the lives of their families.

WHY TEENAGERS BEHAVE THE WAY THEY DO

Age-old Concept of Teen Maturity

Social scientists and psychologists held the opinion that by the age of twelve, the human brain was fully developed to take on responsibilities. Interestingly, their findings corroborated with the age-old concept of teen maturity practised in many pre-literate and literate cultures. At the onset of puberty, a simple initiation rite transformed children into grownups. The initiation rite served as a threshold where children shed their diapers and wore the loin-cloth by learning trades and performing adult functions.

A Flawed Conclusion

Jean Paiget had conducted numerous tests and experiments to determine the intellectual, spatial and cognitive development in children ranging from infants to teenagers. Piaget concluded that children reached the highest rung in the ladder of cognitive development by the age of twelve. Ever since those results became public knowledge, psychologists, psychiatrists, parents, teachers and the police fixed responsibility and blame on teenagers. They concluded that from thirteen onwards children were responsible enough to execute 'formal operations.' Unfortunately, by basing their censure on Piaget's flawed conclusions, parents, educators and law enforcement authorities still beg the question. If the brain is fully developed and mature enough to undertake formal operations at thirteen, then why do teenagers behave so irrationally, and at times, exasperatingly? Is it nature or nurture responsible for the irrational emotional outburst, reckless risk taking, rule breaking, and the pursuit of drugs, sex and substance abuse in adolescence? Indeed, the findings of recent research may not only put to rest the anxieties of parents, educators, social scientists and the law enforcement departments, but may also help to frame a new approach to deal with adolescents in the twenty-first century.

New Breakthrough on Brain Development

Since 1991, Dr Jay Giedd (chief of brain-imaging, child psychiatry branch, National Institute of Mental Health, Bethesda, USA) has been taking a peek inside the heads of over 1,800 kids and teenagers through high-powered magnetic resonance imaging (MRI) machines. His goal is to determine how the brain develops from childhood into adolescence, and on into adulthood. Giedd and other researchers have affirmed that the brain undergoes two major developmental 'proliferation and pruning' (sudden spurt in nerve growth and chopping off brain cells). "During the final months before birth, our brains undergo a dramatic pruning in which unnecessary brain cells are eliminated. Many neuroscientists now believe that autism is the result of insufficient or abnormal prenatal pruning," says Claudia Wallis, in *What Makes Teens Tick, Time,* May 31, 2004.

Unknown to scientists earlier, Giedd's new research has documented a second wave of 'proliferation and pruning' which occurs around the time of puberty and adversely affects some of the brain's highest functions in teenagers. Wallis, reporting on Giedd's research, says, "When a child is between the ages of six and twelve, the neurons grow bushier, each making dozens of connections to other neurons and creating new pathways for nerve signals. The thickening of all this grey matter—the neurons and their branch-like dendrites—peaks when girls are about eleven and boys twelve-and-a-half at which point a serious round of pruning is under way. Grey matter is thinned out at a rate of about 0.7 per cent a year, tapering off in the early twenties."

In the light of this new research, it is unfair to expect mature formal operations from teenagers when their brains are not yet maturely formed. Another factor to remember is that the brain develops from back to front (*see* Chapter on *How the Mind Works*). The brain regions that reach maturity earliest—through proliferation and pruning—are located at the back of the brain, while the frontal lobe, the seat of decision-making is the last to develop, by the time the individual is in the early twenties. In short, the part of the brain that makes teenagers responsible for their actions is not finished maturing—even at the age of twenty.

Coping with Estrogen and Testosterone

Adding to the travails of teenagers, they have further to cope with a heady cocktail of sex hormones which trigger physical and emotional changes in their bodies and minds. While the second pruning goes on, their bodies come under hormonal assault triggered by puberty. The ovaries and testes pour estrogen and testosterone into the bloodstream, stimulating the development of the reproductive systems. The testosterone-like hormones released by the adrenal glands remain extremely active in the brain, regulating mood and excitability. Perhaps, that is why teenagers are prone to skirt with danger, drive recklessly, or challenge rules. Dr Ronald Dahl, a psychologist at the University of Pittsburgh says, "Adolescents tend to seek out situations where they can allow their emotions and passions to run wild. It is a very important hint that there is some particular hormone-brain relationship contributing to the appetite for thrills, strong sensations and excitement." The reason being, the brain region that puts the brakes on risky, impulsive behaviour are still under construction, while the parts of the brain responsible for sensation-seeking thrills begin to function at puberty. According to Giedd, the best estimate for when the brain is fully mature is twenty-five.

Seven Rules for Parents

Drawing on the latest scientific studies of adolescents, Laurence Steinberg, a professor of psychology at Temple University, offers this advice for parents of teens:

1) What you do matters

Many parents mistakenly believe that by the time children have become teenagers, there's nothing more a parent can do. Wrong. Studies clearly show that good parenting continues to help teenagers develop in healthy ways, stay out of trouble and do well in school.

2) You can't be too loving

Don't hold back when it comes to pouring on the praise and showing physical affection. There is no evidence that adolescents are harmed by having parents who are unabashedly loving—as long as you don't embarrass them in front of their friends.

3) Stay involved

Many parents who were actively involved in their child's life during the early years withdraw when their child becomes a teenager. This is a mistake. It's just as important for you to be involved now—maybe even more so. Participate in school programmes. Get to know your child's friends. Spend time together.

4) Adapt your parenting

Many parenting strategies that work at one age stop working at the next stage of development. As children get older, for example, their ability to reason improves dramatically, and they will challenge you if what you are asking doesn't make sense.

5) Set limits

The most important thing children need from their parents is love, but a close second is structure. Even teenagers need rules and limits. Be firm but fair. Relax your rules bit by bit as your child demonstrates more maturity. If he or she can't handle the freedom, tighten the reins and try again in a few months.

6) Foster independence

Many parents erroneously equate their teenager's drive for independence with rebelliousness, disobedience or disrespect. It is healthy for adolescents to push for autonomy. Give your children the psychological space they need to learn to be self-reliant, and resist the temptation of micro manage.

7) Explain your decisions

Good parents have expectations, but in order for your teenagers to live up to them, your rules and decisions have to be clear and appropriate. As your child becomes more adept at reasoning, it's no longer good enough to say, "Because I said so."

Source: Time, May 31, 2004

Two roads diverged in a wood, and I—
I took one less travelled by,
and that has made all the difference.

— ROBERT FROST

Eating Disorders

We may live without books,
what is knowledge but grieving.
We may live without hope,
what is hope but deceiving.
We may live without love,
what is passion but pining:
But where is the man who can live without dining?
(Let's eat!)

— GEORGE MEREDITH

In the decade gone by— the 1990s—a large body of research in eating disorders have led scientists to believe that disturbances in the function of brain neurotransmitter pathways *link* 'eating' disorder and 'substance abuse' disorder (consumption of alcohol and drugs). In other words, like drug addiction, eating disorders must be treated as a brain disease. These scientists are of the view that eating disorders are, themselves, a form of drug addiction since their characteristics satisfy all the clinical and biological criteria for conventional addictions such as smoking, alcoholism and cocaine abuse. According to researchers, the progressively compulsive nature of the behaviour of addicts is to medicate themselves with drugs in the face of adverse consequences to health and safety; similarly, these characteristics find direct parallels in the core eating-disorder behaviours such as dieting, over-exercising and binge eating.

Staying 'High'

At the biological level, medical researchers and scientists point out that strenuous exercise and starvation activate the dopaminergic (DA) reward pathway of the brain. In other words, starving, binging and exercises, all serve as drug delivery devices since they increase the circulating levels of endorphins that are chemically identical to exogenous opiates (used by drug addicts), and these endorphins are as potentially addictive because of their ability to stimulate DA in the brain's mesolimbic reward centres.

Eating disorders are serious addictions, sometimes life-threatening conditions that tend to be chronic. The two main eating disorders are: anorexia nervosa (AN), and bulimia nervosa (BN), the former displays a facility for self-starving and reports a decreasing interest in food, while the latter have increasing difficulty resisting food and become compulsive eaters, who binge on food and then use laxatives, diuretics, enemas, or excessive exercises to stay slim. Persons who are dependent on alcohol and drugs are considered addicted to substance abuse and need to be treated; so also persons with BN ought to be considered suffering from a brain disease and need to be treated accordingly. Interestingly, medical research, backed by statistics, reveals that AN has the most severe consequence with a mortality rate higher than that of almost all other mental disorders.

ANOREXIA NERVOSA (AN)

There is no physical explanation for anorexia nervosa. Nor is there cure for loss of appetite and weight, although if blood pressure drops, and body fat is completely lost, emergency medical treatment includes forced feeding through the nose or veins to prevent sudden death.

Savitri was twenty-five-years old when she died, leaving behind a nineteen-month, old son, Jaideep. One morning, while bathing Jaideep, she collapsed on the floor unconscious. The family rushed her to the hospital where she was declared dead upon arrival. Later, the husband said that he had "felt her gone" in his arms in the car itself. The little baby and the husband, traumatised by her sudden death, are doing their best to cope without a mother and a wife.

Savitri was a good-looking woman, tall, lean, and a great socialite. Six months prior to her death, she joined a *weight-watching* programme, recalled her husband. Her grief-stricken mother said that even "in college she wore *chappals*, and would be dieting in order to mix freely with her friends who were not as *big* as she was." Savitri died of *anorexia nervosa*.

The most common features of anorexia nervosa are loss of weight coupled with a change in behaviour. An anorexic begins a perfectly normal weight-reducing diet, loses weight, and then instead of stopping her diet, eats less and less until she is little less than skin and bones. Some lose more than twenty-five per cent of their body weight within a couple of months, weighing as little as thirty kilos. Anorexia is an adolescent disease—the ten to twenty age-group (although some as young as eight and as old as thirty get affected). It affects young people of both sexes, though ninety per cent of those afflicted are females from well-off homes.

Its Causes

Today's society places a premium on beautiful bodies. Indeed, a resurrection of the renaissance era: a beautiful body—if you got it, you flaunt it. Everything, from apparels to cosmetics, from household appliances to automobiles, from foods and drinks to fertilisers, you name it and you will find it on your television set—beautiful bodies selling the stuff. The impact of these visuals, day and night, on the minds of adolescents is mind-boggling. They spend hours every day preening themselves in front of the mirrors, checking and rechecking their clothes, their physiques, their complexions and their hair. If that is not enough, then there is more of it available in the gossip magazines, the cinema, and the sports icons to emulate from.

Identity Crisis or Narcissism

In Europe and in the USA, people with fair skin, spend hours under the sun burning their skin to darken it. They call it sun-bathing and proudly display the skin tan. Their counterparts in Asian countries like India use skin lotions, pastes and poultices on their bodies to look fair and lovely— the dark tan is considered ugly. They also bleach and streak the hair to look like Westerners. Boys with average build commit a lot of time to exercise in order to look taller and muscular, while girls exercise to look thinner. Boys and girls who are short, and want to look taller, wear shoes with high heels, while tall girls who want to look short wear sandals and shoes without heels. Is it narcissism or is it identity crisis? Or is it both? Spanning three decades, beginning in the 1940s, Erik H. Erikson wrote extensively on the search for *identity* and the crisis of adolescence. Following Erikson's lead, many psychologists through a combination of theory, clinical case studies, and scientific research have determined that the precise course of identity crisis depends on the young person's society, peer groups, and family. Universally, most teenagers are never satisfied with their natural looks.

> If the saying is true that 'how you feel about your body is how you feel about yourself', then it is natural that teenagers who feel terrible about their bodies feel terrible about themselves.

They spend time and money altering and adjusting their body images to gain recognition and admiration from the opposite sex, as well as from their social circles. Social acceptance comes with a price. To compete with oneself in order to measure up to the body images promoted by television, movies and advertising could end up as an obsession. Obsession is a disease in itself.

Parental Maturity

Suffering from low self-image can trigger anxiety and depression syndromes in adolescents. Parental concern, care and counsel are of vital importance at this stage. Parents should offer proper guidance and understanding of the problem. Some parents may deride and censure the child, while others may encourage the adolescent who goes on crash diets, spends hours before the mirror, or burns money on cosmetics, clothes and gymnasiums to groom the *body beautiful*. In the final analysis, the benchmark that determines the maturity displayed by the parents in handling the problem reflects in the adolescent's perception of self-image and personal identity.

Family Therapy

Behavioural scientists consider anorexia nervosa to be a family disease rather than an individual one. According to them, families of anorexics hold high expectations of their children. The anorexic willingly accepts this value structure by setting standards for herself that are extreme. They further state that instead of encouraging adolescents to grow independent, families may want to control them by demanding conformity of behaviour. Salvador Minuchin, in his book, *Psychosomatic Families: Anorexia Nervosa in Context*, has developed family-therapy techniques to help these family members to gain greater individuality and more flexibility in the upbringing of children. Till date, family therapy seems the best treatment for anorexics. According to Kathleen Stassen Berger, in *The Developing Person*, "This approach is instructive for all families that include adolescents. Parents who

> *Adolescents who are level-headed and balanced usually have have parents who care enough to understand them and stay involved.*

recognise their adolescents as individuals, and who realise that family disagreements may be helpful as long as the conflict is discussed and settled, will be able to help their teenagers develop a healthy identity." It is pretty obvious that 'understanding' parents build bridges with their children to provide them a path of hope for the future. Parents have to strike a balance when it comes to parenting teenagers. In some households, parents are orthodox in their approach to raising children, while in other households, they let go of their parenting responsibilities believing that the teens are grown up and don't need the parents around. That's a fallacy. Parents remain the most important people in the lives of adolescents.

Obesity in Children

From the time our children are very young, they need to see us living a healthy lifestyle—taking the time to exercise and to prepare healthy meals, as a regular part of day-to-day living. Probably the biggest obstacle to our doing this is our rushed and overcrowded schedule. How many of us are able to plan even thirty minutes to devote to taking care of ourselves in some way? Perhaps if we realised how important our example is to our children, we would be more motivated to maintain healthy habits.

— DOROTHY LAW NOLTE and RACHEL HARRIS
(Teenagers Learn what They Live)

Anjuli Goel, a Delhi girl was nineteen-years old, five feet tall and weighed fifty-five kilos when she shot herself with her father's revolver. She was up in arms with a weight problem. It was reported that she had tried to commit suicide earlier too, once by consuming rat poison and another time by swallowing mercury from a thermometer. Anjuli had grown up as a plump child who had gone from crash diets to controlled diets, to prayers and fasting without much success. Two weeks prior to killing herself, her family took her to a temple to pray for her 'peace of mind'. May her soul rest in peace.

An obesity pandemic is sweeping across urban India. Doctors, at the All India Institute of Medical Sciences (AIIMS) in New Delhi, warn of a health catastrophe—that death rate among children will shoot up to thirty-three per cent (from nine per cent, at present) on account of cardiovascular diseases caused by obesity alone. The All India Institute of Medical Sciences conducted a study in early 2003, called *Imbalanced Diet and Adverse Anthropometric Profile in Urban Adolescents.* The study revealed that out of the 1,100 adolescent students examined in Delhi's government schools (*Kendriya Vidyalayas*) and the elite private schools, 21 per cent boys, and 22 per cent girls were overweight. And, amongst the overweight children, 24 per cent qualified as obese. The study points out that children in government schools were in better physical shape than their counterparts in the private schools, suggesting that income was related to obesity. The higher the income the fatter the kids. Surveys conducted by the US health department found the rate of obesity in children alarmingly high to declare it as an epidemic sweeping across the country. As people in many countries are facing the problem of obesity, the World Health Organisation (WHO) calls it *globesity.*

Generally, fat babies grow up to become fat children, who in turn will become fat adolescents, and will eventually become fat adults. When babies are overfed, a super abundance of fat cells are produced in the body. Due to such an excess of fat cells in the body, the child's intake of food is a lot more when compared to a child who is not overfed, and whose fat cells are of normal count. When an adolescent or an adult goes on a diet and loses weight, she thinks she has destroyed the fat cells; unfortunately, no. The fat cells, squeezed and shrivelled, remain in the body. No sooner she relaxes on her diet, she puts on the fat faster than she lost it because the shrivelled fat cells revive and soak up all the calories like a sponge.

Social Stigma

Obesity is a physical and a medical problem, be it in adolescents or in adults. An obese person usually exercises less and runs a greater risk of serious illness. However, many obese adolescents get embarrassed by the way their bodies look and move. Physical size and shape during this period affect friendships. Obese teenagers often end up being lonely and unhappy because they know as a fact that they are fatter than their friends. They have fewer friends than other children, and acceptance into a peer group often comes at a price. They get picked on and teased with nicknames like, 'mottie', 'motte-natte', 'fatso', 'football'. The problem gets further compounded when physical appearances create psychological problems. Overweight children also build up phobias about peer acceptance. To avoid humiliating taunts, they further isolate themselves and withdraw from participating in class functions, or group games. As a society we must learn to be tolerant and understanding of others and their problems.

Nicknames or pet names that don't promote a positive self-image, lowers a person's self worth. Shikha, a fourteen-year-old girl who was overweight had learnt to hate herself because she could do nothing right. She was incompetent, awkward and ugly, she told herself. At home she was often rebuffed by her parents for being clumsy, and was teased by her elder brother and cousins for her unattractive looks. In school she was called a few other names which seemed innocuous but to the child they were negative reinforcements of a lowered self-worth. Shikha had to learn new skills to develop her personality without the support of family and friends. She had to insulate herself with Teflon to show others that their taunts didn't hurt her. Shikha read Somerset Maugham and lived his lines, "You have the freedom to laugh at me; I have the freedom to be indifferent to you." Children like Shikha need our support, not our ire in order to develop a healthy self-image.

Causes of Obesity

The causes of obesity could be broadly divided into two parts: genetic and cultural.

GENETIC AND HEREDITARY FACTORS

The Leptin Gene

Since the discovery of the *leptin gene* by Jeffrey Friedman and Rudy Leibel in 1986 at the Rockefeller University, a lot more research has been conducted worldwide to pinpoint leptin's true worth. According to Ellen Ruppel, author of *The Hungry Gene: The Science of Fat and the Future of Thin,* leptin is manufactured in the fat cells—adipose tissue, and it commands the body to eat or to stop eating. This is a very vital step in knowing why some people get fat and others don't. Jeffrey Flier, a Harvard scientist reported that "a decline in leptin is a warning signal to the body that something is amiss, and that the response—a heightening of appetite, a reduction of fertility—is protective." When there's a decline in leptin in the body, it causes people to eat voraciously because the body keeps telling the brain, it's starving; the body craves for food and is never satisfied even after consuming huge quantities of food.

Can leptin be substituted in a pill form? Regrettably, no. Tests conducted on obese people showed that they were immune to leptin which was heralded as a wonder hormone in the mid-1990s.

In another research conducted in the UK, scientists dubbed peptide YY3-36 (PYY), the fullness hormone because PYY—a protein produced by the gut—functions as a powerful appetite suppressant, at least in thin people. But would it benefit the obese and the overweight?

About twenty-four obese and lean people who had volunteered to be experimented upon were given an injection of the PYY3-36 hormone before eating, by Dr Stephen Bloom, one of the researchers, at Imperial College, London. The experiment revealed that the volunteers were able to consume only 30 per cent of the meal. Since the experiment is in its infancy stage, Bloom cautions, "We haven't yet shown you get actual weight reduction. We've only shown you eat less." According to Bloom, the natural levels of PYY3-36 hormone in obese people is at a minimal, which explains why they are hungrier and tend to overeat. Extensive studies carried out by scientists have shown that sleep disorders directly affect hormone levels in the body causing stress, obesity and other diseases (*see* Chapter on *Sleep: Your Health Tonic*).

Heredity Factor

Some scientists are of the view that being fat is in the genes. An individual inherits a body type: it includes height, bone structure, and the distribution of fat cells. They believe you cannot fight with or alter heredity. Others believe that a genetic inclination toward obesity manifests itself in a constitution which is more finely tuned to environmental triggers. Primary among these triggers is the easy access to convenience foods which are high in fat content coupled with a sedentary lifestyle. Most of us are susceptible to overeating and to becoming overweight. Our genes tip the balance for each of us at a different point. Some of us succumb easily, others less so.

The latest figures released by the American Cancer Society, reveal that obesity and lack of physical activity cause as many as one-third of the USA's cancer cases. "Obesity is a factor in about a dozen different types of cancer," said Michael Thun of the American Cancer Society, who co-wrote *Cancer Facts and Figures 2004.*

Cultural Factor

This has to do with lifestyles, personal habits, likes and dislikes. While dieticians are of the opinion that many such factors contribute to obesity, with television and computers being the primary agents. They say that these habits begin in infancy, continue through adolescence, and stay ingrained in adulthood. Social scientists opine that in societies such as ours where the haves and the have-nots coexist, families not only tend to overfeed their babies, but also take a delight in filling the food plates to over-capacity, and urging the child with more and more helpings. Psychologists point out that the proud father shows off his love by the amount of food he can provide, while the doting mother demonstrates her love by the rich variety of foods she can cook, and the children's love is measured by the amount of food they consume. Hence, being overweight is considered being healthy, and it symbolises prosperity.

Watching Television

Without realising the long-term harm caused by television-watching, parents happily switch on the TV set and offer food to keep infants from crying or getting upset. In some homes the child is fed breakfast, lunch and dinner while watching television. "There is no other way he'll eat his food," parents plead in despair. Studies linking television to obesity point out the hazards of the 'eye-mouth' disease. The more television children watch the more they eat. Fat accumulates in the body when the input is in excess of the output. Since most urban children and adolescents don't play outdoors, they're unable to burn the calories. If the intake of food is in excess, it gets stored as fat deposits (adipose tissue). Health care experts are of the view that television viewing prompts children and teenagers to consume large volumes of food because appetite control is asymmetrical—our bodies are better designed to respond to hunger than to satiety. When we are inactive, controlling appetite is not instinctive; it is something we have to impose on ourselves. The less we exert ourselves the more difficult this becomes. The type of foods advertised on television, and the dishes served by fast-food joints are low on fibre and high on fats, salts and sweets which appeal to children. The combination of sugar, fats and salts in one's diet alongwith a TV remote or the computer mouse in hand can only lead to obesity. While the National Institute of Health (NIH), USA, has declared obesity as a national epidemic, it has done precious little to curb advertisements endorsed by children, or aimed at children. On the other hand, Norway and Sweden have placed a total ban on children's advertisement under the banner of exploiting child labour. In both these countries the level of childhood obesity is extremely low, while in countries where television advertisements are least regulated, children's obesity rates are among the highest.

> Since parents use television as a baby-sitter, children grow up on a diet of television which also includes an intake of junk food.

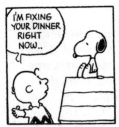 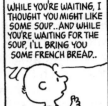 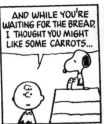 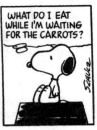

Eat to Live—Slim and Trim

You don't have to feel sheepish or guilty when you occasionally stray from a healthy diet. It is common to give in to your taste buds from time to time. But if you or your children are constantly staring into the refrigerator to grab a quick bite or gulp down some juice or aerated drink, then there's a food problem at home that needs addressing. If your children are plump, overweight or obese they're probably in control of the diet menu. To begin with, you may have to start with yourself and your spouse. Develop an interest in outdoor sports and games. Get to know the calorie count and nutritional value of the foods you buy and stack in your refrigerator. My belief is that the more you learn about calories and nutrition the better you'll invest in quality foods. Below, I will discuss with you some common dietary pitfalls and tell you when they may be a risk to their health, and offer some alternatives.

1. **Why children hate vegetables**? The very sight of vegetables may enrage some children or put them off home food. But if they avoid vegetables they'll miss out on the vitamins and minerals, protective phytochemicals, and the fibre for roughage. Eating fruits alone is a poor substitution to veggies. You may need to make a better presentation of veggies at the table.

   ◈ Don't overcook vegetables. Many children dislike vegetables because they've only had limp, overcooked versions, time and again.

   ◈ Add a little olive oil and spices to vegetables to give it a good flavour.

   ◈ Add vegetables to salads, soups, stir-fries and casseroles.

- Choose a variety of different colours and try new types of vegetables. Start with milder flavoured vegetables, then try crispier textures like carrots or French beans.
- Since children easily copy the negative behaviour of grownups, you should be careful that no adult fusses about eating veggies in front of the kids.

2. **High-calorie cravings:** Children have an irresistible craving for chocolates, ice-cream, chips, or other high-calorie foods. If they indulge in a regular feast of sweet, salty or fatty foods, they're bound to gain weight and run the risk of inviting other health problems. Here's my advise:
   - Stop buying the poison. 'Out of sight' may lead to 'out of mind' solutions.
   - Since most food cravings last for only about ten minutes, be creative and offer distractions to take their mind off those foods.
   - Most food cravings are triggered by stress or boredom; avoid feeding sweet, fatty or salty foods when they are upset. Carrots and cucumbers could be used as good substitutes.

3. **Emotional eating:** Many tweens, teens and grown-ups reach out for food as self-medication when they're feeling stressed, depressed, bored, angry or sad. This habit gets embedded in the brain cells at the time of infancy onward where food was offered as a distraction whenever they were emotionally distressed. A diet of 'comfort foods' that are high in fat, sugar and salt, not only poses a health risk, but also triggers a reflex reaction in children to reach out for foods without dealing with the root of their emotional problems, and they fail to learn healthy ways to deal with negative emotions. Before you teach your children how to avoid binging on comfort foods, you may have to practise a few techniques yourself.

- Keep a diary of what you eat, the amount, whether you were hungry, and how you were feeling when you ate it.
- Reduce stress by regularly practising relaxation techniques like breathing deeply, meditation, or yoga.
- Keep your meal times fixed and eat only at those times.
- Listen to your body and eat only when you feel hungry.
- Eat at the table and not in front of the television since distractions can prompt overeating.

4. **Skipping meals:** When children have to commute to school early every morning, many skip their breakfast either because they wake up late for school, or it's too early to eat. Some grownups skip even lunch or dinner. Either you will end up eating much larger portions to make up for the lost meal, or you gorge on snacks, as children do, at the school canteen. Skipping meals inevitably leads to weight gain. Healthcare experts point out that when you skip meals, you also miss out on nutrients that you may not make up for in your next meal. I believe that children should be in the habit of waking up early enough to have their breakfast in order to stack up all the energy they need to concentrate and focus on the morning's subjects taught in class. Start the breakfast habit, even if it's just a cup of yoghurt and cereal with a glass of milk, or some fruit. People who skip breakfast tend to be heavier than those who eat a nutritious breakfast.

> To ensure that your children's energy levels are high in the mornings, you may have to consider breakfast as the most important meal of the day.

5. **Crazy about carbohydrates:** Children have a weakness for *samosas*, patties, *bhaturae*, burgers, pizzas, pastas, potatoes, bread, cookies, chips,

French fries, or other refined carbs. Foods high in refined carbohydrates can cause blood sugar levels to rise rapidly, which in time may cause problems in insulin resistance, weight gain and even cardiovascular disease. Choose carbohydrates that rate lower on the glycaemic index (a measure of how easily the body turns a particular food into blood sugar). Options include beans, whole grains like oats (naturopathy lists oats as having *antidepressant* value), wheat, barley, non-tropical fruits, sweet potatoes and most vegetables. (Consult your dietician for more information to create your personal nutrition chart.)

- Cook pasta *al dente* (firm, not soft), which lowers glycaemic index rating.
- Eat reasonable amounts. A serving of pasta is a half-cup of cooked noodles, not a plateful.

6. **Drinking calories:** The fast-food outlets, to outdo their competitors, offer free colas, or unlimited refills of beverages to go with the food you buy. Children get into the habit of washing down their meals with calorie-rich sweet beverages which contribute to weight gain, while the sugar increases the risk of tooth decay. Adolescents indulge in downing 'breezers'—a drink made of alcohol mixed with juice or cola. Alcohol is packed with calories, and mixers like cola and juice not only add to the calories, but also are high in sugar. My advise is:

- Don't drink alcohol or soft drinks regularly.
- Avoid eating high-calorie snacks like nuts or chips when you drink these beverages.
- Drink plenty of water throughout the day to keep yourself well-hydrated and full.
- Dilute juice by mixing it with soda water.

7. **Habitual snacking:** When you see someone go munch, munch, munch throughout the day (and some people wake up in the middle of the night to munch, munch, munch), it's obvious that food is uppermost

on their minds. It's also obvious that they don't enjoy or care about regular home-cooked meals, or eating at fixed times since they habitually binge on junk food that consists mainly of soft drinks, chocolates, cookies and chips. Compulsive eating of 'convenience foods' may develop into an eating syndrome which may require medical intervention, not to mention weight gain, scurvy—a disease marked by bleeding gums and muscle degeneration.

- Tease your children's taste buds. Make meals attractive by changing your method of cooking and the ways you present meals at the table so that the children taste a variety of flavours in their meals. Variety adds its own flavour and spice.

- If children are habituated to snacking you cannot stop the habit overnight. But you can change the quality of snacks overnight. Stop buying junk food, soft drinks and sweets. Keep healthy snacks like fruits and vegetables, green salads, low-fat yoghurt, Californian dried prunes, pistachio, walnut, whole-grain crackers and plain popcorn at hand.

- Get them into the habit of drinking water throughout the day to stay filled up—it will kill the beverage-drinking habit. Recently published research in the USA suggests that consumption of *cola* drinks could erode bone density in females. Doctors fear that bone mineral loss from childhood could lead to an increased incidence of osteoporosis.

- To keep their minds off food, introduce them at a very young age to outdoor sports and games like horse riding, swimming, tennis, badminton, football, whatever. TV buffs and the computer whiz kids burn fewer calories and tend to be overweight than the kids who run around playing in the parks and gardens.

Healthcare experts warn that children should never go

on diets or crash diets. Neither should adults, for that matter. You end up paying more than your pound of flesh. Some of the side effects you pick up are: irritability, insomnia, lack of concentration and listlessness, while depleted levels of calcium, proteins and other food nutrients could affect bone density, body minerals and brain growth. On the other hand, obesity embraces heart disease, blood pressure, diabetes, and osteoarthritis. Being self-disciplined will help. Cultivating proper food habits, right from infancy up to adulthood, i.e. eating the right types of food, eating at fixed times, eating normal (small) portions, developing correct sleep patterns, and daily outdoor exercises are excellent habits to adopt as lifestyles. To cope with modern day pressures and tensions, you will have to learn techniques to stay in control of your life, and not to succumb to stress, hypertension and a host of psychosomatic ailments. The practice of yoga, exercises and outdoor games are handy tools to diffuse the steam inside you.

Galvanising Support

Home, school and the local governments should co-relate their efforts at controlling obesity in children and adolescents. A good example is Singapore. When obesity in kids had shot up from two per cent in the late seventies to seventeen per cent by 1992, the City's Health Promotion Board took up a massive campaign. Mabel Yap, Director of the Board's Research and Information Management Division, was reported saying, "We focused on schools, training teachers to impart better eating habits to the kids, modified the food available at the school canteens and embarked on promoting a lifestyle with physical exercises." The campaign was result-oriented: obesity fell to less than eight per cent by 2000. The Delhi government had issued a circular to the city's schools in 2002 *to ban junk foods and drinks* and provide nutritious food in school canteens. The response from schools to that 'circular' wasn't very encouraging since fast-food chains and soft drinks companies have a large stake in those canteens.

School PTAs should take up the issue of student obesity through awareness campaigns and monitor the foods and beverages sold in canteens. At home, parents should find other avenues of motivating children rather than through pocket money and the junk food outlets. Home foods and the foods available in the school canteens must contain a balanced diet. It is heartening to note that in families where parents are nutrition-conscious, the children are not exposed to junk foods and they literally develop a dislike for candy and colas.

Part 2

Building a Learning Foundation

Whenever anyone can succeed in transforming their first steps in reading, or arithmetic, or spelling into a game, you will see children become passionately absorbed in those occupations, which are ordinarily presented as dreary chores.

— JEAN PIAGET
(Science of Education and the Psychology of the Child)

Schooling: The Grey Side

The home-school relations are mostly like a throwball game. There is the home team and the school team, and the child is the ball. Each team throws the child, along with its responsibilities, at the other. "The teachers don't teach any more," scream the parents. *Thuk!* The ball lands with a thud on the school court. "The parents don't discipline their children any more," scream the teachers. *Thuk!* The ball lands with a thud on the home court. While the home team wants to abdicate its responsibilities of disciplining the child at home, the school team wants to abdicate its responsibilities of teaching the child in school. The parents believe that only if teachers would teach in class, the children would enjoy school and wouldn't misbehave. The teachers believe that only if parents were to exercise discipline at home, then the children would want to learn in class. This ballgame goes on for a good twelve years, till the child leaves school. Of course, there are many more grouses and grudges which both teams share. That's where the PTAs come in: not to stop the game, but to keep the game going, amicably.

You see, both teams have, over the years, developed set minds with set boundaries—academics stem from the confines of the schools, say the parents. Behaviour stems from the confines of the home, say the teachers. But children don't function in such straight-laced compartments. On the contrary, children seize such chinks in the armoury of upbringing to their advantage and exploit the situation to their own gain. That's why, in this throwball game, this little 'ball', over the years, gathers its own moss from court to court, and eventually learns to control home and school. In this lose-lose situation every one loses: the child, the parents and the teachers.

WHY THE MESS?

School of Contradictions

A lot of people hold a gripe about schooling, and for a good number of reasons, too. "Schooling is no fun", they say, "at least not any more." Children have had and continue to have a very rough time. On the one hand we send children to school, and on the other, we want to protect them from the grind of bookish slavery. In short, when dealing with the child, we *swear by* the school, and when dealing with the school, we *swear at* the school. Why this contradiction?

Creating this false environment for children perhaps started some time around the beginning of the Industrial Revolution, or at least when it became necessary to protect the young from slave labour in the mines and industry. The British Crown had declared that 'children had no rights'. Effectively, the parents at that time decided to extend child-life as long as possible in order to delay the time when the child would have to enter work in the factories and mills—that dreaded process which signified anxiety and stress. Perhaps, from that time on, we developed the idea that we must protect all children, and in doing so we also cut off their growth. So, what we have is a kind of insane postponement of growth because the growth that the adult envisages is so miserable and stressful that no one would ever want a sweet innocent child to grow that way. "Isn't it *too early* for my baby to...?" is a common doubt expressed by parents wanting to shield their children from falling into a routine of doing things that other children of the same age do. They perceive environment as a big, bad world, and the children need to be shielded from being 'pushed' into, or from being 'pressured' into any activity. Simple chores related to obedience, for instance "sit and finish your meal"; or to follow a routine like doing potty regularly at morning time, brings on an instant refrain of "I don't want to push my baby", or, "I don't want to pressurise my child".

Lack of Coordination

Parents, students and teachers, though working together, work in tight compartments without the oil of joy to lubricate the learning process. Hence, the process of teaching and learning creaks and has become rusty, tedious and irrelevant to contemporary times. Each entity of parents, students and teachers, at times, functions in animosity instead of with understanding.

Children spend almost a quarter of a lifetime in academics. And the end result is despair at being overburdened, and misery because learning is perceived as self-inflicted punishment. While a small percentage of children do succeed in coping with the stress, a large majority of them emerge ill-equipped to deal with life's situations. Urgent help is required.

Parents struggle extremely hard, facing hardships, and making tremendous sacrifices so that their children can succeed in the schools they study in. The end result is frustration and bitterness. Value-oriented parenting skills on how to create 'family support systems' will help parents become pro-active supporters.

Teachers sweat it out day after day, wading through books, notes, homework, methodologies, etc. Their daily personal sacrifices and their work goes unappreciated. The end result is hopelessness. By instilling self-esteem, offering new teaching techniques and pride for profession through regular refresher programmes, as well as, awards and rewards will boost morale and self-image.

Your Ideal School

Look at students who join the IIM or the IIT, the country's premier institutes: they are fully aware of what is expected of them in those professionally-run institutions. They know *why* they are there and *how* they will function. They are focused and goal-oriented, and they motivate themselves, day after day, to achieve those goals. And, yet a few of those goal-oriented students, when they were in school, did not know what was expected of them, neither did they know why they were there or how they were to function.

If, out of the vast ocean of students that study in schools, this minuscule lot of students somehow managed to set goals and stayed motivated to achieve those goals, then why did the rest of the ocean stay placid? Basically, parents and teachers have to pool in their resources together to help the child 'to learn how to learn'. Without teaching the method of learning, how can children enjoy learning? They need the tools to master the skills. Hence, there is frustration amongst children, parents and teachers. Schooling has to be understood as an 'association' of three entities: the teachers, the students and the parents. They become a *triumvirate* to closely coordinate their functions to achieve a common goal—human development.

Working in Collaboration

In order to succeed, the *triumvirate* of students, teachers and parents have to form a 'coalition' and work in close collaboration with one another. The brotherhood of the *triumvirate* lies in the fatherhood of the principals, or headmasters/headmistresses—the management. The fatherhood is the fountainhead of vision, ideology and inspiration. The fatherhood gives direction and inspiration to the *triumvirate*. When the individual entities, namely, the teachers, students, parents, and the principals discharge their independent duties to the maximum, then only its sum total will benefit the common goal of a stress-free, holistic education. Such a 'coalition' can create a win-win situation, making schooling in the twenty-first century a joyful and stress-free experience.

Instilling Accountability through 360 Degree Appraisals

To achieve success, we will have to first throw away the century-old baggage of indifference and ignorance. Indifference and ignorance have made each entity of the *triumvirate* a weak, isolated piece of floating driftwood. In today's scenario, principals, teachers, parents and students shrug off responsibility, and blame one another for non-performance, failure and incompetence. We would not be faced with such a scenario if the principals, teachers, parents and students were groomed and equipped with effective and innovative skills comprising modern techniques, novel methodologies, and regular appraisal formats so as to function with responsibility and accountability. So far, only students are appraised. It's about time teachers, principals and administrators are regularly appraised for their performance. To begin with, students should be allowed to appraise their teachers who teach them.

> *The authority of those who teach is often an obstacle to those who want to learn.*
>
> — CICERO

Don't Push, Pull

Pushing is manipulating. Nobody likes being pushed, whether physically, emotionally or mentally. Neither adults, nor children. In order to push an object one has to get *behind* the thing being pushed. Thereafter, one uses force to push the object forward. Suppose we were to get in *front* of the object and pulled it behind us while we maintained the lead. Would that be more strenuous? It could be. It could also be inconvenient to us. So, just as we push inanimate objects around to suit our convenience, in the same way we push people. Being animate objects, people resent being pushed, including children. If only we could inconvenience ourselves by staying one step ahead, we could pull people along to us and win them over. Isn't that what leadership is all about—staying ahead of others?

Fourteen-year-old Joseph usually sleeps around midnight. Every morning at 6.45 there is pandemonium in the house. Despite his mother's best efforts, Joseph misses the 7 o'clock school bus. He hesitantly wakes up his father who then grudgingly drops him to school. On the way to school, the father chides Joseph for waking up late and missing the school bus. Joseph needs a 'support system' at home to help him reach school on time. Instead of 'pushing' Joseph to catch the bus, which he invariably misses, the parents will have to push themselves. They will have to wake up much earlier in order to 'pull' him along. Both parents will have to wake up at least at 6 o'clock, and set the kitchen and the bathroom in readiness. They will put on some lively music to wake him up. With joy in their hearts, a song on their lips, and a spring in their stride they will help Joseph to get ready for school. Though Joseph is independent, yet his parents should be up and around to offer whatever help is required as he clears his bowels, brushes his teeth, showers, eats a full breakfast, packs his school bag, wears a clean, ironed uniform and reaches the bus stop ahead of time. In this situation, the difference is that the parents do not 'push' Joseph, they push themselves to stay ahead of the kid. They are at hand, no matter what the hour, to offer support, guidance and direction (*see* Chapter on *Quality Time*).

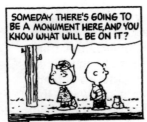
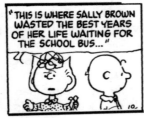
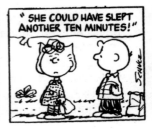

Is Schooling a Game of Dumb Charade?

Why should our children lose out in schools? A large percentage of school-going children end up as losers. Maybe it is time to renovate the educational edifice handed over to us by Lord Macaulay. In renovating the infrastructure, we will need to immediately address the children's needs. The help we can offer through the infrastructure is to teach them *how* to study, and to *think* as they study. Let's draw a parallel between two institutions: the club and the school. One is serious about entertainment, while the other is serious about academics. Both institutions are governed by a code of conduct, and rules and regulations. The more one is conversant with the club rules the more the participation and enjoyment in its activities. When one is ignorant of one's rights and duties, one is at a loss and unsure what the club expects of its members. They become wary of the management, and are unable to recreate, relax or entertain themselves with joyful abandon. And, so it is with schooling. Schooling could become stress-free and enjoyable only if students were made conversant on the basics of how, when and why to study. Why should schooling end up like a game of dumb charade? It is only fair that children should be made to understand the rules of the game they are about to play. Don't we expect too much from the children when we evaluate them on their performance of the dumb charade game even though we have not explained to them how they should play the game? Faced with such a disadvantage many children become high-strung, and fail to enjoy the game or play it well. Many abandon the game. Some abandon hope and commit suicide.

> If children are failing or doing poorly they don't deserve our condemnation; they need our help.

Values in Learning and Education

It is trendy for the departments of education to talk about value-education. The government has set up special cells and allocated special funds to introduce the concept of values in learning and education; the result of their efforts has still to be felt in the schools. Perhaps, there is an error in placement: someone's placed the value-cart in front of the horse, and expect children to ride the value-cart. Maybe, if the horse (the educator) leads the cart by good example, the children in the cart will automatically follow the values in learning and education. Since learning is the process of disseminating information and acquiring knowledge, learning itself is a value.

One cannot be a good teacher unless one is a perpetual learner. Openness to learning, and learning new concepts, new ideas is a sign of a progressive teacher. Teachers who believe that there is nothing new to learn, and all that is there to know they know it all can never touch the highest note of excellence in their vocational calling. Albert Einstein has said, *"It is the supreme art of the teacher to awaken joy in creative expression and knowledge."* To touch excellence, teachers will have to teach themselves by and through the endless process of self-teaching. One of the best ways for teachers to teach and learn is to be intimately familiar with the lives of great teachers, researchers, reformers and learners from whom they can draw inspiration, such as, Gandhi, Radhakrishnan, Vivekanand, Raja Ram Mohan Roy, Vikram Sarabhai, Einstein and others. It is said that those who prove themselves to be good learners in their lifetime, prove to be great teachers of humankind.

The teacher's task is not to implant facts but to place the subject to be learned in front of the learner and, through sympathy, emotion, imagination, and patience, to awaken in the learner the restless drive for answers and insights which enlarge the personal life and give it meaning.

— NATHAN PUSEY (*President, Harvard College*)

Study Skills for Achievers

Somebody said that it couldn't be done
but he with a chuckle replied,
that 'maybe it couldn't' but he would be one
who wouldn't say so till he'd tried.
So he buckled right in with a trace of a grin
on his face. If he worried, he hid it.
He started to sing as he tackled the thing
that couldn't be done. And he did it.

Somebody scoffed, "Oh, you'll never do that,
at least no one has ever done it."
But he took off his coat and took off his hat
and the first thing he knew he'd begun it.
With the lift of his chin and a bit of a grin,
if any doubt rose he forbid it;
he started to sing as he tackled the thing
that couldn't be done, and he did it.

There are thousands to tell you it cannot be done,
there are thousands to prophesy failure;
there are thousands to point out to you, one by one,
the dangers that wait to assail you,

but just buckle right in with a bit of a grin,
then take off your coat and go to it.
Just start in to sing as you tackle the thing
that cannot be done, and you'll do it.

— ANON

Achievers and winners are not born, they are made. They're fashioned by the realities of the schooling environment that demands multidimensional study skills in order to succeed. Don't be taken in by what others say about not comparing one child with the other. Schooling is about being compared and being competitive. Children have to be competitive, and how they compete and fare in class, is compared with other students. Some schools group achievers and winners into special sections to hammer the best out of them; they say it's like fine gold: the more it's hammered the better its lustre. In such a competitive environment, where children are rated losers and winners, it is important they learn the ropes of how to compete successfully.

Time Management

People relate to 'time management' as a module for office executives. But, it's more pertinent for school-going children than to corporate houses. Look at the school children's routine: they have to reach school in the wee hours of the morning on time, attend to six to eight different subjects within fixed time slots, write tests and do homework within fixed time frames, and reach home so that they can carry fresh homework back to school. Compared to what students go through, our office executives are treated with kid gloves. And, then they get to attend 'time management' seminars. Wake up, parents, the schooling structure demands time management. Your children are time-bound, so inculcate in them the sense of routine by adhering to a time-table. Naturally, if your kids are unable to meet deadlines, they lose, and so they get frustrated. No amount of motivational skills will help if they keep falling flat on their faces every time they've to meet a new deadline.

In the following pages, I have laid down a student-programme which I have tested over several years with the brilliant, average and below average students, with tremendous success. They applied these study skills and were able to, not only improve their grades, but also developed their personalities considerably. There's no reason why it shouldn't work for your children. Your children, too, can become achievers by observing, practising, listening, reading, writing, studying, thinking, experimenting and continually assessing all that they study—as laid out in this section.

A Few Basic Rules for the Road

To get your child on the road to study, children are expected not only to work hard but also to work smart. They need to have a focus in order to be go-getters. Though they attend school daily, most students fail to understand the purpose of schooling, and so they end up passing time between home and school, waiting for that period in life to get over at some point in time. When parents get seriously involved in their children's development they seek ways and means to instil a sense of purpose in them. Some of those ideas of instilling a sense of purpose are mentioned below:

- The aim of the study is character building and the goal of study is result-oriented. Students labour hard in order to achieve results. As they sit to study, children should intone the daily study *mantra*: *I am going to get out of my studies what I put into them.* Teachers, books and surroundings help, but in the last analysis, it is all up to the student. They are capable of learning in spite of bad teachers, poor or insufficient books, and difficult physical surroundings. But they cannot learn if they don't apply themselves daily. It is rightly said, there aren't any 'interesting teachers or books', there are only 'interested' students. Encourage your children to develop self-motivating techniques to stay interested in studies.

- Subjects that really count—that are really worthwhile will require hard work. While subjects that are 'easy' in which anybody could score marks will hardly be the kind of subjects your child should be spending prime time on. Teach your child to prioritise between more important and less important work, regardless of likes or dislikes.

- Studying offers a challenge in many ways. This also means that the marks they obtain in the examinations may not always be a true indication of their progress in learning. Teach your children not to get frustrated. In the meanwhile, build bridges with your children's teachers so that they see you as involved parents.
- Stop comparing them or their work with their classmates. Don't demoralise your children. They have untapped potential which has not been fully realised. They have to set high standards and learn to compete with themselves in order to bring out the best in them.
- Help them to set high and yet realistic standards. If you are satisfied with a low level of proficiency, or with general ideas, obviously they will fail to develop a winning edge.
- Regularly test them on how well they have mastered a particular subject, theory or concept. Ask them to 'teach' it to someone (a friend or a family member). Until they are able to pass it on to others, they really have not mastered it.

Motivation

To win, a child has to have a winner's profile. The winner's profile is wrapped around the support system provided by the parents. I believe that motivation comes not from Maslow's principles but from principled parents, because success also has a moral and ethical side to it. If parents lack focus, digress, or cut corners, it becomes that much harder for children to succeed. To succeed, the child must *want* to do it and do it *well*. That is motivation. To be a winner is to be an achiever. And achievers need to constantly stay motivated in order to achieve.

> For children, parents are their primary motivators and leaders.

From the time they are toddlers until the time they are adolescents, parents will have to excite and encourage their children's actions and performances so that they continue to play on a winning wicket. Motivation is the quintessence of all ingredients that makes winners. Day after day, parents will have to renew the motivation *mantra* so that children stay focused as well as enjoy completing the task to the best of their abilities. To stay motivated, you will have to train your children to set goals.

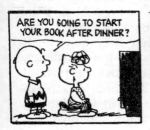 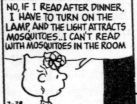 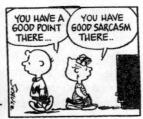

GOAL-SETTING

To be effective and efficient achievers, students should set themselves one-liner goals at the time they sit for their studies everyday. These one-liner goals must be written down on a sheet of paper. They must be defined clearly, sharply and emphatically. Below the one-liner goal they will write a one-line statement on how they will reach this goal. You must guide your children to make this road map so that they know exactly the way to go and also adapt to changes along the way, in case of potholes, without losing focus of the goal. Furthermore, they will also be tight on their target dates. Every night before going to bed you will revise the 'map' with them. In the words of Blanchard and Johnson in *The One-minute Manager*, "Take a minute (to): look at your goals. Look at your performance. See if your behaviour matches your goals." As the children accomplish their goals one by one, they will feel the exhilarating sense of achievement flowing through them. Their motivation will be fed and sustained through these achievements.

Positive Implants

To reinforce your children's performance and behaviour you will have to guide them to exert mental controls to reach their goals. You can do this by planting words into their minds which will flower into actions. People who meditate daily usually read a passage of holy scripture before sleeping so that the holy words they plant in the mind at night will blossom into blissful meditation in the morning. We can learn from this how to channelise the mind to our advantage. Every night before they sleep, show them how to implant in their minds positive and persuasive suggestions. Tell them that they will succeed! They're achievers! That they can do it! And, let them sleep with those thoughts. In the mornings, their first thoughts on waking up will be those purposeful words of conviction and belief in their abilities to achieve their goals. Then let them go ahead and do it! By planting these persuasive success messages in their subconscious and conscious mind, you will help them to constantly stay in focus of their goals and achieve them. Indeed, they can accomplish almost anything if only they set their minds to it.

Characteristics of Achievers

- Achievers never procrastinate. They do not avoid, or postpone unpleasant tasks.
- Achievers have a set routine. The routine is rooted in self-discipline. Routine is about setting a daily time-table and sticking to it, come what may.
- Achievers don't laze around on holidays. Wake-up time is the same as on school days.
- Achievers don't 'crave' for special foods on holidays.
- Achievers set up a 'holiday time-table' focused on extra reading and writing. They prepare for the week ahead, not just the day ahead.
- Achievers neither lag behind, nor do they just stay abreast of the class. They stay ahead of the class.
- Achievers stay organised.
- Achievers are good communicators.
- Achievers rehearse what they learn by discussing/ talking about it to others.

- Achievers are not hooked on to television, or the computer.
- Achievers play vigorous outdoor games to shake off mental and physical fatigue. They play games not to pass the time. They play to excel.
- Achievers have varied interests, other than books.
- Achievers have a positive attitude. Their minds keep juggling with possibilities. They don't give up easily.
- Achievers are popular, outgoing and friendly.

Personal Habits for Aspiring Achievers

If your children have habits that go contrary to the 'characteristics of achievers' mentioned above, don't give up. It's too early to give up, and it's not late for your child to develop new habits. Reading these lists may put you off, thinking that in their present lifetime they'll never achieve these goals. But, come to think of it, each of these traits is not a separate entity; each characteristic is interlinked with the other, forming a chain. One good habit leads to another. All you have to do is get started (which is the toughest) with one habit, and then build on it gradually. Good habits are acquired by constant practice which takes a lot of time, in fact, several months or years because the old habits have to die out completely before the good habits become a way of life. Some of the key study habits your 'aspiring achievers' should acquire are:

- *accurate observation*
- *careful planning*
- *close concentration on work in hand*
- *systematic working methods*
- *perseverance in difficult tasks*
- *an optimistic outlook*
- *promptness in completing each assignment (homework)*
- *regular revision at home*

Importance of Home Study

To understand the concept of 'home study', you have to first understand how the learning machinery works. Many parents are of the impression that the school is for learning and the home is for relaxing. It's not so. School and home have to collaborate in the learning process. At school, the teachers teach subjects and the children gather information. Then, they bring the information home. At home the information has to be assimilated and comprehended. When children revise that information or do their homework, they inadvertently press the 'processing' mode button. It's only through revision, *information is processed into knowledge*. Knowledge is about understanding and comprehension. Learning comes a full circle when information is processed into knowledge. Sitting at home to revise and do homework is an intrinsic part of study.

Self-reliance for Character Building

Weak students blame classmates, teachers, books, whatever for their lack of application, while students who have the winning edge believe in doing their own work. Parents have to guide their children to not depend entirely on the notes the teacher gives in class, or the guidebooks bought in the bazaar, or on summaries and notes made by their classmates. The teacher's notes are connected with the subject matter and should be known. It is, however, not the end of the process of learning but the beginning. The teacher's notes serve as a footstool to do more in-depth study on the topic. Encourage your children to make their own notes which suits their individual style of comprehension.

Guides may provide a source of quick reference to other authors, or may offer some stimulating questions to make students think more effectively. Neither should children memorise verbatim what is written in the guides, nor should they depend on them to succeed.

Summaries and notes made by friends or classmates may be very good for them, and may help them to score high marks, but they are no good for your child. In fact, they may confuse him, and so they are useless to him. Summaries and notes made by others are compiled in the manner that compliments their individual style of arranging ideas to suit their comprehension methods. So, what's good for Annie may not be good for Jenny. Unfortunately, average students lap up the notes and summaries of their companions because they feel it is too time-consuming to make their own notes.

Or, such students may feel mentally incapable to write down their own summaries. Your children will never ride a bicycle by watching others ride them. To ride a bicycle your kids have to get on it and pedal it. The same is true of studies.

An average student may feel that doing his own work all the time will require much more time than using the help which is already provided by others. This may seem true as a short-term policy. But education is never short-term. Achievers look at the total result which is a long way off. They realise that concepts and theories when properly learned in the beginning, even though it may take extra time, make it possible to speed on later. In doing so, they build a solid foundation of their characters by relying on their abilities to succeed. There are students who get fired with enthusiasm and adopt the fastest methods right in the beginning and who, as a result, can never go fast. Remember the hare and the tortoise. The tortoise went along his way slowly and steadily, while the hare ran for a short distance and then stopped moving altogether. All of us are products of an achievement-oriented society; we rear children to be competitive, to be the best, to win. To get average students to perform like above-average students, parents and teachers will have to patiently teach children the techniques of learning smart.

We are what we repeatedly do. Excellence then, is not an act, but a habit.

— ARISTOTLE

The Physical Side of Study

People are always blaming their circumstances for what they are. I don't believe in circumstances. The people who get on in this world are the people who get up and look for the circumstances they want, and if they can't find them, make them.

— GEORGE BERNARD SHAW

Family Support System

Though study is a mental process (*read* Chapter on *The Mental & Emotional Side of Study*), it is the entire human body that gets involved in that mental process. When children excel, the entire family excels, and when children fail, the entire family fails. The education of children is not done in watertight compartments where children are expected to perform their study duties regardless of family support. Parents have a duty towards their children in seeing that the home environment is study-friendly. Translated in practical terms, it means that children have to stay in good shape, mentally and physically, in order to make the learning process easier and productive. Also, parents have to supervise children so that they maintain excellent balance in regard to study, physical exercise, food and sleep. There are winners and there are losers, but they are not born like that. Some children win at sports, games, studies, dramatics, music, dance, cooking—at everything! You name it and they're good at it. How, you've wondered, do they manage to succeed in so many skills, while your kids lose at whatever they set to do? To get your children ride the success bandwagon get them to do what achievers do and they, too, will win.

14 Best Kept Secrets of Achievers

1. Sleep

Find out how much sleep your children need, and they should have it. If they need eight hours let them take eight. Seven hours will leave them tired. But if they cut short that hour of sleep and spend it in study, it may be uselessly spent since it will hamper their concentration. They may even find it difficult to keep their eyes open. And if they need seven hours of sleep, then they shouldn't take eight. (To understand the importance of sleep, *read* the Chapter on *Sleep: Your Health Tonic*). Lying down in bed to study is a waste of time. It may feel comfortable to stay in bed and read the newspaper or a novel, but definitely not to study. Achievers NEVER study in bed. A word of caution: Those who read books or watch television in bed habitually may develop orthopaedic and posture problems.

2. Food

Make sure that your children eat a balanced, high-fibre diet and drink plenty of water. Children should not binge on food (*see Chapter on Eating Disorders*). Eating too much will make them feel sluggish or heavy. And, by eating little, the pangs of hunger will remind them that they should be nibbling on something. You shouldn't offer or tempt your children with food or delicacies while they study. Tell them, never to nibble when studying. Meats are too heavy to digest and will make them lethargic. Non-vegetarians must be careful about the intake of meat; poultry and fish are better substitutes to red meats.

3. Climate

Here's a good alibi for losers: the weather never agrees with them. Experts agree that 70 degrees Fahrenheit, or 21 degrees Celsius, is the ideal temperature to study in. While a few homes with access to air-conditioners may be able to create the ideal temperature for studying, the schools in which those children study will not be able to offer that ideal climate. The Indian climate, during some months of the year, can be awful, really awful. Achievers don't make excuses about the weather or the climatic conditions they have to study in. They develop the right attitude and accept the day's temperature as it is. With this attitude they do not waste time or energy fretting and fuming about power cuts and other uncomfortable and tedious conditions they have to suffer. Through good weather and foul, winners stay focused.

4. Recreation

This is a tough one for parents to instil in average performers that when they have to concentrate on their studies, children should never recreate while studying, and never study while recreating. The electronic age has brought us gizmos such as computers, simulators, cellular-phones, head-phones, music systems, portable disc players, Walkman, television, treadmills, steppers, walkers, etc. to distract even the most committed of students. Your commitment to ensure that your children have study-friendly environment at home means that all the distraction-friendly electronic gizmos are out of the study room during study time.

Outdoor games played with friends every evening for an hour will help clear off all the fatigue accumulated in the body and mind. While playing, if they forget completely about the books and concentrate on playing the game well, they will in all probability get back to their books, after a shower, fully refreshed and will be able to produce much more than had they tried to work straight through, without this break. If your children get so tired after playing that

> Children have to fully understand the value of playtime; so they don't spend that time chatting with friends, or gossip about school as they watch others play.

they need to rest in bed, then you will need to advice them about it. Just as achievers never overeat and get sluggish, so also they never play games so vigorously that they get too exhausted to study.

5. Time Out

Achievers take small breaks of ten minutes after every hour, especially when they study for a long stretch of time, say an hour or two, at the maximum. They stretch their muscles for better blood circulation and relaxation, or take a drink of water, or visit the bathroom. The ten-minute breaks are not meant to excite or distract the mind, but instead to refresh the mind and body.

6. The Place of Study

Arrange the study area in the manner that the study-table never faces the window. Children cannot concentrate by looking out of the window. At the same time, they should never walk around the balcony or the terrace with a book in their hand. They will achieve much more in fifteen minutes sitting at their desk than they will in one hour of walking on the balcony or the terrace. It is not possible to walk and make notes, or consult reference books, or memorise a passage. If at all a child has to walk around due to medical reason, then let him choose some light reading at that time, instead of serious study. All serious study must be done at the desk.

7. Lack of Privacy

Most homes do not have the luxury of appointing a private room as children's studyroom. Children should not be made to feel that they are studying under a handicap; instead they should be encouraged to make the best of a given situation. Teach them how to build a 'mental partition' between them and the others with whom they share the room, so that they train themselves to have their solitude and not get distracted. Point out to them examples of children sitting by the sidewalks and studying under street lamps. If children living on the pavements can create a *mental cubicle* out in the open streets, in the face of so much noise and distractions, it is possible for our children to create their own private zone in the midst of family distractions. Your children have got to be just as motivated as those street kids are to do that. This is the stuff winners are made of—create your own island for study.

8. Sitting Posture

Winners can be suckers for punishment! They choose simple straight-backed chairs (without arms) to sit on as it is the best for wide-awake work. It doesn't allow for lazy, sloppy or lounging postures which hinder alertness. It enables them to get close to their work, and at the same time to be at their desk in a position in which it is easy to write and take notes and consult reference books.

9. Lighting

There should be enough light in the study-room. The fluorescent tubelight, which emits white light is evenly spread and gives a cool feeling to the eyes. Lights should be so fitted that they are neither harsh on the eyes nor hurt the eyes. They should not cast shadows over the books or on the place of work. Arrange the table lamp (if you find it to be useful) in such a way that it does not cast a glare on the books. Shadows or glares strain the eyes and your children could suffer from tired eyes.

10. Study Tool-kit

Structure your own time in such a way that the children learn by your example how precious time is, and how quickly it passes. Before they sit to study, they should make sure that the study desk has all the tools they will need during that period of time. This includes textbooks, notebooks (the class-notes and the personal notebooks), references books, dictionaries, pen, ballpen, pencil, eraser. Nothing else. No electronic gizmos as mentioned earlier, no comic books, pictures, magazines, trinkets, or foods and drinks.

11. Handling Daily Homework

The grind of the daily homework breaks most of the average students' backs, but not the backs of winners. By 2.30 p.m. after lunch, while the average student has a siesta for a

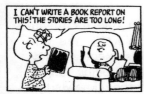 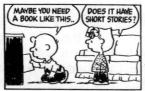 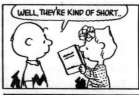
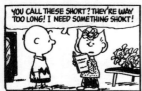 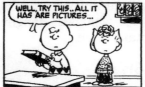 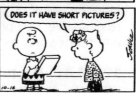

Achievers find the afternoons the best time to concentrate on the homework, while the losers snooze.

couple of hours because he is tired after his ordeal in school, the winner gets to his desk and starts his study. All that the teachers had taught in class comes back to him in a rush since it is all so fresh in his mind. He revises the class work and finishes off his homework. The phone never rings nor do the doorbells at that hour, and if it does, either others attend to it, or he's brief and to the point. By 5 o'clock in the evening he is ready to go out and play with his friends. By 7 o'clock when his parents come home from work he is relaxed to meet them and spend time chatting with them (summarising all that he learnt that day), without the pressure of homework gnawing at all of them. As the house settles down until suppertime, he will do some extra reading or revision, or indulge in some hobbies. On the other hand, the average student, after the siesta also may go out and play. By 7 o'clock when his parents come home from work, the first thing they may do is to remind him about his homework, which in all probability he will reluctantly bring forth. The parents fume and fret as they sit with him to coach him or to do his homework to save him from the teacher's wrath.

You will need to closely supervise your children's study to see that they don't let the homework accumulate or pile up. It is common to see average students waiting till the last day before the homework is due, then they begin work on it. Most times they conveniently forget about it, and when they remember, it is so late that they mostly make a hash of it. The fact that a week was given doesn't mean that they have to use seven days to do the work. You will have to coach them to keep up with each subject as they go along. Be sure that they understand what is being taught each day so that there will not be gaps in their knowledge later on. And, if they are absent or miss class, hold them responsible to find out what was taught and if there was any homework, to make it up.

12. Make Haste Slowly

While doing homework, winners have different approaches for different assignments. Certain assignments may require them to first study the principles and then attempt the written exercises. Average students *skip* learning the principles and finish the written work itself. In their haste to get the homework over and done with, they will soon forget the principles that hold those theories together. At a later date, when they revise those lessons for the examinations they may have to start memorising the principles from scratch.

13. Time-table: The Ultimate Key

Achievers make a time-table and stick to it, while others keep making time-tables on time-tables to no effect. On school days the time-table is more or else in place. Setting the routine for the holidays and staying with it is what is most important. The holiday time-table has longer study hours because achievers would like to revise and review the entire week's matter taught in class.

If you know your children's strengths and weaknesses, you will also know which subjects require more effort and which ones, more time. You will also know when they are fresh and when they are likely to be tired. Divide the day in such a way that they give the best time to the things that are *most important* and then to the *most difficult*. Thereafter, give each subject the time and attention it requires with ten-minute breaks after every hour. Lunch break could be for an hour, followed by

> *Achievers never shift the morning wake-up time on holidays. They wake up at the same hour as on school days.*

another long duration of study until tea break or playtime in the evenings. The study hours after lunch, will slow them down, so they should attend to those subjects that don't need sharp concentration or any memorising to be done. Writing or copying notes is best done at this time. Hobbies and other talents could also be nurtured at this hour. The time you allot for each of the subjects should be sufficient to enable them to achieve a substantial amount of work. There are some subjects like math and science which may require a certain minimum time. To leave such tasks in the middle would mean starting all over again from the beginning. On the other hand, science and math subjects should not take such a long time that mental fatigue sets in and renders them inefficient to cope with other subjects. When they are tired of one subject (not because they don't like it but because they have worked at it hard and long), a change to another subject can provide the relaxation that the mind needs. Attending family functions, social gatherings, or outings. should also be taken into consideration when you are planning their holiday time-table. You must make sure that equal importance is given to studies and to family get-togethers—neither should be compromised. Studies will sharpen their academic edge, and the get-togethers will sharpen their social edge.

14. Revision

The importance of revision cannot be undermined. Revision is as important to students as stocktaking is to the local grocer or the *500 Fortune* Business houses. When students revise they also review all that they have learnt. Revision cannot be done on weekdays. Students spend the weekdays in studying, reading, comprehending, making notes, memorising and completing the homework. Revision is usually done on weekends and on holidays. Hence it is very important to enter a special time for revision in the holiday time-table. That special time must be spent to revise and review the entire week's matter, and read reference books from the library and make special notes (*see* Chapter on *Examinations: the Final Countdown*).

Learning to Learn
(At School)

The child who quits has a brain and hand
as good as the next, but he lacks the sand
that would make him stick with a courage stout
to whatever he tackles and fights it out.

He starts with a rush and a solemn vow
that he'll soon be showing the others how;
then something strikes his roving eye
and his task is left for the bye and bye.

It's up to each boy what becomes of him;
he must find in himself the grit and vim
that brings success; he can get the skill
if he brings to the task a steadfast will.

No child is beaten till he gives in;
hard luck can't stand for a cheerful grin;
the boy who fails needs a better excuse
than the quitter's whining "What's the use?"
For the child who quits lets his chances slip
just because he's too lazy to keep his grip.

— ANON

It is sad to note that due to the vast syllabus which is off-loaded on to the students within a limited time-frame, there is no time to teach children the basics of how to learn. Since students have to swim through the syllabus without being taught the basics of swimming, most drown or wallow, while some improvise along the way, and a few master the skills required with the help of their parents or tutors. Teach your children, step by step, how to master the skills of learning as mentioned below. Teach them to master the many learning skills required while they are in the class, especially since you are not around to supervise how they apply themselves. When children are taught responsibility at a tender age, and have developed the ability to work on their own with a minimum of parental supervision, you can be sure those kids will measure up to your expectations in the classroom, too (see Chapter on *Choosing a Nursery School*).

Breakfasts Ensure High Energy Levels

Winners have high energy levels. They start the day with a large amount of force and vitality stored in the brain, nerves and muscles. In the class, they feel an unlimited supply of energy welling up, which can be transmitted into stamina and will power. Winners are not born that way; they make themselves so. They are determined to put in extra effort to get extra profit. They are ready to run that extra mile. To 'run that extra mile', as the saying goes, winners make sure that they stack ample stamina to do it. Winners know that soon after the morning assembly, the first three to four periods are the toughest and the most important ones of the day. They will need all the physical and mental energy to stay focused and concentrate on those subjects. Before leaving home for school, early in the mornings, they eat a hearty breakfast so that by the time they reach school their energy levels are buoyant and high. On the other hand, since losers don't wake up early enough, their mornings are never organised. Mornings are their worst moments. It is one mad rush trying to beat the

Winners don't eat to enjoy the breakfast. They eat it because they have to eat it. Eating is a functional activity.

school clock and avoid getting punished for late attendance. They carry pocket money to catch a bite in the school canteen, which they will do so in the first break—only after those three most important periods are over. Their energy levels are very low. Hunger pangs keep gnawing at their insides. While the teachers are giving their classes, they find it next to impossible to stay focused or to concentrate on the subjects taught. Losers are unable to muster their will power to make the effort to copy what is on the blackboard, because whatever the teacher wrote on the blackboard, they were unable to connect it with what she had said in class, since they weren't paying attention. We've heard the old rhyme, 'For want of a nail the battle was lost'. Here, it was for want of a breakfast the entire day was lost.

Pay Attention in Class

In class, they should give all their attention to the teachers. Average students allow themselves to daydream or to doodle on their books. Those with a winning edge over others, even if they know much of what is being taught, pay careful attention in class because they know that repetition is very essential to learning. They make notes on the new light thrown on the subject by the teacher. While paying careful attention, the good student is also *selecting*. Some of the things said in class are of prime importance for an understanding of the matter. Other remarks by the teacher are made in passing in order to provide some relaxation for the class. This selection, of which comments are essential to the matter and which comments are offered as relaxation, is very important when it comes to taking down notes in the class.

Take Notes in Class

Taking down notes is an art. Most students don't know what notes to take in class. Since it is impossible, and neither necessary, nor useful to take down everything, students must be selective in taking down appropriate notes. Things that are in the textbooks or can easily be found in reference books need not be copied in class. The attentive student knows when the teacher provides the class with a new insight into the matter, he makes a note of it so that he can study it further. Often the teacher makes connections between different points that can be found in books or gives suggestions for further reading. These points should be noted.

When the teacher gives a talk which is not in the textbooks, then the only thing a student can do is to try and write down a brief outline of the talk and fill in the details later to the best of his ability. Often it is useful to take down notes quickly on rough paper, and after class to copy them out neatly and to integrate them with other reading that may have been done on the matter, or with one's own thoughts which have developed from discussion and reflection.

> *It is essential to make a note of all that the teacher writes on the blackboard if one wants to gain maximum advantage.*

When the teacher puts something on the blackboard it is often a sign that she considers it important. Since she spends time doing this, it is not hard to copy it down.

A Quick Review

As soon as class is over, in the midst of the noise, achievers quickly make a brief mental review by recalling the gist of what the teacher just said. It is an established fact that *we forget most of what we hear almost immediately after hearing it.* Hence the sooner we repeat the lesson or recall it to mind, the more chance we have of remembering what was taught. Remember your friend who rattles off jokes after jokes and keeps the group in splits, while some of us cannot remember a single joke, or have trouble remembering the punch line? To remember a joke or an anecdote you've got to tell it to someone as soon as you can, and then share it with someone again. The more often you tell it the more confident you will become and embellish it as you go along. Apply the same method to the daily class stuff.

In Sync with Your Teacher

To be in sync is to be in tune with the teacher. But if you or your children hold animosity or hostility or indifference towards the teacher, then it will be next to impossible to get the best out of the teacher. Winners have a clear idea of what the teacher expects them to take away from the class. The teacher teaches from the point of view she has in mind; the brilliant student too shares the same outlook and draws maximum profit from it.

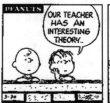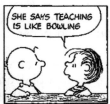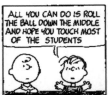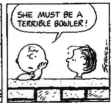

Teachers Need to be Role Models

Most teachers don't only teach students, they perform numerous other roles. To a large extent, teachers' roles are undermined by most people. While many of them are a dedicated lot filling the roles of teacher, counsellor and guide, some unfortunately are in a profession they shouldn't be. The dedicated ones do try their very best to encourage children to come out of their shells. In these stressful times, they may have to try harder to help children lighten their bags of mental and emotional troubles which weigh them down. To help the children respond positively, parents and teachers may have to band together on a one-to-one to work out strategies such as devising exercises as chores (even games) that offer opportunities:

- ❖ To exercise responsibilities
- ❖ To understand another person's perspective
- ❖ To be sharing, caring, cooperative and helpful
- ❖ To be pro-social, friendly and be liked by peers
- ❖ To be less impulsive and more self-controlled
- ❖ To be able to analyse and understand relationships
- ❖ To be able to resolve conflicts and negotiate disagreements
- ❖ To be able to communicate well

It has been proved time and again, when educators and parents work together to lighten children's *bags of woes*, then children begin to do well in academics, and their social behaviour in school and at home improves by leaps and bounds. It is almost like unlocking the child's fetters and setting him free to fly. It is truly a rewarding and a marvellous experience to watch a child who is set free and flying high. Winners are not shackled by emotional handicaps, and if they do get bogged down, they fall back on other emotional strengths to stay afloat despite the eddy of turbulence. Unfortunately, children who fair poorly academically and/or have behavioural problems in school usually are those who are burdened with emotional and mental baggage and have no buffer to fall back on. All grownups need a cushion for support whenever they fall. Children need them, too.

In closing this chapter, it would be appropriate to point out Erik H. Erikson's views contained in his book, *Identity: Youth and Crisis*, on inspirational teachers, "Good teachers... know how to alternate play, work, games and study. They know how to recognise special efforts, how to encourage special gifts. They also know how to give a child time and how to handle those children to whom school, for a while, is not important and is considered something to endure rather than enjoy, or even the child to whom, for a while, other children are more important than the teacher. But good parents also feel a need to make their children trust their teachers, and therefore, to have teachers who can be trusted . . . Again and again in interviews with gifted people, one is told spontaneously and with a special glow that *one* teacher can be credited with having kindled the flame of hidden talent. Against this stands the overwhelming evidence of vast neglect."

Learning to Learn
(At Home)

You've got to have the goods, my boy,
        if you would finish strong;
a bluff may work a little while,
        but not for very long;
a line of talk all by itself
        will seldom see you thru;
you've got to have the goods, my boy,
        and nothing else will do.

The fight is pretty stiff, my boy,
        I'd call it rather tough,
and all along the route are wrecks
        of those who tried to bluff—
They could not back their lines of talk,
        to meet the final test,
you've got to have the goods, my boy,
        and that's no idle jest.

— ANON

The Mental and Emotional Side of Study

Nobody ever told parents or children (the two 'associates' of the school *triumvirate*) that *real study* takes place only at home (after school hours). Most parents are of the impression that since they pay a hefty fee to the school, all the learning, studying and education of the child should begin and end in the school itself. Except for the residential/ boarding schools, nowhere in the world this is true. Children have to revise at home what is taught in class. Some schools with populist notions experiment with the theory of the school handling all the study-responsibilities, and the parents are delighted that they don't have to bother with teaching children at home, but when the students fare poorly at the State Board exams, they quickly revert to the old-fashioned school-home study partnership.

Children go to school from home, and come home from school carrying a heavy bag. Not necessarily stacked with books alone. Their minds are cluttered with emotional debris. They carry it with them as they shunt between home and school, and back, while the parents and teachers treat it as non-existent. This emotional debris could be identified as:

* *depression*
* *anxiety*
* *stress*
* *hatred*
* *rebellion*
* *loneliness*
* *frustration*
* *fear*
* *anger*
* *jealousy*
* *regret*
* *pain*
* *boredom*

These bottled up emotions ultimately find their outlets in many destructive forms, which in turn earns them the rebuke of the authorities either at home or at school, or both (*read* Section 4, Part II).

> *When children fair badly in school it is not usually poor IQ the cause of it, it is poor self-esteem.*

Emotions affect Performance

It is a documented fact that emotions can impede or enhance learning and school performance. Studies point out that if anxiety is too high, the child's concentration on the problem-solving situation will be impeded, and if anxiety is too low,

> *Keeping a happy frame of mind is very essential to learning.*

he will probably not be motivated to undertake a solution to the problem. Hence, moderate anxiety levels foster good school performance. The precise relation between anxiety and performance depends on the task.

According to O'Neill, Spielberger and Hansen in the *Journal of Educational Psychology*, "For well-learned or non-complex tasks (e.g. signing one's name, tying a shoe, pushing a button on request), the optimal level of anxiety is quite high. By contrast, when a student is just learning a task (e.g. learning to drive a car, learning to play tennis), or when the task is extremely complex (e.g. solving calculus problems), the optimal level of anxiety is quite low." For new or complex tasks, he performs best when he is relaxed but alert and attentive. Some researchers are of the view that children who frequently think about sad events may not perform and learn as efficiently as children who think about happy events.

According to research conducted by Mischel, Ebbeson, and Zeiss in the *Journal of Educational Psychology*, "Emotions have also been shown to influence children's ability to delay gratification. Delay of gratification, a person's ability to wait for a valuable reward rather than accept a less valuable reward immediately is an important indicator of self-control in individuals, and is regarded as a critical factor in school achievement." Since self-control helps children to cope with anxiety and stress, the techniques could be taught to children at a very early age (*see* Chapter on *Exercise Self-control*).

Poor concentration, poor memory work, poor application to studies, distractions, etc. are mostly manifestation of some of the disturbing factors mentioned above. Teachers and parents, on catching a child doing a wrong, usually punish him. Such a child is labelled as a non-conforming child. The police also do the same with criminals. This further reinforces negative behaviour. Teachers and parents may have to stop playing cops and work for long-term results. They will have to go deeper into the child's mental and emotional recesses to touch his soul and heal his emotions so that he will begin to positively respond to studies. A cheerful child is a giver while a sulking child is a receiver. With some tender, loving, care and patience we could help children become cheerful givers.

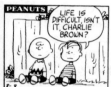 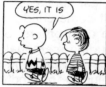 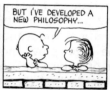 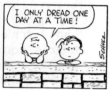

Coping with Anxiety and Stress

If children experience high levels of anxiety and stress, can they cope with it on their own? Or, can they be taught and helped by parents and teachers to cope with it? Psychologists are of the view that children are unable to cope with anxiety and stress on their own due to the complex nature of their behaviour in coping with stress, hence the need for parents and teachers to step in. Experts in the field of social behaviour recommend several techniques that can be clubbed into three separate formats:

1. Doing meditation and yoga exercises for *breathing and relaxation*. When doing yoga exercises, the child should actively participate by concentrating intensely on what he is doing, namely relaxing different parts of his body and mind.

2. Cognitive control: Psychological research carried out by Meichenbaum, Turk and Burstein, point out that telling children to think in generally positive way has not been effective in reducing anxiety and stress, but *focussing on specific pleasant thoughts* has. The *Art of Living* by Sri Sri Ravi Shankar shows how the power of *positive thinking* can radically change people's lives.

3. Learning social skills and how to *control the environment*. Social competence—the child's sense

that he is master of his environment—encompasses both social and intellectual skills that have been acquired. Authoritarian parents seem best at fostering competence in children. These parents are warm and loving; they foster independence but set limits, demands and controls on their children's actions (*see* Chapter on *Teenagers: Face of the Future*).

Everyone experiences anxiety, fear, sadness and depression, happiness, joy and elation, but some children seem to have higher achievement motivation than others, because several factors come into play, including personal standards of success, fear of failure, or hope and belief in success. Most teachers will agree that the influence of emotions on day-to-day activities is evident in children's school performance. Donald Meichenbaum and his colleagues have developed a set of questions/statements to help children develop coping skills to deal with emotional problems. The following examples of self-statements can be successfully used to reduce stress and anxiety at different times in a stressful situation:

Preparing for anxiety or stress

- What do I have to do?
- Am I going to map out a plan to deal with it?
- I'll just think about what I have to do.
- I won't worry; worry doesn't help anything.
- I have a lot of strategies to call on.

Confronting and handling the pain

- I can meet the challenge.
- I'll keep on taking just one step at a time; I can handle it.
- I'll just relax, breathe deeply, and use one of the strategies.
- I won't think about the pain; I'll think about what I have to do.

Coping with feelings at critical moments

- What is it I have to do?

- I was supposed to expect the pain to increase; I just have to keep myself in control.
- When the pain comes, I'll just pause and keep focussing on what I have to do.

Reinforcing self-statements

- Good, I did it.
- I handled it well.
- I knew I could do it.
- Wait until I tell other people how I did it.

As can be seen, these statements focus on specific ways of coping with stress rather than merely thinking good thoughts about oneself. By following these tested guidelines and procedures, students will be well prepared to cope with anxiety and stress when it arrives.

Exercise Self-control

*There's no thrill in easy sailing,
when the sky is clear and blue;
there's no joy in merely doing
things which anyone can do.*

*But there's some satisfaction
that is mighty sweet to take,
when you've reached a destination
that you thought you couldn't make.*

— ANON

The key word that sums up the stuff winners are made of is self-discipline. Every one admires the winner for his discipline. As we admire the winner and watch his behaviour closely, we will notice that he somehow has developed *control* over his passions and emotions. He is not impulsive. Children by nature are impulsive. Parents take delight when little babies do things impulsively. As this impulsive nature goes unchecked they grow up having their way. Psychologists who study behaviour have devised numerous games to train children to develop self-control and self-restraint so that they

> *Students who have not been exposed to self-control games as toddlers will have a major disadvantage over those who have learnt to be self-restrained and self-controlled.*

become better adjusted to take on life's challenges as young adults. Nursery schools and children's activity centres must incorporate lots of games and activities to develop self-restraint in toddlers, as part of the daily curriculum. Such exposures leave an indelible mark on the children's personalities and characters. We have witnessed the results of such exposures through our work with toddlers; they're overwhelming. When these toddlers grow up to be teenagers they emerge emotionally stronger, pro-social, confident, and display a tenacity to complete their tasks, among other qualities.

In his book, *Emotional Intelligence*, Daniel Goleman, (should be read by all educators and parents) very well illustrates 'The Marshmallow Test'. The teacher (experimenter) offered a proposal to the class of four-year olds. A tray of appetising marshmallows was laid out before children. She told the class that she had to leave on an errand but would return soon. Those who would wait until she returned would have two marshmallows, otherwise they could help themselves to one marshmallow. About a third of the class gave in to their impulses almost the very second the teacher left on the errand and helped themselves to the marshmallow. The remaining toddlers restrained themselves, even to the point of squeezing their eyes shut to resist the temptation of giving in to the impulse. These preschoolers were rewarded with two marshmallows when the teacher returned.

Simple games like these have far-reaching consequences in later life. Goleman points out that the faculty of Stanford University who carried out this experiment tracked down those same children some twelve to fourteen years later, who by then were adolescents, graduating from high school. The *Report* pointed out:

> "Those who had resisted temptation at four were now, as adolescents, more socially competent, personally effective, self-assertive, and better able to cope with the frustrations of life. They were less

likely to go to pieces, freeze, or regress under stress, or become rattled or disorganised when pressured. They embraced challenges and pursued them instead of giving up even in the face of difficulties; they were self-reliant and confident, trustworthy and dependable; and they took initiatives and plunged into projects. And, more than a decade later they were still able to delay gratification in pursuit of their goals.

The third or so who grabbed for the marshmallow, however, tended to have fewer of these qualities, and shared instead a relatively more troubled psychological portrait. In adolescence they were more likely to be seen as shying away from social contacts; to be stubborn and indecisive; to be easily upset by frustrations; to think of themselves as 'bad' or unworthy; to regress or become immobilised by stress; to be mistrustful and resentful about not 'getting enough'; to be prone to jealousy and envy; to overreact to irritations with sharp temper, so provoking arguments and fights. And, after all those years, they still were unable to put off gratification."

TEACHERS ARE ROAD MAPS

When parents invite discussions at home, it becomes easier for children to ask questions in class. Most children are shy of asking questions from the teacher because they're afraid they'll be snubbed or yelled at because that's how they're dealt with at home. When parents 'befriend' their children and are easy to get along with, it becomes easier for children not only to ask questions in class, but also seek the teacher's advice outside class hours. When children ask teachers for guidance and direction, they make them feel that they're interested in their subjects. It also demonstrates that your children have confidence in the teachers and want to work along with them. While average students feel hesitant, shy or indifferent to ask their teachers for help, *winners* are convinced that without the teacher's guidance they would lose their way, or waste a lot of time. Every chapter of each subject is a new terrain for a student. The teachers, with their experience in the subjects, will be able to tell the students which books are worth reading and which are not. She will be able to guide which portions of a subject require more attention and which can be done more rapidly. Like a road map, she will be able to point out the short cuts that connect different chapters.

SKILLS TO MEMORISE

Going by the amount of volumes written on enhancing memory skills, one would think that by now all the kids would have it easy. But it's not so. Memorising a poem, a formula, a theorem is time consuming. But memory work becomes a lot easier when you enjoy the subject (*see* Chapter on *Ways to Pre-empt Learning Disabilities*). Trying to memorise poetry verses, or maths and science formulae can be very tedious when the mind is dissipated, disturbed or when the student is not interested or motivated to do it. All studies, whether concept learning or rote learning, have portions which have to be committed to memory.

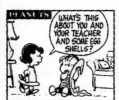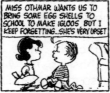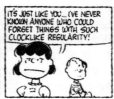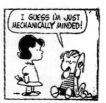

© 1961 United Feature Syndicate, Inc.

How to Memorise

When you have to teach children how to memorise, remember the following points:

1. Memory work does not start with the memory but with the intellect. *Think* first; then *understand* what they are trying to memorise. Help them to *organise* the matter before they begin to memorise. For example, they may want to group similar words when they have to memorise vocabularies. If it is a

grammatical rule, then they may want to put it in verse or associate it with some other rule in the same language or the same type of rule in another language. To ensure proper understanding you may have to consult a dictionary.

2. When they sit to memorise, they shouldn't spend a long time at it. Frequent short periods of about ten minutes will be much more valuable than an half-hour period. Explain the matter to them using imagery so that they understand it. When the matter begins to make more sense to them then they can increase their time working on it at one sitting.

3. Memory work should always be attempted at the beginning of the study hour when their mind is fresh, not at the end of the study hour when they are mentally tired.

4. The more they immerse themselves into the work of memorising the more successful they will be. While the mind thinks, allow the mind to create appropriate pictures if possible. They should *see* the words, *speak* them aloud with the mouth and voice, *hear* them with the ears, and then *write* them down. And all this while, the mind stays carefully fixed on the meaning for, if it goes wandering, they will not succeed in memorising the text.

5. Finally, you must test the kids by asking them to recite the text to you or to write it down from memory. Note down those parts where they are weakest and then give special attention to the weak areas.

Postscript

Since our education system puts a premium on cramming the entire syllabus, which parent wouldn't want to invest on books, CDs and CD-Roms offering novel techniques on memorising? Don't feel bad if you already have a shelf full of material and your children still struggle to come to grips with developing memory skills. Nothing is wrong with the material you've purchased; it's good stuff. If it's not working on your kids, it's because they are either emotionally

> *Many children see study time as punishment time; and punishment is related to pain. You will have to teach children to shift their focus from the pain zone and make study their pleasure zone.*

disturbed, or they are not interested in the matter they're trying to memorise. Suppose their favourite television serial was being aired at the time they were memorising; however hard they try, they just won't be successful. In either case, the *emotional brain* instantly hijacks all the inputs sent by the *thinking brain* by placing their disinterest, or anxiety (pain) levels on high alert. To beat the emotional brain at its own game, children will have to find enjoyment in what they are memorising. That's the toughest technique you could teach your children: to improvise methods to find joy and pleasure in their studies in order to blunt the anxiety signals sent to millions of nerve centres and the nervous system. To begin with, this will not be an easy exercise, but once they get into the habit, the switchover becomes automatic. Remember the time you had a headache and you asked your child to sit by the bed and gently rub your head? As she rubbed your forehead, you then felt the soft caresses as she played with your hair, and talked to you affectionately. After a while you smiled at her and told her your head was feeling much better. This was her healing balm. She blunted (hijacked) the pain signals by sending pleasure signals to the millions of nerve centres in the brain and to the nervous system. We have this power within us, let's put it to use. You've got to apply the healing balm to help your children to touch this power within them.

Encourage Reading
Habits

*Few children learn to love books by themselves. Someone
has to lure them into the wonderful world of the written
word; someone has to show them the way.*

— ORVILLE PRESCOTT (*New York Times* critic)

Parents and teachers often find themselves breathing down
the necks of children to read, read, and read, while children
shun books, like one shuns the virus. We all want students
to cultivate a reading habit. But how will they do that? Isn't
it amazing that students spend all their years reading books
in schools and colleges, and yet they are never taught the
art of reading? Says Jim Trelease, author of *The New Read-
Aloud Handbook*, "Reading is an accrued skill like swimming.
True, there are rules and strokes to learn but that doesn't
take much time. The only way to 'get good' at swimming is
to jump into the water and swim. And the only way to get
good at reading is to jump into a book and read. The more
you do it the better you get. The better you get the more
you like it. The more you like it the more you do it, *ad*

infinitum. But children will never get better at reading without doing it, and they won't do it if they hate it." Just as students have to be taught *how* to learn, so also they have to be taught *how* to read. The 'how' is taught by luring children into reading by giving them books that excite, entertain, amuse and inform in the way their appetite is aroused. According to Trelease, most parents and teachers view reading as something dry and artificial, to be learned by rote, filling in the blanks, or circling the correct answer.

Surrounded by so much of printed material, children waste valuable time just browsing through books out of boredom. To teach children to *want* to read, you will have to be very selective about the quality of books you recommend or gift to children. To give children dull, trivial books is a sure way to kill their appetite for reading. The old saying is, 'We don't have time for the good books; we have time only for the *best books*' (*see* Chapter on *Language Development*).

The Art of Reading

Carol Otis Hurst, in *Once Upon a Time ... An Encyclopaedia for Successfully using Literature with Young Children*, says, "If a child comes from a home in which reading prevails, he or she will probably reach out to more solid stuff eventually: books on a variety of subjects by excellent authors and illustrators, the numbers of which are legion. Unfortunately, although the situation is improving, most children do not come from such homes." To teach children how to read, parents and teachers will have to groom themselves on reading skills so that they can read to children like the way they would want them to read. Parents and teachers must read aloud with meaning and feeling to children, no matter how old they are. Just as an oyster takes a grain of sand and makes a pearl out of it, so you should take the cold words from the printed page and make them warm and alive by the way you read them aloud. The transformation of cold words into alive and emotional ideas by reading aloud is called *interpretation*. Interpretation is a very loaded expression. Interpretation calls for *voice quality, pitch, inflection, melody, force, pause, speed (rate) of words, emphasis and rhythm.* Without going into the details of interpretation, I'll attempt to broadly explain the meaning behind the art of reading. Great literature (take the example of *Ramayana* and *Mahabharata*) is great because it speaks with vitality about the great things in life. The author of great literature has re-created life's experiences on paper. You, as the interpreter of those printed words, must find the author's meaning and understand the characters about which he writes. You must know their hopes and fears, prides and vanities, feelings and emotions. You must know what songs they sing and what sentiments they applaud. You must know what gods they worship. Then you must make them talk, walk and live so realistically that the children see them as living people—see them as you see them. The art of reading lies in the art of interpretation—your listeners must feel what the characters are experiencing.

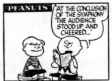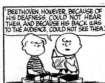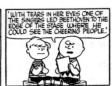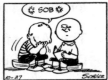

© United Feature Syndicate, Inc. 1955

Reading with a Purpose

The reading we do should have a purpose. Seeking information is a purpose; recreation is a purpose; learning a language is a purpose; and studying is a purpose. Purposeless reading is reading done when something comes into our hands (like magazines in the reception room of a doctor's clinic), and we read them because we have nothing better to do.

Besides reading with a purpose, we should know what our purpose is with regard to the particular book in our hands. The ultimate purpose will determine how we approach the book. We may merely skim through it or we may skip through it. We may read it rapidly or we may really study it.

Types of Reading

I will elaborate on the number of ways children can improve their reading skills. It is best to work on these techniques during the holidays when they have some free time and you feel relaxed.

Skimming is a fast process, and it is basic to all other reading methods. It gives us a bird's eye-view of the whole subject. It tells us whether or not the book is worth reading at all, and if it is, just what we can expect to get out of it. Skimming means reading for thought. It is a method in which the reader becomes very conscious of signs that indicate special thoughts. Some of these signs are the indentations that indicate new paragraphs. One way of skimming is to read only the first and last sentences of each paragraph. This will generally give us the skeleton of the author's thought. Another sign is the use of *italics* or **bold**. And then there are indications through the use of new paragraphs and sub-headings, or through the use of words such as, *first, secondly, therefore, however, on the other hand, in conclusion.* These are used to call our attention to significant words or passages. If after skimming through a book we find that it is worth a careful reading, our skimming has not been a waste of time. It has helped us to know what to look for when we read it the second time, and this will make our second reading much more profitable than one slow reading could hope to be.

Fast Reading

Winners regularly practise fast reading. Those who enjoy reading, develop the habit of fast reading, automatically. Here is how you can train yourself. While you may read carefully as you read for ideas, you must never read tediously. Winners train themselves to see all the words but read only those that carry essential ideas. This means that they omit words such as articles, adjectives, adverbs and prepositions. They hold on to nouns and verbs that carry most of the meaning. After having finished reading a chapter, winners summarise briefly what they have read so that ideas stay firmly in their memories. Winners who read quickly for comprehension actually get more out of their reading than the plodder does. Winners read ideas, while the plodders read words.

Rapid Reading

This means reading all the words but concentrating on the main ideas and the progress of the thought without paying too much attention to the details. Leisure reading is mostly done in this manner. Students may do fast reading and rapid reading when they indulge in recreational reading, that is, when they read light material like magazines, novels and newspapers—NEVER when studying.

One part of rapid reading is a purely mechanical process of seeing more and more on the printed page. Some see letters, others see words, and winners see sentences. A cluster of letters of the alphabet make a word. A cluster of words make a sentence, and a cluster of sentences make a paragraph. When studying an unfamiliar foreign language, it is an uphill task as one struggles to put together first the letters, then the words, and finally the sentence. Good vocabulary and language usage are important ingredients to rapid reading.

Eye-Mind Coordination

The mind can only take in at one time what the eye sees; so it is of some importance to increase the eye span, that is, the number of words that the eye sees at one fixation. As the eye moves across a printed page, it stops and then moves on. It sees only when it stops. The more often it moves the more time it will take to read a line of print. Students will have to push themselves to see phrases in clusters when they read newspapers and magazines. When reading a short story or a novel, set a time limit for a fixed portion of a book, say fifty pages and place a marker there. Setting the alarm to ring after one hour, the reader must try to finish those pages within the time set. Do set reasonable goals and do not dilute them. A conscious effort will produce better results than any amount of slow, effortless reading.

Parents as Role Models

It is a good habit for parents to read a passage or a story to their children every day. Many parents would like their children to develop good reading habits. They regularly subscribe to topical magazines and daily newspapers and they consider themselves to be avid readers. Unfortunately, many parents, under the pretext of 'no time', do not indulge in reading novels, short stories or poetry and they expect their children to develop good reading habits. Parents should not only develop reading habits but also develop a discussion habit. They must guide their children in conversation and discussion at the family dining-table where a novel or some topical matter of importance is talked about. This practice will have three benefits:

- It will arouse interest in the children to read the novel, or the article in the newspaper or magazine.
- It will encourage the children to discuss at the table whatever they read. In this manner the children will naturally 'review' the subjects they have read or studied.
- It will put an end to TV watching while eating meals.

You have realised by now how important it is to inculcate the reading habit in yourselves so that children at a very young age will enjoy reading books. Instead of bringing home toys of violence, movement and speed, LEGO, blocks and picture books are the better alternatives in instilling the concept of constructive playing, and toying with books while sitting in a place. Reading to your children regularly will draw them to books. As they reach higher classes, more and more books are heaped at them for their consumption, and they are expected to handle the load without breakdowns. The next chapter, *Principles of Study*, will succinctly tell all that it takes to master study skills to become winners.

> It is so much easier to get children interested in books when they're infants than when they get older.

Principles of Study

You are the fellow who has to decide
whether you'll do it or toss it aside.
You are the fellow who makes up your mind
whether you'll lead or linger behind—
Whether you'll try for the goal that's afar
or be contented to stay where you are.
Take it or leave it. Here's something to do,
just think it over. It's all up to you!

What do you wish? To be known as a shirk,
known as a good man who's willing to work,
scorned for a loafer or praised by your chief,
rich man or poor man or beggar or thief?
Eager or earnest or dull through the day,
honest or crooked? It's you who must say!
You must decide in the face of the test
whether you'll shirk it or give it your best.

— ANON

READING TO STUDY

Reading to study is serious reading, and many students are

unaware of it. Serious students do not indulge in 'rapid reading' when studying. The reading techniques mentioned below, if mastered, will definitely help the eye-mind coordination and improve the speed of reading-to-understand, a skill so important for children to grasp since the number of books that makes the annual syllabi is voluminous.

When attempting to read a new subject which is hard to understand, it is natural for a student to run into difficulties. With his best efforts at concentrating on the text he may have problems understanding some of the points. Tell your child, that it's no reason for him to stop. He should keep on reading. These small dark areas which he does not understand are to be expected. At times they get cleared up as one reads on since the picture becomes clearer. But if he stops every time to find the meaning of words and sentences, he is bound to give up reading. On the other hand, if the mind stays stuck on the dark areas while the eye moves ahead, taking in more words and phrases, then those passages also will make no sense. Read to him and show him by example how the mind should move on, keeping pace with the eye movement. Plodding through the book kills the spirit making studies that much more tedious. School and college books come packed with ideas, hence the need to read and re-read the books for better understanding.

> It is beneficial to read the book the second time at a good pace than to plod through it laboriously.

The purpose of study is to understand the subject from the author's point of view. A 'questioning mind' on the part of the student is very essential to serious study. Reading to study involves writing notes, jotting down points, and even making summaries of the chapters read. Comprehension becomes easier when students train themselves and develop the ability

- to spot the most important word in a given sentence
- to spot the most important sentence in a given paragraph
- to summarise the chapter into a précis form

All this is very time consuming but so rewarding in the long run; indeed, it is a lifetime asset for winners.

Reading to Understand *(3 techniques)*

- Look for main ideas.
- See which subordinate ideas prove or support those main ideas.
- Try and find the connection between ideas.

Identifying the Causes for Slow Reading
(at 100 wpm or below)

- *Inability to recognise words:* This may be due to inverting the order of letters or mixing the symbols of letters in one language with the symbols in another language, or an over-emphasis on individual letters in the process of reading.
- *Very low vocabulary:* Too many words which are unfamiliar.
- *Vocalisation:* It takes the voice much longer to produce a word than it takes the eye to see it and if these two operations are always combined, the eye will have to slow down.
- *Pointing to words:* The hands should be kept off the page when one is reading.
- Too many eye fixations.
- Regressive eye fixations (backtracking).
- Over-emphasis on oral reading: Oral reading is necessary and must be worked at, but silent reading is much more necessary for comprehension. Oral reading should come only after a passage has been comprehended.

Identifying the Causes of Poor Comprehension

- *Limited intelligence*: There is not much any one can do if a child thinks with difficulty, except to keep trying to do as much as one can.
- Undesirable physical factors, such as noisy surroundings, poor lighting, very high or very low temperatures, distracting sights.

- *Over-emphasis on oral reading:* If one is concentrating on sounds, then one is sure to miss the meaning.
- Failure to adjust reading techniques to the reading purpose and the type of material one has in hand. For instance, to apply the techniques of reading fiction to scientific books will hinder comprehension.

Formula for Quick Comprehension

- Find the main idea
- Select significant details (leaving aside what is insignificant)
- Answer questions, summarise and organise in a sequence
- Arrive at generalisations
- Follow directions
- Predict outcomes
- Evaluate critically
- Understand phrase meaning, as distinct from the meaning of the words that make the phrases up, for example, 'an eye for an eye'. This is also true of the meaning of sentences, paragraphs and the whole selection

How to Make Notes from Books

Lots of students spend a lot of time filling notebooks with volumes of notes. Many would never bother to refer to them once they are written, leave alone reading them. So a lot of precious time is unnecessarily wasted; after all making notes is time consuming.

There are three kinds of notes: (i) copying the text just as it is in the book, (ii) making a summary of the passage read, (iii) reference to the passage in a book.

1. When children own the textbook, or if the book is easily available in the school library, then there is no point wasting time copying the text just as it is in the book. If they make photocopies of books in the school library, make sure to write summaries of the important texts. Lose sheets of photocopied notes are very difficult to revise after a while.

2. Making a summary is a useful exercise because it involves personal effort, concentration and it reinforces the essential ideas of what they have read. It helps students to relate those ideas to other reading they have done and to their own thinking on the subject.

3. The exact text is copied when the author has put his ideas in such a way that it would be hard to summarise them. At times the author's use of idiom, metaphors, comparisons and examples are so compelling that if not copied exactly, their true meaning would be lost. In the case where the book is easily accessible, then small indentations could be written on slips of paper and placed in the book to serve as bookmarks.

Many students are in the habit of underlining the text pages; they also write short notes in the margins of their textbooks. This is not a good habit. It not only ruins the book but it also distracts the reader from concentrating on the contents when read at a later date. Teach children to keep their textbooks neat and 'readable' at all times.

Use of Reference Material

Reference books are absolutely essential to round off the understanding of the subject matter. In addition to studying from the textbooks, winners constantly refer to the reference books. Unfortunately, many students avoid reference books not because they are lazy, but because no one ever bothered to teach the student the method to use such books. Parents and teachers must teach and encourage children to use the dictionary, encyclopaedia, and the library so that the child's horizons of learning become limitless.

Examinations: The Final Countdown

If you think you are beaten, you are,
if you think that you dare not, you don't,
if you like to win, but you think you can't,
it's almost certain you won't.

If you think you'll lose, you've lost,
for out in the world you'll find
success begins with a fellow's will—
It's all in the state of mind.

If you think you are outclassed, you are;
you've got to think high to rise;
you've got to be sure of yourself before
you can ever win a prize.

Life's battles don't always go
to the stronger or faster man;
but sooner or later the man who wins
is the man who thinks he can.

— ANON

OVERCOMING THE FEAR OF EXAMINATIONS

Fear grips even the brave-hearts at the time of examinations. Believe me, if you don't feel the tension, you're not fully ready. It is common to see children nervous and tense before and during examinations. A lot of the tension is passed on by the family members also. Without understanding how our body systems function, we try to fight tension, and end up losing. It's a trigger built inside the brain—very essential to our survival; so forget about a brain surgery! I will show you in this chapter how you can help your children overcome their nervous tension, and use the trigger to your advantage.

All athletes and sportspersons who compete to win suffer from nervous tension just before the event. This nervous tension tones their muscles and helps them to stay in a state of razor-sharp high alert mode. It helps them to concentrate better and to perform exceedingly well. If they did not build this nervous tension within them, they would, in all probability, perform poorly. They use nervous tension to their advantage by converting it into nervous energy. They do not let the tension break them as it does to average performers. Whenever the human entity's performance, whether it is competitive sports and games or examinations, comes under the glare of the public eye, the reptilian brain takes over the systems by sending SOS signals which throw humans off balance. If the cerebral cortex (thinking brain) does not come to the rescue and balance out the red alert signals or the fight-or-flight messages sent by the reptilian brain, then fear takes control of the entire body systems: physically, mentally and emotionally (*see* Chapter on *How The Mind Works* for a detailed understanding). The three main categories of the fear symptoms which affect the physical, mental and emotional are listed below:

Physical

- Rapid heartbeat
- Stomach nervousness, nausea, dysentery
- Hot flashes—feeling of faintness
- Mild vertigo
- Hyperventilation—gasping for air

- Eye tearing or a running nose
- Fever build-up
- Joint ache, and pain in neck, shoulder or back

Mental

- Loss of memory, including the inability to recall facts and figures accurately
- Thought blockage—the mind going absolutely blank like a mental paralysis
- General disorganisation

Emotional

- A sense of being overwhelmed
- A sense of having lost control—helplessness
- Panic state
- Feelings of terror
- Embarrassment and shame

Make Tension Work for You

The best way to help children overcome psychosomatic breakdowns is to learn lessons from the sportspersons who are their icons. Since the mind and body naturally build up nervous tension, there is no point in fighting it off. Instead, help them make it work to their advantage; convert tension into an energy force—just like their favourite sportspersons do. The tension inside the body builds up to something similar like a winding mechanism in a mechanical toy. The more the tension in the winding mechanism the better it is for the toy's motion.

So also it is with us. When we are taut with tension, our physical and mental systems are at a razor-edge performance level. This tension is good for us—up to the point when we know how to harness it and use it to our advantage. Most of humanity succumbs to this tension because they keep fighting it off. Since we cannot pre-empt or shut down the *fight-or-flight* signals sent by the *reptilian brain* to the billions of impulse centres inside us, we will have to neutralise the fear impulses which will otherwise drive us into the *flight* mode. We will have to make a conscious effort to feed our subconscious mind with positive inputs of determination, enthusiasm and belief in ourselves. Like our sports icons, we must learn warm-up techniques to keep the tension under control so that it is released in measured doses to complete the task successfully. Achievers develop their own warm-up techniques. We, too have to do the same. It means we will have to talk ourselves into winning; we will have to think positive, believe in ourselves and remind ourselves that we are capable of achieving what we've been working on so hard for so many months. We have to give ourselves a good pep talk time and again. *Auto suggestion,* when used like a *mantra,* will release positive juices in the brain ushering a *flow* of confidence to the entire body systems. We will feel a surge of confidence within us. It will give our minds a razor-sharp edge to perform at peak level.

> *People who feel good about themselves produce good results.*
> — BLANCHARD AND JOHNSON (*The One-minute Manager*)

The Will to Succeed

Many bright students before taking an exam already know that they will do badly. They study so hard throughout the year and at the time of giving their exams they break down. Success or failure begins first in the mind. Deep in the subconscious mind the fear of failure or the will to succeed gets nurtured. These negative or positive inputs trigger the billions of brain cells to respond to acts of failure or acts of success—to despondency or to confidence. Some of us give up with or without hurdles. Some run through the hurdles knowing that they will *not* succeed. And, some overcome hurdles and achieve success. Achievers think and talk positively, and like jugglers juggle with ideas and options on how to overcome the hurdles. Losers, on the other hand, think and talk negatively or cynically and lack the *will* to find solutions. Achievers look for opportunities while losers look for alibis.

> *We are the products of our own thinking. We are the products of the negative or positive stimulants which our brain cells get accustomed to respond to.*

Motivation to Take an Examination

The will to act upon a particular course of action gets its stimulation through motivation. Many parents believe that the best form of motivating children to do well in exams is by dangling baits or by offering bribes to them—"If you study hard and do well in your exams I will buy you a ..." (see 'Use of Reinforcement' in the Chapter on *Disciplining Children*). Motivation is not about baits and bribes; instead, motivation is an in-built, self-sustaining, goal-oriented, feel-good mechanism that keeps going on and on. The power to motivate ourselves lies in the brain—and not in material objects. We have to believe in the power of the brain. The human brain is such a marvellous piece of creation that we have inherited. To maximise on its powers, we have to know more about its functions and capabilities. Without the road map, most of us are ignorant of its inherent powers, and so we choose to wallow in misery. Its capacity is unfathomable. Through research we have learnt that the power of the brain to process information is staggering. Compare it with the fastest computer built. The computer can only make connections one at a time. By contrast the brain can connect to several twenty-eight billion nerve centres in a span of about fourteen-thousandth of a second (14 milliseconds) as researched on mice, and twenty-thousandth of a second (20 milliseconds) in humans. This awesome power is lying dormant and untapped in most humans. Many of us would rather believe that we are born underprivileged and mediocre than capable go-getters.

> Within each of us lies the power to mobilise our abilities and to destroy our fears. We have the power to convert failure into success, and to turn defeat into victory.

EXAMINATIONS: YOUR PASSPORT TO SUCCESS

The Final Preparation

Your children have been preparing themselves for this moment—to take an examination. Achievers are adequately prepared to take the examination. Since they studied regularly throughout the year, they do not need to study right up to the last minute. On the other hand, the average students wait for the last week before the exam to complete their course of study. They spend sleepless nights trying to cram through volumes of what seems like unending subjects. With so little time on their hands and such a vast syllabus to cram, they hit the panic button. As the countdown to the examination day (D-day) begins, fear takes control of all their faculties and they go through the motions of studies and revision in a daze. They are worried, anxious and in a confused state of mind. They already know that they will do poorly or fail in the examinations. They pray for miracles to happen, that somehow they scrape through the exams.

All students know that sooner or later they will appear for tests and examinations every year. And, yet only a small percentage of the students know how to go about preparing for the tests and exams in advance. The approach to prepare for tests and exams is not the same as one approaches the on-the-spot painting competition. The approach to study-preparation should be long term. Once again, look at the athletes: they take time out to train throughout the year. Our approach to preparing for the exams should be that of a marathon runner. The marathon runner maintains a sustained speed and stamina to cover long stretches of distance before reaching the finishing line. So also students will have to develop a sustained work-tempo the year round, in order to reach the finishing line successfully.

Revision—The Mother of Learning

I hear, and I forget.
I see, and I remember.
I do, and I understand.

— ANCIENT CHINESE PROVERB

Achievers use the 'exam preparation time' to *revise*. Revision time is not spent on learning new matter. New and unfamiliar matter is learnt during study time on regular weekdays. Revising for tests and examinations means going over the matter already studied. Students, who play the fool throughout the year, wind up cramming the text during the time assigned for revision. Teachers and parents should emphasise this difference to the students so that they fully understand the concept of daily study and revision for exam preparation. They should never mix up the two concepts.

Exam preparations have two types of revisions. There is *oral* revision and there is *written* revision. And both go hand in hand.

Oral Revision

Achievers rely mostly on the notes they have made. That extra time they had spent during study hours making comprehensive notes was worth the investment. They are familiar with their notes since they have gone over those notes at the weekly, monthly and quarterly revisions. It saves them time wading through the textbooks and other reference books. Since they have studiously adhered to the time-table they had earlier chalked out, there is no new material to learn. At the same time, revision is not a passive activity. With more understanding of the subject come more insights. When a new thought occurs, they quickly peg it to what they already know. They improvise as they go along, assimilating and enhancing their horizons through new techniques of understanding and memorising.

Written Revision

Oral revision is fifty per cent of the preparation. The other fifty per cent is the written revision. Winners know that without simulators, pilots could never master the art of flying a plane, so without written revision they could never master the art of writing the exams. Excellent speakers, who are sought after, train themselves through several practice sessions to deliver their speeches in the exact mode they would address the audience. While boring speakers take the audience for granted and speak without preparation. Students appearing for exams know that the mode of delivery will be *writing*, hence they will have to prepare themselves likewise. Achievers jump into the pilot's (simulator) seat by getting hold of question papers of the previous years and practise answering them within the set time-frame. They set aside a few minutes at the end to review all that they wrote. 'Practice makes perfect' is the old adage made new when achievers give themselves that winning edge over others. The more they attempt 'mock' test papers the sharper their comprehension powers become and greater the ability they develop to complete the papers accurately and rapidly. Hard as it may seem to the average student, but doing these exercises is working *smart*.

Regret and Remorse

Average students spend a lot of time like unfocused waiters in a busy restaurant, rushing hither and thither, back and forth, pretending to be busy without serving the guests or attending to their needs. Such students pull wool over their parents' eyes by announcing that they are studying when, in reality, they play the fool. When the results show that they did poorly, they cover their tracks with alibis and excuses, regrets and remorse. This is one of the most wasted emotions in human enterprise. It projects a weakling. He first reneges on his responsibilities and thereafter refuses to be held accountable. The common refrain failures sing sweetly is: "The harder I work the tougher it is to pass," implying that he was okay and did his best, but his teachers/examiners are not okay, and were out to victimise him.

We look for before and after
and pine for what is naught
our sincerest laughter
with some pain is fraught
our sweetest songs are those that tell of saddest thought.

— PERCY BYSHE SHELLY (*Ode to a Skylark*)

TAKING AN EXAMINATION: YOUR HOUR OF RECKONING

Self-indoctrination

The chapters above, if put into practice, would help you to activate your *thinking brain*. But that is not everything. To be inspired by the Muse of Learning in the examination hall, your *reptilian brain* and the *emotional brain* will have to work in sync with the *thinking brain*. The *emotional brain* must be activated to keep the *reptilian brain* in check so that it does not set off a series of alarm bells ringing and your *thinking brain* gets overwhelmed by distress signals and is rendered paralysed by fear. We do not want the *thinking brain* to shut down. Try to block all emotional debris from cluttering your mind (*see* Chapter on *How the Mind Works*). At this point, the pep talk comes in handy. You literally indoctrinate yourself to believe in your abilities. Look yourself in the mirror and tell yourself that today is going to change the course of your destiny. You are going to put your best foot forward. You have prepared yourself thoroughly for the exam ahead of you. Come what may, you will not let yourself down. You will do your very best. As you give yourself this pep talk, smile at yourself. Stay cheerful, and with a song on your lips and spring in your feet, greet your family as you eat your breakfast and get ready to strut off to write your exams.

Make sure you leave home well ahead of time so that you do not get stuck in traffic snarls. All your writing equipment is checked and ready, so also are your admit card, identification papers and your wrist-watch. Of course, you would know much in advance and make a note of the date-sheet, time, and venue of examination.

Code of Ethics

A person cannot do right in one department whilst
attempting to do wrong in another department.
Life is one indivisible whole.

— MAHATMA GANDHI

True, examinations are make-or-break situations. If we do well in the exams, we will score a very high percentage enabling us to attend the best colleges, and later be employed in the best companies, and our road to success is guaranteed. On the other hand if we do badly, we may end up in a third-rate college or in an unknown vocational training college and then end up on the lower middle class rung, struggling to make a living for the rest of our lives. If the goal of study is result-oriented, then the hour of reckoning is the precise hour when we sit to write the examination. All studies are the pursuit of knowledge. The pursuit of knowledge is the pursuit of truth. Gandhi had defined God as Truth. Indeed, if we use unethical or unfair means in any form to pass the examinations, we have not only failed in the pursuit of knowledge, but have sinned against God. In the case of public examinations, the law comes down with a heavy hand on such delinquent students. Being blacklisted by the Board of Controller of Examinations, the student will carry the failure's stigma for life.

In the Examination Hall

This is your moment of truth. You have prepared well for this moment and you will deliver well by indoctrinating yourself that this is going to be your finest hour. You will be mentally alert and physically fresh since you have rested well. As you have trained yourself to be punctual and proper, so you will arrive slightly ahead of time. When the exam paper is given to you, read it fully in a very calm manner. Keep your excitement in check. You do not want your *thinking brain* to get overwhelmed by the emotional brain with thoughts of overconfidence or despondency. If the question paper is easy, then don't jump with joy doing mental somersaults; this is not the hour of celebration. Finish the question paper well, first. If the question paper is tough, don't get miserable or give up without a fight. You owe yourself a fighting chance in order to win. This is that chance. You will begin the question paper by answering first only those questions which you feel very competent in handling. After that, you will attempt your second best question. As you sail through these answers, the juices of confidence will begin to flow inside your body systems and when you begin to warm up feeling good about what you are doing, your *Muse* will automatically take over and guide you to handle the difficult questions. You must attempt and answer every question and complete the question paper on time. Though you will write rapidly, your answers must be written neatly, precisely and methodically—keeping a regular check on your watch. Finally, you will fully revise your answer sheets before handing in your papers.

Appendix

Appendix:
2 Case Studies

ARPITA'S SEARCH FOR IDENTITY

Rani's Story

Rani Sachdev came from Mumbai to discuss her daughter's problem. Arpita was a third-year MBBS student in Mumbai. In a soft voice she started to say that she didn't know whether it was her or the daughter who had the problem. "Let's put the cart and the horse in the right order, so start at the very beginning," I told her. Here's her two-hour story in brief: Her husband, an engineer by profession, had worked for an engineering company for close to thirty-three years. He was vice-president, projects. About six years ago when management gurus talked about restructuring and downsizing, her husband read the writing on the wall and decided to 'look around' for new openings. When he was offered a job in Manchester, UK, they began to talk about moving to the UK with Arpita's schooling top on their list. Arpita was against moving to Manchester. The parents assured her that there were excellent schools in London and she could study and live there. But she was adamant; she wanted to complete her studies in Mumbai. A year passed by—squabbling, arguing, discussing. Arpita was the apple of her father's eye, so he wouldn't leave without her. Meanwhile, with 'young blood' being infused in the management, her husband was getting tense and stressed out. She feared that once he resigned from the company he would vegetate. Rani had to force the decision on the family. She began to pack her bags, as she made arrangements with her relatives to accommodate Arpita in Mumbai, and locked up their Peddar Road apartment. Rani and her husband moved to Manchester. In the five years, Arpita never visited them, though the parents would come to Mumbai regularly.

During the past year Arpita got romantically involved with a young man from Kerala. When Rani got to hear of it from the relatives, Arpita denied it. Now, the relatives told Rani that they wouldn't accommodate Arpita any more for the burden of responsibility was too much on them. On her fourth visit to Mumbai within ten months, Rani forced the truth out of her and insisted on meeting the young man. Rani met Rajan Thayil in a tight apartment in Kurla (a suburb in Mumbai). Rajan was a medium-built, pleasant young man who lived with his parents and younger brother. Driving back to Peddar Road she didn't know whether to scream, laugh it off, rant, cry, or what. Whom to blame? The feelings and thoughts weren't positive. If she had voiced her opinion, Arpita would pounce at her. So, she kept quiet. The next day she left for Manchester, giving Arpita the keys of the Peddar Road apartment. Soon, she and her husband were back in Mumbai—within two months. Arpita and Rajan had set their wedding date. Rani had resigned herself and prepared her husband to accept Rajan in the family. But, while the wedding arrangements were going on, barely a week before the wedding, Arpita attempted to kill herself.

It was past midnight, and Arpita wasn't home. Her mobile was switched off. Both parents were worried sick. Rani gave her husband a sedative and put him to sleep while she kept vigil. At two-thirty in the morning Arpita walked into the house, looking upset. She walked past her mother, went to her room and slammed the door shut. As Rani softly shut her bedroom door, she heard Arpita shouting into her mobile phone.

It was eleven-thirty the next morning and Arpita hadn't surfaced. Rani knocked on the door without a response. Her sixth sense sent a tingling sensation down her spine. With the help of the house servants they forced open the door. She saw Arpita in bed, lifeless. They quickly bundled her in the car and rushed her to a private clinic in the neighbourhood, and had her stomach pumped. As she waited for Arpita to revive, she called Rajan.

When Arpita regained consciousness there was pandemonium. She screamed incoherently, and accusingly pointed at her mother. The doctor and the nurse asked Rani to step out of the room. Holding Rajan's arm she told the nurse that her mother had driven her to suicide since she was against the marriage. On being discharged, the clinic recommended Arpita to a psychiatrist. After weeks of arguments she finally saw one. Thereafter, she talked to a couple more.

Rani was very confused. The more accommodating she was towards her daughter the more the divide between them. She couldn't fathom why Arpita had turned against her. Why she hated her so much? "I want my daughter back. Can you help me," she pleaded. I told Rani that I could only answer those questions after I met Arpita, but she would have to call for that appointment herself. Rani felt defeated. "She'll never call you," she said, "because she doesn't think anything is wrong with her." So I left it at that. A fortnight later, Rani called from Mumbai saying that Arpita was visiting some friends in Delhi. In case she got in touch with me, I should "*never* mention our meeting". A few days later, I received a call from Arpita Sachdev asking for an appointment.

Arpita's Story
1st Meeting

My parents are very selfish. They live for themselves. They abandoned me and settled in England; they left me here on my own. I had to live with those horrid relatives and follow their silly rules. Nobody understands me. My aunt never liked me; she was stricter with me than with her children. My Mom paid them well, you see. They could do anything and nobody bothered; but everything I did was reported to my parents. My mother is a great manipulator; she gave everybody the impression that she was for the wedding, but deep down she hated Rajan. She hated his apartment, his family, his job. He doesn't have a house on Carmichael Road, so what? But, he's hard-working and ambitious. My mother thinks he's an opportunist. She didn't have to say it, I know her mind, after all, I'm her daughter. She never liked Rajan one bit and I hate her for that. You know, I tried to kill myself. How? I took twenty-two valium pills. I wish I had died. Would I do it again? No, I don't think so. You know I've seen three psychiatrists since then. I'm all right now. Of course, this was my first attempt; I've never tried to kill myself before. You think I've done it before? You're wrong. No, I was never in love. When I was in school, I even toyed with the idea of becoming a nun, so, you see, no boys. Rajan's my first love. I'm wasting your time, you know. Am I wasting mine? No, I don't think so. You're easy to talk to. Oh, you must meet my mother; she's so damn calculating and domineering. What's the difference between my mother and Rajan? That's a stupid equation. I'll tell her you'd like to meet her.

2nd Meeting (the next day)

Last night you kept me awake. You had upset me. How could you equate Rajan and my mother? Okay, you said, what's the difference? To me, it's the same thing. I love one and I hate the other. One is selfless and the other is selfish. She thinks about her image in society, while he thinks what will make me happy. Of course, I'm sure. For Rajan, I come first—then his family. Yes, he's a family man, that's why he brought his parents and younger brother to Mumbai. After marriage where will I live? In Kurla, where else? So, why I took the valium? My Mom's the cause. You see, that night my Mom-in-law got really upset. According to Rajan, she said that woman-to-woman she sensed that my Mom was against the wedding and that was a bad omen. His Mom's assessment was right. My mother is evil, I know. Rajan worked out a compromise. Since his mother and my mother had reservations about the wedding, the date should be postponed. I told him not to be a jackass. They'll all come round after a while. Here I was fighting my family to marry him, and there he was telling me to postpone the date. But he's like that. He wants everyone happy. Then I realised he was adamant about the postponement; nothing could change his mind. When I looked at the watch, it was six-thirty. I had class to attend, so I took a pill to sleep. I was feeling so sad. I cried and cried into my pillow. I felt very lonely and wanted to sleep but couldn't. What do you mean, 'jilted'? By whom? Rajan wasn't jilting me. He only wanted some more time. Yes, it was a terrible feeling—being alone and lonely; but not jilted. What a mess! I told myself, to hell with it; if only I could sleep, and kept taking the pills one at a time, I think.

So, what happened after I took the pills? I woke up in this clinic and saw my mother hovering over me. She nauseated me; so I told the doctors to get her out of the room. Of course, Rajan was at my side. He gave me the strength I needed. How he got there? I don't know how he got there. Rajan being afraid? What has he to be afraid of? You think the police would question him? Why? I don't think he was at my bedside to save his own skin. So, you see my Mother took me to this private clinic to keep it hush, hush. Wasn't she clever? Are you trying to be philosophical now? You're saying that to know differences I must first identify similarities? Okay, I'll try and think about differences and similarities.

3rd Meeting (three days later)

I want to tell you that Rajan and I didn't talk much since yesterday, and you're the cause of it. Why? Well, I asked him if he was at my bedside to save his own skin, as you put it. He went ballistic. He wanted to know who had planted that stupid idea in my head. He asked me if I was seeing another shrink, and I told him I was. What (surprised)? You're not a shrink? Thank God. I'll tell him you're not a shrink. You see, I promised him I won't see any more psychiatrists. He doesn't have faith in them, and it's a waste of time and money, according to him. You're right, Mom did a clever thing by taking me to that clinic. It saved her from a scandal and it saved Rajan from being questioned by the cops. You know what I just did? Oh, my God, I put my mother and Rajan on the same level. Okay, there's another thing that came to my mind last night. It's rather confusing.

I think you need to know. In Class XI, I had taken a fancy to a guy studying in Campion School. Yes, that's the time my parents wanted me to join them abroad, instead I fought them tooth and nail and I stayed back for that jerk. When he ditched me, the earth below me gave way and I wanted to die. I even thought of cutting my wrists but didn't have the guts for it. Why are you smiling? What's a 'trigger?' So, you think that's the 'trigger' you've been looking for? (suddenly she sees the flow) ! Good heavens, each time I don't get my way with guys—each time I get, jilted, rejected, scorned— at that point I want to kill myself? I'm such a miserable creature. Now what? You're asking me to be a detective? I should make two lists, one of my Mom and one of Rajan and you want me to assign motives to their actions? That's weird. That's not going to prove anything. Why do you insist? Okay, I'll think about it.

Curtain Call (six weeks later)

When they came to meet me, Rani and Arpita were together and smiling; it was obvious that the hatchet was buried between the mother and daughter. Rani got back her daughter, I guess that was reason enough to smile. Their immediate plans were to take a month's holiday on a European cruise liner. There was no mention of Rajan at all. Rani had also told her relatives to find a buyer for the Peddar Road apartment. After the cruise, Arpita would complete her studies in Manchester, and would settle down permanently in the UK. Her parting words were, "I learnt a lot from you, especially about a calf following the herd, so I'm going where I belong." On her way out she left an envelope on the table. It contained the 'assignment' of assigning motives to the two people she loved and hated.

"To Sir, with Love,

Doing the 'two lists of assigning motives' was the toughest exercise I have ever done in my life. You're very subtle in the way you have guided me. For a couple of weeks, I tore pages and pages as I wrote, then rewrote and tore some more pages, then rewrote and wrote again the two lists about my Mom's love for me and Rajan's. At first, this exercise made no sense at all; there was so much venom inside me. I never realised that writing would cleanse me and make me see things in a clear light. I cried my heart out as I was losing out on one—the love of my life; and my heart ached as I saw through my tears a mother's pain of holding on to me. Yes, Mom is dominating, decisive and blunt. She intrudes into my space and makes huge mistakes all the time without admitting to them. If she hasn't changed in all these years, she will not change now. I've searched and searched for 'motives' for her rude actions and behaviour, and concluded it's simply a mother's prerogative. I, too, paid her back in the same coin—tit for tat. The difference being that my hatred took me away from her, while her dominating behaviour kept me in her orbit. She likes to control people around her—Dad, me, everyone. Through all her faults, her love was without fault. I can accept her the way she is only because of that quantity called, motherly love. She loved me and believed in me even when I was nasty to her.

About Rajan, you helped me see him in a new light. One of Mom's 'instincts' about him proved right. I didn't realise his love for me would be an anchor to assist his family. His caring for his parents and younger brother—which I was ga-ga about since I saw those actions virtuous—came first. (My thoughts are so clear on this, but I'm confused on words.) The night I took the pills to kill myself was not because of Mom as I'd believed, but because he contradicted his love for me. He chose his family instead of me. Shamelessly, I kept throwing myself at him while he shunned me. No man is worth dying for. I feel so much stronger today. Rajan and I have drifted apart and I am not upset about it. I think his family is convinced I am a suicidal nut-case. I can move on without carrying his baggage of ill feelings. He used me as much as I used him—I used him to get even with my Mom. I am still caught up with a niggling thought: first, I lost my parents to gain Rajan; now, I lose Rajan to gain my parents. I guess, it's better this way than to have lost both, or my life. I'm not feeling empty inside; I'm filled with hope. I have my life ahead of me, and this thought makes me feel upbeat and good. Writing this made me go back in time. I won't look back again. I'm moving on. Thank you, Sir, for being there for me."

— ARPITA

After reading the letter, I folded it and put it back into the envelope. There was reason to smile. Arpita had set herself free.

MEETING A FATHER'S EXPECTATIONS

Yashovardhan Mittal's father was a practicing high court judge. Yashovardhan rang me up and said that his uncle had given him my number and he was calling me to ask for an appointment. The sixteen-year old was punctual. His opening statement was, "Uncle said, you wanted to see me. Here I am. What do you want me to do?" I was taken aback. I recalled Dinesh, whom he called 'Uncle', telling me a couple of months ago that a good friend of his, who was a high court judge, was having a problem relating to his son, and to do something about it. I'd told Dinesh to tell the lad to give me a call. And now here we were face to face. As he was studying in Class X, I asked him about his best subjects. "Maths and science," he said promptly. With a wave of his hand and a chuckle he said that he only studied during the exams and he'd score hundred per cent in maths and close to ninety-eight per cent in science. The rest of the time he devoted to cars which were his passion. So, where was the problem? "My problem, sir, is my father," he said. "He's such a nerd. He's constantly at me, and then blames Mother for spoiling me. He doesn't talk; he commands and orders around. He thinks we're criminals and the home is his courtroom. He says he has earned his reputation through hard work, and I'm just lucky at the tests and exams. The roof above our heads he has earned by toil and dedication. A number of times he has called my mother 'stupid' and 'brainless' He's too much. Get him off my back. You know, sir," he added mischievously, "should I ask him to see you?"

"You want your father off your back?" I asked him. "Sure, that's what I want. If only you could do that I'd breathe easy." I had his interest when I assured him the easiest thing to do was to get his father off his back. Yashovardhan was in high spirits. He was expecting me to instantly pick up the phone and order the judge to back off, or lay off his son. He was probably imagining his father's expressions and reactions to my orders and was grinning away when I interrupted his thoughts. I explained to Yashovardhan that his father was a learned judge with a reputation of being a no-nonsense guy, so he couldn't be ordered around; instead, he should use *subtle strategy* to get *even* with his Dad. He liked the idea of *getting even* through subtle strategy. I gave him a blank sheet of paper and a pencil to jot down the points.

To start him off, I asked him how he'd managed to be so punctual for the meeting, he said, that's the trait he inherited from his father. And, he came in a car. I asked him if his driver was outside on that cold wintery morning? Yashovardhan said he drove his own car. "How could you afford the car?" I asked him. He admitted it was his father's car he was driving. "How did you get the driving licence at sixteen?" I asked. His Dad had arranged it. "And you live in a spacious bungalow on Pandara Road?" Yes, his Dad was allotted the bungalow on his appointment as justice of the high court. I then told him a parable of the landlord and a tenant.

In Nizamuddin, there lived a landlord who was looking for a tenant to live on the first floor of his house, and there was a tenant who was looking for a house to live in. The landlord who lived on the ground floor was happy to see the tenant move in, and the tenant was happy to move into a well furnished and comfortable house. A few weeks later, the tenant began to get annoyed with the landlord for prying and interfering in his life. But the landlord was only making sure that his first-floor apartment was used well and managed well by the tenant. The tenant was fed up of being told, "Keep the music low; don't hit nails in the wall; don't waste the water; don't have loud parties; don't keep pets; not to park the car too near the gate; don't move the furniture at night." That was too much for the tenant to bear. The poor tenant felt miserable and unhappy; he whined and whined to people about his nosey landlord. Would he ever be able to get the landlord off his back, wondered the tenant?

"Did the tenant have a solution to his problem?" I asked Yashovardhan. "Sure," he said. "If the tenant was not happy with the landlord he should find another house."

"Suppose that tenant is you and your father the landlord, are your ready to hand over the car keys and driving licence, and walk out of the comfortable bungalow you live in? That's the surest way to get your Dad off your back in a jiffy. But if you continue to live under his roof and use his property, he's going to be minding you and telling you off from time to time. So, come to think of it, you don't have many choices. By your whining you've put yourself in a 'shape up or ship out' situation. Either you'll have to shape up to your father's expectations, or ship out and make your own rules." Yashovardhan did not expect the story to take such a turn; he was so shaken that he quietly excused himself and left.

A week later Dinesh called me and told me that the kid liked the story of the 'Nizamuddin landlord'; but he was too embarrassed to get back to me since he had left in a huff. I called up Yashovardhan and told him to come and hear the second story I had on *How to get Your Landlord Eating out of Your Hand.* He liked that and we set the date.

That morning Yashovardhan was again punctual. "You punch hard," was his opening statement. Since he was here again, I knew he was ready for more. As we got started I asked him to write down his father's strengths. When he asked, "Not mine?" I told him that at this point, his strengths didn't measure up in his father's view. To get his father eating out of his hand, he would need to know the stuff his father was made of, his qualities of discipline. In identifying his father's strengths he would have identified his father's expectations, also. And, in measuring up to his father's expectations, Yashovardhan would not only win him over to his side, but also learn to discipline himself. The lad started writing. When he finished, he handed me the paper; there were four main behaviour traits and umpteen qualities. We took the four behaviour traits which were the main arteries that fed the qualities of the man. According to Yashovardhan,

The judge was a voracious reader, while Yashovardha read only his class textbooks. The lad didn't like reading. He said, fiction novels bored him since he found them to be 'predictable'. As he was extremely good at maths and science and loved the subjects, I suggested a few titles related to science fiction, and a few biographical novels. He promised to try one. I quickly loaned him my copy of *A Beautiful Mind*.

Yashovardhan's father was tidy and methodical. Boys are boys and that's why God made mothers—to clean up the mess. Immediately, we worked out a programme where neither the house servant, nor his mother was to keep his room clean. He was going to do it all by himself. He would wake up a little early to get used to the idea of making his bed, caring for his clothes and keeping his books in order. His father kept all his books on a shelf very orderly, said the lad. I was beginning to sense respect in his voice towards his father.

The judge was organised and structured. Yashovardhan was ready to discipline himself with the help of a time-table. On school days, his time was pretty much structured; it was on holidays that he lost time deciding on what to do and never got to doing much. So, we worked out the same waking hours as on school days and went right through bedtime, putting structure to his weekends and holidays.

Yashovardhan's father was a religious man. Every morning he meditated and said his prayers. He fasted every Tuesday in obeisance to Lord Hanuman. This was my toughest moment, to inspire the lad with the sense of the sacred. For starters, Yashovardhan agreed to stand for a minute in silence in the small prayer room in the house; he didn't know how to pray, and wondered whether he was an agnostic or an atheist. He got red in the face, but finally agreed to bend down and touch his parents' feet and take their blessings every morning before leaving for school.

I liked the look on his face. His eyes had that glint in them which comes from having a sense of purpose. We both knew he had prepared a fool-proof *subtle strategy* to get even with his father. Not for a moment did I doubt his zeal in executing the plan of action at home. But I had to warn him about the time it would take to get his father off his back and eating out of his hand. I had to be careful not to dampen his spirits. When I asked him how long could he hold on to the action plan? He said, he'd follow the plan till his father came round. And, after that? He had nothing to say. I explained to him that his father wasn't going to be taken in by short spurts of good behaviour. His father would bide his time to satisfy himself that his son lived up to his expectations. He would take his own time to check and cross-check, mentally, to verify any inconsistencies in his son's new behaviour pattern. That could be time consuming. So, once the action plan was on track, don't give up midway, or get frustrated because your father won't buy any of that 'good behaviour' stuff. Yashovardhan wanted to know how long it would take him to reach his goal? We put it down to ten per cent of his age. Being about sixteen-years old, it would take sixteen months to melt the judge. Yashovardhan sighed with relief. He was expecting a lifetime of struggle. According to him, a year passes by so quickly, so what's sixteen months?

Six months later, Yashovardhan phoned me to confirm if I'd received the invitation to his parents' wedding anniversary? There was a note of pride in his voice when he said he was organising the entire party, and I must attend. I, too, was looking forward to meeting his parents. When he introduced me to his parents, the judge put his arm around his son's shoulders saying, "You've done wonders with Yasho. You've made a man out of him." I told him the plain, simple truth, "He admires you so much; he wanted to become like you and didn't know how to."

And a woman who held a babe against her bosom said,
"Speak to us of children."
And he said:
"Your children are not your children;
they are the sons and daughters of Life's longing for itself.
they come through you but not from you,
and though they are with you, yet they belong not to you.
You may give them your love but not your thoughts.
For they have their own thoughts.
You may house their bodies but not their souls,
for their souls dwell in the house of tomorrow,
which you cannot visit, not even in your dreams.
You may strive to be like them, but seek not
to make them like you.
For life goes not backward nor tarries with yesterday.
You are the bows from which your children
as living arrows are sent forth.
The archer sees the mark upon the path of the infinite,
and He bends you with His might
that His arrows may go swift and far.
Let your bending in the archer's hand be for gladness;
for even as he loves the arrow that flies,
so He loves the bow that is stable."

— KHALIL GIBRAN *(The Prophet)*

Bibliography

This bibliography has a two-fold purpose. The first purpose is to give due recognition and thanks to the numerous thinkers and writers whose books, journals and magazines the author has delved into and used as authentic research carried out by these great masters to reinforce his own theories and beliefs. The second purpose is to offer a list of books to read which you may find stimulating and enlightening.

Adele Faber and Elaine Mazlish : *Liberated Parents, Liberated Children* (Avon Books).

Albert Bandura and C.J. Kupers : *Journal of Abnormal and Social Psychology* (1964). *Alive,* March, 2004.

Anthony Robins : *Awaken the Giant Within* (Simon & Schuster, 1992).

A.P.J. Abdul Kalam : *Ignited Minds – Unleashing the Power within India* (Penguin Books, 2003).

B.R. McCandless and E.D. Evans : *Children and Youth: Psychological Development* (Dryden Press, 1973).

Barbara Brenner : *The Preschool Handbook.*

Cathi Cohen : *Raise Your Child's Social IQ* (Advantage Books, 1999).

Colin Rose and Gordon Dryden : *Learning Fundamentals* (Big Fish, 2001).

Daniel Goleman : *Emotional Intelligence.*

David Elkind	:	*The Miseducation of Children.*
Debashis Chatterjee	:	*Light the Fire in Your Heart* (Full Circle, 2003).
Desmond Morris	:	*The Human Zoo.*
Desmond Morris	:	*The Naked Ape.*
Echhart Tolle	:	*The Power of NOW* (Yogi Impressions, 2001).
Ellen Ruppel	:	*The Hungry Gene: The Science of Fat and the Future of Thin.*
Eric Berne	:	*Games People Play.*
Erik H. Erikson	:	*Childhood and Society* (second ed., Norton, 1963).
Erik H. Erikson	:	*Identity – Youth and Crisis* (Norton, 1968)
Ernst Edzard	:	*Sleep* (Godsfield Press, 1999). *Harvard Business Review – On Human Relations* (Harper & Row, 1978).
Hilary Rodham Clinton	:	*It takes a Village* (Simon & Schuster, 1995)
Jacob M. Braude	:	*Complete Speaker's and Toastmaster's Library* (8 volumes) (Prentice Hall).
Jean Piaget	:	*Science of Education and the Psychology of the Child* (Orion Press, 1970).
Jerome Durack, S.J.	:	*Some Principles and their Practice.*
Jim Trelease	:	*The New Read-aloud Handbook.*
Jodi Mindell	:	*Sleeping through the Night* (Harper Collins, 1997).
John Gray	:	*Men are from Mars, Women are from Venus* (Harper Collins, 1992).
John Welwood	:	*Love and Awakening* (Harper Collins, 1996).
Kathleen Stassen Berger	:	*The Developing Person* (Worth Publishers, 1980).
Kenneth Blanchard and Spencer Johnson	:	*The One-minute Manager* (Morrow, 1982)

Laurence
Steinberg   : *10 Principles of Good Parenting*
                             (Simon & Schuster, 2004).

M.J. Costelloe S.J.   : *Montessori, Discovery of the Child*,
                             (Notre Dame, 1980).

Martin Waddel   : *Owl Babies* (Candlewick Press, 2000).

Mischel, Ebbeson
and Zeiss   : *Journal of Educational Psychology* (1972).

O'Neill, Spielberger
and Hansen   : *Journal of Educational Psychology* (1968).

Rabindranath   *An Anthology*, edited by Krishna Dutta
Tagore   : and Andrew Robinson
                             (Picador India, 1999).

Robert A. Johnson   : *Owning Your own Shadow.*

Robert J.   *Setting Limits*
Mackenzie   : (Prima Publishing, 1998).

Salvador Minuchin   : *Psychosomatic Families: Anorexia
                             Nervosa in Context*
                             (Harvard University Press, 1978).

Steffen Krachmer   : *Quantity Time: Moving Beyond the
                             Quality Time Myth.*

Stephen R. Covey   : *The Seven Habits of Highly Effective
                             People*, (Simon & Schuster, 1994).

Steve Metzer   : *It's Time for School* (1997).

Steven R. Yussen   *Child Development*
and John Santrock   : (William Brown & Co., 1978).

Susan Forward   : *Toxic Parents*, (Bantam Books, 1989).

Theodre D. Wachs   : *Child Development.*

Thomas Harris   : *I'm Okay, You're Okay*

Wayne W. Dyer   : *What Do You Really Want for Your
                             Children* (Arrow Books, 1997).

Wesley C. Becker   : *Parents Are Teachers*
                             (Research Press, 1971).